Martin Penalver is English-born with Spanish history throughout his family. Born in 1968 in Colchester he lived in nearby Clacton-on-Sea as a child before moving to London. Noted at an early age for his writing skills and imagination, Martin soon found some of his work gaining attention. The poem 'River of Dreams' won a national placing and was published. He also won critical acclaim for further poems: 'The Shadow Dancer' and 'Letter to the Lord'. In addition Martin edited and wrote for 'Gazetta di Castel di Frinton', and currently writes for the 'Gacetta Sporting de la Vista'.

'Ticking Of The Clock' is Martin's second published book and is the sequel to the award-winning 'In Search Of An Angel'. It is the second book in the trilogy 'Laws of the Angel'.

www.martinpenalver.com

ISBN: 978-1-905988-82-2

Cover design by Sue Cordon

Published by Libros International

www.librosinternational.com

Dear Jean,

TICKING OF THE CLOCK

The second book in the trilogy 'Laws of the Angel'

Martin Penalver

Thanks for your support.
I am glad your knees are better
lots of love
Martin xx

Libros
INTERNATIONAL

Acknowledgements

To Rosalind: You inspired me to write 'In Search Of An Angel'. You inspired everyone who knew you. Thank you for giving the world so much more than you could ever take from it. This book is dedicated to you.

To my dear mum and dad, Bob and Pam: I hope I have made you as proud of me as I am of you both. I love you both very dearly.

To my brother and sisters and extended family: So many smiles shared, I love you all beyond compare.

To those friends who have judged me not: I am so fortunate to know you all. A special mention to Billy Bush, Dave Poulton, Stuart Skee and Darren Tobyn. Thank you for simply being yourselves and wonderful lifelong friends.

To Ross Mayo: You have experienced a journey many of us could never imagine and come through with a smile. Thank you for sharing your story with me. Best wishes always.

To Carol Cole: My heartfelt thanks for all the hours you gave to the edit, for all the fun that we had, and for crafting so much with your incredible talent. It has been a privilege working with you and this book is all the better thanks to you.

To Sue Cordon: Once again you designed a beautiful cover with patience and understanding. Thank you so much.

To Ken, Kelly and all the Libros team: Thank you for believing in me.

To my blue-eyed baby girl: If I could reach up and hold a star for every time you've made me smile, the entire evening sky would be in the palm of my hand.

Finally to you, the reader: May your Angel guide you towards your dreams.

In memory of Rosalind Annie Inns
26th June 1922 - 7th June 2008

You inspired me and you touched so many lives.
I still see you smiling across the fence and
I will never forget you.
You have your wings now, Roz.
You are where Angels belong.

And so the Angel was born out of love.
Earth had its youngest.
To fly, she must find the other wing.
The one who would truly deserve all she could give.

Martin Penalver 2009

Time is a gift we all are given at birth. Through our creation and throughout all known history, all is counted in terms of time.

But do we understand time? Do we know its limitless boundaries and do we understand its precious value?

Your brief life is measured meticulously with time. It counts for all you do whether you realise it or not. From the moment your eyes open in the morning to the final vision you see last thing at night, time is your Lord and Master.

You the learned, you the learner, it matters not, for time will give you every chance to follow your dreams, for that is its absolute gift.

But time will one day take all away from you. That is its absolute truth.

Then time will pass onto the next. They will have the chance to write upon the blank sheet that time presents them.

So who am I?

I am many things but you will learn that I am you. I am the teacher for a moment and you are the reader.

Walk with me now through a fragment of time. A mere thirty years, a little over a quarter of a century, in a world where thousands of centuries have passed and many more will come to pass.

One slice of time will illuminate so much, for you will know the power of the gift and how one act will affect the fabric we weave.

You all judge time by the hands on the face of a clock.

So let it begin…the ticking of the clock.

Preface – 2002

'I want to find an Angel.'

On the morning of December 8th 1980, the child Steve Bidante uttered these words through a sea of tears. The boy became a man, and through fate, followed his destiny as he went – in search of an Angel.

* * *

'As an Angel it is forbidden to directly interfere in the worlds we oversee. Our influence can only be through guidance, together with a gentle touch of fate and destiny. We have the gift to offer choices to the ones we wish to help and guide.

'Many, with eyes unfocused, will not see these things and that is the way of it.

'We can only represent what we are as sentient beings. We are, after all, fundamentally made of the spirit of you. Emotions are what we hold and cherish. Many good and many bad make up the composition of Angels. We are, in essence, a reflection of dark and light with the balance of emotions in our being.

'I represent the emotions you would call Love, Harmony, Serenity, Power, Will and Authority, and I am spoken of as an Archangel. My gifts have been woven over eons to the point of divinity, yet I have not walked on Earth for three hundred years.

'There was a time when the influence of your clock had no effect on our being. Now that has changed and the Laws of the Angel must be obeyed.

'It is nearly time for me to walk once more on the beautiful planet you call Earth. It may be for the last time. Even I cannot know.

'I can tell you this. The journey of Steve Bidante was so much more than he could have known or imagined. His actions and belief and that of Andréa Sekhova created a miracle: the child born out of pure love. The infant that all white Angels had wished for was found, and our last hope was born.

'There is much to know of the Laws of the Angel and much to explain. The events within these pages will do much to tell of this, but first we must go back in time and let the story unfold. It will be the decisions and actions of others that will determine our and your destiny. Now is the time to open your mind and soul and to believe.

'The clock is ticking.'

CHAPTER ONE

2003

As Steve Bidante made his journey to the forest of Boubin the two Angels paused to speak with each other.

'Do you think he will complete his task?' Helena Sekhova asked.

Rose Gardener smiled as she replied, *'Of that, there is no doubt. He knows now and understands. Now love will do the rest but I must ask you something, Helena. Tell me, did Andréa know that she should not have been able to bear a child?'*

Helena's lips formed an ironic smile as she pondered the question. *'No, I think not, although…I cannot say that she did not doubt it sometimes, when her soul spoke to her. But the Angel coin guided her well and ultimately did all we asked of it.'*

'So,' Rose nodded slowly, *'if all comes true as it is said, then they will raise the girl to become who she is destined to be.'*

'Yes,' Helena replied in a soft tone as she touched Rose's arm affectionately, *'that is all of our hopes but now…now we must seek the Angelis Mortis and ask for what was taken from you so long ago. Now we must redeem your soul.'*

* * *

Steve Bidante saw that there were about ten big log houses separated from each other by small wooden fences. Within he saw soft lights and open fires that sent plumes of smoke upwards into the night air. His eyes scanned for number four and, when he reached it, he hesitated before edging closer to the window. Peering through a small crack in the curtain he saw the silhouette of Andréa. Momentarily paralysed by her beauty he froze, watching until she had moved away from the light and into a room behind.

Taking a deep breath Steve walked to the door and, grasping the small brass knocker in his hand, paused one last time to utter the words *'Here we go'* into the night.

The knocker dropped onto the door, its dull thud vibrating within him as the noise carried into the forest. The sound of her footsteps approached before Andréa pulled the door open until the chain behind reached its length.

Steve looked into her eyes for the first time in what seemed like forever; the blueness of them shone out like two moons as he spoke her name.

'Andréa.'

Initially she seemed to react like a rabbit caught in headlights but after a few seconds she relaxed and, without a word, undid the latch and opened the door. As the light glowed from behind her, he stared his destiny in the face. She held out her hand and guided him silently inside.

The two of them stood in the centre of the warm room where a blazing fire flickered in the corner and lit up her face. It was Andréa who broke the long silence.

'I was told you would come.'

'I was told you are the answer; that you have the answers.' Steve looked at her longingly.

'Maybe; maybe you do too.' She smiled. 'Now, come and sit by the fire.' She took his hand and guided him to a chair where he watched the flames dancing while she went into the kitchen and returned a few minutes later with two mugs of hot coffee.

'I saw you, Andréa.' Steve's voice cracked with emotion. 'I saw your image at my grandmother's funeral and soon after I found another coin, the same as the one you gave me. It was then that I knew for sure.'

Andréa looked down at the floor as she replied, 'I knew a long time ago, I think. When I met you, I knew. When we shared our time together, I knew.' She looked straight at him. 'I always knew.'

As he watched her beautiful lips speak those words, Steve Bidante knew that everything he had seen had been true.

He reached out and took her hand. 'It seems *you* are my destiny, Andréa.'

She squeezed his hand as a tear fell down her face. 'And you. You are my miracle.' She stood up motioning for him to follow.

'Come.'

Andréa guided him through the kitchen and into a long, narrow hallway. A sensation of familiarity enveloped Steve. He knew this place. He knew the shape and the smooth walls. Opening the door to a room at the back, he saw a large bedroom with a double bed set against the far wall. The room was dimly lit and he strained his eyes as Andréa pointed to the left where there was a child's wooden cot.

'There, go see,' she whispered.

Steve walked over to the cot and peered inside and there he saw a baby with blonde, almost white, hair and blue eyes that gazed up at him as she lay gurgling in the cot.

'Come, pick her up,' Andréa said softly.

He stood, unable to move. He *knew* this little girl. Of *course* he knew her. He'd seen her in his dream but not like she was now, but as she would become. Steve picked her up gently and held her, feeling her soft marshmallow skin and her warmth against his face.

'But…' he mumbled, overcome with emotion, 'I thought I could not have a child.'

Andréa moved in front of him and Steve saw the tears running down her face, not sad ones, but ones filled with joy.

'I could not have children, Steve. That is what they told me. But you…you were my miracle; she is *our* miracle, born out of love.'

He thought back to those last weeks when he and Andréa were together. She had put on weight yet he hadn't even thought about *why*. Everything unfolded in front of him as he held the gift of life in his arms, tears of joy and happiness streaming down his face, the creation by two souls whose destiny was decided by events in time.

* * *

The two Angels climbed the many steps towards Prague Castle with an ease belying their appearances. Upon reaching the top they paused momentarily to gaze across the panoramic landscape of Prague before passing the blank-faced guards at the gates of the castle unnoticed.

Walking through into the main courtyard they sat and waited as the sound of the last tourists' feet rattled the cobblestones around them, clouds of misty air from their mouths floating transiently under the soft glow of the gas lamps. The two women gave off no such vapour or sound. To the passers-by, they were invisible.

When all was quiet, they rose and glided silently across to the vast archway leading to the doors of St Vitus Cathedral. With a touch of Helena's hand the great door clicked open and the two slipped inside sealing the door behind them.

The cathedral was now empty, magnifying its vastness. The silence was interrupted only by the gentle movement of flames, flickering from the many candles which guided the two women to the chancel of the cathedral where, in front of the high altar, they stared fleetingly at the royal mausoleum knowing that below, in the crypt, the royal tombs of Czech kings and queens and patron saints were interred. Now was the time.

Rose closed her eyes and held out her arms as Helena whispered a prayer to the Angelis Mortis. After a period of gentle chanting Helena's call was answered by the taker of life and souls. Rose fell into a trance-like state as the words of ancient Latin were spoken, a dim glow emanating around her statuesque figure. When Helena fell silent Rose slowly dropped, rag doll-like, to the floor where she lay for several moments whilst the ghostlike aura faded from around her. Upon opening her eyes Rose whispered the words with emotion.

'My soul is redeemed.'

'Did you hear the words?' Helena said softly as she helped her up to the nearby pew.

Rose looked at her vaguely. *'I heard much, but the sensation diluted all but a little. Two sons survived the crash,'* she added in a weary tone, *'I do not understand.'*

Helena had heard all. *'Then you will know that there were two sons. Rose, our task is not complete. We have to find the other.'*

'Yes...' Rose replied in a puzzled tone, *'but if two sons survived the crash and Steve was one, how are we to find the other? And why would the Angel of Death tell us such things?'*

'The Angelis Mortis is neither dark nor light for death comes to both,' Helena whispered thoughtfully as she recollected the words. *'She did not tell. She simply said as she would to those with black hearts in the same situation. We must hope that the coin of Angels will guide us. We must go back in time to find the future. There is much to learn.'*

Rose was silent, looking ahead to the mausoleum as her soul gained a new found energy. With the return of a glint in her eye she looked quizzically at Helena.

'Then it seems my work, our work, is not yet done. We have still one more part to play.'

They stood, as Helena took Rose's hands in hers. *'We must find the other son and his child, for I learnt that he has followed the path already unknowingly. His daughter is to bear a son. If all is true, that son is the second half Angel and, with the child of Steve and Andréa, perhaps saviours of all that is good on this Earth. We cannot interfere, only guide as*

19

it is written in the laws.'

'*Then we must hope that this son and his child will be of purity,*' Rose answered with apprehension, '*and we must pray that we find her first, that she will not be corrupted, and that the child too will be born out of divine love.*' As Rose spoke, her returning soul filled her with emotions hidden for over half a century. Her face strained with the new found sense of concern. '*We have so much to learn of this yet we cannot fail. We must not fail, so much depends on us.*'

'*We will not fail and neither will she,*' replied Helena, confidence resounding from her voice. '*Even now she is surrounded by love which will protect her, and her gifts will guide her on. When the boy is born they will find their way to each other and they will save us all. It is foretold.*'

'*Of that,*' answered Rose with a wise look, '*we must hope with all we are.*'

With that the two Angels slipped away on their final journey.

CHAPTER TWO

August 2007

Stefano sat alone. His gaze was fixed on the glass of wine that he held almost tenderly in his hand. In the background the soft sound of Classic FM wafted around the penthouse apartment he was in for the weekend. One of three properties Stefano owned. The house in Knightsbridge was home for his wife Nicole this weekend, while his daughter Francesca would be relaxing now in the farmhouse in Italy with his parents. He wished he was there right now, in San Piceno, at home.

He sighed before gulping down the glass of Montepulciano in one hit. It did not taste anything like as nice as normal. No depth, no character, no feeling. Stefano Riza felt the sad similarity to his world. The glass of wine reflected him at that moment.

Instead of hurling the glass at the vast mirror that adorned the rear wall of the spacious lounge, he softly lowered his hand to hear the sound of crystal glass on crystal table creating a reverberating 'ting' that is normally associated with celebration. Not now. The phone call had changed everything.

Taking the envelope in his hand he stood and walked over to the French doors. Pushing them open, he stepped out onto the vast balcony to view the Point Clear summer evening. He had loved this place when he and his family had come to view it; Point Clear, what a beautiful name, which surely did justice to its location. A quaint seaside village set seven miles from the town of Clacton-on-Sea. It had exclusivity but also the beat of life close enough to touch.

With numbness he had never experienced before, Stefano gazed out at the golden sands which filled the eye like a never-ending carpet waiting for the red of the sunset to turn the landscape into something any film premiere would be proud of.

The beautiful creek stretched out beyond, separated only by the small sandy stretch of land, home to a bird sanctuary. The only images that broke this constant arc of peace were a simple wooden rowing boat moored up with ageing rope and a crooked jetty that connected the land with the water. Tranquillity reigned supreme. It was, and always should be, a place to reflect, relax and refresh. Yet, at that moment, he hated Point Clear. He hated England. He hated himself.

Leaning over the iron railings, Stefano peeled back the lip of the envelope which had remained sealed for twenty-seven years and slid out its contents. Breathing in deeply, he began to read.

LAST WILL AND TESTAMENT OF ME STEFANO RIZA

He scanned the address and then noticed the flat he was living in back then was as much a part of history as the content that followed.

I hereby revoke all former Wills and testamentary dispositions hereto before made by me and declare this to be my last Will and Testament.

*I appoint **Emilio Riza** of Fourteen Via Escalo, Ascoli, 3157 Italia to be Executrix and Trustee of this my Will (hereinafter called "my Trustee") but if he should fail to survive me or be unable or unwilling to act then I appoint **Cesare Bertolini** of Via Terenza, St Piceno 2890 Italia to act as Executor and my Trustee pursuant to the provisions of this, my Will.*

Stefano paused and, for the first time in what seemed like forever, he smiled. It was not a smile we would be familiar with, not a smile of joy, or of happiness, nor contentment. Those days, those smiles had gone. This was a wry smile. He spoke softly and his breath carried his words out into the August night. 'Emilio, Cesare....'

The pain of the car crash in 1980 that had cost the lives of his brother and his dearest friend resurfaced and simply added to his desolation. Seven long years had passed from that horrific night before he had met Nicole Simione and rediscovered a love for the world.

Back then, his life had been so different and now here, of all places, he had opened up a can of long suppressed worms without even knowing it. Stefano cast his mind back to the day he was given the will. Emilio, smiling, long tousled hair, film star looks, laughing as he handed him his sixteenth birthday present. Stefano had opened the envelope then and stared, unsure of what exactly his brother had just given him. 'It is always good to have things planned out,' Emilio had said, laughing. Stefano knew then and knew even more now. Nothing in this world can be planned. Time allows only guesswork.

It was so long ago now, so long ago that even the memory of his comrades had faded like the sun, only to be awakened by the flimsy sheet he held in his hand. He had envisaged the end so many times. The journey from Rome to England, two people, two lifelong friends who were probably listening to music, chatting without pause, embracing the moment as they always did, before the lorry changed their lives, ended their lives, ended their friendship, stolen a brother, taken a friend, broken so many hearts along the way. The years that had passed from then until he met Nicole had been as empty as the darkness of space itself, yet now in this deep abyss he had been close to falling into, Stefano felt an emotion at last: tears of pain and suffering.

The moments passed as the droplets of yesterday fell.

Eventually the tears ceased to fall from his vacant stare. So much had been decided in that fragment of time. That was then and this was now; the years had been kind to him for he had met Nicole the saviour, mother of his beautiful daughter Francesca. The prominent facts on the sheet of paper now screamed out at him: his will was outdated and pathetic. He had not thought of death for so long.

The sky was as inky black as his soul. Tonight could not be the night. His plan could not be executed. It would not be fair, not until he had changed his will.

Suicide would have to wait.

CHAPTER THREE

The day of Sunday December 7th 1980

And the voice inside her head said: 'The boy must stay.'

Agnes Bidante turned and turned again, looking for the voice. There was no one there.

'Steve MUST stay.' The voice spoke once more and this time she simply listened before uttering a single word in reply – 'Cyril.'

* * *

John Parsons was an angry man. His weekend had been ruined and, although he had staff to blame, he also had himself to blame. That was how he felt.

Three staff had called in sick Friday evening as he was trying to relax at home in Sheffield. It meant that, even with back-up staff, he was still a man down and the goods were due for delivery before Monday morning. It was his company, his problem and – his biggest contract.

After spending most of Saturday morning and afternoon at the local hub overseeing the other two drivers and their loads, John then scanned the paperwork of his own load. There were twelve pallets and sixteen cages of goods to three drops, one local, the other two bloody miles away; just his luck. He called the branches before calculating the routes and decided that if he left today he could do the local drop first and head down to London in the morning before the Ipswich drop. If all went well he would on the road home sometime Sunday afternoon.

'Fuck this business,' he thought as, with his index finger, he swung the dial of the phone back and forth. He had to call the stores to see if the warehouse bays would be open. After all, it was a Sunday and shops generally did not open on Sundays.

Two calls later and he felt a tad happier despite a small sense of disgust. Of course the two stores were open; not technically, of course, as in the front bloody doors. No, the staff had informed him that both shops used Sundays to *'merchandise and restock'* as they put it. If there was one company that would think down those lines it would be T Healy & Sons Hypermarkets or whatever their damned name was.

A few years previously and John had been a much happier man. When he got the contract and met Terry Healy he found his drive and determination refreshing, not to mention the extra income intoxicating. Delivering to his shops gave a stream of constant business, everything nice and local. John's pockets were being lined by Terry's business on top of all the other bits and pieces. It was all good.

But he had found that each new shop meant he had to expand in sync. One new shop meant one new truck to cater for the growing distribution. That was fine, he thought at first, until the shops began to get further away, like the bloody London store and the Ipswich store. That meant more diesel and more wages, more hours, more hassle, more fucking everything.

Then the first bitter pill had come. At last year's *'review'* as Healy had *'kindly'* put it John had found himself in an uncomfortable position. Sitting across from the main man himself he had been told in no uncertain terms that the price *had* to drop in order to *compete*. The fear of losing the contract worried him into agreeing a slightly better rate, at least for Healy and his company. It was not until a few hours later that he contemplated: 'If he is getting bigger then why should I be getting poorer?'

Since then, the contract had gnarled him, the whole ethics had, yet now he could not afford to lose it. The loans on the new lorries and trucks had to be paid and it looked like T Healy & Sons were only going one way – up. He had to cling on for the ride.

After dropping the first load off, John settled down for the evening with a glass or two of whisky. He enjoyed a drop of the hard stuff and when the alarm went off early next morning he pushed the snooze button before his wife pushed his wake button by shaking him from his slumbers. Not much of a driver himself these days, he climbed into the cab grudgingly and, after a moment's pondering, decided to go to Ipswich first and then head back to London. On the A1 road to Ipswich he called up a pal in Tottenham and told him he may drop in depending on the time. He now had a place to stay if things got behind schedule and, the way his head felt, it could well be that way.

Whether it was bad luck or bad planning one could not say but John found himself stuck in traffic on the A14. The three and a bit hour journey took over six and he had not stopped, with the exception of traffic jams. He felt tired already and there was still London to go.

Making a decision, he settled for a late brunch and a snooze before the journey to London. It was mid-afternoon as he set off. After stopping to fill up he treated himself to a small bottle of Scotch and the comfort that he would stay over the night in Tottenham and get loaded. *'Work hard. Play hard,'* he said out loud as he moved onto the A12.

He would have trouble recalling what happened in the next hour but it would cost him dear.

* * *

Emilio Riza was singing along with music that was blaring

from the cassette player on the floor. It was typical: in order to talk they would have to shout, but they had to have the sound full-blast to hear it over the droning of the Fiat 133 that Cesare Bertolini was driving with typical Italian conviction.

The last week had been a good one for the two boys. After arriving from Italy they had stayed at Point Clear with Emilio's mother. Good Italian food and plenty of red wine had made the laughter flow. Now they were travelling the eighty odd miles to Stratford where they would help Emilio's father with the café for a day or two and install the second-hand coffee machine they had collected from Harwich Docks that morning. After that, they would return and collect his mother who would by now be much missed by her husband at the café. The apartment in Point Clear still needed much renovation but it was in a lovely spot, albeit too desolate at times.

In the seconds that led up to the moment, Emilio saw nothing. His head was leaning forwards towards the tape recorder as he inserted the latest Julio Iglesias cassette into the slot. Cesare stared in horror as the image in his rear-view mirror gave him a momentary vision which warned him of the impending doom.

The lorry was coming up too fast. Cesare saw in that fraction of a second – when time slows beyond substance – that the driver was not aware of anything that was about to happen. As a last reaction Cesare hit the horn and saw the face behind snap his head forwards. Their eyes met momentarily as the driver swung the wheel suddenly to the right. It could have avoided the accident had it been seconds earlier. Now it only compounded it.

The left steel bumper of the juggernaut shunted the right rear side of the Fiat, the force sending the car hurtling forwards towards the barrier like a flicked paper ball. Emilio glanced up at the sound of the horn before the shunt allowed him to witness the last microseconds of his young life. The barrier arrived in a blur and the car smashed into it.

Emilio saw no more. On impact his head was instantly

propelled towards the dashboard and thudded into it with a sickening crack as his skull disintegrated. Cesare witnessed the horror before the driver's side crumpled inwards towards his body. Metal hit flesh with disastrous consequences as his body became part of the machine coated in blood.

They were both dead in a moment.

In a horrified daze John Parsons watched destiny. By trying to avoid the car in front he had clipped it before veering across the carriageway and hitting another car head-on killing instantly the couple inside. The next thing he knew, he was being helped out of the lorry by a fireman.

* * *

Terry Healy picked up the phone at around 9pm. He listened carefully before mumbling a few words and putting the receiver back on its stand. He turned to Jenny with a grim look on his face.

'I cannot bloody believe it,' he said with a snarl.

Jenny looked up from the sink where she had been rinsing some vegetables in preparation for their supper. 'What? What's happened?'

'That was the police,' he answered in a stern voice which accentuated his northern accent. 'One of our drivers, the bloke that owns the bloody firm in fact, has crashed one of his lorries that was delivering to us and he's killed four people.'

'Oh my God,' Jenny stuttered, face aghast, 'that is so terrible. How...?'

Terry's expression was blank. 'I have no idea. They just informed me that it was one of *our lorries*, 'he snorted in contempt at this point, 'one of our lorries had hit two vehicles resulting in four deaths and... the driver has been found to be over the bloody limit.'

Jenny felt sick inside as she thought of it. 'Those poor people,' she said in a soft voice, 'poor innocent people, all dead...'

'That's true enough,' replied Terry, 'and very sad it is too but we have to act, Jenny, we have to act.' His voice rose as he repeated his words, displaying anger upon his face. 'I am going to terminate the contract,' he declared finally. 'I cannot have this type of thing being associated with us, bad for business.'

He looked at her for approval and Jenny found herself nodding in silence. She could not think of any words to say in reply. *'Bad for business?'* She found herself wanting to vomit with disgust.

CHAPTER FOUR

The night of Sunday December 7th 1980

Late that evening in East Ham, London, a policeman and policewoman knocked on the front door, grim expressions etched on their faces.

After a moment the door opened revealing the image of an elderly lady illuminated by the hallway light.

'Agnes Bidante?' The policeman croaked her name.

'Yes?' She instantly looked confused.

'I am afraid I have some grave news,' the policeman began. 'There has been a terrible accident…'

As he explained, Agnes Bidante aged right there on the spot. Her already frail frame shrunk under the weight of their news. She had lost a son, a daughter-in-law and now…what of Steve? How would she…?

The policewoman could not contain herself as her eyes met the young child's. He appeared from nowhere to stand at the top of the stairs. Pyjamas of claret, face of innocence, eyes rubbing sand away, just watching, absorbing the scene and understanding in the way only a child can. The scene became slow motion – heads turned in unison to watch one face looking down at three – a vacant, confused stare which tore into them all. The policeman grunted the final clichéd words.

'We are so sorry, Mrs Bidante.'

The door shut but, before they had reached the gate, the policewoman spoke in tattered tones, her voice cracking as she broke down. It was not the first time she had witnessed such a task but the child, his eyes sand-filled and soft, awoken from a dream, shown the harshness of a sinister nightmare. She was haunted – soft hands rubbing eyes – seeing death arrive at the door. It was too much to bear. She sobbed the words that the boy upstairs was about to realise. 'That poor boy has lost his parents.'

* * *

Stefano Riza ran his finger across the steamy window of the Stratford café etching a face on the pane. From the kitchen, his father Mimo moved methodically, mop in hand, out into the cafeteria wiping in stiff circles whilst mumbling curses under his breath.

The dank, dark night outside made the streetlights dance like fireflies as Stefano's eyes scoured the pavement for signs of activity. He was bored. The day had been like most other Sundays in the café: hustle and bustle, as the locals drifted in and out, chatting about their days and weeks whilst Mimo poured coffees, created meals and barked at Stefano to serve a little more quickly.

It was always like this when Mama was absent. When she was not around, the café seemed a less organised place, or at least his father seemed a less organised man. He had consoled himself that, by the evening, he would have the company of his brother and friend whilst Mimo would have a newer coffee machine to toy with for the rest of the night. Now though, time was getting on and there was no sign of Emilio and Cesare. He hoped privately that they arrived before his mother took the long walk from their home in Point Clear to the payphone. He could imagine her distress if she called in to check up on everything and his brother had not arrived. She would either go mad with worry, or mad with anger. Either way it would mean more bad vibes for his father and he seemed in a black mood as it was.

The street was deserted when the orange lights gave way to a brighter beam. Stefano wiped a larger circle in the window just in time to see the swirling blue rays of the police car as it pulled up across the road. He could make out two expressionless faces in the car as they looked across to the shop. Glancing around, he saw his father stop mopping and bring the handle up as if he was going to lean on it. A resounding knock on the glass of the door fixed his gaze on the policemen staring through at him.

Before Stefano could rise from his seat, Mimo had passed him and was at the front door awkwardly flicking through a large set of keys. He saw his father's hand tremble a little as he pushed the correct key in and pulled the door open.

A gust of cold wind followed the policemen into the café. They shot him a look as the first policeman asked his father if he was Mimo Riza. Automatically his father replied that, yes, he was and would they like a coffee or something to eat?

They refused the offer and sat uneasily at a table opposite Stefano. The eighteen-year-old's mind raced, trying to think of reasons why these policemen were here, now. Had there been trouble? Emilio and Cesare could be a couple of tearaways at times, he knew that. But apart from odd scuffles with some of the local English there was not much room for serious crime. His father would have none of that and they knew it. No, by the look in his father's eyes it was something different.

Mimo's voice called out to him to come out back. He obeyed, avoiding eye contact with the two men as he did so. Mimo stood, two bin bags in hand, staring blankly at him as he entered the kitchen. 'Take these out and then take a walk,' he said firmly. Stefano sensed something alien in his voice and did not answer straightaway. 'Stay close, Stefano, but do not come back until the car has gone, understand?'

Perhaps after a day like today and being a runner for his father, Stefano might have backchatted to such a blatantly uncaring request. Now he could only say the words, 'Yes, father.' Something was very wrong.

* * *

A gentle drizzle fell on the street as he turned the corner and headed down towards the off-licence. After buying a pack of Hubba Bubba gum, Stefano wandered over to the bus shelter across the street and perched himself on the seat where he went about manipulating the gum in order to create a larger bubble each time. Each burst as the bubble broke made him more determined to make a larger one. It was not a favourite pastime by any means but, as his mind wandered, it was the only thing he could focus on.

After some time he headed back around the corner towards the café. The car had gone. Instead of quickening his step he slowed, putting each foot inside the crack of the paving slabs, again in order to fill his mind with something, anything but going back to the café.

Mimo sat alone, his head in his hands. Stefano saw from outside the door that his dirty white vest was wet with tears. He hesitated before finally plucking up the courage to push the door open. The sound of the small bell rang in his ears as his and his father's eyes made contact.

'Dead,' the word was spoken with a crackling hoarseness. 'They are both dead, Stefano.'

His father's eyes had a glazed madness in them. Stefano stayed motionless for an instant as he tried to digest the bombshell that the words had delivered. He heard himself shout the word, 'No' as he approached his father but Mimo held out a hand which deflected his step and made him halt immediately.

Mimo dropped his head onto the table and muttered in grief. Stefano heard the words, 'No, no. The car, no, it cannot be true.'

'Papa,' he said hesitantly as the overwhelming impact of it all sank in.

Mimo raised his face and Stefano saw the deepest anger imaginable flare from his expression. 'NO!' he yelled making him take a step back in fright.

Emilio had been his favourite and Stefano knew that. It was the way in some Italian families, but now all he wanted to do was to hold his father. All he felt from his father was bitter sadness, anger and rejection.

Silence raged and danced around the room before the loud trill of the telephone interceded. It rang with a ferocity that screamed for it to be answered, instantly creating seconds of panic as the two sets of eyes spoke a thousand desperate words. They both knew who would be at the other end of that line. Eventually, with the expression of a broken man, Mimo reached out his hand to take the hardest call of his life.

Stefano turned and ran out of the door.

CHAPTER FIVE

1980-1982

The small Italian village of San Piceno has seen its fair share of events over the last half century. Set just thirty kilometres north of the Gustav Line, the battles of the Second World War had left scars which, like the village and surrounding land, had healed slowly as the years passed.

The main road into the village runs alongside the River Mesti which cuts like a blue vein into the landscape. Four decades on from the horrors of war and San Piceno had returned to its natural state. Young trees and flowering plants replaced the bomb craters that had once pitted dark holes amongst the debris of destroyed houses and lives. To walk into the pretty centre of San Piceno nowadays, you would have been hard pushed to find any remnant of the past. The population of just a few thousand knew of course. The piazza, located in the centre of San Piceno, acts as the heart and from there sprout windy streets leading into every nook and cranny of this part of Italy. There, in the centre, the granite memorial to those lost remind the tourists of the village's history but San Piceno is not a hub for tourism. The rows of shops, cafés and restaurants are circled by the houses that stretch beyond and upwards into the surrounding hills serving as home to generations of Italians who have never moved away. It is, in every sense, a timeless small Mediterranean village, now re-blessed in its own innocent beauty.

The community is small enough for everyone to know of each other's business and life. The Riza family were no different. Stefano's grandparents still resided in the east of the village and when Mimo had married Eva Terboni and moved to England in the mid-fifties to start a new life the word had spread of their adventure. For the remaining population, hearing that they had moved to London to open a café might as well have been moving to the moon.

Mimo's and Eva's roots were in San Piceno however and at least twice yearly they would return and stay at the family home. Mimo made sure that he looked after both his and Eva's parents financially helping them to live a good life which, in turn, made the name Riza well respected.

When the funeral took place in December 1980, the whole village took to the streets. Emilio had been a popular child and Cesare Bertolini, who had lived in San Piceno up until that fateful day, was much loved. The basilica was full to the brim and people spilled out onto the cobblestone piazza as the families walked alongside the coffins of two lost souls. There had not been such a sad day in San Piceno for many a year.

After a heart-rending ceremony the two young men were laid to rest in the graveyard overlooking the village. Later many people, including close friends and family, asked Mimo and Eva to return, to leave England and its hand of death behind, but the two decided that they would go back and forge on with their lives, perhaps because the overly solicitous attention of the village was too much for Eva to bear. They left in tears, returning to Stratford with Stefano to try and rebuild their lives after the loss of Emilio.

* * *

Upon their return the family of three kept their grief as private as possible in the daily world of custom and gossip. Of course word within Stratford from the café locals extended and sympathetic glances were shown, but few pried into their anguish. The English way was different and that suited Mimo and Eva who said less and less to each other while submerging their broken hearts into work. For Stefano, the void was complete. He had few friends of note, choosing to wander alone for the most part between helping in the café and travelling down to Point Clear as his mother silently continued to build up the home she had wanted to make for them all.

As with tragedy, time can seem twofold. It has the ability to soften the agony as its hands move on yet it pauses on certain dates to amplify events. Each December, the family would return to San Piceno to pay their respects whilst reigniting the flame that burned daily. For Stefano, the loss of a brother and friend was burden enough. To see his parents suffer not only their own private grief but also the severance of the closeness he had taken for granted was a lesson in itself.

* * *

After two years of work and little else, Mimo informed Stefano that he and Eva were going to buy into another business which they wanted the twenty-year-old to become involved in. Stefano was not surprised. It almost seemed that anything to fill the slightest void of memory would suffice. His father had learned of a small company that made plastic fly blinds. As it was situated just a few miles down the road in East Ham, the business seemed to present a good investment at the knock-down price it was up for. When Stefano accompanied Mimo on a visit he could see why.

Set in a small industrial estate of the Roman Road, the factory was in need of restoration. The asbestos roof had cracks and chunks missing out of it and, inside, the machinery looked aged and decrepit. They were shown round by the manager, an enthusiastic young man named Darrell Britton, who cheerfully demonstrated the making of the blinds. Colourful strips were stapled on slats of wood and then covered with a strip of plastic to hide the staples. The blinds were sold to hang in doorways and keep out insects in the summer. Stefano had seen these blinds before and, despite the need for a lick of paint and much more, he took to the place immediately. He could imagine working here and it would give a sense of purpose, other than to ache for the loss of a friend and brother as he did so often.

* * *

A few months later, in a small, dusty office on the outskirts of East Ham's town centre, Stefano sat with his parents. A chubby, balding solicitor sat in front of them explaining the finer details of the contract they were about to sign whilst an old lady, who must have been the owner, and a boy, a good few years younger than him, sat alongside.

When the man had finished talking, he produced a sheaf of papers and at this point, feeling bored, Stefano excused himself to go outside and take a 'breather'. After a stern look from his mother he got up and walked out of the office into the grey street.

A few moments later, as he sat on the steps, the boy appeared and sat down beside him. Stefano nodded in acknowledgment but said nothing, taking a cigarette from his shirt pocket and striking the match on the pavement. As he inhaled the smoke he was aware that the boy was watching him. Stefano initially ignored him, choosing to gaze at the passing traffic and hoping his parents would hurry up.

Every now and again he took a fleeting look at the child who was now pacing up and down the steps. He surmised that he must be in his early teens and therefore even more bored than he was. But there was something different, not a familiarity as such, but an understanding of him. The boy kept looking until, finally, Stefano broke the silence.

'Is there something wrong with me? You keep staring,' he said in a neutral tone. The boy dipped his head down at

Stefano's words and shuffled from the bottom step onto the street, kicking a small stone as he did.

'It's not you that's wrong,' he said after a brief pause. 'It's everything.'

Stefano realised what he had seen earlier in the boy's expression. It was not rude, not angry, but a deep underlying sadness which was now apparent in his whole body language.

'Well, sorry to hear that.' Stefano spoke softly as sad thoughts returned. 'I know what you mean.'

'Do you?' The boy's reply was laced with hurt. 'The business your mum and dad are buying, it was my mum and dad's, and that's my granny up there, see?'

Stefano contemplated his words, trying to make sense of them. The boy looked lost and lonely. He felt for him. 'Where are your parents then?' he asked.

The boy hid his face momentarily to shield the tears before regaining his composure and turning to look Stefano straight in the eye. 'My name is Steve, Steve Bidante,' his voice trembling, 'and my parents are dead.'

* * *

A hush replaced the whispers as the final Archangel entered. Over eons the vast hall had seen meetings of the sentient beings on a much wider scale. Now, however, the fragile balance between dark and light bringing mistrust beyond knowledge meant that the few dozen witnesses were those of the purest. The other Archangels waited for her address.

Galgliel let her smile light the room as she raised her hand and spoke to those present.

'The message is true. We have found the other son and so have found the other key to the legend of the half Angels.'

There was a murmur of wonder in reply as she continued, *'I must return to Earth, as must you in good time. For now we have many of our own watching and listening, gathering knowledge, and sharing it with those we can. The two sons have met in a brief moment which neither will remember nor forget. Their paths will separate now only to rejoin in many years if all is as foretold.'*

It was Gabriel who spoke first. *'Divine sister, is it to be that the boy you speak of will be the father of the half Angel? Would that not bring disarray into time? The birth of a child now would make the hopes of their coming together unlikely.'* He gazed at the Archangels for whom time had become irrelevant. *'The human element of the clock would make the age between them difficult to ignore, am I not correct, Galgliel?'*

With a gentle nod Galgliel responded. *'What you say is true, my love. The clock which ticks has always been part of the essence of humanity. But its hands have reached up and out to touch us now. It is for us to now treat time with a new found respect, for its power will decide all on Earth.'*

Turning to address the remaining Angels, Galgliel spoke with authority not heard for millennia. *'The answer is no, he will not be the father of the half Angel. It will be that of his child.'*

Pale shadows from their mouths resonated in tandem with the Angels' voices as more whispers resounded within the hall. As Galgliel moved from the centre it was the Archangel Raguel that asked the question all others were thinking.

'How long, Galgliel, how long will it be, how long do we have?'

Her answer carried coldness akin to the crystal blue of her eyes.

'We are bound by the Laws of the Angel. We cannot directly interfere; only give essence of what we are from patience to love, from harmony to hope. Future events will affect us all. The thin threads of time are all but severed in the eyes of an Archangel for the years remaining will seem like a single moment to us. Both dark and light await the outcome but, even in human terms, there is little time.' With sorrow Galgliel took a deep breath. *'As you know in the Laws, it is fifty Earth years*

before the soul of a deceased human can gather the strength to appear in the form of an Angel. That is nothing for us, yet it is a little short of the time we have left.'

CHAPTER SIX

'The soul begins as a blank canvas. Life is both its paint and its brush.
Fear not strokes of sadness and pain, but let all colours touch your heart.
For at the end its picture will always be simply you.'
   (Galgliel's scripture entered into the chronicle of Omniangels)

Terry Healy was a successful man, of that there could be no doubt.

Unlike some that are classed as successful, Terry was given nothing by accident nor by inheritance. Everything that Terry had earned had been off his own back. He was proud of his roots and he was proud of his determination and drive.

Born in the town of Worksop to his parents Margery and Terrance in 1958, he had grown up as the only child in a small terraced house under the meticulous guidance of his mother. His father, a gruff man who had served his country in the war, said very little to him, except in matters of discipline. Then a belt or a smack of the hand would suffice. Those moments filled Terry with fear and, as he grew, he swore he would never treat his children in that manner.

Nevertheless, what his father did say and do carried meaning. Terrance had seen hard times but had always been an honest man. Working in the coal mine in nearby Manton Wood as a youngster he had then served in the RAF up until the end of the war before working in the steelworks in

Sheffield. There he would remain until his death in the early seventies.

Worksop was a good place to grow up as a child. Set in the Bassetlaw district of Nottinghamshire there was plenty to do for a young boy. He would spend many hours of his youth hanging around the River Ryton which was a short walk from his home set at the northern edge of Sherwood Forest. Countless days saw Terry and a clutch of friends traipse the river banks in search of adventure whilst the deep greenery of the famous forest enabled him to act out scenes from Robin Hood.

After leaving school Terry did not follow his father into Sheffield but preferred to stay locally in Worksop. After a decent but undistinguished education, Terry found employment at the nearby OXO factory where many school leavers began their working life. At weekends he also worked in the local store 'Baker Brothers'. The shop sold all manner of goods from foodstuff to nails, from wool to tents. It was a glittering cave of wares and was always bustling.

Compared to his weekly job, it was much more interesting and Terry was absorbed in learning about the products, the prices and, eventually, the profits that the shop made. He worked honestly and hard, putting in more effort in two days than he would in a whole week at the factory. The owner, Mr Baker Junior (his older brother had passed away a year previously), liked Terry. He liked his timekeeping and he liked his curiosity. It reminded him of himself as a child and he liked that. Terry's enthusiasm was rewarded when he was offered full-time employment and from then on he threw himself into his work with a new found passion. Over the next three years Terry listened and learnt from Mr Baker, digesting his knowledge and wisdom whilst carefully putting forward new ideas when the time was right. The two developed an almost father and son relationship which reaped dividends as the shop became more successful and the two became closer and closer.

It was late one evening as they carefully packed the items from outside in the rear warehouse that Mr Baker put to Terry what was to be a life-changing idea. Leaning on an old broom handle Mr Baker smiled as he said, 'I am not getting any younger, Terry. Would you be interested in becoming a partner and sharing the burden?'

Terry listened carefully as Mr Baker explained his thinking. For a sum of money which seemed a lot at the time, Terry could hold a stake in the shop. Mr Baker said that he could get the sum of money for Terry by borrowing it from a bank and then Terry could pay the loan back out of his share of the profits. It would mean a lot more hard work but it was a chance, a chance for Terry Healy to own a part of something at just nineteen years of age.

So, in 1977, Terry Healy became a partner in Baker Brothers. He worked hard over the next year and took the shop to new heights as Mr Baker watched on. He started promotions within the shop, offering discounts on some essential items and sales throughout the year. Word soon spread and the shop became the busiest in its history. Terry felt he was born to the trade.

In 1978 Mr Baker was suffering from ill health and, after much discussion and soul-searching, agreed with Terry that he could go on no longer. Now in his late seventies, Mr Baker was no longer able to cope with the workload and so offered the business to his trusted partner. After more negotiations with the bank, Terry bought out Mr Baker's share of the business and worked harder than ever to make the shop successful. He renamed the shop 'T Healy & Sons'. Not that he had children. It was upon the advice of his teacher Mr Baker that he did so. 'It reads much better to the public,' Mr Baker said. 'It sounds more of a family business.' And Terry agreed. Besides, one day he might have a son to share the business with.

Mr Baker's untimely death in late 1979 hit Terry hard. He had lost both a friend and confidant. He swore to improve further and dedicate his success to his much loved teacher. A year later and he had four shops, three in the Worksop and Nottingham area and one in North London which had been recommended as a good starting foothold in the big city. With more success his next choice of venue was purely down to fate. The next store he invested in was bought impulsively after a visit to a small village just outside Ipswich. It was there he had spent a weekend in a place called Stebdon and where he met a woman he fell in love with.

* * *

Stebdon is just a few miles from Ipswich town; a scenic village set amongst two or three other small villages. Terry and two old school friends had taken the weekend off to go on a camping trip and Stebdon was the choice. It was known locally for its pretty lake which ran through the hilly backdrop of cottages and natural beauty. On a fine spring evening he and his friends pitched their tent on the small but friendly campsite and wandered into the village centre in search of fun. After sampling a few pints of local ale and chatting, they were informed that on Friday nights the main attraction was the weekend dance held in the village hall. The three young men grinned as they entered to see plenty of fresh-faced females, all of whom seemed to take an interest in the strangers. It was there that Jenny Cross first came to Terry's attention.

Whilst his pals cavorted with the first girls they could get to dance, Terry bided his time watching the mixture of lads in smart suits and girls in summery frocks dancing. The one girl that stuck out seemed to be the focus of many boys' attention. She was of slim build with a slightly pale complexion that seemed to complement her flowing soft blonde hair which danced upon her shoulders as she accepted the odd invitation to the floor. It was after a little more ale and a few nudges from his friends that Terry worked up enough courage to ask the girl to dance.

46

When he did she grinned, perhaps at his accent, perhaps at his awkwardness, but dance she did. From that moment onwards he was smitten and, as they left the floor, he asked if he could walk her home later. In a matter of hours he had found love. On the way home he asked if he could see her again and also if they could write to each other. She accepted. Jenny liked him from the outset. He was a well mannered man with a slight resemblance to a young Clark Gable, even if his accent was a little unusual. They agreed to keep in touch and from there Terry found an even greater determination to expand his growing business.

After a few trips to the town of Ipswich he found an ageing shop that was a viable purchase, hence he bought it impulsively. It gave him even more of a reason to be there and over the next months he travelled as frequently as possible to Ipswich and any spare moments he could muster would be spent with Jenny.

Her parents liked what they saw in Terry Healy. Here was a man who worked hard and seemed successful. On their first meeting her father's words were set in stone in his mind. 'We want to see our Jenny with a good man, a man who will provide. You understand that, don't you, Terry?' he had said.

Terry felt jubilant. Work was one thing he was very good at. Some of his mannerisms were a little more difficult to identify with. He was not the most romantic for he had never really had a girlfriend, let alone a girl as pretty as Jenny. But in those days things were different and, whilst Jenny liked many things about Terry, the small things she did not like did not matter so much. Her parents approved, he was a good man, and she would be secure. They would court for another year before he found the courage, and came up with the romantic idea of proposing to her on the banks of the River Ryton, back in Terry's hometown. Jenny duly accepted and in the summer of 1980 they married.

Jenny had envisaged starting a family soon after saying their vows but such was Terry's drive to become more successful that it would be another six years before their first child. In that time two things were to happen: Jenny pined for the family she had thought part of marriage and Terry avoided the subject as much as possible. It was not that he did not wish for a family, especially a son to make the name T Healy & Sons. No, it was not that at all.

It was the fact that Terry suddenly found something out about himself. Now he had it all with the exception of family he found a fear: the fear of failure. This drove him onwards over the next six years to work harder and harder, and to open more and more shops until by the time Terrance was born in 1986 they had eighteen shops spread across the country. And now Terry Healy had unknowingly discovered, inherited, a potential disease: greed.

CHAPTER SEVEN

1987

The bar on Via Nazionale was bustling as Stefano entered. Swerving past the mass of lattice-style wicker chairs filled with a mix of chattering Italians and many other nationalities, he made his way towards the entrance which had a large polished wooden sign above: 'Simione's'.

Outside, the pungent scent of bougainvillea hanging from the trellis wafted up his nose, as bright a smell as the sight of it on this fine evening. Inside the bar was even busier. Table upon table were full and the noise of a hundred voices rang out at once in melodic relaxation. Stefano veered in between tables and oncoming customers until he found a spot at the bar where he ordered a double espresso, looking around hurriedly as he did so.

'Are you trying to stay awake or just a busy day?' She chatted over the noise as she slid the drink towards him.

He saw her now; his attention had focused at her words and now he took in her features. She stood tall and slim, crimped black hair flowing midway down her back, her features unblemished, complemented by a carefree smile. As he took the coffee he saw coal-black eyes shining at him.

'Well?'

Stumbling on his words, he replied as casually as he could muster, 'I ordered the coffee to keep me awake for the journey to San Piceno. Have you heard of the place?'

She shook her head as she took his money. 'Well, I hope it works. Long way to go?'

He heard the words stumble out as he remained fixed upon her beauty. 'Four hours from here – if I catch the fast train or, indeed, the last train which is why I *was* in a hurry.'

'Oh,' she replied unemotionally, 'well, best you hurry your coffee!'

She turned to serve and, knowing that time was about to run out on their brief conversation, Stefano impulsively blurted out, 'Please…I said I *was* in a hurry, which was before I saw you. What's your name?'

'Nicole,' she answered in a clipped voice laced with cuteness, 'and I must get along. In case you had not noticed, it is extremely busy in here and my father, the owner, does not take kindly to me chatting with strangers while working.'

He caught a mischievous glint in her eye which simply ignited his desire to know her further. 'Nicole, please let me meet you after work and talk with you.'

She considered his request for an instant before replying, 'What about the train you have to catch?'

'It can wait.'

* * *

Over the next hours Stefano did some thinking. More thinking than he had done in his life, it seemed. For the past seven years he had done little thinking. When he had done, Emilio and Cesare always came to the forefront with the living grief of his parents a close second. Now his world was obsessed with something else: the girl in the bar.

Love had never taken Stefano's heart. Now, as he waited, he could feel a crescendo of butterflies that sent his stomach into turmoil making him nervous, yet elated, and yet scared as hell. As he sat a little distance from the bar itself, he pondered a multitude of outcomes. What if she had a boyfriend? What if she simply did not like him? What if her family did not like him? So many questions came to mind and each time he tried to find a positive answer. He *must* win the girl over. His occasional glance was initially just to assure his heart that he had not made a mistake, not judged his instinct too quickly, but soon he found himself unable to look anywhere else.

After the longest wait of his life, Stefano felt both composed and full of ideas, and a nervous wreck. He knew this minute chance could be all he had to touch the heart of this princess yet now, as the moment arrived, he felt dormant emotions explode with firework fury sending a shiver down his spine and creating beads of perspiration on his brow. When Nicole approached the table she looked as serene as the River Mesti on a warm spring evening. Her persona rubbed off on him immediately and, as she sat, he felt a surge of confidence simply because she was there.

She sat across from him, placing a bottle of wine between the two of them and poured two large glasses, smiling languidly as she did so. 'You never told me your name, sir. A little rude, don't you think?'

He was caught off balance and the confidence of a moment ago vanished. Damn! I didn't! Her smile twinkled under the dim lights as he realised she was playing with him. Trying to keep a cool Italian head, he replied casually, 'My apologies. I was intent on meeting you and nothing else came into my mind.' He picked up his glass. 'Stefano is my name and I raise a glass to us meeting and your beauty.'

Her cheeks took the colour of the wine as crystal touched crystal and their eyes met. The look held for the briefest of time but he felt the electricity between them flow. Conversation came easily and, before they knew it, time had moved into the early hours, noted only by the appearance of Nicole's father who greeted Stefano gruffly with a tired nod before flicking out the main lights and leaving them to it.

After more wine, together with leftover antipasti, their tongues had loosened. Stefano told of many things: the loss of his brother, the grief of his parents, his life in England and his yearning for Italy, especially San Piceno.

Nicole listened eagerly, feeling herself relax in his company. He was both handsome and charming and, unlike many of the men who had struck up conversations with her, he seemed honest and selfless. She had been in Rome all of her life and knew nothing much of life outside the city. This man seemed different to those she had met and, as he described San Piceno, she visualised a beautiful place. She wanted to go there with him, a man who, just a few hours ago, had been a stranger.

Tiredness took over as the clock passed 4am. Stefano noticed her eyelids getting heavier, making him aware instantly of the night's end. Not wanting to leave at all was one thing but, being a gentleman, he must do so.

'You should sleep,' he said in a soft tone. 'I will go, but only if you promise me you will see me again.' He pushed his hand towards hers. 'I mean... only if you want to, of course.'

She felt a leap inside her soul and tried to control her emotions but with little success. 'You have nowhere to go, Stefano, so, please, stay here. We have a spare room out back and I have no work tomorrow so...' the barriers crumbled, 'perhaps we could go to San Piceno together?'

With a last effort to cling to reason, Stefano smiled like a child as his heart exploded. 'I would love that.' As soon as he heard his words he wished he had foregone reason and simply replied, 'I love you.'

* * *

The following day they made their way to San Piceno by train. Once outside Rome, the journey cut through the wide valleys and mountains. As they gradually gained height, picture-postcard views flew by but each of them had eyes only for the other.

A little under four hours later, the train drew into the small sleepy station and the two jumped off, Stefano overflowing with joy at being back in the place that felt like home and Nicole with a feeling of adventure that just a day ago would have seemed impossible.

Stefano pointed out the sights as they walked, hand in hand, through the diverse streets, some as wide as those in Rome, others too narrow to allow a car through. Approaching the village centre, they crossed a wooden bridge which curved over the River Mesti. She stopped, leaning over to watch the water, rushing, gurgling towards its eventual destination, the ducks and other birds feeding off its rich content. Nicole felt a new sense of freedom.

Her mind finally gave up comparisons of Rome as they passed the piazza of San Piceno. In Rome such a piazza would be full of people going this way and that, but here, here there were just a handful of people, all beautiful in their own individual way. Men sat alongside each other, soft wrinkles upon their bronzed faces which all seemed to be cracked into relaxed smiles as they discussed matters of interest only to themselves. Women were locked in high tempo conversations which could be taken for arguments, yet appeared to always end in laughter. Families wandered together, children skipping freely as they chattered like the birds. Nicole fell in love with the village in a moment.

Stefano led her to the east of the village where his grandparents lived. The house stood wide and tall with long wooden shutters flung open, flowering plants dropping from below them in a cascade of early autumn colour. Here, in the mountain region, the temperature was cooler than in the city but, for September, it was still remarkably warm and, in addition, the two felt an inner warmth which made them loosen their clothing as they wandered towards the house.

For Stefano it was always wonderful to come back. The blinds business was always quieter at this time of year in England whereas during the English summers it was nearly impossible to return. As his grandparents came outside to greet him, he felt both joy to see them again and pride at his return with the stunning woman alongside him.

After embraces, kisses and words of happiness, the four of them sat down for a simple meal of spaghetti and bread. Stefano ate this sort of food in England but nothing could compare to the divine tastes his grandmother could conjure up. The spaghetti was dressed with garlic and minced boar, and the bread freshly baked. His taste buds stood in tribute as he ate, laughing and sharing the stories of months gone by, culminating with his best story: the story of yesterday and meeting Nicole. As he described the events Stefano felt elation; his soul was free.

* * *

For three days and nights they stayed in separate rooms in Stefano's grandparents' home in San Piceno, learning more about each other and, on the second night, making love. It was not planned and happened when they least expected it. As the moon rose above and the stars danced across the dark landscape, they sat together on the hill above the house looking down to the village below. The quietness was stimulating, as were the surroundings. With ease they came close, each craving the scent of the other. Touch turned into lust as they kissed, their bodies becoming entwined in passionate intimacy. He caressed her and she him, their hands exploring each other as their eyes shone like diamonds before he entered her, the explosion of excited delight overcoming them both. Some time later they lay panting and glistening with the heat of love. Each of them was silent, each sharing the silence while a thousand thoughts raced through their minds. Each had found happiness in the other.

* * *

'Tomorrow I will go home and you will return to England – and then?' Her voice was hoarse with the grief of parting.

She had stood up and was gazing into the River Mesti, her reflection hovering shakily as the water moved on by, flanked by flowers and life. He remained sitting where they had both been a moment ago, the bread and wine by his side. He was in the Garden of Eden, but not for long now; soon they would leave, not only this place of perfection, but each other. His insides ripped and he felt lost.

'I want to be with you forever,' was all he could say in response as he got up and walked quietly to her. Slipping his arm around her waist he said the words that had been trapped within from the first moments – 'I love you.'

She did not answer but stood, beauty personified, gazing into the passing river, deep in thought. When she did finally speak, her voice carried great resolve.

'I will one day move with you to England if that is what it takes for us to have a future, but I am not ready, yet...' She turned to face Stefano and he saw tears welling up in her eyes. 'I love you too and I give you my heart. That love will guide us.'

He held her there by the river as he cried with her at the loss they both felt. Torment ran riot within him. He did not want to leave, to make her leave, to live in England. There was little choice.

So it was, by the River Mesti in San Piceno, that Stefano and Nicole swore a bond of love that would bring their hearts together as one. All that stood in their way was life itself.

* * *

In England the rains fell and he felt isolated. The only comfort in between endless days at work and weekends in the steamy café were trips to Italy and the visits of Nicole. Both sets of parents were in favour of the other which was a blessing and made the infrequency of time together bearable.

As spring came Stefano had to work more at the factory. New machinery meant that the colourful curtains were being made faster than ever. He threw himself into his work, seeking out new accounts before driving to London and further to deliver the blinds himself. The business thrived and grew and when Nicole could visit he would drop everything to share every possible second with her. They would go to Point Clear and stay together in the apartment which was becoming more and more of a home and a retreat from the smoky atmosphere and toil of the capital.

It was there, on a delicious August night, that Nicole fell pregnant. Alone and out in the open the two made love by the lapping water. Uninhibited in their longing for each other they became one and created a child. Several weeks later, after discovering she was pregnant, Nicole telephoned Stefano to break the news. He was overjoyed and flew to Rome before they both announced the news to their families.

After talking, the two agreed to live in England and in the autumn they married, Nicole choosing San Piceno as the venue for their wedding. On the afternoon of their joining, the village turned out in their droves creating a carnival atmosphere. Nicole, accompanied by her father, walked up the aisle looking radiant and as fresh as the sun itself. The two lovers exchanged vows and swore allegiance to each other in the same church that had been the scene of such sadness in a previous time. As the sunshine combined with the deluge of flowers and rice fell upon them, Stefano knew he had found wholeness, and promised he would bring her to San Piceno, their paradise, often.

As throngs of people shouted and cheered and cameras flashed in their smiling faces, the shimmering figures stood some distance back, smiling and sharing in the occasion like any other. They felt the love surrounding the village that day and they absorbed the elation before them. And next to them, scarcely visible in the sparkling sunlight, stood the faint silhouettes of Emilio and Cesare, barely strong enough to project an image at all, but whole enough to witness the wonder of love.

It was a match made in heaven and deserved to be blessed by the Angels that watched.

CHAPTER EIGHT

'Those of you who doubt the words "fate" and "destiny" will never question such things when seeing the miracle of a new life.'
(From the scriptures of Galgliel)

1988

After giving birth in her native Italy, Nicole watched on as the timeless moment took place. Stefano cradled the baby in his arms stroking the infant's soft skin, wanting to squeeze her chubby arms, wanting to ruffle her mop of deep black hair yet he remained unable to do anything except smile, and to continue to cry.

Nicole was tired but elated. The labour had lasted over fourteen hours and at one point a Caesarean was contemplated, but eventually, with superb work from the maternity nurse, the six-pound baby girl had been delivered. The devotion for the man she now shared a child with was as deep and loving as a woman could wish for. Despite her tiredness Nicole felt energy inside that warmed her throughout – the energy of true love.

'Francesca,' she said softly, causing Stefano to look towards her. 'Francesca is beautiful, no?'

Stefano smiled warmly. 'Beautiful.

'Francesca.' He repeated the name. 'That is so beautiful; she is so beautiful. Our child, our creation,' he added in a whisper.

The door of the hospital room opened as the nurse returned. She gave a warm smile in the direction of Stefano before turning to Nicole. 'It is time to rest now.'

As her words settled in Nicole's ears, a wave of drawn-out tiredness enveloped her. She nodded and looked at Stefano. He leant over the bed and kissed her softly on the cheek, running his fingers through her long dark hair as he did so. Pausing for a moment, he then dropped his head slowly towards his newborn daughter; a feeling of overwhelming love covered his being. His lips touched her fragile forehead. He felt the small baby wrinkle against his warm kiss. Pure delight ran through his veins.

'I will be here in the morning, darling.' His gaze returned to Nicole. 'Then we will go home... Our family will go home.'

* * *

Recognising the nurse as she passed him in the corridor, Stefano suddenly felt small, meagre... It had been her work that had aided the birth and now, here, he had a chance to thank her. Before she had moved too far on, he called out in Italian, 'Mi scusi.'

She turned back at his words and he now saw a wisdom that belied her youthful appearance. A feeling of humbleness washed over him as he spoke. 'I wish to thank you, from the bottom of my heart, for all you have done on this day. I, we, will never forget you.'

The nurse smiled with a warmth that radiated through him. 'She will be a beautiful child, Stefano.' She said his name and he felt familiarity as she spoke it. 'I am happy to help bring such a gift into the world.'

Stefano approached, kissing her on both cheeks and, as he did so, thought of a gift to bring when he came to collect Nicole. Yes, a beautiful bouquet of flowers, he decided. As he withdrew, Stefano glanced at her name badge and memorised it – Rozalinda Gardner.

* * *

Stefano almost glided along the white corridors of Pescara's Santo Spirito Hospital until he found a payphone and dialled the number for his grandparents in San Piceno. Although sleep deprived, he could not wait until the one and a half hour journey back home was completed to tell his family of the news. The beep of the ring tone was interrupted quickly by the voice of his grandfather, answering in the typical Italian manner. 'Pronto?'

He took a deep breath. 'It's a girl! It's a girl!' The words blurted out in pure joy. Stefano's ear then became witness to his grandfather who dropped the phone with a hefty clunk before repeating his statement with the enthusiasm of a child. Stefano pushed his ear to the phone to hear the impact of his news. He heard his grandmother shouting excitedly before Vicente spoke again. His voice was echoed by all in the room. 'Congratulazioni! Congratulazioni!'

He spoke for a short time to each of his elder family before clicking back the receiver. Now he must call his mother and father. Now he could give his mother a moment she would cherish forever.

Before dialling the number Stefano paused. He felt a new emotion rise to the surface. One he had not contemplated. He tried to control this feeling but it would not be subdued. Placing the phone back on the hook he tried to stop his stomach turning over. He could not. At the moment of unblemished joy of fatherhood he realised the utter sense of loss that his parents must have felt on the day that Emilio had died.

Before, at just eighteen, he had not *truly* understood the loss of a brother as he had not understood the change in his parents. He had faced a thousand memories of Emilio and Cesare but they had all been from his perspective. Now, with a daughter of his own, he felt utterly aware of his parents' heartache. He suddenly feared telling his mother and father. Francesca could never replace his brother, he knew that. She could only be a gift from God that would be adored and treasured by all. He was now a parent as well as a son. A new found clarity ran through his veins. He understood his parents' despair over the last eight years. He understood his mother's vacant stares whenever there had been a family celebration. He understood his father's lack of emotion since that day. Their sense of loss was the ultimate. No parent should lose a child in their lifetime. The sadness of death should only be witnessed by the children as age takes their elders to '*cielo*'.

Eventually he summed up the courage to make the call. A different ring tone and a longer gap before a voice answered. 'Hello?'

The silky tone of his mother's voice resurrected the tears and sentiment. 'Mama – Stefano.'

'Stefano?' she replied, her voice quavering slightly as it travelled down the line. The one word she uttered explained so much. He now knew his mother and father so much more. The quaver was a part of her being; her voice could not lie, or tell of the apprehension she felt at the sound of her son's voice. She could not bring herself to ask for news. She feared such news since the day of Emilio's death in case it carried the same message of tragedy. Stefano understood now.

'Mama, it's a baby girl.' He stopped momentarily; was he understanding her tension or misjudging his own? After a brief pause he continued, 'She is fine, Mama. She is well and so beautiful, Mama; so beautiful.'

The line remained silent and that silence echoed inside Stefano's mind. It expanded into what seemed like minutes, hours. He wiped the back of his hand across his forehead. He was perspiring profusely.

He spoke into the silence. 'We have named her Francesca, Mama.'

'It is a beautiful name, Stefano.' Her voice carried a smile to his ear. He looked up to the ceiling, his face beaming in relief. 'I will call Papa; he will be overjoyed.' Her voice broke up slightly as she added, 'It will mean so much to him, Stefano.'

He heard the crack in her accent, the pain in her words. They meant so much more then he could have comprehended before. He felt desperately happy, yet desperately sad.

'I love you, Mama.'

'And I love you.' He heard the clunk of the phone resting against the sideboard. He waited.

After a moment he heard his father's gruff voice. 'È vero? Una ragazza?'

'Si, Papa.' He found himself laughing aloud. 'It is true and it is a girl.'

'I am very proud, son, and Nicole, is she alright, are they alright?'

'Everything is fine, Papa. They are both tired but wonderful, as am I.'

Whether it was the distance between them or simply the moment, Stefano could not be sure. He felt the awkwardness, but did not know how to deal with it. Another silence followed, this time not through emotions, but through the distance of both Father and son and the miles that separated them. Mimo was the first to speak.

'We are delighted, my son, and we cannot wait to see you both... you three,' he added clumsily.

Listening to his father as a father now himself made it easy for Stefano to digest his words. He knew the hidden meaning, just as he had done with his mother. This time he felt stronger as he replied, 'We will be there as soon as things are arranged here, Papa.'

An awkward pause ensued before Mimo spoke again.

'I understand. As soon as you can, please.'

Stefano nodded and clicked the phone back onto the hook. There was no ending to the conversation, no '*I love you, Papa*'. They did not do that anymore. They had not done that since the death of Emilio, since the death of the word *love* in

62

his father's heart.

Walking out of the hospital Stefano breathed in the fresh evening air. It was still warm despite being March. The sea air from the Adriatic gave the gentle breeze a salty perfume making him lick his lips as the thought came to him.

'England,' he said aloud.

Everything he had known was in England, yet everything he loved was here, in Italy. Life in London had been tolerable, but, since meeting Nicole, that was all it had become, tolerable. Home was Italy, at least in his heart. Despite the decision to live in England, Stefano knew it was not really his home. It was not *their* home.

Yet, because of his father, he knew at that moment that Francesca would have to begin her life in England.

* * *

When, in the winter of 1988, Jenny Healy gave birth to their second child she was overjoyed. Many might suggest that the firstborn child always holds a special meaning to some parents, not that all children are not special. But for Jenny, the birth of Holly was the most joyous moment of her marriage.

The bond was there from the first moment she held the small fair-haired bundle in her arms. Because of the season, and because she was such a gift, Jenny wanted her named Holly. She of course loved Terrance but somewhere deep inside over the last two years she had felt that he was more her husband's child than their own. She felt angry at herself for feeling this way but she could not help it. From the day Terrance had breathed his first lungful of air, Terry had been smitten.

His name was Terry's choice, naturally as he put it, a son and heir to the empire he was working so hard to build for them all. Jenny did not object, nor resent his enthusiasm; he was the perfect father to Terrance, allowing him more time than he had allowed himself all the years they had been married. He still worked like a dog but took his son wherever he could. Terrance became the centre of his universe and he loved nothing better than to carry him in his arms and sit him behind the counter of the shop once known as Baker Brothers. Here Terry would chat to him all day long, serving old faces and sharing his pride with them all.

Those early years were the happiest she had seen him. The fact that she did not get many moments of romance or love hurt a little but she told herself it was for the greater cause of the family. Her parents seemed to accept this; it was the way of things and Jenny was not a selfish woman. She knew there must always be sacrifices in a marriage and, after all, Terry worked only for the good of his family.

So when Holly was born Jenny found many things. She found that Terry did not have room in his world for another child to dote over. This, contrary to making her feel disappointed, made her feel more alive than ever. She had a beautiful girl to cherish with a face that listened to her every word. She had found a best friend and loved Holly in the same way Terry loved their son.

By the time Holly entered the world, T Healy & Sons had twenty-four shops. They had spread across the North of England mainly, but started to open a few more branches in the South. As the business grew, Terry controlled senior staff appointments and gave excellent bonuses to them if the stores under their control had success. He had one major weakness though which stole time from his family: he did not trust anyone quite enough to be the main buyer for the company. He took the mantle and in his mind groomed Terrance to be his successor one day. The growing size of the company made it easy to hammer down suppliers and he spent many an hour on the phone or in his office, his Sheffield accent barking at hapless salesmen and reps who knew that, despite the low prices, the turnover would make a big difference to their respective companies should they do business with T Healy & Sons.

For his part, Terry was a very fair man. He had instilled in his veins the morals of Mr Baker and, as such, always treated people with respect and dignity, once the tough end of the deal had been achieved. After many a blunt, even aggressive, bargaining session he would be the first to put one hand in his pocket and the other around the shoulder of his new or current supplier and buy them a good meal or give them a gift for their wives. Terry Healy drove a hard bargain but did things the right way.

* * *

Now a larger family, the year of 1988 was to bring a vast change in their lives and show many sides to the husband Jenny had married.

'Honey, I have been thinking,' she mentioned casually one rare afternoon when all of them were together. The two children were sleeping and peace reigned in their Worksop home.

Terry looked up from a wad of sheets he had brought back from the office. 'Yes, love?' he replied with a blank expression.

To get him alone for a day was one achievement; to hold any degree of attention could well be another. Jenny struck like a cobra.

'Well, darling…' she began tentatively, 'the family is growing…'

'Grown you mean, Jenny, grown,' he interrupted with a steely look in his eye.

She sighed, exasperated already. Once again in their marriage he decided the shots. 'For God's sake, grown then!' she said with a fierceness that made him sit back and take notice. 'The point is, I think we should move, into a bigger house, in a different town.'

Her outburst silenced him briefly. Seeming to realise that he had offended her with the family numbers' issue, Terry moved across and sat next to her on the couch showing another side of his character. 'If that is what you want,' he said in a tender voice, 'then that, love, is what we will do. Business is good, we have the money, so you say where you want to live and we can begin to look.'

He kissed her on the cheek. She felt both jubilant and downtrodden at the same time. He would do that for her but they would not be having any more children. End of story on that one. As she looked at him, Jenny imagined one of his meetings with a desperate salesman and pictured him saying the words, 'And that's that!' She bit her lip and pushed the thought away, concentrating on keeping her calm.

'I would like to perhaps move somewhere nice in London, or anywhere nearer to Stebdon. I think it would be good for the children, don't you?'

'Mmm,' was his initial reply as he pushed himself up from the sofa, 'I'll have a good think about that, love.' Seeing a glint of frustration he added hastily, 'You know, we will have to think about relocating offices, that kind of thing.'

She nodded, admitting both victory and defeat at the same time. They would be moving, but ultimately he would decide.

* * *

Four months later and four new shops later (the company objective was now a new shop a month) Terry and Jenny settled on the new home. London was the destination and Hampstead the place. They had looked at three properties in the area once Terry had decided it was the perfect location, both for the family and also the business. He was elated when Jenny agreed it was for the best. She privately thought of more trips to Stebdon and Hampstead at least halved the journey.

The house was beautiful: five bedrooms with three bathrooms and steeped in luxury. The short distance to Hampstead Heath made good sense for the children and the area was very much in demand. Jenny never questioned the need for an extra bedroom. She just imagined that most of the houses would have at least that number.

Initially Jenny concentrated on making the house in London a home with her own personal touches. Spending time with the children was a pleasure, although demanding, as Terry was working longer and longer hours. When she could, she would take the children to Stebdon and Terry would join them on odd weekends. As time passed, that became less and less but she did not mind. Sometimes it would just be her and Holly who would chatter away to her in the car whilst the 'two men', as Terry referred to him and his son, would 'be off to work'.

In hindsight Jenny would reflect on that period of both children's lives and their marriage as a whole. Perhaps if she had been a stronger, more aggressive woman, she could have stopped the slow fracture that was growing within the family but the little girl from Stebdon was not that kind of person. She watched as Terrance grew, developing more and more of his father's traits but with less of his selflessness. Instead of nipping it in the bud she let Terry be her son's guide and found herself concentrating more of her time and energy on Holly.

It was to be a decision she would regret.

CHAPTER NINE

*'Doubt in us in your darkest moments and the world will doubt
with you. Believe in us when you are strong and the world will not
matter. For all know of the word Angel.'*

(From the scriptures of Galgliel)

1988-1995

The goodbyes in Simione's were both long and emotional.
Nicole clung to her parents, tears streaming down her face,
whilst Stefano held baby Francesca in his arms feeling
distress at the scene before him.

Nicole's mother, Maria, was beside herself, weeping as if
her daughter was leaving forever. The two had exchanged
promises of frequent phone calls and visits before her father,
Paulo, a big man with a big heart, crumbled like a cookie into
his daughter's arms, setting off more wails and many more
tears.

Stefano felt awful witnessing the scene. When it was his
turn to say goodbye he felt guilty as hell. Both Maria and
Paulo understood the family reasons behind the move and
there was no anger, no accusations of stealing Nicole or any
such thing. It just did not help. Holding Francesca simply
caused more kissing and sobbing. It was a dark moment
before a new beginning.

Nicole had promised she would come to England with
Stefano and now she was honouring that pledge. He loved her

more than life itself at that moment and swore that one day they would return to Italy.

It was with the heaviest of hearts that the three boarded the plane to England.

* * *

Upon the family's arrival in England, Mimo and Eva greeted them with embraces and kind words, doting on Francesca. Stefano watched on, smiling at their joy yet noticing that both his parents suddenly looked much older.

Eva looked drawn and haggard. The beautiful woman she had once been was a thing of the past, gradually destroyed by the death of a son and the overwork which followed to try and avoid the pain. Even with Stefano's help with the blinds business, Mimo had worked himself into the ground. Then there were the trips to Point Clear, the café, the factory, the heartache and the strain on their marriage that ultimately had caused his recent ill health. He looked like a man who had run out of ideas and energy. Stefano swore he would never let that happen to his family.

* * *

That night the family sat down to discuss future plans. It was Eva's wish to return to Italy. As they sat in the café, blinds drawn, Francesca nuzzled up on Nicole's lap asleep whilst Mimo told of their wishes.

'For many years we have worked day and night to achieve what we now have, what we want you to have,' he began solemnly. 'The recent times have made it more difficult. My health is not what it was, Stefano.' His eyes were softer than Stefano remembered, weaker, tired. 'Your mother has known for a long time that this day would come. We want nothing from you and offer you all we have. All we ask is that, from the profits, you help us to make a life in our remaining years, back in San Piceno.' His voice began to falter at the name. 'At home.'

Seeing Mimo becoming upset, Eva took over the mantle. 'Stefano, Nicole, you are now a family, you have a beautiful daughter and your whole lives ahead of you. Mimo and I have spoken for many hours recently.' She moved her wrinkled hand onto her husband's and smiled at him. 'We have not spoken that much for a long time...' Stefano had not seen such affection between them since he could remember. His father's eyes welled with tears as they pulled such emotions from each other once again.

'You know both businesses, my son,' Mimo spoke proudly, 'you will do well and you will have a good life here, as a family. All we have worked for will one day be yours; we just ask for things to be this way now. We cannot go on anymore.' Mimo let the tears trickle freely down his face.

'Papa, please,' Stefano had never seen him like this, 'please do not be upset, we will do our best and we will raise Francesca here. One day we, like you, must return to Italy. This will be our home for now but it will not be forever. We have a promise to each other to keep.' He looked at Nicole, who smiled reassuringly and nodded.

'Your father is upset because we made a wrong choice and he does not want that for you,' Eva said.

'I do not understand, Mama.'

'I will do my best to explain to you. It is the least you deserve, Stefano.' The warmth in her tone reminded him of the early days, the days when she smiled and felt the joy of being a mother, the days before her heart had been torn in two.

'When we arrived here we had many dreams, dreams we shared together. You and Emilio were born to us and our lives were full of happiness. We worked to create our home here and the home in Point Clear to settle in one day. It all seemed so different to San Piceno and we thrived on the space and freedom. When Emilio was taken away, everything changed...' Eva closed her eyes, as if to seal in the pain. When she opened them again Stefano saw a watery gaze that had held tears of grief for so long. A wave of her hand stopped him trying to intervene as she swallowed hard and continued.

'When we returned to San Piceno for the funeral we found so many caring people and that is where our first mistake lay.' She glanced at Mimo who returned her look of sadness. 'We mistook the care and love of our own people as intrusion. We had forgotten how it felt to have many people who care around us, so we decided, instead of selling up and moving back home, we would return to London and be left alone in our grieving. It was a terrible mistake.'

'We had changed, son.' Mimo whispered the words.

'At first we noticed nothing, we were too busy dealing with our pain,' Eva went on. 'The seasons passed and you grew, while we also grew…apart. What we want to say is this: England has changed, is changing. Do not change with it. We made the mistake and so nearly lost each other. London is a city and the people do not have the closeness of a village. They have forgotten many things and you must not let that happen to you. Return home often and never forget to be close to each other, to share all your secrets and *never* hide from each other. It really does not matter where you live. The only difference is that, in a city, it is easier to forget how to be close.'

* * *

'Are we doing the right thing?' Nicole whispered as they lay together in the darkness.

'I do not know,' replied Stefano. 'I feel torn in two. One part of me knows we belong here, the other in Italy. We will return, darling, I promise that.'

She stroked his hair and kissed him gently. 'It does not matter where we are, my love, as long as we are together. Let us never forget that.'

'And let us never make the mistake that my parents made.'

'Never…'

They held each other and fell into a gentle sleep whilst in the room next door his parents did the same, for the first time in nearly a decade.

* * *

A month later and his parents left England for the last time. There were more tears and hugging, now for Stefano as he watched his mother and father go. Everything was changing.

Stefano had planned meticulously for the move and now began to implement his ideas. With Nicole taking care of Francesca, she could not offer much help in the café so he employed a local lady Wendy to oversee the day-to-day running. Wendy was East End through and through, with a humour that attracted the customers, as well as a talent for organising that made her a pleasure to work with.

Previously the blinds business had been Stefano's main concern but now he knew he would have to divide his time as well as save enough money to send to his parents. Then there was the home in Point Clear to maintain in addition to travelling back and forth to Italy. It was not going to be easy. After discussions with the manager Darrell Britton, Stefano made the decision to entrust him with the overall running of the factory. He had been there for many years and knew the place inside out. Stefano knew he could count on him and in addition he hired a part-time secretary, a woman named Sue, to keep an eye on the books. The mother of two had a degree in accounting and was ideal. His final change was to hire a representative for the company. He would not have the time to seek new customers so he put out an advert for a sales rep, offering a commission-based position in the company. Out of the many that applied, one stood out. A young chap with an Italian background arrived, brimming with confidence. An hour later and Nevallo Green had got the job. The choices Stefano had made were to prove wise.

The first year went by in a flash. The café boomed and the blinds business thrived. Enough business came in to make the payments to Mimo and Eva, as well as maintaining a good lifestyle, and securing a few visits back home in between to visit both sets of parents. Mimo looked ten years younger and he and Eva had rediscovered their love for each other. Things seemed to be going perfectly.

* * *

The letters had long ceased to arrive in Lindholme Prison; and the visits had stopped long before that. They had been filled with pain anyway, sitting behind a glass screen looking at the hatred in his wife's eyes. After the first two years of receiving a maximum fourteen year sentence for manslaughter, John Parsons received his divorce papers and then the visits stopped completely. He received a few pictures of his son and then… nothing.

On the day of his release in 1991, John had served eleven years of his sentence. He was, in every way, the perfect example to many of drink-driving and its horrors. Four people had died because of him and he had suffered the grief quietly. He had lost his family, business and dignity. He could probably have kept his head down and been granted parole much earlier, but the combination of goading combined with the collapse of his marriage made him an angry man for the first few years and any chance of early release was soon quashed with incident after incident.

As the years moved on he adapted to prison life. He had little choice. He came to terms with the guilt and began to read from the bible. He started to dream and in those dreams he faced many demons. The world outside seemed a lifetime ago and the thought of it numbed him. There was nothing there for him anymore. He had killed innocent people and, like a man who has killed, he found it easier than he expected to admit the *death* of his marriage and his family. He had nothing to leave prison for.

On the morning of his release, John Parsons stood alone outside the bland surroundings of Lindholme. The Doncaster rain was ceaseless and he was soon wet through. Just one man with a few pounds and a tatty case walked towards the bus stop. His time had been done, now his journey must begin.

The next few months saw John attempt to resurrect his life. He did not get in contact with his wife. That was far from his mind. He went through the motions, trying to get work to maintain the scruffy bedsit he had located. Each time he got as far as an interview he would feel the look and sense that his past was still haunting him. No one wanted to employ a murderer to drive for them, especially when the murders had been committed whilst driving.

He had been prepared for it though. Picking up scraps of work, he paid his way and put by a little. The bottle returned and he drank from it whilst holding the bible in his other hand and repenting to it. His only solace was the hope that he could be forgiven. His time in prison had not all been a waste. He knew the names of the relatives of those he had killed. They were now his redemption. He relied on it.

He finished the letters and sealed them carefully before tucking one inside the other and scribbling the name and address of his wife on the outside. If all went well, he would not return and she would know of his sorrow and pain. It was the only way.

* * *

Wendy was tidying up at the café when the last customer entered. She puffed out her cheeks briefly. It had been a long day, and it was always annoying when a 'trailer' as she called them arrived. The man was thickset and short. He was almost bald, a wisp of hair remaining which he had pushed forward in an attempt to cover his shining pate.

His eyes darted around the café making him look more

suspicious than a 'usual' customer. She summed him up in an instant. He was looking for someone and somehow that *someone* had something to do with the café.

'What can I get ya, love?'

He studied her carefully. She could feel his intense look and it made her a little uneasy. 'Are you having anything, love? We are nearly closed, ya know.'

'I'm looking for someone,' he said cagily.

'Ain't we all, love, ain't we all.' She didn't feel threatened but rather irritated now. 'Who you looking for? Perhaps I might know them.'

'I'm looking for a Mimo Riza,' he said after a short delay. 'I was told I would find him here.'

'You would have...' she answered, 'a year or so ago.' She toyed with the idea of telling him about Stefano but her East End instinct kicked in. 'He and his wife left last year, moved away, love.' She tried to look vague. 'No idea where they are now.'

He seemed to accept her explanation, looking annoyed with himself. 'Who owns it now then? You?' he asked in a curt tone. 'I *need* to find them.'

Whatever it was that this man wanted, she did not feel comfortable now. 'Yeah, love, me and my old man own the place. When they sold up we never asked where they were going. You don't, do you?'

'Thank you.' He seemed convinced enough. 'If you see them, can you just do one thing for me?'

'Sure.' She shrugged.

'Tell them that I am so sorry; John Parsons is so sorry.'

* * *

John Parsons did not get to see Mimo or Eva. His trail for the relatives of the Bidante family ran dry as well, ending up in a graveyard in Clacton. There he found the headstones of the two people whose deaths he had been responsible for. He laid flowers and repented, bible by his side. He bumped into a local lady named Roz who kindly told him that there had been no descendants.

His mission had failed and soon after the bottle would take over completely. John Parsons was to sink into the shadows with a tainted heart and corrupted soul.

* * *

It was a few days before Wendy recollected the visit. Stefano was in the café and chatting with Nicole about arrangements for the weekend. The mention of seeing his parents jogged her memory.

'Oh, Stefano, I meant to tell you, there was a man who came in the other day. He was after seeing your father.'

'Did he leave a message?' Stefano took little interest.

'Yeah,' she replied, 'wanted to know where he was now. I said I owned the café; was not sure about him, ya know.' She grinned and Stefano slipped his arm around her.

'You're a good woman. Is that it?'

She racked her brain for a moment. 'Yeah, he said his name was John Parsons and he said to tell your dad he was sorry. That was all he said.'

Stefano thought. John Parsons. Something about the name was kind of familiar.

He shook his head after a pause. 'No, never heard of him.'

CHAPTER TEN

'There is no Archangel of time, for time mattered not to us, until now. Like the intricate working parts of the clock itself, humanity will make choices that decide where the hands will guide them, and now, ultimately, us too.'

(Archangel Galgliel spoken in the halls of Angels)

1996

Edward Sonning sat at the long oak table while his wife Hayley bustled around at the stove. She called up to their son William that tea was ready before taking a fresh cotton tablecloth in her petite hands. The scent of slow-cooked beef casserole entered Edward's nostrils from across the kitchen as he watched his wife. Hayley gave her husband a loving smile as she shook the cloth, creating a breeze which momentarily lifted her long brown hair.

As the cloth fell into place, he digested her beauty and felt himself gulp in the subtle fragrance of her perfume, that familiar scent that still reminded him of their first meeting.

All his life Edward had been an uncomplicated man. From his youth in the small village of Stebdon where his father owned the largest farm, to his adulthood where he learnt his trade: farming naturally. Life in Stebdon had always been simple, easy and straightforward. The population had hardly risen over the last twenty years and the people were still warm in comparison to some of the bigger towns and cities Edward had visited through farming affairs. Hayley, humming gently, collected up the cutlery as he reflected the fact that meeting the woman who would become his wife had been simple. The local dance at the village hall and the simplest of requests: 'Will you dance with me?'

He had been twenty-one years old then. She was just twenty. Neither really knew anything of the world, just the local village, its people, its customs and togetherness. Now at forty-six years old and with a son in his twentieth year, Edward knew a little more of the world. Not because he had wanted to but because the big wide world had come in search of him.

With the gentle sound of ladle upon stoneware, the aroma of dinner grew significantly. Edward gazed out of the lead-paned window into the front yard and beyond past the four-row Acme planter. As far as his eyes could see, carefully tended fields lay containing crops of potatoes that would grow into the next generation of income for him and his family. Far to the right, the glass of nine greenhouses reflected the last rays of sun across the dark fields of finely combed earth. Edward knew this business inside out. His father had taught him and he had taught his son.

Beyond and afar lay the village of Stebdon. Grey-stone buildings blended with the green of surrounding trees and lush grass in the warm evening light. In the centre of the scene the old church clock face looked over the cobblestone square in the village centre. Crooked and twisting streets led out from the square towards quaint shops and houses. Victorian street lamps now flickered on in the main high street giving an almost Dickensian soft glow, their light reaching out to the narrow stream which ran alongside the high street east to west before winding its way down and out past the farm and the village itself.

William bounded into the kitchen in tandem with the large pot of casserole arriving on the table. His tanned young face bore an enthusiastic smile as he pulled out the large aged wooden chair to the left of his father. 'Hydroponics, Dad, that's the way forward!' He spoke with an energetic tempo before casting a cheeky grin his mother's way. 'Hi, Mum.'

'Hi, darling,' she replied, sitting down to the right of the head of the table. She clasped her hands and waited for the two men of her world to follow suit before she began. 'For what we are about to eat, thank you, God.'

Edwards's eyes met his son's as he opened them. He saw a sparkle of accomplishment shining through as William continued to speak. 'Dad, I've been looking into it and hydroponics really is the way forward. We can maximise our output tenfold and from there, who knows?'

Never a man to rush into things, Edward ladled the stew onto his plate slowly whilst thinking at a pace akin to the serving speed. William grabbed a slab of bread and tore at it, fresh white teeth ripping through the dough impatiently. Hayley said nothing, just smiled at her husband and waited for the stew to come her way.

Eventually Edward spoke after taking the first warm beefy mouthful of stew. 'Son,' he said gently, his country accent predominant, 'this family has been in this village for many years. We've always done well by ourselves and we've always had a good reputation within the village. Now why do we want to be talking large words and things like hydroponics? There's no need or place for that in our family.'

William gave his mother an exasperated glance as he spooned the stew towards his mouth. He chewed at speed before swallowing down the rich food. 'Good, Mum, real good.'

Hayley smiled and spoke the words her son wanted to hear following his briefest of compliments. 'Why not let the boy speak, Ed, at least listen to what he has to say?'

Edward chewed on another mouthful whilst wiping a piece of bread around the edge of the plate to soak up the juices. William took his chance.

'Dad, it's not the biggest investment but the potential is vast. We have the greenhouses already and with some Ebb and

79

flood benches, solution tanks and plumbing, lighting, sensors and an aspirated box we could start to mass-produce. There's a massive market, Dad. Sonnings Farm could sell real big, you know.' He waited for an answer but seeing there was none he continued, 'Dad, we could have a mass-production of lettuces every thirty-five days!' William reached across to hold his father's arm.

As Edward felt his son's touch something inside wanted to pull away, to show anger at his son. He did not, instead he let his son hold on and speak. 'Just think about it, Dad, that all I'm asking.'

'I'll think about it, son,' Edward replied slowly as he glanced at Hayley who smiled and nodded quietly with a look of satisfaction. Confrontation had been avoided and her son and husband had spoken of serious matters. She ate with a new found appetite whilst the cogs within each of the men's brains turned rapidly.

* * *

The bell jangled gleefully welcoming its visitors through the ageing lead-paned door. Above the entrance, quaint black stencil writing stood out on the old wooden fascia: 'Guild Toys and Treats'.

Stepping inside, the two children accompanying Jenny Healy were instantly spellbound at the wonders within. Jenny took a moment to breathe in the shop's smell, a nasal mixture of so many wonderful things. She could never put her finger on that aroma; was it age maybe? Or the odours of all the toys, the jars and boxes of sweets combined? It was still there all these years later, an almost exquisite smell that hadn't changed since she was a little girl, and never would in this wonderful shop. She noted how much smaller it now looked inside than the last time she had visited. It measured perhaps twenty-five feet in depth and around ten feet in width but contained so much in such a small area. Wooden cabinets lined the walls whilst the floor area was precisely covered with children's delights. Large teddy bears and soft toys sat on the cleanly swept boards making a fluffy passageway to the scarred old counter at the rear of the shop. Either side of that were housed an array of toys and gadgets. Recapturing her childhood, she smiled and turned to watch her children experience the sensation for the first time.

'Terrance, Holly, what do you think?' Jenny asked the question with an inner smile. She knew at that moment the two children were in a world of their own.

Terrance had been gazing upwards since he had walked in the shop. His eyes were fixed on an array of Airfix model planes which hung from the ceiling at the rear of the shop, their kit packs stacked neatly below on the shelf. In front over a dozen marionettes hung, all positioned for purpose and effect. A Hornby train track ran around the whole of the shop, set just below the ceiling. Tiny puffs of smoke came from the small chimney as the steam engine whistled gently in tandem with the constantly moving train. The left-hand side of the shop ceiling had Christmas toys, again hung with delicate care, small lights set in perfect placement to add to the beauty.

Holly wandered from shelf to shelf. Occasionally she would vent a gentle gasp at the contents before her. She had never seen so many boxes of games. Pretty doll's houses with all the 'doll' family present gazed at her, willing her to take them home.

The two children were transfixed. A jingle from the bell above the door beyond the counter made Jenny turn around. The owner Albert Guild appeared, nudging his glasses up a notch onto the bridge of his pointed nose as he made his way forward to greet them. In his late fifties, he shuffled a little, adjusting his waistcoat as he did so.

'Well, hello there,' he welcomed them in a playful tone, 'and what can we surprise you with today?'

Jenny smiled back as she walked towards the counter 'Hello, Mr Guild.'

Albert looked extra hard through his thick lenses as his right hand moved through grey wispy hair. His bony, talented fingers which had created many a toy in the days before plastic click and fix designs now scratched his scalp curiously. 'Mmm, now let me think. Do I know you?' His kindly eyes stared at her as he twitched a grey brow in inquisitive exaggeration.

Jenny grinned with amusement. 'Albert Guild! Don't say you don't remember me?'

Albert was not quite finished and pretended for a few more seconds that he had no idea who the woman in front of him was. Holly took her eyes away from the rows of shelves behind the counter. She had been mesmerised by the array of sweet-filled jars containing a kaleidoscope of colours. Now she was intrigued by the wise-looking man. 'Mummy, does Mr Guild not know you? I thought everybody knew you!' She gazed at her mother with as curious a look as Albert Guild had just delivered.

As Albert pushed open the small gate that separated the counter from the main shop, Jenny giggled. With the two children looking on, the old man held out his arms and Jenny fell into them with a childish squeal of laughter.

'Little Jenny Cross! How could I not remember you! The girl who spent nearly all her pocket money on fizzles and gobstoppers and would *never* leave this shop!' Albert let out a boom of laughter which oozed delightful warmth and kindness.

Holly pulled at her mother's arm gently. 'Mummy,' she whispered, 'that's not your name!'

Jenny moved back from the warm clinch, her face as alight as the children's had been upon entering. 'No, darling, that was my name when I was a little girl like you, before I married Daddy.' She looked into Albert's soft brown eyes. 'Albert, I would like you to meet my children. This is Holly, my youngest, and over there standing like a statue is Terrance, my oldest.'

82

Albert diverted his attention to Holly. 'Well, it's a pleasure to meet you, young lady. I must say you are very pretty, and how old are you?'

Jenny felt warmth transcend within. She could remember Albert Guild saying something similar to her many years before and now the words were rich in nostalgia.

Holly poked her hand out further from her red woollen coat so that her small fingers could form the offering of a handshake. 'My name is Holly, Mr Guild, and I am eight years old. It is very nice to meet you and I like your shop very much, very, very much indeed.' She repeated the words with perfect conviction as she smiled up at Albert.

'Why, that is very kind of you, Holly.' He took her petite hand in his and softly shook it so as not to hurt her. 'A pleasure to meet you too!' Albert looked towards the little boy who had now begun to wander, oblivious to the attention, towards the Action Men toy section. Jenny called out to him. 'Terrance, come and meet Mr Guild.'

Terrance ignored her voice and Jenny spoke again, this time in a slightly harsher tone. 'Terrance Healy!'

Terrance turned, his face showing contempt at her voice like a gluttonous child being interrupted from a midnight feast. 'Mum, I want some of these toys.' He pulled at an Action Man figure which did not give way, seeming almost to resist his greedy clasp. 'This one for starters!' he said giving it another tug to force it free from the wire display that held it in place.

'Don't force it, boy.' The voice of Albert echoed around the shop, seemingly gathering loudness until it reached the ears of Terrance. He froze on the spot, his hands dropping to his side.

Normally Holly would have shivered with fear, but not today, not in this shop and not with this nice man. Jenny flushed with embarrassment. 'Come here, Terrance!' Terrance obeyed and shuffled slowly towards the counter mimicking Albert's earlier natural shuffle.

'I'm sorry, Albert,' Jenny muttered in a defenceless voice. 'He's like his father, he normally gets what he wants.' She suddenly felt small. She was that little girl in the shop again and, as she heard her own words, she actually felt ashamed. That was it, ashamed.

As Terrance stood next to his mother, his head dropped for a moment. Albert waited. He had been in the company of children for over thirty years. They would come and go in his shop, good kids and bad kids, poor kids and rich kids, generous kids and greedy kids. He knew how to deal with the Terrances of this world. He had liked Jenny Cross as a child. She had been one of the good kids, generous and happy. Holly looked to be a clone of her: long blonde hair that dropped over the shoulders, button-nosed with dimpled cheeks and a warm smile which was complemented by clear blue eyes. As he looked at Terrance he saw a sulky child with sallow eyes and thin mean lips. His pointed nose seemed almost to push his cheeks back, giving his expression one of gauntness. His basin-style haircut did him no favours and Albert knew that, without meeting his father, this boy in front of him was from that side of the cabbage patch.

'If you want something in this shop, Terrance, you just ask and I will help.' Albert said the words in as kind a tone as he could find, for the sake of Jenny more than the boy. 'See, the toys are mine at the moment until someone buys them and they don't like to be moved without me saying so.' He looked up at Jenny and grinned.

Holly giggled and Jenny found herself laughing. 'Say sorry to Mr Guild, Terrance, and we'll have a look at the toys you want.'

After a few seconds Terrance raised his head and looked at Albert. His mother's words and temptation of the impending gifts made it easier to be nice. 'Sorry, Mr Guild,' he said in a meaningless tone.

An hour later and the counter was amass with toys and treats. Three Action Men figures, two Airfix kits, a train set and five extra boxes of accessories to complement the main purchases. Terrance looked smug and content as he stuffed his face with the coconut 'tobacco' that Albert had given him to sample. Holly had selected one marionette, a hand-carved Pinocchio character, as well as a big teddy that she had spotted on arriving. She had a selection of sweets carefully wrapped in crisp white paper bags. Jenny had simply chosen a box of fizzles and a jigsaw puzzle of Stebdon for nostalgic purposes. She had not completed a jigsaw for years and had not even thought about it until the box called out to her. She had to buy it.

Albert shuffled around as he popped the purchases into brown bags of all sizes. It was going to be a good day today. Jenny had spent more in the time she had been there than he had taken all week. A couple of children had been in and bought sweets but, on the whole, toy sales had been slower than normal this year. Times were moving on and new crazes were on the horizon. Computer games that Albert did not understand or want to sell. They had no beauty or imagination. Not in the same way as an inanimate toy did. Albert Guild's toys had to be made to come alive and he liked it that way.

Jenny paid the bill and gave Albert a long hug. 'It's lovely to see you again, Mr Guild,' she said in a much more childish voice than she expected. The magic of his shop still got to her, even now.

'You too, Jenny Cross.' He whispered the words to her before breaking from the affectionate clinch. 'And it's very nice to meet you, young lady, and you, young man.'

Holly beamed while Terrance took little notice. His eyes were fixed firmly on the bags.

After saying goodbye, the three left the shop and turned left into Copse Way where the car was parked. As they approached, a few children moved away from the gleaming Range Rover, their eyes looking in awe at the owners. Jenny smiled at them as she picked the keys out of her handbag. She felt her phone vibrate as she did so. Taking the mobile out, she flicked open the front. It was Terry.

'Hi, darling.' She greeted him warmly whilst opening the

boot and pointing to the children to put the toys in there. 'No, sweetheart, we'll be a couple of hours. I've taken the children out for the day into the country and treated them to some toys.' The children got into the car and waited as Jenny finished the conversation.

She started the Range Rover and began to drive slowly out of the village. It had been a few years since the last visit but Jenny never tired of the landscape that surrounded this unblemished part of England. The old-fashioned stone set buildings lined the narrow streets leading from the village centre. Her eyes searched for signs of change but, instead, found a warmth growing inside as she saw little or no difference. The picture house stood on the corner of Gables Street, its coating of warm red paint mingled with the fresh flowers that adorned the entrance. The village hall looked smaller than she remembered. It would of course, for it was years ago that she would run there excitedly for the weekly disco and dance. Everything had a feel of prettiness; no, familiarity, that was it. A familiarity that made Jenny Cross *feel* closer to this place. She found herself missing it terribly already.

'Mum.' Terrance's voice sounded from the back seat breaking her thought patterns. 'What did Dad want?'

Still deep in thought, Jenny glanced out of the window as they passed a sign which read 'Thank you for visiting Stebdon, please drive carefully'. Her husband had not wanted anything really. He had not asked too much about her or the children either. She took one last look in the rear-view mirror and sighed gently before replying.

'Well, darling,' she said, trying to sound as excited as possible, 'Daddy has just bought up two more shops.'

The Range Rover left the green fields and farmland behind as Jenny Cross and her two children left Stebdon.

CHAPTER ELEVEN

2002 – six years later

Stefano was on the way to Point Clear when his mobile phone rang. It was Nevallo.

'Hi, Nev, how are we doing?'

'I think I may have some big news for you, my friend.' Nevallo's voice rang with excitement. 'My commission could just be shooting to the stars!'

Stefano smiled. Nevallo had been a godsend to the business, bringing in new clients faster than old ones were disappearing. The years had not always been easy, with many companies bending under the weight of cheap, imported goods that were infiltrating the market. The public were buying and the government were showing no signs of tightening the laws on imports. For Stefano that had caused a few problems, to say the least. The wages were higher in England, the red tape tighter and, just when it was getting tough, the Far East began to saturate the markets with items that were inferior but cheaper, thereby offering copies of almost everything, his blinds included. Without Nevallo's skill at selling the 'British & best' angle, Stefano doubted he would be able to survive long-term.

'So tell me,' he laughed, 'you do well enough already, what is the big news?'

'I think I have got you T Healy & Sons,' Nevallo almost yelled. 'I suppose you have heard of them?'

The news sank in and immediately two feelings ran through Stefano's mind: one was the size of the business, which would be massive; the other was a fear of that size. He had heard stories about T Healy & Sons. They paid late and expected early. A tougher company to deal with, there was none.

He was not entirely sure. 'How do you feel about it, Nev?'

'I met with Terry Healy yesterday,' Nevallo explained. 'Bit of luck really, but I found him to be an honest man. He liked the fact our blinds are made in England and he knew of them. The meeting was one of the easiest in *some* ways.'

Stefano raised his eyebrows. 'Some ways?'

'Yeah,' Nevallo replied slowly, 'we have the deal but on their terms: ninety days' payment and seasonal discounts, etc, etc. It could change the company, Stefano.'

Stefano puffed out his cheeks. 'Whew! Ninety days? That could be a problem.' He thought of Nicole, of the years that had passed and of Francesca, of her future. 'I'll have to have a think, okay, Nev? It is a huge decision.'

'Take your time,' Nevallo replied with a chuckle. 'We have two weeks.'

* * *

'Stefano, I don't know,' Nicole's reply was uncertain, 'I just think, do we need that much business? They are big, maybe too big for us?'

He could not argue. He was wary too. The temptation was there. The money would mean a golden future for his family but it would also mean a change in everything. The number of blinds they would be selling would mean more staff, more hours, perhaps moving into a larger building. There were many things to address. The one thing that niggled him more than anything was the timing. They had discussed selling the café and plodding along with the blinds business. There was enough money in that to do well. He had promised one day that they would return home. If they took the contract what would that mean in terms of that promise? How long would they stay in England?

'Look,' he replied calmly, 'you and Francesca are due to go home next week. When you're there perhaps you could talk with Papa and see what he thinks? He may have good advice.'

'Alright, darling,' she answered peaceably, 'the break will give us all time to think.'

* * *

After visiting Nicole's parents in Rome, a week later mother and daughter headed for San Piceno. The village was at its busiest in August, the month of festivals, and that is where Francesca first met Domenici.

Nicole and Francesca were at the children's regatta which saw all manner of boats sail along the River Mesti. The children were allowed to design their own efforts which, as long as they floated, could be used. The idea was just to have some fun with plenty of water and wetness. The river was shallow enough on the stretch that the regatta took place to allow a boat to float but for a child to swim safely.

The banks were packed with people and laughter resounded that afternoon; Francesca giggled as she watched the young sailors push their boats into the water, many slipping over even before they had begun. She walked the few steps along the bank side as each boat started to bob along. After a short time she, like many of the watching crowd, was soaked as jets from toy guns sprayed from the yelling children on board their vessels.

As one boat came near she heard a voice shouting in her direction. 'Hey, give me your hand!'

She found the voice. It came from a boy who was leaning from the port side, a lively grin on his face. *He is so handsome*, she thought, slim build and olive-skinned, with long locks of jet-black hair flowing down his back onto a crisp puffy white shirt like an ink spot spilling onto paper. He wore swashbuckling trousers which matched the colour of his hair. He looked ever the pirate that the flag attached on the makeshift mast behind him signified. She blushed and took his hand.

A moment later she was on board the small vessel. It was perhaps the size of two small rowing boats in length with the height of a miniature galleon. He took her by the hand and led her to the front of the ship, spraying people with a water pistol as they went. He passed her another pistol and, between them, they shot spurts of cold water, intermingled with laughing and squirting each other.

The boat did not make it to the finishing line, not that it mattered. The boy who was trying to steer failed miserably, the ship veered onto the right bank of the river sending all its crew scattering across the deck. Francesca felt scared for the briefest of moments until she felt a strong arm around her waist. The next thing she knew she was lying on the river bank, soaking wet and staring right into his eyes.

'Domenici Virone at your service.' Gleaming white teeth shone at her from the pirate.

'Francesca Riza.' She blushed again. 'Thank you for saving me.'

'Come on,' he said after a moment, 'let's go down to the finishing line; they're cooking food!' He leapt up and offered his hand, pulling her to her feet. They ran down the side of the bank and across the bridge to where a large marquee had been erected. They headed to the centre where rows of tables split the marquee into two. The happy strumming of live music sounding from the back of the hall made the atmosphere joyous.

Domenici called out, 'Mama, Papa!' Francesca turned to see his parents smiling from the other side of the tent. 'Come, meet my family,' he stopped to look at her affectionately, 'if you do not mind.'

'Of course not,' she beamed. She felt at home and excited by his vitality. 'Lead the way, my pirate!'

'This is my father, Maurizio,' he said by way of introduction as Francesca saw an older version of Domenici, as handsome as well, 'and my lovely mother, Cinzia.' The lady smiled warmly; Francesca instantly took to her. Her beauty was stereotypical Italian, latte skin with jet-black hair complemented by raisin-coloured eyes but, more than that, she had a glow about her, a kindness that needed no words to show that she cared. Her exquisiteness seemed effortless.

'This,' Domenici continued in a proud voice, 'is Francesca, my girlfriend!'

She heard the words and simply laughed but did not say anything to the contrary. She liked him immensely already and found his cheeky ways very attractive.

'Well, we will leave you two to it,' said Cinzia. 'Just don't go far, Domenici, we have dinner later.'

'Of course, Mama,' he replied, grabbing some Parma ham and melon from the nearby table. 'Come, Francesca, let's eat!'

The next hours were almost a dream for Francesca. They found a spot near some woodland to the west of the river and there they sat eating the food whilst Domenici chatted enthusiastically. He was fourteen, one year older than her, and had lived in San Piceno all his life. His father was a doctor and his mother a school teacher just outside the village. As he spoke she sensed the happiness in his tone and she found herself wishing that she lived in the village, with him. Young love was growing by the minute.

'So,' he said between mouthfuls of ham and melon, 'how come I have not seen you before? It is a small enough place.'

'I do not live here, not much anyway,' she replied, wishing more than ever that she did. 'I am here with my mother now and my grandparents live up beyond the hill.' She pointed as he nodded. 'My father is in London where we live and we have another house on the coast in England. It's kind of nice,' she added somewhat weakly.

He was intrigued. 'London? What is it like? I have never been to England!'

Francesca thought before she answered, 'It's good, in some ways. We have a nice home and we do well, but…' she found it easy to share her feelings with him, 'I am Italian and when I am here… with someone like you… I feel…'

His lips touched hers from nowhere. She did not fight, but instead opened her mouth and let him kiss her. She was not sure if she was doing it right. She had never kissed before but it felt right, he felt right. The kiss lasted for… who knows? All she knew was that she staring at him now. The kiss had finished and she felt a tremble. A small shaking inside her stomach that she had no name for. She felt her face redden.

'Will you be my girlfriend? I never really asked you.' His eyes shone.

'Yes, I will,' she replied with a shy smile. Whatever was happening to her, it felt strange but wonderful.

* * *

'He is so lovely, Mama,' Francesca crooned.

'I don't care; you should have let me know where you were,' Nicole scolded her.

Francesca felt light inside; her mother's anger was not real, not as real as it was at other times. 'Mama,' she replied in a childish tone, 'you know you don't have to worry about me here. This is San Piceno, not London.'

Nicole hid a smile from her daughter. She was right and she was not angry at all. She was pleased that Francesca was happy and the boy sounded very nice. 'I am just saying…'

'Be careful.' They said the words at the same time before bursting into laughter.

'I will be, Mama, I will be.'

'I am very happy for you, darling,' she replied affectionately. 'Now, let us go and eat with Grandpa and

Grandma. I need to have a good chat with them.'

* * *

'Mama, may I go out for a little while?' Domenici stood at the door of the kitchen looking a little shy as Francesca sidled towards him, a big grin on her face.

'So you are Domenici?' Nicole asked with a welcoming look.

'Yes, Mrs Riza,' he replied in his most polite voice, 'it is a pleasure to meet you.' He glanced at Mimo and Eva. 'Good evening to you both.'

Nicole liked what she saw and smiled as she nodded to Francesca. 'Go on, and don't be late and…'

'Be careful!' Francesca finished the sentence off. 'I will. Bye, Mama, bye, Grandpa, Grandma.' She quickly kissed them all before gleefully following Domenici outside.

Nicole sighed. 'Young love, ah? He seems nice enough.'

'He is a good boy, Nicole,' Eva answered. 'We have seen him about and his parents are good people. She could do worse.'

'I would like her to meet an Italian,' Nicole agreed. 'Maybe a little early though for my liking.'

'Let her have her fun!' Mimo laughed and Nicole noticed the change in him. He seemed so much more relaxed and healthy, a new man in comparison to the one that had left London.

'Of course.' She smiled in reply. 'Just being a mother, and talking of which…I need to speak with you, Mimo, regarding some advice.'

He raised his eyebrows good-humouredly. 'You want advice, from me? What do you think, Eva? I am no marriage counsellor.'

'Mimo, stop that! Please, Nicole, tell us what advice we can give you and know we will do our best,' Eva intervened reassuringly.

Nicole laughed out loud at the two of them. 'It's nothing like that! Not a problem between Stefano and me! Not at all, we are very happy and Francesca is doing well at school. Her languages are excellent and her life in England could not be better. One day we want to return as you know. For now everything, well... nearly everything is perfect.'

'Nearly everything?' Mimo asked, looking bemused.

'Yes, nearly, it's about work, Mimo, the blinds factory in fact. We spoke recently of perhaps selling the café and then using the spare time to run the factory as well as having more free time to travel and enjoy things. Just the other day, our rep called us. He has a large contract which he wants us to take.'

'Is that not good?' Eva interrupted.

'I'm not sure. I mean, in some ways it would be much more business and it could mean a chance to earn good money for a few years, but... I don't know. It would mean so much more work and organisation. They are talking about two hundred thousand blinds a year, just for them!'

'Whew!' Mimo took in the figures. 'That is a lot of extra work! I see what you mean. Are they a good company? Do you both know anything about them?'

Nicole nodded. 'They are one of the largest, if not the largest chain in England now, Mimo. The only thing Stefano does not like is their terms of payment, ninety days, which could stretch our budget at times.'

'I see,' he answered thoughtfully, 'that is a long time. What does Stefano think?'

She smiled. 'He wants the best for us.'

'What is the name of the company?' Eva commented, 'Perhaps you will know them, Mimo?'

'They are called T Healy & Sons,' Nicole responded. 'Do you know them?'

Eva stared at Mimo who sat frozen in time. His eyes snapped at Eva's and then towards Nicole. She saw anger and sadness at once in his gaze; in Eva she saw only a heart-broken stare.

'What? What is it? What did I say?'

'Nicole,' Mimo spoke first, 'what I am about to tell you must go NO further! Do you understand? I mean NO further. You must promise not to tell even your husband.'

Nicole felt nervous. Something in his voice carried alarm which she had never witnessed from his lips. 'I… I will not say anything if that is your wish, but that is a hard thing to ask me to do, Mimo, to keep something from Stefano.'

'If you feel it is unfair, Nicole, please, we will say nothing.' Eva's voice was compassionate.

'No, no, I will do as you ask. It must be important for you to ask such a thing of me.'

'Then I will tell you,' replied Mimo. He looked at Eva to support him in his decision and she nodded.

'We have no love for Terry Healy, Nicole.'

'You know him?'

'Not really,' his expression was showing the strain of age suddenly, 'his business was smaller then…' Nicole watched as Mimo lowered his head, almost cowering at the memories that suddenly overwhelmed him. His breathing became heavy before she heard him summon up a heartfelt gulp and glance up. 'It was the driver of a lorry of Terry Healy's who killed Emilio.' Each word uttered from his lips seemed to reopen a wound that would never heal. 'He showed no remorse, Nicole.'

'Oh, my God,' Nicole replied looking horrified, 'but, if I tell Stefano this, he would never deal with them.'

'NO!' Mimo shouted so loud that she jumped back a little. 'You must say nothing, Nicole! Don't you see? We never want Stefano to know about the crash in detail, at least not what happened and how. It is enough for him to have lost his brother. It has been painful enough for us. We do not want to burden him with anymore pain than he has already suffered.'

Eva took Nicole's hand. 'Mimo is right. It is not about the contract, Nicole. It is something we promised ourselves many years ago. We went to the court to see the man who did this.

He was put in prison and that was that. There was no remorse. Terry Healy did not even come to the trial. To tell Stefano this would make him relive the pain and feel the anger, as we have done for many years.'

'Alright,' Nicole conceded, 'I agree with some of what you say. It can do no good to bring this up with Stefano, but it can surely do no good for me to know he is dealing with a murderer?' Her gaze portrayed mixed emotions as the steely look of anger at the thought of meeting this 'murderer' gave way to the guilt that shone in her eyes at hiding such a thing from her husband. 'How would I be able to live with that secret?'

'I am sorry… we are sorry,' replied Mimo.

'I will simply say I do not feel right about the idea. That way he can make the choice and I will know I have done what I can. That is the only way I can think of things.'

'I agree,' said Eva. 'Nicole, you are a wonderful woman and wife and we love you dearly. Please do not feel any guilt for knowing. You asked and we have to be truthful with you. If one day Stefano asks then we will tell him. Until that day, we swore to never mention it.'

'I understand. I love you both too, very much, and I will tell Stefano I do not agree and hope he will take my opinion into account.'

* * *

The shrill ring of the telephone woke Stefano from his slumber. He stretched his arm out and picked up the receiver, still half asleep.

'Yes?'

'Hey, Stefano,' the confident sound of Nevallo's voice rang in his ear, 'you'll never guess what, my friend?'

'Please tell me,' he replied with a sleepy smile. 'We have another contract offer?'

'Eh, not quite actually,' his tone changed, 'time's up, boss.

We need to make a decision. I just got off the phone with Mr Terry Healy's main non-food buyer. We have until the morning to take up the business or…'

Stefano sat upright. 'Or what? Nicole is not back for another few days. Why tomorrow?'

'They have a buying party heading out for the Far East the day after. Basically, that means that if we don't sell to them then they will look for a similar product over there…I guess.'

Stefano's mind raced with the options open to him. 'I… I said I would discuss it with Nicole when she returns and has had time to think and discuss it. She may not agree, Nev. You know, she is my wife.'

'I agree,' he said sympathetically, 'but you let this one go and you may never get the chance again. Surely Nicole will understand?'

Stefano rose unsteadily and walked to the window of the Point Clear apartment. Outside the sun was just dipping on the horizon. It was going to be a beautiful evening. It would have been heavenly if Nicole was here, if only she could be here now…

He let the thoughts tumble around his mind as Neville waited at the end of the line.

'Alright,' he said finally, his voice cracking with uncertainty, 'tell them we look forward to doing business with them.'

CHAPTER TWELVE

'The deceased and his faithful companion had to pause, despite his thirst at the sight before him. The woman who sat on the path was dressed in a simple robe, her head tilted down away from the glaring sun. "Excuse me," the deceased said, "I am looking for Heaven. Is it ahead?"

The woman smiled. "Right on up the lane, just the way your feet are taking you."

The deceased walked up the dusty lane as his lifelong companion trailed paw by paw in his wake. A hundred metres later he saw the marble building and smiled. Fountains of clear water sprayed from the ornate statues that adorned the perimeter. Walking to the gates he saw two guards who barred his way.

"Welcome to Heaven." Looking down at the scraggy dog one of them added, "No animals allowed. This is not their Heaven."

The deceased paused in shock at his harsh words. "But... then I will not stay. But I ask, on my behalf, for just a drink?"

They shook their heads. "No animals."

The deceased turned and looked at his companion before he made his choice.

Perhaps twenty minutes passed before he saw the woman again, but now she was far on up the hill he had headed to rest his and his dog's souls upon.

"You again?" he muttered. "You told me Heaven was this way and I followed your words."

The woman smiled and the deceased saw no hidden secrets. "I did not lie. Follow the road as I said."

The deceased did not question her words and gave his soul one more chance. His dog followed him with no argument. Within fifty steps he saw another gate, a simple wooden affair that was only noticeable by the shimmering winged guards at the gate. Beside them was a trough brimming with fresh clean water.

Upon approaching, the deceased spoke with a dry tongue. "Can my animal drink with me from the trough? I was refused a moment ago at the gates of Heaven because of my dog, but the woman back there told me to keep going."

Galgliel smiled as she lifted her hand and watched the dog sprint to the gushing water. "Of course, all life is welcome in Heaven."

The deceased stumbled as he watched his companion feast on the clean water. "But...I thought..."

"You chose well because it is in your soul. You turned away from the gates of Hell."'

(From the scriptures of Galgliel)

Francesca burst into the apartment at Point Clear, her face aglow as she sang out. 'I'm in love! I'm in love!'

Stefano appeared from the kitchen smiling broadly. 'My girls are back! How are you, darling?' he said embracing Nicole before turning to Francesca. 'And what is this about love?'

Nicole raised her eyebrows in amusement. 'Our daughter has discovered her true love, at the tender age of thirteen, sweetheart. Long may it last.' Her face told Stefano to play along with her.

Francesca leapt into his arms. She was growing so fast and weighed more each time he held her. As she nuzzled into his collar he found himself realising how quickly time passes. One day it would be a man, like this new boyfriend, who she would be embracing. That was not yet; for now he would make the most of these moments.

'So tell me, little one. Who is this man in your life?' He said it in a voice that carried a playful tone.

Francesca's innocence bypassed his tone as she pulled him

by the hand and motioned for him to sit with her. 'Oh, Papa! He is just the best!' she crooned, her expression dancing with the joy of a new found emotion. 'His name is Domenici, he is *Italian*,' she expressed purposely, 'and he is wonderful! Isn't he, Mama? Tell him, tell him!'

Nicole, laughing, joined them on the sofa. 'He is a very nice boy, Francesca, a little young perhaps, but then…so are you, darling.' She ignored the serious look that Francesca gave her. 'I think he's nice and we shall see what happens. Perhaps,' she looked lovingly as Stefano, 'perhaps the two of you will be like your father and me one day: very much in love.'

'I know we will, oh I hope we will! I am going to go and write him a letter to tell him!'

With that she leapt up leaving Stefano gazing, bemused, at Nicole. 'Write a letter? What happened to her out there?'

Nicole giggled. 'It's young love, Stefano, let her be. She will maybe forget him with time or maybe they will last and see each other on our visits. It's good for her.'

'If you say so, darling,' he replied hesitantly.

'Anyway,' Nicole took his hand, her expression becoming more intense, 'that's not all that happened. I spoke with your mother and father about the contract from Healy's.'

Stefano shifted awkwardly. 'And…what did they say?'

She steadied herself for the white lie that was coming. 'They said that they think you should make the choice, or should I say, we should. They asked me to tell you what I thought and then let you make your mind up.'

He hesitated, trying to word his reply tactfully. 'In normal circumstances I would have to agree, but…'

'I don't think we should take it, darling,' Nicole intervened forcefully. 'It doesn't feel right, not with all we have talked of and planned for the future.'

A tiny slither of defensiveness arose. 'When did you decide this?'

'In Italy,' she answered. 'We said one day we would return and being there made me wish for that again.' Squeezing his hand she added, 'We don't need the money, Stefano, and we have Francesca's future and our families to think of. It would be good for us all one day to go home.'

He could feel his stomach squirming; the doubt and even guilt of the decision magnified more than ever.

He stared at her with sorrow. 'I signed the contract while you were away.'

The silence that followed yelled in his ears. He saw a look that he would never have imagined, a look of a woman who had just been told by her lover that he had cheated on her. He wanted to change everything, to say anything, but no words would come out.

Nicole could have burst into tears, yelled and screamed in anger, stabbed him with harsh words, but she did none of that. Instead she tortured him with the look of one brutally hurt before saying just a few icy words.

'You made a promise, you said we would decide together, we would use the time to think.' Her eyes filled with tears as her hand slipped from his. 'I always trusted you.'

Trust had become *trusted* and as she got up he knew he had damaged everything; how much remained to be seen. Stefano felt like a man cursed as he felt the other side of the power of love.

* * *

Changes were coming to the world, some subtle, some created, some natural, but all changes.

Suicide bombers in Israel, Pakistan and Moscow killed a total of 112 people and left many injured as dark thoughts and greedy policies bred an old but newly invented anger.

Individual actions of pure madness made the news as one woman in Texas was found guilty of drowning her five children and another American in Virgina shot six people at school. The loss of the Queen Mother at one hundred and one years of age was mourned worldwide, whilst natural disasters increased with a major earthquake in Taiwan and Central Europe was ravaged by floods.

The news channels covered story after story in dramatic light. Yet hardly any network really analysed the Near Earth Asteroid of 2002 which missed the planet by 75,000 miles, about one third of the distance to the moon. Some news, it seemed was meant for certain ears only. Yet whilst the events in outer space were taking place largly unnoticed there was also a miracle of its own kind occurring on Earth that was only barely noticed and, even then, it went by unquestioned. The half Angel was born silently to the joy of the watching Angels.

* * *

In the spa town of Karlovy Vary, Andrea Sekova lay resting in a dreamy haze as the last days and hours returned to her mind in brief images: flashbacks of Steve and England, combined with the discovery of her pregnancy, the guidance of the woman, the new home in the forest and the void in her world since then. As brave as she was, it had been a trying time for her beliefs and faith. The once pure love had been tainted by the man in England. When she had discovered she was pregnant by him, the choice to say nothing had been painful. When she had heard the voice of the stranger in her subconscious she had chosen to follow the words that guided her. The woman had appeared in her dreams; her soft voice seemed to speak directly to Andrea's heart.

She remembered entering the hospital and the initial pain of birth before a calmness surfaced. As the cries of the newborn infant rang out she felt her soul set free. It had been an almost out-of-body experience as she found herself watching the events from a different perspective. She heard the nurse's whisper of a miracle, a birth they had not seen before, one that should not have happened. She saw them smile at her reassuringly afterwards and then she arrived back in her own body.

She felt the warmth of being alive once more and, with that, the completeness of another. Her arms were wrapped around the soft white blanket that contained the tiny bundle of life.

'What will you call her?' They were the first words she heard in this 'new' life.

It was then she realised that, through the last nine months, she had never even thought of a name; no, that was not entirely true, she had contemplated it briefly but found a fear rising within, as if it was not time to think of such things. Now, as she held her daughter, she knew the reason why. She should not have been able to bear a child. That should have been her destiny until fate intervened. Seeing the nurses and hearing their words had clarified that. It did not matter now. She was a mother and the child was healthy.

'Her name will be Dusana.' She smiled through hazy tears. 'It means spirit, soul.' The name came easily to her lips, as if it had always been on them. It was then that she thought of Steve and wondered for him. Would he know? Would he feel anything as his daughter was born? The words of the woman echoed in her subconcious: '*He will come if all is as it should be.*'

She still loved him with all her heart. She had tried not to, a fight she could never win, in the end surrendering to her sanity and faith. There had been a magic that only love could create, and with that came the frailty of humankind. She did not blame him for that. If the words were true then one day he would find her... find them both.

A few days later she returned to the forest and began her life there as a mother. The emptiness that had become a part of her disappeared, to be replaced by the gentle crying of Dusana and her needs. Very few people saw them; those that did commented on the baby and how radiant Andrea looked. She found an inner happiness in the solitude that followed, a sense of contentment that one would get if all in their life had been achieved. It was not that Andrea wanted things in her life, she had not lost her drive, she had simply found her Angel and now she hoped that Steve would find his. She could not have known that even as those days passed he was deep into his search.

* * *

'I'm sorry.' Stefano stood in the doorway of the bedroom. Nicole turned a page before glancing up, as if the issue from earlier held little importance. She had not thought of anything else since he had told her earlier about the contract. It was not that that bothered her, it was the pain of being ignored, cheated, by the man she had given her life to.

'I am too, Stefano,' she replied icily, 'I really am.'

He watched as she looked back at the pages in the book, discarding him in the process. For the first time in their relationship, he felt the garden of togetherness turn into a desert of barren selfishness. It was his fault and his fault alone. He tried again.

'I am sorry, really I am. I should never have said yes. It was wrong of me and I got involved with a deadline. My only defence is that I *wanted* to wait, truly I did.' She arched her eyebrows in an attempt to make him feel even worse. 'Please, Nicole, you have to believe me.'

His desperate tone awoke her senses and eroded the barrier that had formed through hurt. 'I do believe you. I'm just hurt, you must understand that.' She put the book down and gave him her full attention. 'We made a promise, Stefano, and I kept that promise. That is what hurts me.'

'I will call them and cancel the contract.' He sat with her, staring directly into her eyes.

'No,' Nicole retorted in a steely tone, 'you've made the choice and even though I was no part of it, I am a part of you. We'll take the contract and see where that takes us.'

Her words seemed surreal as Stefano heard them. He had made the choice. It was to be his burden.

CHAPTER THIRTEEN

February 2003

And the storm moved in from the East. Innocence came in search of hope in an ever changing world laced with greed.

* * *

Jan Kowalik shuffled the leaflet inside his pocket with his fingers, running his nails across and up and down the sacred sheet he now possessed. He ran, fleet-footed, to escape the town centre and find a spot in order to unfold the important document. It was, in reality, just a leaflet but he had paid six złoty for this piece of information and for a man, a boy really on his income, this represented an expensive piece of business.

He slipped down the street and behind the church almost gasping for breath, not out of physical exhaustion but out of pure, unadulterated excitement. He gently caressed the leaflet before slowly unfolding it.

He knew the town of Karczew inside out; how could he not? He had spent the last eighteen years of his life here, in a town of roughly ten thousand people. He knew the numbers because he had listened and learnt. He'd learnt enough to be able to barter for this document in his hand. His ticket to freedom and a new life for him and his sister Basia, a life they both deserved, instead of rotting in this place.

He gazed in wonder at the writing on the unfurled sheet that he held. Languages looked back at him, languages that he had never seen but, being a clever person, he had calculated for this before the six złoty left his palm to be replaced by the paper.

The drunk in the bar had been French and he had informed Jan, through another Pole who spoke a little English and a little French, that it was simple case of working out the currency and the languages. He also informed Jan (at no extra cost) that the money was not exactly applicable to Polish people because they were not in the organisation called the EU. Jan, being smart, knew that Poland were applying to join the EU and would eventually get in this organisation anyway so he absorbed that, and when the Frenchman added, 'You will be one of the first to seize the opportunity,' Jan just nodded in agreement because he knew that anyway.

He saw names of places he had never heard of but they were not what interested him. It was the figures to the right of the document and some wording next to them. He stared, slightly amazed at the moment and feeling sure now that he had done the right thing by himself and Basia. He said the figures in a whisper for he did not want anyone else to discover his secret. *'Fouve ponds fiffetee, moreee than thew minimum wagy.'* He stopped and waited while his mind worked it out. The figure, he discovered after some clicking and crunching within, was... could it be? Twenty-six złoty an hour. The six złoty he had paid for the piece of paper now seemed great business for it held the evidence of such riches. It was going to be his meal ticket out of this place.

He felt the tears of joy run down his face as he ran down the cobbled alleyway which led him towards home. Pushing the door open with zest, he greeted his father who as usual rocked gently in his chair, greeting his son with a bronchitic cough. The smell of burning wood mixed with lime and chalk from the furnace filled his nostrils, usually a welcoming odour, but not today. Today he had things to discuss with his family and, with the enthusiasm of a child a decade younger, he ran into the kitchen and wrapped his arms around his mother before planting a kiss onto her. She squealed in surprise and partly anger at being disturbed whilst Basia, who stood to her right with a mixing spoon in her hand, simply looked in amazement at her brother.

'You must come now, Mama,' he almost screeched in Polish. 'You too, Basia, we must talk.' He sounded breathless and his anguish, as they saw it, rather than his excitement, made them drop the tools they held and follow him into the sitting room.

'Father, Mother,' he began, 'I have some great news! I met a man today from France and he gave me some information.' He did not wait for any comments. 'There is some work for me and Basia abroad and the pay is as much as twenty-six złoty an hour!'

Basia's eyes lit up. She had not heard of such an amount of money in her sixteen-year-old world. Jan's mother also looked taken aback for she knew the value of twenty-six złoty and also knew it had been a long time since her husband had brought that much home in a day, let alone in an hour.

Jan's father was the first to speak. He coughed heavily before pulling himself up a little from the rocking chair and easing his head forwards. 'Where is this work?' he asked with conviction. 'You say abroad?'

Jan nodded. He had been ready for such a question and he had many answers. Firstly out of respect for his father he would be gentle. If that did not work he had harsher answers. He touched his father's arm as he replied, 'Father, the work is in England. They need young people to work on the farms. We can go there and work and save money to send home, don't you see? It is the chance we have been waiting for! If Basia comes with me I will look after her and we will earn double the amount!'

'England?' His mother interrupted with a look of doubt. 'That is a long way away, Jan, and you are just a young boy!

I do not know,' she looked to Basia with concern, 'and as for her? You are not old enough to take care of yourself, let alone Basia.'

Jan had expected such a comment from his mother. Of course she would be concerned and, as his father nodded in agreement, he used his next tactic.

'England is a good place, you both know that,' he said with a new fierceness and determination in his voice. 'It is as safe as any country and there is work which pays much more than I could ever earn on that damned fruit stall! What am I to do here in Karczew? Should I work like Father in the mines and become contaminated? What will Basia do as she grows up? Work on the streets selling herself?' As he said those words he felt guilt and lowered his voice once more. 'I am sorry. I just want to do the best for us all and it is a chance for us, for us all. Please let me help.' His eyes filled with tears.

His father grunted as he slumped back into his chair to ponder Jan's words. Jan regretted his outburst. His father had worked hard since he could remember; up until he became too ill and his lungs had become diseased from the dust and dirt. He had not meant to insult him.

Eventually his father spoke. 'How long will you be going for?'

Jan was ready once again. 'We will go for six months and then see how it is. Father…' he added looking at him with kindness, 'we can make all our lives better and get you the best treatment; we can make you well again.'

A decision was not made that night but in the morning, as they ate rolled oats with hot milk and bread, his parents told him that they had agreed. He sensed that his mother had been the one to persuade his father; no doubt a little of what he had said about his father's health and the money had convinced her.

He smiled and tried not to show how he felt inside. He wanted to jump up and down, to go crazy and hug them all but he knew he should not because he was now a man with responsibility for his young sister and his family. So he simply nodded and began to plan in his head the next steps.

* * *

It was a cold February morning as the two left the house. Jan had planned the trip as best he could and during the previous evening had checked and double-checked all the belongings he would take for them both. He had their passports and, after some bargaining which had cost more precious złoty, he had obtained the necessary papers as well as a mixture of essential items. A penknife, an old portable transistor radio, plenty of clothes as he knew they would be expensive in England and a copy of the book The Polish Peasant in Europe and America 1918-1920 written by Florian Znaniecki and William I. Thomas. He felt it may help him on his travels.

After checking that Basia had plenty of warm clothes in her small rucksack they set off for the town centre. There Jan met with the Frenchman who had sold him the bus ticket. He greeted them both with a smile and commented on how pretty Basia looked. Jan felt a tinge of possessiveness at his words but Basia simply smiled with innocence and thanked him as she pushed her blonde hair back shyly.

Jan gave the Frenchman the fifty złoty he had promised him. The sum was for 'passage and protection' as the Frenchman had told him whilst they planned the trip.

His name was Jean-Philippe and, as they sat in the coach on the way to Warsaw, he ran over the details once more as both Basia and Jan listened intently.

'We will take the Polish Euroline to Berlin which will only take about four hours and it is the cheapest way,' he said with a knowledge that Jan did not have. 'There we will get the train to Paris where I will leave you.'

Jan nodded. 'Will you show us which coach to take to England?'

Jean-Philippe laughed. 'You will take the train! There is one that runs through a tunnel under the sea and will get you to London. From there you must find your way to this place called Ipswich.'

The coach rode over bumpy, pot-filled streets on the way to Warsaw. Jan gazed outside at the passing views. Snow lay thick on the barren fields and, as he watched and soaked up the sense of adventure that he had waited years to feel, Basia dropped off to sleep, leaving Jan to ask more questions about England and the journey ahead.

Jean-Philippe informed him that England was a green place with much rain but little or no snow. He sneered a little when describing the English people as 'arrogant' but Jan knew that some French did not like the English and Jean-Philippe must be one of them so he just nodded in agreement and listened more. He felt alert and excited. They arrived at Warsaw and Jean-Philippe directed them to the correct train. Jan calculated that most or all of his money and savings would be spent on the trip. Basia had some more money which her mother had given to her but Jan decided that would be kept for emergencies. Besides, once they were in England, the money would be worthless anyway and they would have lots of 'real' money to spend as they wished.

Four hours later found the three of them in Berlin. Jan had woken as they entered the city and was amazed by the change of landscape. Warsaw had been old-looking, decrepit even, compared to the vast shining buildings around them now. He wondered how it was that two places so close together could be so different.

As they made their way to the train Jean-Philippe instructed them that he should do most of the talking if spoken to. He explained that, although they would be fine, it was not totally legal what they were doing. Basia did not understand but Jan did and promised that they would say as little as possible except, if asked, that they were visiting friends and family in Ipswich.

The Frenchman guided them onto the train. He had no

concern as to what happened to them both once they arrived in Paris and a part of him doubted that they would even get through to England. He said nothing though; he had no grudge against Polish people and these two in particular. If they wanted to go and work in England it meant that it would be two less foreigners in his country and he was fine with that.

Over eleven hours later the three arrived in Paris. It was dark outside now and Jan and Basia had got little sleep on the train. The carriage was the cheapest of the ones available and, although much more luxurious than a Polish train, it was still a little cramped. Jean-Philippe seemed to be fine with it all. He was nearly home after all. He had a rucksack full of cheap drugs and the days he had spent in some pissholes in Poland had been worth it.

The huge station at Paris was as big as anything Jan and Basia had ever seen. As they gazed upwards in amazement at the lattice steel architecture their guide led them to Paris Nord and asked Jan for the remainder of his złoty explaining that he would have to pay for their tickets in euros, the new currency of Europe. He took the currency and shoved it into his pocket for another day, another trip to Poland. When Jan asked him why England did not have the 'new currency of Europe', Jean-Philippe snorted and explained that was because the English as he had told them earlier were arrogant and stuck in their ways. 'They will regret it,' he said with a confident smile but, as he handed over the euro notes, he felt a tinge of envy towards the islanders. He and many of his people had been saddened by the loss of the franc. He was not going to let that show to two Polish kids though.

A short time later and Jean-Philippe bid them goodbye. Now it was all up to Jan, now he was in charge. The responsibility was a little daunting. So far they had not been asked anything by anyone. Their guide had made him feel safe, he realised that now as they stood on the platform. With a smile that belied his fear, Jan brushed his sister's hair with his fingers and put his arm around her. They looked a lonely pair.

The train was much more modern than either of them had ever seen. Jan whispered to his sister not to look too amazed as they settled down on comfortable seats. 'We must look as if we belong,' he told her. She whispered back that many of the other people 'did not look like them.' And Jan had to agree. He was of slim build, standing at just under two metres tall and, with his light brown short hair, must have appeared a little daunting to these well-dressed people around him with their fashionable hairdos. His old woollen sweater and faded black jeans looked tatty in comparison to the other passengers' smart clothing and Basia, despite her slim beauty, looked to be dressed like a woman with an outdated wardrobe. No one else wore a long dress and shawl like she had on. She even looked foreign to him. He decided there and then that once they had some money he would buy them both 'European clothes' so they too could look as smart as the people around them.

One moment of tension arose on the train journey. It should not have been a moment of fear as the ticket collector was merely checking tickets and Jan had both of theirs safe and sound. It was the way the official looked at them that worried him. When asked for his tickets he said *'Oui'* and *'Merci'* in as French an accent as he could muster. His practice on the journey as he copied Jean-Philippe seemed to pay off as the man clipped the tickets and handed them back gruffly causing a shiver down the spine. After ten minutes had passed Jan calmed, guessing he had not run and told the authority on the train that they had two 'illegal' passengers.

The train terminated at London's St Pancras station where Jan and Basia disembarked onto the platform of their new world. Masses of people rushed this way and that, all seemingly intent on getting to their destinations as fast as possible. After some finger pointing from several rail officials they found their way onto the tube which took them to Liverpool Street Station. Now they had to get directions to Ipswich and, amid the madness of so many people, Jan waited for the right person to wander past before finding the courage to ask, 'Ipswich please?' The middle-aged couple looked bemused initially as the man threw a look of contempt their way and muttered something to the lady. She seemed sympathetic and after a moment pointed directions.

Liverpool Street Station looked as big as Paris to the two of them. With good fortune they caught the last train of the evening which left at ten thirty. Had it not been for the help of the couple then they would have surely missed the train and been stuck in an unknown part of London for the night. It was past midnight when they arrived at Ipswich; Jan had no idea what to do next. The station was deserted.

He held his sister's hand as the cold wind picked up around them before spotting a lighted window a short distance away. As they approached, it looked like a waiting room of some sort. Despite his uncertainty, he told Basia that they would have to rest here until the morning and then head for the place of work. She did not argue with her older brother. She, like him, was cold, dirty and tired by now and the waiting room looked warm and welcoming. Jan pulled out a small bag of home-made cakes his mother had given them and the two ate ravenously.

Within minutes Basia was asleep on the bench beside Jan, her head resting on her rucksack. He took out the leaflet with care and ran his index finger downwards to the piece he wanted to read. Tomorrow he would take his sister and they would earn more money than they had ever known. He smiled to himself even though, at that moment, he felt very scared.

Nodding off into a dreamy slumber, Jan visualised the place they would be tomorrow: a place called Stebdon.

CHAPTER FOURTEEN

He saw them approaching from a distance: two sodden shapes, trudging towards the iron barrier that prevented access to the farm.

Edward Sonning had been sitting by the window eating breakfast when the two figures came in sight. The view from the farmhouse stretched between the two rolling hills either side of the lane which gave the only entrance directly to the farm.

He gave a grunt and stood up. After pulling on some wellington boots and grabbing his body warmer from the hook, he opened the door and went outside to look for William.

Bright rays of sunshine cut through the early dawn mist as he passed the vast array of greenhouses.

Walking the hundred or so metres, Edward lifted the latch of the gate and made his way down towards the two shapes. He saw that they were speaking with Billy and Ethan, the two men in charge of the checkpoint that had been set up. Exhaling an air of exasperation he trudged over to the wooden outhouse that served as security headquarters to the two men.

In spite of the warmth that the sun now threw downwards, Edward saw immediately that the young boy and girl standing in front of him were cold and wet through. The girl shivered from what appeared to be not only the freezing cold but also from fright, whilst the boy, who could not have been much older than she was, argued with the two men in a language he could not understand.

'What the hell is going on here?' Edward said loudly, interrupting the heated discussion. Billy Jones turned around at the voice of his employer and gave an apologetic look. 'Sorry, sir, didn't hear you coming,' he said in his slow local accent whilst flashing a glance in the direction of Ethan who said nothing. 'These two folk, sir,' he continued, 'well, they just turned up a few moments ago demanding to be let in. Of course I…we told them they need the proper authorisation, sir.'

At that point Ethan, whom Edward had not liked from the first time he set eyes on him, butted in. 'The boss says to check everyone and these people are not even from around here, Mr Sonning,' he snarled, 'and as for this boy…well, whatever he's saying it's with a foul mouth, you can just tell.' The expression on Ethan's pock-marked face seemed to indicate that he wanted to kick the boy back down the hills and probably would have, had Edward not arrived.

Ignoring Ethan's remarks, Edward spoke directly to Billy whilst looking the two children up and down. 'Can you not see that wherever they're from, they're wet and more than likely hungry?' Billy shuffled awkwardly as Edward continued. 'We're not barbarians, are we, gentlemen?' His voice gathered an authoritative tone. 'Boy,' he continued, pointing at Jan, 'where are you from?'

Jan, who had been standing quietly during the exchange, his arm protectively around Basia's shoulders, seemed to understand his request. 'Polska,' he answered proudly.

Edward scratched his head in disbelief. He concluded that the young girl hiding behind the boy must be his sister. After a moment's contemplation he looked at Ethan and Billy. 'Well, there's nothing for it. These two are coming to the farmhouse and we'll get them some food and a wash.' He paused. 'Then we'll get to the bottom of this.'

'Shouldn't you find the boss first, Mr Sonning?' Ethan interjected. 'He may have the answers.'

Edward glared at him. 'While I'm on this farm, Ethan Dobbs, I AM the boss and these people are on MY land, you understand?'

'Eh, yes, Mr Sonning,' Ethan replied timidly seeming to shrink back.

Edward turned and gestured for the two to follow him. Jan scowled as he held out his hand for Basia and went to follow him.

Ethan had one last dig ready for Jan. 'Perhaps you would like to take this with you, Mr Sonning,' he said holding the yellow leaflet out. 'Apparently this boy seems to think it is some sort of job slip, or...' he added with a sarcastic sneer, 'perhaps the foreigner thinks it's his passport.'

Edward took the now grubby leaflet and began to walk towards the house with the two in tow, opening up the piece of crumpled paper as he did so. He did not speak until they got to the door when he called out to his wife. Gesturing for Jan and Basia to take off their shoes and follow him in, Edward glanced back outside as he closed the door, muttering, *'What the hell is going on?'*

* * *

Hayley took Jan and Basia upstairs and, after showing them the spare room, gave them both towels before demonstrating how to use the shower. Although they had had to make do with sharing a bath back at home, they enjoyed the luxury of a separate shower, each standing under the hot jets of water seemingly forever. While they cleaned up, Hayley found a jumper and trousers for Jan from William's wardrobe although she doubted they would be a very good fit but would have to do. For Basia, she sorted through some of her clothes that she had kept from a more youthful time and selected a pretty floral dress that she hoped would suffice. She surmised that the clothes couldn't be worse than the two already had on.

A short time later the two were clean and dressed. After their

116

initial meeting with those two obnoxious men, perhaps England would turn out alright after all. Jan's one remaining concern was the language problem.

Hayley smiled as they entered the kitchen where she had prepared some food. Basia looked much better after her shower and the clothes amplified her young beauty. She had tied her wet hair up, accentuating her jawline and making her blue-grey eyes stand out even further. Jan looked a little gawky in his new get-up. The trousers were a little short as were the arms of the jumper. It was alright for now, Hayley thought, but she could not imagine him wanting to be seen by many people in such clothes.

She waved over to them to sit at the table and set down scalding hot chicken soup with a plate full of crusty bread. Jan immediately tore into the bread washing it down with gulps of soup whilst Basia gave a smile of thanks before following suit.

Edward had gone back out in search of his son and, while Hayley watched the two, she ran a number of questions through her mind. Why had they come to this farm of all places? It was not exactly a famous place in a big town. How had they made their way here? Her husband had explained that they had come from Poland but knew little more than that himself, except that they spoke little or no English.

It was just as she had just served them second portions that Edward came in with William trailing behind him looking sheepish.

'Well, son,' Edward began, 'here are your two friends from Poland. Why don't you introduce yourself?' His voice had a hint of the sarcasm that Ethan had spoken with earlier.

'Don't, Dad,' William replied with an embarrassed look. 'Er, hi,' he said uncomfortably as he pulled up a chair and sat opposite them.

Jan guessed he must be the person behind the leaflets but said nothing and just nodded as he gulped down some more of the hearty soup. Basia just smiled.

Edward looked at his wife. 'Well, Hayley, I've had a little chat with our son and he wants to explain how and why these two people are sitting at our table,' he glanced at William sternly, 'don't you, son?'

'Well,' William cleared his throat, 'it's a sort of mistake, kind of, and, well, it might not be actually.' Hayley looked bemused and he knew he was making little sense. 'The thing is,' he continued hurriedly, 'since the hydroponics effect and extra sales, we've had to expand, as you know. So we have more work for the locals and I figured...' he looked at his father uneasily, '...I figured it would be a good move to expand our net of employees, but not quite like this.'

'So he decided to print hundreds of these,' said Edward handing Hayley the leaflet. Her eyes ran down the sheet as William tried to justify his actions.

'Mum, Dad, I did not expect this leaflet to end up in bloody Poland! I thought that by canvassing we may get some other labour in, you know, maybe people who were working in England, or even France on farms who may want some seasonal work.' He hesitated now. 'It was just an idea and we're getting more and more demand, especially as we're looking to expand with new accounts.'

Hayley could see that Edward was annoyed by his son and she too, felt a little angry. 'William, this whole thing seems to have got a little out of control,' she said in a motherly tone. 'When we agreed to the hydroponics it helped produce more but how far do we go? Your father and I think that already things have changed... too much.'

Edward snorted bad-temperedly as he handed the leaflet back to Jan. 'Too bloody right. We didn't need the extra work and, since you came up with this *great* idea, we've been chasing our tails. And if that wasn't bad enough we now even have a bloody checkpoint out at the front of the farm run by that idiot Ethan.'

'The checkpoint was set up for exactly that purpose,' William reasoned. 'When I sent the leaflets out I thought we should be prepared, and we *should* be. If business keeps growing we will need more people, Dad. Besides, I read that the European Community is joining up with each other and that means more competition and more opportunities. I was doing it for *all* of us.'

'That's all very well, darling,' intervened Hayley, 'but what are we to do with these two? They have nowhere to stay and… can we be sure they are here legally?'

William visibly relaxed in his chair. 'I have thought of all the avenues. Now that we can produce more than enough lettuce and potatoes, the farm will thrive. We have plenty of free space down by the parking and delivery bay which we can utilise in the future as boarding quarters should we need to.' At this point he searched for a look of reassurance from his father but, receiving none, continued, 'If things improve further we must be ready, don't you see that? I'm just planning a secure future for this family, and more business means more jobs for the people of Stebdon.'

Edward muttered something under his breath. Hayley felt for him. It had always been a simple case of farming for her husband and he, like she, did not fully understand their son's desire for such expansion. They had brought their son up as well as any parents could and he had turned into a strong man with bright, enthusiastic ideas. She did not want to dampen that spirit and, as a mother, she naturally only wanted the best for her son, as she did for her husband.

'William, you must understand that your father also wants the best,' she began tenderly, 'but he understands fields, not hydroponics, and he understands farming, not mass production.' She looked at the four faces listening and felt compassion for them all as she thought, *'If there is a wind of change coming then we must all hold together.'*

* * *

William promised to take care of the new guests but that night they stayed in the farmhouse, sleeping in the dusty attic while he organised other accommodation. Jan had made it clear using a mixture of hand signals and the odd word that he and his sister wished to stay and work on the farm. In the morning William greeted the two of them and, after a hearty breakfast of bacon, eggs and fresh bread, motioned them to follow him outside.

With a reassuring grin, William led them into the first greenhouse. Inside there were a few women who greeted all three with smiles of curiosity. Lines of foam trays ran the length of the greenhouse, each floating in a type of broth that contained essential nutrients for the lettuce to grow. Jan and Basia gazed, awestruck at the number of lettuces growing in just one greenhouse. Hundreds of green plants coloured the path down to where he showed them some equipment which they did not understand. William pointed to several instruments, trying to explain their uses. They nodded as he spoke, neither able to understand him but both eager to impress.

As they left, William stopped to speak to one of the ladies, telling her that, from the next day, she would be teaching the girl to plant the seeds and pack the lettuces that were ready. He felt that Basia would be well suited to the work. The cycles in each greenhouse were preset for each batch of lettuces to grow. Once they had reached the required growth they simply needed to be picked and packed.

Jan would be working outside. William had asked his father if Jan could work as a general farmhand to which Edward had begrudgingly agreed. With a spring in his step, William took Jan and Basia back down to the gate by the large outhouse. Billy was alone there and greeted the three with a grin indicating he was happier than the day before.

'It seems our friends have settled in then, sir,' he said in a friendly tone. Jan liked this man. His weather-beaten face looked honest, his smile kindly. He somehow reminded him of a friendly face from home. The other man that he didn't like was nowhere to be seen and privately Jan hoped he would never have to see him again.

'Indeed they have,' replied William with a smile. 'Is the caravan ready, Billy?'

Billy nodded. 'As you requested, sir, on the edge of the delivery area and out of the wind.'

'Good,' said William signalling for Jan and Basia to follow him. 'Thank you, Billy.'

He took them out through the gate and turned left, towards a large empty piece of land fenced off on all sides with just one opening acting as the entrance. A mixture of tyre tracks from various vehicles had destroyed the grass, leaving a compacted area of sticky mud. The enclosure was empty except for a small caravan He led them to the door and showed them inside. The caravan was adequate for two people, the kind you might take on a short break. Inside were two small bunks and a seating area on one side with a toilet and kitchen area on the other. Basia's eyes lit up as she looked around, familiarising herself with everything. Jan was pleased as well and, although he did not share his sister's childish delight at their new home, he realised they were lucky to have been treated so well in this foreign land.

He held out his hand. 'Thank you,' he said slowly to William who shook his hand, pleased at their reaction.

* * *

Over the next week, Jan and Basia settled in to life on the farm. Elaine, the woman in charge of teaching Basia, showed her how to plant the seeds in trays being careful to put the right amount in each whilst mothering her along, chatting enthusiastically as she sat packing lettuces. Basia loved the work and found Elaine a joy to be around despite not understanding her too well. Each day that passed she would pick up a new word or two though and each night she chattered excitedly to Jan about the day. Jan proved to be extremely useful to have around and Edward took to him from the start. Willing to work hard, he might not have known what he was being told but he followed the lead shown to him out on the fields and was soon doing the manual labour of two men. His determination and eagerness shone through and, by the end of the first week, he was thoroughly competent at sorting through and packing the potatoes whilst always being ready to offer a hand to anyone.

Each evening Jan and Basia returned to the caravan with ham, cheese and bread that Hayley had given them. On the Saturday she took them into Stebdon village, as beautiful a place as Basia had ever seen. Her eyes gazed at the shop windows with glee whilst Jan memorised certain shops where he would spend his wages, and thought of how much he would have to tell his parents about when he could call them.

It was explained to them that they had to work a week in hand so the following Friday Jan and Basia queued at the checkpoint that once a week also acted as a pay booth. Ethan sat behind the makeshift counter handing out pay packets in small brown envelopes. As Jan collected theirs, Ethan gave him a look of disdain as he pushed the packets towards him. Opening them, Jan saw the English money and, after counting it out, returned back to the counter.

'You've been paid, you greedy varmint,' Ethan spat venomously. 'Come back next week, if you're still here.'

Jan produced the leaflet and pushed it angrily towards him, pointing to the figures on the sheet.

Ethan glanced with a wry smile at the piece of paper, running his fingers through his greasy black hair. He looked up and pointed to Elaine who was standing just behind Basia. 'Can I borrow you a minute?'

Seeing Jan's look of anger and Basia's confusion, Elaine went to the counter where Ethan had a piece of blank paper and a pen. 'Look, here's the minimum wage for their ages, right?' he said impatiently, pointing to another sheet. Elaine looked: *£3 for 16 year olds and £3.80 for 18-21 year olds.* She nodded as she saw the figure of £5.50 on the sheet that Jan had given him.

Ethan sat back looking satisfied. 'Well, explain that to them and also that I have to work out the wages, right? So they get that amount minus one hundred pounds for their accommodation. We don't want to do things wrong, do we?' he said with a dangerous glint in his eye.

Elaine felt a trace of sadness for the two as she took them to one side and explained what he had said. Eventually Jan understood and Basia did not seem to care. He worked out they had worked forty hours each and instead of £220 each they had just £172 pounds between them after the deduction of rent. He felt a little angry but, seeing Basia's lack of concern, smiled and thanked Elaine for her help. He knew they had no choice and that Ethan knew that as well.

And so it was that Jan and Basia's new life in England began.

CHAPTER FIFTEEN

*'Follow your heart for it will lead you true. Follow your head to
never really know you. For the head may lead you to your goal, but
the heart's journey will lead you to your soul.'*
                        (Taken from scriptures from the Hall of Angels)

2004

William Sonning pulled his tie straight and took a deep breath.
The man in the mirror was about to embark on the biggest
negotiation of his twenty-eight years and he was feeling the
pressure. If this came off then the future of Sonnings would be
secure. His parents would have their dream retirement and he,
William Sonning, would go down in history within the village
of Stebdon.

After splashing some water on his face, William left the
toilets and walked back into the plush reception area of T
Healy & Sons where he sat and waited. A few reps over to the
right-hand side of the gurgling fountain centrepiece were
whispering strategies, papers in hand, as they waited their
turn. The only other sounds were the constant ringing of
phones and the continual answer of the receptionists: 'T Healy
& Sons, what extension number please?'

After what seemed like another good hour he heard his
name called out.

'Mr Sonning, please follow me.' He checked himself one
last time and followed the lady into a plush lift which raced up

to the very top of the skyscraper.

Terry Healy's office was the stuff of dreams, at least for the child who wanted to have his own. The room was immense, with what appeared to be a conference room leading off to the right. It was minimalist, but very classy. Terry Healy, the man who owned England's largest chain of supermarkets, sat behind a huge oak desk. This was it.

'Take a seat please.' He glanced up at William but did not make any other gesture of welcome. This was Terry Healy's territory. William sat down; he could feel the moisture on his palms.

There was a silence in the room as Terry flicked through a pile of papers. William felt each turn of the pages; his tender was in there, and the question was how many others was he competing against? Any confidence he had before was slipping away, page after endless page.

'So,' Terry broke the icy silence as he stopped midway through, pushing the remainder of the sheets to one side, 'Sonnings Farm, ah?'

'Yes, sir,' William answered politely.

'My wife is from Stebdon originally, you know.' William was sure he could see a gentle smile forming. 'A very nice village indeed. The question I have to ask is this: do you feel you can cope with the figures we're requesting and the potential figures based on our growth?'

The calculations had been rehearsed in William's mind. 'Yes, sir; with the expectancy of your growth, in line with our hydroponics programme, I can foresee no problem at all. We are familiar with your terms and conditions as well, sir.'

Terry nodded in approval. 'We have to run a professional business, Mr Sonning. That means deliveries on time, no fuss, no mess. We do not take kindly to failure. Your contract will be reviewed at the end of each season and weighed up against many factors including price, reliability, service and so on.'

Your contract. He digested the words. 'Does that mean, sir...?'

Terry stood up and held out his hand. 'Yes, it does indeed, Mr Sonning. The contract is yours.' He smiled as they shook hands. 'I know the village of Stebdon and I am happy with both the price and the fact we can support your farm...BUT...' William noted an iciness form around the word as Terry continued, '...the fact is though I plan for my son Terrance to take over many of my buying duties over the next couple of years, when he is ready, of course. He may not have such affection for your village, bear in mind.'

'We won't let you down, Mr Healy,' William replied solemnly.

'Good, well best we get on. You have a farm to reorganise!'

William held his emotions inside until he reached the car park. Then he leapt up and punched the air. 'Yes!'

Terry Healy watched from the window above as he thought back to the first time he met Jenny. 'I like Stebdon,' he muttered before returning to his work.

* * *

The old barn at the back of the house was filled with workers as William arrived for the meeting with Ethan alongside him. There was no sign of Edward.

Jan and Basia stood a few rows back from the front and waited for him to speak. The past few days had seen a buzz around the farm as small caravans had arrived, filling the old car park to brimming point before more came to be set up on the empty fields. With the caravans had come people, trickling in slowly at first; some local, some from further afield. The news of the contract with Healy's had sent a positive vibe around the farm and village. Basia had spoken with Elaine who had seemed elated by the news. It meant that the whole village would have plenty of work and, if Elaine was happy, then so was Basia. Jan did not share her feelings but he kept his thoughts to himself. He had liked things the way they were and he knew that Edward had done as well. A part of him had planned that, as soon as they had earned enough money, he was going to take Basia for a 'holiday'. It was time to go home.

Ethan clapped loudly to silence the gentle hum of voices. Once he had their attention he glanced at William who stepped forward, smiling broadly.

'Thank you all for coming today, ladies and gentlemen. I am pleased to announce a new dawn for Sonnings Farm. Our contract with Healy's supermarkets will mean a change in the way some things are done. It will also mean much more to the village of Stebdon!' He paused, allowing Ethan to applaud his small speech before a few others did the same and soon the barn was filled with the gentle clapping.

'Many of you have been here for some time,' William continued as silence returned, 'but many of you are new. We will have a system for new workers which is to be run by the man standing to my left, Mr Ethan Dobbs.' He waited for some applause which did not follow before he went on hastily, 'Eh, Mr Dobbs will be delegating our senior workers with their responsibilities for new recruits. Tomorrow morning, at nine o'clock, could all staff employed for at least one year visit the office to collect your information sheets which will list necessary instructions. If you have any questions then Mr Dobbs will be happy to answer.' He smiled at Ethan who returned the compliment through cracked black teeth.

'I hate that man,' Jan said out loud to Elaine and Basia as the three walked towards the caravan. Elaine gave him a sharp look. 'You shouldn't use the word hate, Jan; it's not a good word. Anyway, I think it is good for the village…even though I have never seen so many foreign people before.' She paused, looking sheepish. 'Sorry, no offence to you two, of course.'

As they reached the caravan Elaine motioned them to come closer. 'I have heard,' she said in a whisper, 'that Ethan suggested they put the foreign workers up on the farm so they can charge them rent. That way they will make even more money.' Her eyes darted around in case someone else was in earshot. 'I also heard, and no offence to you again, that the village didn't want outsiders staying in it anyway.'

'They don't mind them spending their money in the village though, do they?' Jan said with a snarl. His mind was made up at that moment. The sooner he could take Basia home the better. They had earned enough money in the year they had been there to put a lump sum by, enough for a good while in Poland anyway. He liked Edward Sonning and William for the most but Ethan, Ethan was awful and so were some of the others on the farm. He had seen the way they looked at Basia and heard some of the comments. It could only get worse with all these new people.

'It is good for the village,' Elaine surmised before kissing Basia goodbye and leaving them to their own devices.

Basia studied her brother's face. 'You seem angry, Jan. Is everything alright?'

'Yes,' he replied in a firm tone, 'I just don't like it here anymore.'

* * *

Jan was to be in charge of three workers. Ethan had grinned as he gave him his sheet which had the details of two Romanians and one local man. 'Perhaps you will be able to teach them English,' he remarked sarcastically, 'if you can speak it yourself yet.'

Basia was more fortunate. Still only seventeen, she was to remain under the tutelage of Elaine, thus making her days the same as before. From the start, Jan struggled with his new recruits. The two Romanian men were of a similar age to him and spoke barely any English. He had to show them with a mixture of hand signals and practical demonstrations what had to be done. The local man was something of a character. His name was Mark but everyone referred to him as 'Rusty' on account of his ginger hair. Upon first meeting him, you could sum him up a Caucasian Bob Marley. Swaying dreadlocks adorned his pear-shaped face which was half hidden by the growth of a carrot-coloured beard. He lived on the outskirts of the village in an old coach which he had converted into a mobile home. There was not a day that went by, rain or shine, that he could not be seen strolling along in shorts and sandals like some lost reggae singer looking for his band. Jan did not dislike him; he was amiable enough, if not a little tedious at times. If he was not telling any woman that breathed how beautiful they were he would be telling Basia the same. Apart from that, he spent most of the time singing to himself, oblivious of the real world. Whenever Jan tried to get him to do anything he would joke and pretend he could not understand him. At first it was fine but, after the hundredth 'What? I do not understand your Polish accent', he wanted to pull his dreadlocked hair out and stuff it down his throat.

* * *

During the next few months the farm grew busier and the once barren area where Jan and Basia's home sat was now full of caravans and all available space had been taken. Jan found out that what Elaine had said was true. He was standing outside the office one night when he heard Ethan commenting on the amount of 'rent' that they had earned that week. 'It pays for a good bloody quarter of those rodents we have here.'

The contract kept the place busy from sunrise till sunset. Lorry after lorry arrived to collect potatoes and lettuces for Healy's. The hydroponics was doing a roaring trade and the labourers on the fields were also kept busy from dawn till dusk. Ethan could be seen strolling around barking out orders at his subordinates whilst, on a rare occasion, William would tour the farm inspecting his new found success.

One morning Jan saw Edward Sonning walking down to the gate alone. He had not seen him for some time and stopped work to walk swiftly over to him.

'Morning, Mr Sonning! How are you?'

Edward gave him a fleeting look as he continued to walk. 'Oh, hello, Jan; not too bad, my boy. How are you and...'

'Basia, sir,' Jan interjected, 'we are doing well. How is Mrs Sonning? Well, I hope.'

'She's fine,' he replied casually. 'are you enjoying the work, Jan?'

'I like it, sir,' he lied, 'although it is strange here now, with the new contract and workers...a little different,' he said carefully.

Jan saw a look of concern etched on Edward's face. 'It's changed, Jan,' he said in a grave tone, 'and I don't think for the better. The extra business is one thing, but...,' he looked over to where caravan upon caravan were squashed together like battery chickens, 'I think the farm has lost its identity and as for that idiot Ethan Dobbs... I have no idea who he thinks he is these days.'

Jan did not answer. He detested Ethan with a passion but it was not his place to say that, not to Mr Sonning. He stood rather awkwardly waiting for Edward to continue. Edward in turn looked at Jan, a gaze of sympathy crossing his face.

'You know something, Jan,' he said in a sad but soft tone, 'I admire you and your sister for making the journey here and working so hard. I often think that you must miss home. This place must seem like a prison to you sometimes.'

Jan again thought carefully before replying, 'It is hard sometimes, sir, but you have been very kind to us. It is not our home, but it is not a prison to us either.'

Edward clamped a strong hand on Jan's shoulder. 'You're a good man and I tell you that I wish I could say the same.' Edward's voice was tinged with sadness. 'It feels like a bloody prison to me these days.'

* * *

There was a thud on the caravan door followed by a voice. 'Kowalik, you are wanted down at the office, sharp.'

Jan pulled himself up from the sofa and slipped a pullover on. 'Do you want me to come?' Basia said with concern.

'No, you stay here. It will be nothing, probably that idiot wanting something stupid.'

He ran down the path towards the faintly lit office. Nodding at Billy he went inside to look for Ethan. He did not have to look far as he heard Ethan's booming voice. 'Ah, Kowalik, you have a phone call on the office line. Best hurry, probably costing one of your people a lot of money!'

Jan grimaced twofold. Any contact with Ethan brought hatred to his heart but he was worried. No one had called from Poland since they had arrived because of the cost; something must be wrong.

Cagily he lifted the phone to his ear and whispered his name.

'Jan, oh Jan, it is terrible,' his mother's voice was panicky, 'they take him away, your father is so ill.' Seeing Ethan eyeballing him curiously he kept a calm face and replied gently in Polish.

'Mama, tell me slowly, where is he? What happened? Please stay calm, I will help.'

He could hear Julita trying to gather her composure and he wished more than anything that he was by her side, not standing here, miles away with Ethan's inquisitive gaze upon him.

'He, he has been ill for a long time, as you know.' Julita eventually spoke, her voice faltering. 'He has been getting worse, chest pains, no breath and yesterday, blood.'

'Blood, what do you mean blood?' The fear rose in his voice as he glanced across to see Ethan's lips curl into a smile.

'He coughed up blood, lots of it. Jan, I was so worried. I called the doctor and he said he has to go to the hospital, he looked so serious!'

More sobbing followed as Jan's heart sank. His mind raced as he searched for solutions. He could travel back with Basia as planned, but what good would that do now? The money he had saved would not be enough. The second thought was that he could help. That would mean sacrifice. Having left home with a head full of dreams, he now knew what sacrifice was.

'Mama,' his voice did not waver, 'go to the doctor, the hospital, and tell them that you want the best treatment possible and that we will pay for it. I will send the money I have to you. I have saved many hundreds of pounds and we can use that to make him well. You must do that, Mama, okay?'

The sobbing calmed a little, in response to his tone. When Julita spoke again it was with passion and love. 'Oh, Jan, you are a good boy. I am so proud of you; your father is too, you know.' She checked herself, fighting back another outburst of tears. 'But what of you and Basia? When will you come home? We miss you so much.'

He had not said anything of his plans and that was the only thing he could be glad of now. The acceptance of his fate was upon him. They would have to stay, for how long, he did not know.

'We will come home as soon as we can, Mama. I will send all the money you need until Papa is better. Then,' his voice quavered, 'then we will come home and be a family.'

'I will go and tell them, my son,' she answered with a new found strength, 'I will tell them to do their best and I will tell them that my son and daughter are rich enough, in both money and in love. I love you, Jan, very much. Tell Basia I love her too, okay? Tell her it will be alright, okay?'

'I will tell her, Mama.' Jan's eyes stung now at holding back the sadness. 'I will call you in two days and you can tell me what they say. I will wire the money then. I love you too, Mama.'

He put the phone down and nodded a gesture of thanks to Ethan as he left the building. His heart and mind were in turmoil. He felt empty at having to stay on the farm, his dreams shattered. He had taken his little sister on a journey to a place where no one knew or cared for his family. Loneliness enveloped him and his mother's words gave him no sense of glory. The only sense of pride he felt was not letting Ethan Dobbs see his tears. He would save them a few moments more before he reached a quiet place and sobbed his heart out.

* * *

Two days later and, after paying the money over the counter at the post office, Jan walked to the nearby phone box. He perched a pile of change on the shelf and dialled the number.

'Mama, it's Jan, what news do you have?'

'They have done an X-ray, Jan,' Julita replied with relief. 'I told them we would have the money and they agreed to do the X-ray and move him into a better hospital in Warsaw.'

He steadied himself. 'What did the X-ray say?'

She sounded vague in her reply as she shuffled through some papers. She was not a woman of medical knowledge. 'They say they think he may have something called asbestosis. The X-ray showed something called "plaques" on his lungs. I do not know what this means but they tell me that it is from the work he has done.'

'Can they do anything? Can they make him better?'

'They say it is not the most serious problem of this type, not like something called…' she thought for a moment, 'ah, not mesothelioma, no, not that.'

'Well, can they do anything, Mama?' Jan felt a little frustrated; it did not sound good.

'They will give some medication and they will monitor him. He must stay in the hospital for now.' She sounded more cheerful than Jan felt as she went on, 'You tell Basia. You tell her, Jan, and you tell her we love her and it will all be alright, you tell her that.'

'Alright, I will, Mama,' he lied. He had not told Basia anything thus far. He did not want to scare her and now, even more so. He would say as little as possible and just keep sending the savings they made to Poland. She would understand one day, when their father was better.

'We will talk soon, Mama,' he replied tenderly, fighting back the sting of tears. 'We love you both.'

CHAPTER SIXTEEN

'The soul is at its most open with your waking thoughts. Take a moment to think of all the beauty around you and be humble, for you exist in a wonderful place which is full of magic moments. They are there, all around you each day; just open your eyes.'

(From the Scriptures of Galgliel)

2005

She was alone on the beach. A carpet of golden sand stretched beyond, sifted by the blue-green tide that frothed at her feet. Despite three years having passed, Andréa knew this place. She was back in Clacton-on-Sea.

There was a warm and gentle breeze that pushed her black hair back as she strained to take in the entire coastline. Far in the distance she could see another lone figure past the distant pier which jutted out into the sea like an aged finger pointing towards the horizon.

Her heart felt free and she felt safe, despite the strange emptiness around her. Her initial instinct of looking around fearfully for Steve or Dusana had passed now and her curiosity had compelled her to understand this place and her reasons for being back here. Andréa knew enough of the world and fate to wait for events to take their natural course.

The shape in the distance was getting closer. She decided against walking towards it but instead and on impulse, taking a handful of smooth pebbles that lay near her feet, she began to skim them across the water's surface. The grey oval stones skipped along the waves, leaping and dancing in a way that reminded her of Dusana skipping towards her, face alight with pure joy and love. Her heart felt full of love and happiness.

The breeze dropped and sunny warmth enveloped Andréa as Helena Sekhova approached. Her grandmother had changed since their last meeting, yet she was even more beautiful. Her skin beach-brown, her hair sea-crest white, as if she had become a part of this place. She wore a sheer white robe, scattered with golden butterflies that seemed to dance with each stride she took towards her.

Andréa held out her arms and the two embraced with easy affection. She knew that Helena could not be existent in terms of flesh and bone, yet she could feel her and hold her with a realness that life could not give. Andréa laughed with a joy beyond words as she held her grandmother once more.

As they broke gently away from their clinch, Helena put her arms on Andréa's shoulders and gazed lovingly into her eyes. Andréa felt her Angel look into her, warmly seeking her heart and glowing inside her.

'My beautiful Andréa,' her voice carried an Elfish splendour, *'it has been a little while but you look so happy... so complete.'*

Andréa's blue eyes shone with contentment. 'I am truly as in love with my heart and the world as I can be.' A warm tear trickled down her cheek. 'Thank you for guiding me, for showing me the way.'

'I showed you your destiny,' Helena replied, *'but you, my child, you held the faith to seek it. I should thank you, my darling Andréa, for fulfilling the prophecy and creating the child born out of pure love.'* Helena paused, her silky words hanging in the air as she shared her wisdom.

Andréa nodded slowly. 'I felt incomplete sometimes…as if something that was not yet missing would be one day.' She felt shivers down her spine as she thought of what her life could have been. 'I feel blessed in every sense; she is an amazing little girl and he, a wonderful man.'

Helena let her hands run from Andréa's shoulders down to her hands as she spoke. *'The child had to be born from the deepest love imaginable and forged from that. She was to be one half of the future, guided by the coin of Angels.'*

'I felt and feel that,' Andréa answered, 'but I do not understand some things. One half of what future and what parts do we play in this?'

'Dusana will grow with the gift bestowed upon her,' Helena replied joyfully. *'She will touch hearts and infiltrate even the hardest soul with love. One day she will join with the other half of the coin; it is destined that they will find each other. Together they will take this world back to its true beauty and prevent many bad things that could corrupt humanity's future. They will not know this and we cannot tell them, for it is fate that will be their guide and we can only be their guardians for now.'*

'What should I do?' Andréa asked willingly.

'The time has come for the coin to guide another,' Helena replied gently. *'You will wake tomorrow and know how this is to be done. All you need do is what you have always done, my sweet Andréa. Follow your heart.'*

* * *

Warm probing rays of sunlight flickered through the leafy canopy of the forest, dancing their way into the window. A patter of tiny feet was followed by a gentle creak as the little girl climbed up onto the bed and scrambled upwards towards her parents.

Steve awoke to feel her small, soft fingers ruffling his hair. His first impression of a new day was the vision and innocent beauty of his daughter, her penetrating blue eyes gazing at him with the wonder of innocence. He smiled and pulled her close to him, planting a soft kiss upon her forehead.

Dusana snuggled between them as his hand slid across to

Andréa, fingers stroking through her hair and down behind her ear which, in turn, had the effect of waking her from her dreamy slumber.

Sitting up, she greeted Dusana with a soft push and a squeeze of her little belly. Dusana giggled and wrapped both arms around her mother, nuzzling her nose into her nape.

'Darling,' Andréa began, 'I had the most vivid dream... vision last night: the coin and much more.'

Steve gave a gentle look of concern. 'Are you alright? It wasn't horrible or anything?'

She smiled as Dusana nestled in between them, listening intently. 'No, not at all, I just know that I must give my coin away. It is time.'

Looking a little confused, Steve nevertheless accepted her words. He knew her and her visions well enough to understand the sincerity he saw in her expression. 'Do you know to whom and where?' he asked.

She contemplated for a moment, searching her subconscious for the answers. 'Yes, I think I do,' she replied with a grin, 'we should go and see Harry.'

Harry... It was now Steve's turn to smile. As soon as he heard the name he realised it had been more than a year since he had seen his great friend. Goodness, how quickly the time had gone. Harry, entrepreneur antique dealer and the life and soul of any party, one of the funniest people alive, a man who had been the best friend Steve could have wished for. Casting his mind back, Steve remembered first meeting Andréa, how she had given him the pretty coin as a gift of her love, and how he had been so wretched in return. That coin had become his only connection with the woman he had loved and, if not for Harry, it would have remained just that: a coin of unknown identity that was only worth keeping because of the girl who had given it. It had been Harry who had noticed the coin and explained its meaning as the coin of Angels. If not for him then Steve's search for an Angel would have never been fulfilled. Now the coin would bring them all back together. He had not seen Harry for over a year and his great friend had never seen Dusana. It seemed right.

'Then, sweetheart,' he replied as he kissed her gently on the lips, 'we will arrange to go to London and see Harry.'

* * *

A week later, on a fine summer's morning, the three boarded the plane at Prague Airport for the journey to London. Steve had called Harry and arranged to meet with him at his shop in London which then could be followed by a trip around the West End and a night in a good hotel before returning to Clacton the following day and Harry's for the night. Steve had also decided to make a small detour on the way to visit the cemetery on Gorse Hill to pay his respects to those he had lost.

The sight of all the planes taking off and landing had Dusana staring in wonder and, as they made their way onto the Airbus for her first ever flight, she skipped and leapt around with unbridled enthusiasm.

The plane climbed powerfully into the sky whilst Steve closed his eyes and reflected. It was his first return journey to England since fate had guided him to Prague, Andréa and his destiny. He felt Andréa's hand clutch lovingly onto his and opened his eyes to see Dusana's face pressed up against the window in awe. She had seen little of the world except the town of Boubin and the forest in which she had grown up. The wonder of planes and flying made both Steve and Andréa grin with the innocence of parents sharing yet another joy.

Once the plane levelled off and the seat belt signs had been turned off, Dusana was allowed to roam the aircraft. She beamed through crystal eyes at her mother as she danced in the aisle. *'Já letím!'* They both laughed as Steve added, 'I am flying, and that is what you must say in English, clever little one.'

She laughed back gleefully before running up and down the craft as she spread the word 'I am flying! *Já letím!' t*o anyone

139

that would listen. Even the grumpiest businessmen could not help but laugh at the splendour of the small child as she shared her innocent gift of natural love with them.

A few hours later and a journey by train from Stansted to Liverpool Street, followed by another by tube to Oxford Circus, saw a different side to Dusana. Initially staring in both wonder and natural curiosity at the train and vast amounts of passengers, she became withdrawn on the tube as she clutched both parents' hands glancing warily at the other travellers.

As the three walked up and out onto the busy streets of London, she seemed to absorb the atmosphere and she trembled a little. Andréa noticed and knelt in front of her, pulling her soft coat close around her as she did. 'Dusana, are you alright?'

Dusana shook her head from side to side sending her white blonde hair into the wind that had whipped up as they left the tube station. *'Maminko, já se bojím,'* she voiced with a fearful look.

Andréa hugged her warmly and whispered in her ear. 'There is no need to be afraid, my Angel. This is just London and it is different. You will get used to it and you are with us and safe, okay? We will see Uncle Harry soon!'

'Arry.' Dusana seemed to relax as she repeated his name in her accent before taking both parents' hands again as they made their way towards the impressive shop front of *'HTT antiques and valuable objects'*.

* * *

A surly-looking security guard was standing just inside the door as the three entered. Steve introduced himself and asked for Harry whilst Andréa held Dusana's hand tightly, fearing that her curiosity could prove costly in a shop full of expensive wonders. After a word on the internal intercom the guard motioned to them to the door at the rear of the shop. 'Please go through, it's the first door on the left.'

The three made their way as directed and there, in a vast study, sat Harry, magnifying glass close to his eye, poring over a large stone of some kind. Steve cleared his throat tactfully. 'Well, well, well,' Harry flashed a toothy grin, 'if it's not the return of Steve Bidante. Last time I saw you, old mate, you were going to let me know if you wanted a lift back from the airport... which you obviously didn't! Come here, you!'

The two friends held each other tightly for a brief moment before Harry turned his smiling face towards Andréa and Dusana. 'I have to say, Andréa, you look more stunning than ever. Does he know how lucky he is?'

Andréa laughed, her face glowing red as they embraced. 'Been a long time, girl,' he whispered into her ear. 'I am so happy for you both... you three,' he added as his attention turned Dusana. 'Well, I have to say I have never seen quite such a pretty girl in all my days and what, may I ask, is your name, little girl?'

He winked at Andréa who grinned from ear to ear. Dusana did a dainty curtsey, as if rehearsed for royalty as she replied timidly, 'Dusana – Arry!'

The room filled with laughter as the friends reunited. Eventually Harry motioned for them to sit down. Dusana leapt onto his lap and begun pulling with inquisitiveness on his tie.

'So,' Harry began, 'why did you want to meet me here, Steve?'

'Just one of many reasons really, mate.' He glanced at Dusana who was now rolling the tie in the palm of her hand. 'We wanted to see London and show her and... well, I'll let Andréa explain.'

As Harry's eyes flitted across to Andréa, she searched inside her bag and produced the coin. 'Harry, your knowledge of antiques unravelled the meaning of the coin and for that,' she let loose an uninhibited wide smile, 'I thank you. Something now tells me that I, we, should come to you and leave the coin in your hands.'

'Eh, okay,' Harry said uncertainly, 'knowing the way you two think and all that has gone on, I am not going to doubt that you have good reason.' He picked the coin up and twisted it between his fingers as he added, 'What exactly am I going to do with it?'

Steve looked at Andréa with the same puzzlement as Harry. She shifted slightly in her chair trying to remain composed. 'I know it may sound silly, Harry, but it's simple really. Just hold onto the coin until the right person comes in and tries to buy it from you. You will know when and you will know who. I trust you so, please, trust me.'

There was a pause before Harry let out a puff of air. 'Well, if that's what you want, then that's what I will do. Although, I have to be honest, I have no idea how I'm going to know. Shall I put a sign up and just wait or what?'

Andréa looked startled. 'No!' The tension in her voice made Dusana jump. 'No, Harry, you must not do that. You must keep it locked away and only sell it or pass it on when the right person comes for it.' She looked with sincerity at Harry who, in turn, fell under the spell of her words. 'You will know.'

CHAPTER SEVENTEEN

A knock at the door ended the discussion. Harry called out for the visitor to enter and a soft voice with an unmistakeable Irish lilt accompanied the visitor's entrance. 'I hope I'm not gatecrashing your party, but I did get an invite!'

Stunned at the familiar voice, Steve spun round in his chair to see the grinning face of Pat Reilly. The Irishman had befriended him as a child and since then they had forged a strong friendship that had seen much emotion. It had been Pat who had fought to keep Ray Skee alive those few years ago as fate struck in their lives. Now, with some clever planning on Harry's part, the brain surgeon had arrived right on cue. Steve shot Harry an appreciative smile as he stood up to greet his friend. 'Harry, that's brilliant. Pat!'

He grabbed his old friend as the two backslapped before recovering a degree of decorum. 'Darling, this is Pat Reilly, the one I told you about.' Steve grinned as he added, 'A great and wise man who loves his Guinness.'

Pat didn't give her time to answer as he boldly walked up and kissed her on both cheeks. 'Bejaysus! What a flower you are! It's an honour to meet yer at last, Andréa, to be sure it is.'

She melted immediately under his Irish charm and warmth as, smiling, she replied, 'Thank you, Pat, I've heard many good things about you from Steve. It's lovely to finally meet you.'

Pat grinned affectionately as he looked at Harry and then Dusana, still perched on his lap. 'Surely it cannot be.' He feigned astonishment. 'I thought I would never see such a thing as a living Angel but it seems I am wrong.' Turning to Steve he imitated a gasp. 'She cannot be yours, can she?'

Before Steve could retort, Pat let out a booming laugh and slapped Steve on the back. Turning back to Dusana, he said, 'Well, my precious one, you have a wonderful father and mother, let me tell you.' Pat looked around the room. 'So, what are we doing here, wasting time or going for a pint of Guinness?'

'We're all finished now, Pat,' Andréa replied, her eyes passing one last time over the coin. 'Steve, if you men would like to go to catch up I'll take Dusana shopping for a while and meet you at the hotel?'

'A finer woman you will never meet,' interjected Pat as his gaze followed hers to the coin. 'Ah, the coin, I guess? Harry told me all about it, Steve. Seems to have served you well whatever it is doing back here.'

'It did indeed,' Steve replied in a heartfelt tone, 'and now Harry will take care of it. So, let's go and catch up. Darling, we won't be long.'

Pat lifted his eyebrows in the direction of Harry and grinned as they watched Steve say his goodbyes to the girls. He had never seen his friend like this and Harry's silent response echoed his thoughts.

* * *

Andréa and Dusana made their way out of the shop and onto Oxford Street. Immediately Andréa noticed two things which unsettled her. One was that Dusana wanted to know *everything* and the other was that more than a few people seemed interested in her daughter.

Dusana tugged at her mother after just a few steps. *'Maminko támhle ten pán?'*

'Who is who?' Andréa answered as she followed her daughter's pointed finger. It was aimed towards the pavement where Andréa picked out the beggar. He sat hunched, his clothing filthy, his face contorted as he tore into a burger with blackened teeth. Andréa felt repulsed as she attempted to cajole Dusana away. 'It's a bad man, come, come.'

As she pulled gently on Dusana's hand she became aware that the tramp suddenly seemed to notice them and stopped chewing. His neck seemed to click into one rigid place, frozen in time, and now Andréa saw his stare. He had the most powerful opaque green eyes. Those eyes were fixed on Dusana.

Feeling uneasy at his intense fixation, she whispered in Dusana's ear urgently, 'Come now, we must be getting along.'

Dusana ignored her as she stared back at the man, a gentle smile appearing on her lips. As she did so, he smiled back, the cloudiness disappearing to be replaced by tears. He dropped his food to the floor and fell forwards, hands stretched out, in front of Dusana.

People were beginning to slow around them, the scene taking their attention as they first looked at the beggar and then to the girl he seemed to be worshipping. Andréa panicked, grabbing Dusana firmly and snapping at her, 'Now, we go!'

She dragged her for the first few steps before Dusana started to walk again in tandem with her. Andréa glared at her as the crowds moved on with their usual tasks. 'Don't disobey me, Dusana! I tell you to go and you go! This is not Boubin, it is not safe here.'

She looked down at Dusana feeling a little ashamed at her outburst; the girl looked up, her face sad at her scolding but etched with honesty as she spoke without words – *He is not a bad man*.

* * *

Nicole and Francesca were trying to snake their way through the bodies that had congested the street ahead when they noticed the scene.

'Mum, look at that!' Francesca gaped, open-mouthed, 'that man, and just look at that girl!'

Nicole took in the scene: a beggar lying face down in front of a small girl whilst the girl's mother seemed irate. The beep of the green man at the crossing interceded as Nicole pulled her daughter towards the crossing.

Francesca glanced back but remained silent as the moment engulfed her. She would never speak of it but for the rest of her life she would not forget seeing the girl with the wings who glowed.

* * *

The three friends spent a few hours in the bar catching up on all that had gone on in the past year. They spoke emotionally of Ray and of Sharon, who was now, as Harry explained, *clean*. Steve described Boubin in its true splendour. He told them that it had seemed perfect from the moment he stepped inside Andréa's house and saw Dusana for the first time. The decision to sell his house had been an easy one. Many memories were left in England whilst a new life awaited him in Boubin. He had picked up a little work with computers, enough for them to get by in their humble, yet happy world. Andréa, he explained, had work as a masseuse. She was skilled and had plenty of work not far from home to keep the three of them. As Steve described his life he felt inside that he had made a perfect choice in leaving England and so many emotions far behind.

Harry seemed happy with his lot. Jack and Charlie were growing up and Sophie and he were going through a *purple patch* as he called it. Business was fine and he felt in tune with his inner self. The last comment brought a grin from both men, knowing Harry's defiance of anything but logic in time gone by.

Pat, for all his work, had now gained more national

recognition in his field of neurology. Outside of work he was also noted for not being able to pick the right woman. He seemed a little envious as he told of a handful of diabolical dates with women that had the other two in stitches.

Time flew by and Steve ended the meeting after a glance at his watch. No one had mentioned Laurence or Susie throughout and that suited him down to the ground. They surely knew the pain that it had caused him when he found out his friend had betrayed him for the woman he had planned to marry and he appreciated the silence on the matter. Besides, those days were a part of history and, anyway, the last he had heard they were not getting on so well. He was glad the subject had not been brought up.

* * *

Andréa had taken Dusana to a multitude of shops including her daughter's new favourite, Hamley's, where Dusana found a perfect child's playground. After having to practically drag the little girl out, the two went for burgers and shakes before they returned to the hotel. By the time Steve returned, Dusana was out like a light, leaving the two to a relaxing night with a bottle of wine, courtesy of room service. On a bright Wednesday morning they left London feeling refreshed and ready for the trip ahead.

Harry had left his car for them in the compound by the shop as he had taken the train home to Clacton the night before. They would meet at his place later that evening before he took them back to the airport on the way to work the following day. Soon the three were on the road heading towards Clacton.

As Dusana dozed, Steve and Andréa said little, each wrapped in their own memories of a place where so much had happened before. Steve tried to contain the surge of memories that were flowing like a swollen river through his mind whilst Andréa pondered a return to a place she never imagined she would see again. Unbeknown to Steve, she had once sworn she would never go back to England, the place where her heart had lain shattered like a crushed shell on the beach. Time had taken nothing away from that promise, but love had. Now was now, and all was different.

They arrived back in good time and Steve pulled into the train station to get some flowers. He had chosen to go back there, as if revisiting his destiny, to see if the woman from his long past dreams was there, but it was just a young girl who wrapped several bright bouquets.

Gorse Hill remained unchanged, yet, on the journey back to his home, Steve had noticed subtle differences. There seemed many more houses and much more traffic in the country he had once called home. At least back here, all around seemed to have escaped any such transformation.

As Steve pulled up in the car park between the two cemeteries, Dusana pressed her nose to the window, spotting the play area off to the left. As Andréa opened the car door she was off like a shot, legs like pistons, giggling for all she was worth.

'Dusana…!' Steve called to no avail.

'Don't worry, darling,' Andréa smiled compassionately, 'I'll go with her. This is your time.'

Steve breathed in the sweet fresh air and gazed around. The large willow trees, now flourishing in Garden of Eden green, swung gently in the warm wind as if welcoming him back. Bright flowers paraded high along the hedge line of the cemetery on the right, while the scent of freshly cut grass intoxicated his senses. Despite the reason for visiting, Steve could feel the power, the intensity of this place, so much history, so many memories; it felt good to be back.

Standing at the grave of Ray Skee, Steve felt almost surreal. The loss of his friend on that fateful day still seemed unbelievable. In fact, the whole situation seemed incomprehensible. He should have been on that bike with Ray, he should have been dead. But now, amongst those he held so dear, there was the gravestone of his friend. After some time whispering tear-filled regrets, Steve visited firstly his grandparents' graveside before walking the short distance to the grave of his parents. He knelt at the base of the headstones, delicately placing each bouquet as he did so. In a whisper of a voice he prayed and spoke to his parents just as before. This time though, he spoke of joy and love and all things full of hope.

As he finished speaking, Steve closed his eyes letting the warm breeze massage his face. In a trance-like state, his mind seemed to open and he heard a voice deep in his subconscious: 'Daddy, who are those people?' Steve snapped his eyes open before staring open-mouthed.

In front of him he saw the shadowy images of those lost in the past. Just as he had seen them at the funeral of his grandmother, they now stood in front of him. Some of the images were the same: Ray Skee, dressed for the festival he never saw and his grandfather Cyril who stood proudly in full uniform from a war long finished. But now there was his granny and the two that made his heart beat faster: his parents.

They stood together. His parents, lost so long ago yet now side by side before him. His father stood tall and proud, his strong facial features amplifying snow-white hair, with powerful deep grey eyes. His mother, petite, yet so strong, curled black hair touching her soft tanned face which exuberated kindness, love and yet now, at this moment, sorrow.

Confusion took over as he felt Dusana's voice close by. He looked across the field and saw her in the distance by the swings, Andréa rocking her back and forth. Returning his gaze to the figures in front he whispered, 'Can you see them too, darling?'

In his mind he felt her nod, as she replied in Czech, *'Ano tatínku, já je vidím.'* Of course I can see them, Daddy.

Any vision Steve had experienced before now paled into insignificance. The connection with his daughter was so real, yet, as unbelievable as the figures that stood in front of him, a parade of ghostly silhouettes, lit by the backdrop of the sun. One now moved forward slowly but not a blade of grass moved beneath her.

'Mum,' Steve caught his breath at the sight of her, 'I never thought...'

Her lips curled into a smile which he instantly remembered from his childhood. He was a boy once more and she shone with the same motherly glory that she had been to him. The child in him awoke as he wished so hard that she had never gone.

'Hello, boy.' Her voice carried the familiarity as if spoken just a moment before. She, like his granny, had always referred to him as *boy.* The warmth in her tone crystallised his insides setting off a magnitude of passion, love and so, so many questions.

'Mum,' he began as he stretched out a hand towards her. It touched nothing but warm air.

'Mum,' he repeated, distraught, 'why did you go? Why are you here? Why...'

'Shh,' she said softly, *'accept the gift you have, boy. You chose to see me. I, we have little time. You must listen carefully, Steve.'*

He nodded silently, his eyes focusing on every detail of his mother and father that his mind could capture.

'You must return home and not bring Dusana back here for many years. It is too dangerous here for her. Your task is done here.'

His heart filled with many things that he could not identify. 'I will do as you say but it all seems so much to not come back. Why?'

She sighed, much the way she used to when he asked one question too many. *'There is much to know of the Laws of the Angel and there is no time to explain now. We are soon to be expelled from the Earth as the new darkness comes. In old times it would take half a century for a sentient being of good heart and soul to show itself as a living image on Earth, to cross the divide. Things have changed now and my energy will be vanquished but I have to give you something, something whole and real which will drain my life force.'* He saw the sadness as she added, *'It is all I can do, for you will not see me again.'*

Steve remained quiet, his being simply yearning for anything more she could say. When she spoke again, it was about Dusana.

'My little grandchild, she can see me, can't she, through your mind?' Her image floated, glowing, as she said the words. Steve could almost feel Dusana smile from the distance as he looked to see her playing. Steve's mother, Dusana's grandmother, followed his eyes taking in the beauty of one she could never touch.

She broke the connection he had felt as she said, *'One day she will see me as a whole being, if all comes to pass. But for now, Steve, take this, put it on her and know it will protect her. You will understand.'*

She offered her hand to him and Steve went to take it in his but felt only air, combined with a sudden coolness, as the ghostly hand passed one of flesh. He opened his palm to see the object she had left in his palm, a pretty necklace with a silver pendant.

'I must go, boy, I love you all, we all do, and you will understand…The time has come with Andréa.' She began to grow fainter.

'Mum, please, will I see you again? What should I do?' He wanted to shout to her to stay but knew it would be no good.

'You spent many years of your life searching for the Angel and you found her… Now you must protect her.'

He hung on the last words he would hear before she and the others faded into nothingness.

Steve snapped back to reality seeing Andréa and Dusana walking towards him. He beckoned to Dusana who skipped over and stood before him with an almost knowing smile. Pushing her long, silky hair back, Steve slipped the necklace around her soft neck before clicking the link into place.

As Dusana gazed at him, Steve saw the immediate impact of his mother's gift. Her azure eyes had always been so penetrating, yet now the silver of the pendant somehow seemed to deflect, almost soften, that stare. He swallowed deeply as he remembered where he had first seen the pendant. He relived the vision that had haunted him for so long; the dreams where a daughter he never knew of stood before him, wearing this very same necklace as she whispered the word he would now never take for granted: *'**Daddy.**'*

The sound of Andréa's voice brought him back to reality. 'Darling, that's lovely. Where did you get it?'

Still staring he said in a knowing, yet sombre voice, 'It was my mother's.'

CHAPTER EIGHTEEN

September 2005

The black limousine pulled up alongside the fountain that marked the courtyard outside Number 3 Hampstead Heath. From within the mansion, Lorraine made her way from the front room, up the marble spiral staircase towards the master bedroom.

'Joey is waiting, Mrs Healy,' she said, knocking softly at the door.

Jenny acknowledged the call, and a moment later made her way downstairs giving Lorraine a weak smile of thanks. 'Good morning, Lorraine,' she said faintly as the latter held open a long black leather coat for her.

Slipping her arms inside Jenny gave a gentle sigh as Lorraine attempted to make small talk. 'Are we going into the city this morning, ma'am?'

'Mmm,' replied Jenny absentmindedly, 'for a change.' She muttered to herself rather than in reply.

She took a quick look in the immense mirror that dominated the entrance hall. Even at forty-four Jenny still possessed great natural beauty. Her slim physique was complemented by a kind, youthful face and natural soft blonde hair that touched her shoulders setting off her blue eyes. There could be no doubt that Jenny was an attractive woman, but today, as in many of the days of the last years, she did not see the woman in front of her. The laughter lines around her eyes were interlaced with sadness. The glance lasted mere seconds before Jenny turned and left the house to the sound of the large oak doors closing, which in turn created an echo of empty space that epitomised her sense of loneliness.

She climbed into the back of the limousine and greeted Joey with the usual short exchange of dialogue: 'Good morning, Mrs Healy.' 'Good morning, Joey.' He did not ask where she was going as he knew she would inform him if it was anywhere different than usual. As he drove towards the West End, Jenny opened her mobile and texted Holly. She had nothing to say really. There was nothing different about today with the exception that, since Holly had left for Loughborough University, she had found herself lonelier then ever. When Holly was around Jenny felt whole, alive. Holly was the mirror of herself in her youth and her daughter's zest for life far surpassed her husband's and son's desire for work.

The streets of London sped by as they made good headway. As Joey steered the limousine to the kerbside near Oxford Circus, Jenny thanked him and, as usual, told him that she would call when ready. Joey nodded mechanically before the car glided off, leaving Jenny surrounded by movement and life but, inside, alone.

Friendly voices greeted her as she entered each familiar shop. The usual haunts in the area: H & M, Topshop, United Colours of Benetton, Shellys, Miss Selfridge and John Lewis. Shop assistants scurried to her bidding, recognising one of their best customers instantly and pandering to her every whim. It was here, in these places, that she found the most attention and, being a woman of kindness and good manners, she was always polite and friendly, yet she also found herself agitated by the attention. It was not 'real'. She was a currency to each store and that made her resent the false flocking of the staff. These were the only places she knew that actually made her *want* to be alone. Perhaps that is why she came here so often, to exchange one version of emptiness for another.

Whilst trying on the umpteenth piece of clothing, Jenny heard her mobile hum telling her she had a text. The mobile suddenly took precedence as Jenny delved into her handbag. After retrieving the phone, her face found a rare glow as she saw the name of her daughter in the inbox. The simple text read '*Thank you mummy, love you too. All good here, will call at weekend.*' Somehow just those few words meant something special, instantly dissolving the monotony that she was feeling.

For a short time she felt elated. It had been just a simple message but from Holly, the daughter she adored, the shining star in her world, it carried a warming sensation. With several bags under her arms she made her way to the plush Rimini's Restaurant at the top of Regent Street and signalled for her usual glass of white wine.

Sitting by the window, she sipped her drink and watched the world go by. So many people, all in seemingly such a rush to be going somewhere while she sat feeling bored and empty, so much time but so little to do with it.

Out of habit she played with her mobile phone, instinctively scrolling down her contact list and letting her mind talk quietly as she saw the names. Debbie Threadgold, Teresa Jameson, Mollie Broadhurst. Each name brought the same gut reaction: fair-weather friends. The list was full of rich people who, like her, had more money than they could ever need or wish for, but, unlike her, wished to talk about it constantly, to compare notes on purchases and people; to sneer down at the lesser beings, those 'who were not of the same stock'.

She shut the phone and tossed it back into her bag as if it had suddenly become almost too hot to hold. It was not Terry's fault things were like this, she told herself. He wanted the best for her and the family. Of course he did, and he worked all hours to get it. He too resented the dinner parties and functions that they had to attend, the false smiles as they listened and endured all manner of upper-class snobs who cared not for the Northern man and his family. They probably begrudged his success but, being the type of people they were, they would swarm with honey-coated tongues to greet them, in the hope of seeing some of his companies' monies flowing into their bank accounts in a fashion similar to the expensive bubbly that they so freely shared with '*such a great man*'.

No, Jenny loved her husband and knew that he loved her deeply in return. She felt selfish to even be thinking of such things, but then she knew the one thing she did not like in Terry would never be eradicated, for it was rife in their son. The drive that spurred him on had led to an inbuilt fear of failure and that had been passed down to Terrance but in a different sense. She loved her son, but despised his single-minded view toward money. Where her husband worked for what he perceived as a worthy cause, her son worked purely out of greed and the instrument of power that it gave him.

Terrance, unlike the rest of the family, thrived in an atmosphere where people fussed around him constantly. His arrogance had grown with each passing year and Jenny felt a tinge of guilt. She had known it so long ago, even in the toy shop with Mr Guild. She had felt an embarrassment that her only son could be so driven and selfish. With a sad realisation, she even knew that he looked down on her nowadays. She was not the earner and her status in the family was below his, at least in his eyes. She knew that no mother should feel such a way but his emotions, if he actually had any, were the opposite of Holly's outwardly loving ones.

Slipping a handsome tip to the waiter with a waxwork smile, Jenny set off out of the restaurant towards the plush antique shop just off Oxford Circus, her mind a muddled mess of uncertainty and insecurity. She knew she would change nothing, for nothing could be changed. A stranger brushed past her, knocking her off balance a little as he walked head down, briefcase in hand, rushing to be somewhere. There was no apology, no smile, and, as she glanced around, she realised that most people were just like him.

Then she saw him.

Two doors away from the antique shop was a McDonald's and by the side of the entrance a man crouched holding a cup in front of him. She only caught sight of him briefly, but took in his image immediately.

He was filthy, with sodden clothing that hung shapelessly off his skinny frame. His hair and facial growth gave him the look of a Neanderthal which, in turn, disguised any hope of guessing his age. In that fragment of time their eyes locked and then…he smiled.

The smile travelled towards her, complemented by an amazing set of pale green eyes that hit her with impact. There was no bitter sadness in those eyes, no longing or begging. Just the most beautiful smile she had seen for as long as she could remember. She smiled back before natural shyness intervened, causing her to bow her head and walk past him. She could feel her breathing intensify as she reached the entrance of the shop and she dialled up Joey.

* * *

Jenny sat alone at the dining table whilst Lorraine cleared up the dishes from dinner and informed her that Terrance had left a message saying he would be away until the weekend. His job of being head buyer for T Healy & Sons meant that he was seldom home. For all she knew her son could be anywhere right now. She also knew that, like clockwork, her husband would arrive home after ten, kiss her before pouring a drink, taking a shower and perhaps making some late-night calls or watching some TV before heading for bed. Soon after that he would be grunting in his sleep until early next morning when the routine resumed.

She thought about the man, who had slipped almost with ease into her subconscious. It was not what he was or where he was that had niggled at her. It was *that* smile. It had been the most genuine smile she had felt in forever. She made the decision.

* * *

Once out of the solitude of the limo, she inhaled the evening air and put up her umbrella before heading towards McDonald's. The steady rain made the streets appear shiny with a wet lacquer that amplified the footsteps of passers-by. People splashed their way hurriedly along, umbrellas hitting other umbrellas sending plumes of spray onto anyone unfortunate enough not have one.

As she neared, Jenny checked her step and paused. She had not really decided what to do once she got there, or even if the man would be there. That was the first thing to do. Check. Using the umbrella as a kind of camouflage, Jenny sidled along to within sight of the shop. He was there.

She watched the wretched man from the distance. He was now soaked through but still in the familiar position she had last seen him in. Since that time she had unpacked, bathed, eaten and relaxed while he had crouched or knelt in front of the shop, begging. How much could he have been given? How much could it be worth to be in that situation? She could not understand, and now she was here again she was not sure if she wanted to understand.

A part of her urged her to leave now, to turn and call Joey who would be there in an instant and take her back to the warmth of home. It told her that a lesson should be learned from this worthless man and, now it had, she should return and bathe in the luxuries that life had given her. She listened to the voice and found herself agreeing. Perhaps that was all it was: a fortunate event to teach her a lesson on self-esteem.

Her eyes never left the man as she thought. Despite the voice telling her to go, she still stared. He had no idea of her presence; his view remained steadfastly ahead as he waited for a passer-by's kindness or guilt or anything that resulted in money, damned money.

She saw the two young men strolling confidently along the street and she saw the look of utter contempt that they gave to the beggar as they came close. She saw the right foot of the nearest man lurch out, making heavy contact with the beggar's midriff. She heard the grunt of pain from his mouth and one of the men say, *'Piece of fucking scum'* before the other man kicked the beggar's paper cup away and the two resumed their journey, now heading towards her.

As they passed her, neither gave her a second look. She, unlike the beggar, did not stand out. Their fresh young faces brimmed with a confidence that a good job in the City and a fat pay packet gave. She found herself filling with hatred that these two men, with so much good fortune, could be callous enough to hurt someone much less so. Before she knew it she was next to him on the floor. She gathered the cup as he blew out air, trying to regain his breath. With just one hand she scooped up the money beside him and saw that there could only be a few pounds at best. A few pounds were all this man had gained in hours of freezing isolation from the people around him. Tears of pity welled up inside as she placed the cup back in front of him and spoke.

'Are you alright?' she began carefully. She had seen his smile earlier but now felt a tinge of fear. After his assault, what if he was dangerous? She checked her feelings and felt ashamed. 'I saw what they did. Bastards.'

'It's not the first time,' he grunted as the breath came back into his lungs. 'The suits are the worst, I don't know why.'

He shuffled himself upwards and back into position as he looked at her. A vague familiarity showed in his face making Jenny feel self-conscious. 'Let me go and get you a hot drink,' she said in a sympathetic tone which was also laced with awkwardness.

After queuing in McDonald's she brought two cups of coffee out. Whilst inside she had regained her composure and determined that she would talk with the man.

As the steam of the coffee rose up into his face, he gave a thankful grin. Jenny felt that radiance once more and it lit up a flame of compassion in her stomach.

'Thank you,' he said as his lips touched the hot liquid. 'I saw you earlier today, didn't I?'

'Yes, yes, you did,' she replied, somehow feeling special that he had remembered her. 'Why are you here and why do people do that to you?'

She watched as some of the coffee overflowed from his overeager sips and ran down his beard onto his dull khaki windcheater. He seemed unaware or uncaring about it and replied almost nonchalantly, 'It's not all bad. Like I said, the suits seem to be the worst but some people are really kind.' For the first time Jenny saw a look of sadness in the green of his eyes as he added, 'I have no choice, you see.'

'But why, I mean how?' she asked. 'Where do you live, where do you eat?'

He answered calmly, seeming less bothered about his plight than her. 'I live all over, I suppose,' he replied with uncertainty, as if trying to remember himself. 'I do it as I have no choice, not at the moment anyway.' He shot her a look of submission. 'I'm not the only one, you know; there are loads like me out here.'

Jenny did not reply. She knew that, but she could not bring herself to say to the man that he was unique, at least to her. His smile had made a difference to her day. She felt her phone vibrate and, after excusing herself, looked at the number. It was Joey.

'Mrs Healy? Are you alright? It's been over an hour and I was becoming a little concerned.'

Jenny looked at her watch realising that time had escaped her. 'Sorry, Joey, I'll be ready in five minutes. Meet me at the antiques shop, please.'

The man heard of course, but did not comment on the fact that she did not want to be collected near him. Jenny had not meant it that way; at least she did not think she had.

'My name is Jenny,' she said lifting herself up. 'I hope I can see you again if that's alright.'

'I'll be here, or there, or somewhere nearby,' he answered, and again she saw that smile as he spoke. Such depth, such inner meaning, which made her crave to know more about him and his life. 'My name is Oliver,' he added.

'That's a nice name.' She fumbled for her bag as a thought entered her mind. 'Here, Oliver, please take this and I hope it will help.'

She held out two twenty-pound notes in front of him expecting his hand to snap out at any moment and take them from her with an uncontrollable desire, but he did not.

He sat and looked at the notes; she could almost see the battle raging in his mind. She was confused. 'Take it, please,' she said again, pushing the money nearer to him.

Eventually his eyes cleared and he looked at her. 'No, thank you, but I cannot.'

'But I'm only trying…' Jenny spoke apologetically.

'Wait!' he interrupted.

She watched him use one hand to roll up the sleeve of his other arm displaying the bare skin, his eyes now letting watery emotions shine from them. She saw the numerous needle marks dotted like a dartboard as he spoke.

'Thank you, but I can't take your money. I will just do more of this.' His voice quavered. 'Now, please go. Visit me but never offer me money again, you understand?'

Jenny nodded humbly and walked away. She found her heart aching for Oliver, the homeless heroin addict.

CHAPTER NINETEEN

'The world does not change, people do. The world does not change. You do. The world cannot change but people will try to change the world. The world cannot change so do not let them change you.'

(From the scriptures of Galgliel)

'Andréa, we need to talk for a moment.' They had reached the second willow, its fronds whispering in the breeze in a language that spoke only to the wind; yet now that wind picked up and swept towards her, shifting her hair back gently as her blue eyes met his. She knew he was going to speak of the past, of the memories of their meeting in this town. She remembered the beauty and love they had shared, of his betrayal with Susie and her attempt at forgiveness, a forgiveness that had been impossible to imagine but was now, in hindsight, her redemption.

'Here is a place we both know,' he began passionately, 'a place we could both picture, even if we were on opposite corners of the planet, a place that has brought us both happiness and heartache. I lost you, Andréa, I know I did.'

'Steve, stop, you don't have to say this…'

'No, I must, I have to,' his voice cracked like a dead branch, 'I still, even now, do not know if I have won you back. Not entirely, and I probably never deserve to, for you gave me beauty, and in return I gave you pain. That was until…'

She could see the pain in his eyes and hear the torture of his voice as he paused. Taking him close in her arms she whispered the words, 'We are together now, all of us, that is all that matters.'

The fearless boy resurged. The woman before him had shown him the preciousness that love could bring yet he had hurt her so selfishly. Still she forgave him. He felt his tooth cut into his lip as he replied, 'I know, and for that I will be eternally grateful to you and destiny. I just cannot hide anything anymore, and neither should you. I know that without Dusana we would have been lost. You would have made a new life for yourself and perhaps I would have; perhaps…'

A droplet of blood fell from the fresh cut of his punctured lip, the emotions ripe and meaningful as he went on. 'Look at me, Andréa, flesh and bone, a human, weak and frail, designed to make mistakes, to learn, and then one day, die. That is me, you and all of us. I have learned something that you can never take away from me and I never want to be taken. I learned what true love is and that means that this exterior can go to hell, for what remained would be love. Utopia is a word but you, you are my Zahir. I ask one thing of you only and in return will give all. I want you to… I mean, will you marry me?'

Her teardrops diluted the blood as she moved close and kissed him. Dusana watched, an innocent child, knowing the moment was sacred.

'I think I can do that now.' She smiled. It had been a long journey and it would continue to be fraught with many things, but no longer uncertainty.

'Yes, Steve, I will.'

* * *

The morning of the wedding was blessed with sun as the small contingent made their way deep into the forest. A handful of locals joined Harry and his two sons, Jack and Charlie, who, along with Pat, had travelled from England to witness the scene. In the centre was a large opening where a temporary trellis network had been erected along with seating and canopies for the guests. The sun's rays poked through and bounced upon the floor giving off a beautiful illumination which seemed to dance with the music that welcomed them all.

It was Harry who stood next to Steve holding the ring in readiness for Andréa's entrance. Dressed in matching Italian suits, the two exchanged a brief grin as the tempo of the music changed.

Steve chanced the briefest of glances back to see his future wife make her way up the makeshift aisle. Andréa looked utterly radiant as she approached; her arm linked to that of Pat Reilly and behind them Jack, Charlie and Dusana, marching in step under the guidance of a delighted local lady.

As Andréa drew level, the two turned to each other. He swallowed hard at her beauty. She looked absolutely stunning in a gleaming white dress, woven of the finest fabric, and cut from her shoulders to hug her figure and trace down to the floor. The fairytale was real.

The priest began the simple ceremony which was spoken in the twin languages and contained a short prayer along with two pieces of classical music which Andréa had selected. Then, in front of the small gathering, the priest pronounced them man and wife. The two kissed to the sound of gentle applause as the music began to play in a joyous manner whilst the small congregation of witnesses danced, drank and ate long into the afternoon and evening. The setting was serene and beautiful and the day full of celebration and magic. It would be a day that Steve and Andréa would never forget and, for Harry and Pat, a day they never believed could ever happen.

* * *

It was near to dusk as Harry and Pat leisurely wandered

through the forest. Ahead ran the three children: Dusana playing 'It' with Jack and Charlie to many squeals of delight.

'Ah, a good day, Harry, a good day indeed.' Pat, looking relaxed, lit up a cigarette. 'I never thought I would see such a day, mind.'

Harry flashed his grin. 'Me neither, my friend, but now I am here, well,' he sighed gently, 'I can see the attraction. It's so tranquil and pretty and the air...'

Pat blew a cloud of smoke towards him. 'Can't say the air smells much different to me, but I agree on the place. It reminds me of Ireland and home. You know, the green valleys, the steam of peat fires and...' Pat stopped as he saw Harry's expression change. It sharpened instantly as he glanced into the copse ahead and touched his lips with one finger.

It had suddenly gone deadly silent up ahead. The chirps of the children had ceased. Something was wrong.

The two arrived within the leafy copse together, Harry's face flushed with concern, Pat's red from the sprint. Together they witnessed the scene in awestruck amazement.

She held Dusana, close to her bosom, whilst the other hand gracefully stroked the foreheads of the two boys in turn. The children were transfixed, yet totally calm as the men stared open-mouthed.

She stood tall and nimble at around two metres, yet her height simply added to the imposing magnificence that she radiated. Her figure was as slim as a candle, lit gracefully by a torrent of fiery red hair which flowed to her slender waist. Her skin was as white as the dress she wore and there, there rising from her back, creating the softest of breezes, were her wings. Beautiful plumed crystal white feathers which fluttered ever gently, causing her hair to dance like an electric storm against the whiteness of her being.

'Bejaysus.'

Harry remained speechless.

Her eyes lifted at the sound of Pat's voice, two blue cream orbs as she motioned with a wand-like hand to come forwards.

Helpless and unable to resist, the two moved towards her.

As they approached, the copse became dark edged, as if she had sealed the darkness in a circle with her glow. The gentlest gust from her wing beat pushed two feathers from her wings before they bobbed boat-like on the wind's current and floated gently to the floor at their feet.

'It is true,' she spoke in an Angelic voice, *'what you think is what you see.'* She smiled, lantern-like at the children beneath her. *'They accept it, for they are the purest of humans. You must simply let yourself feel the same.'*

'But,' Harry looked stunned, 'who are you?'

She let her lips curve serenely upwards as she replied, *'You know who I am, and I know who you both are.'*

'Jesus, Mary and Joseph,' Pat murmured, 'she's an Angel, a real-life Angel.'

'My name is Galgliel,' she answered in acknowledgement as she lowered Dusana to the ground. *'I am known as the Archangel of many things, of which none are important to you. I am here however to give you both a message, for you are important to me – to us all.'*

Neither man dared speak or move. After a moment Galgliel continued. *'You have good hearts and good souls, so hear my message.'* Turning to Harry she went on, *'You have the knowledge of the coin and your intervention has proved wise, as it will again. Never doubt that. My message is simple. See what you really see, and release the ghosts from your soul. It will be only then that the beauty you know of can appear.'*

Turning to Pat, Galgliel offered an almost remorseful stare. *'Your pain was shared, Pat Reilly. The loss of one can be more than many and I felt that with you.'* Pat felt a tremble at the memory of Ray Skee as Galgliel continued, *'You have a depth, a quality that many an Angel would wish for. You have it now, and because of this I can give you this message.'*

The Archangel closed her eyes and clasped her hands close to her mouth. Into the opening of her lily-white palms, she whispered before turning her hands flat, fingers pointing towards Pat. A single beat from her wings created a silvery breeze which joined with her words, creating a wisp. The copse lit up as another beat from her pure wings sent the wisp upwards, shimmering and swishing, a sealed secret from an Angel. There was no impact, no injection, as the words of Galgliel found their mark. Pat felt the most delicate sensation within his ears, the softness of Turkish delight against his lobes before his mind felt the message.

'Your faith has always been true, Pat Reilly, and you will be rewarded with the most important of honours. You, and you alone, on this Earth will know the identity of both half Angels. Use your gift well and see that no harm comes to them.'

The power of her wings lifted the leaves and blossoms from the surface creating a wondrous snow from nature which leapt ballerina-like into a mesmerising dance.

For a moment or two there was nothing but colour, before the wind subsided and the scene returned to normal leaving three children and two men gazing up at an Archangel in flight.

CHAPTER TWENTY

Jenny's trips to London remained the same, in the sense of her routine at least. She would wake alone; eat breakfast alone before some small talk with Lorraine as she waited for Joey to arrive. Everything was as it was, but now the trips into the city had taken on a whole new meaning. No longer did she awaken with dullness in her heart, craving the time she would spend with Holly. Now she had a sense of purpose, and a friend: Oliver.

She would find him in his usual spot, cup in hand, head raised, voice desperate at some, head lowered, voice silent when he sensed danger. She did not offer him money again after that first meeting. Instead they would share time with a coffee and a burger, while she listened to his stories of the streets. He did not give too much away, painting a picture of London which had no shining lights and glitzy stores, rather the hidden colours that are not seen. The grey mornings with a cardboard box for a duvet, the search for food and, predominantly, drugs, the fights for space and guarding of territory. This spot was Oliver territory, come rain or shine, insults and abuse. For many regular passers-by, the sad-looking figure of Oliver was as familiar as the golden arches of McDonald's he sat under.

The first few meetings had been fulfilling for Jenny. She found she had more in common with Oliver than she did with either her husband or her son. Oliver spoke with a depth and clarity on each and every subject he chose to speak of. He never mentioned money or possessions. His voice portrayed a brutal realism of the world in which he lived, where objects of wealth had no place and the only use for money was to eat, drink, and feed his addiction. At times, Jenny found it hard to deal with, to think of no home, no bed, no warmth and, above all, no foreseeable end to it all. She would watch Oliver as he spoke of the streets and of desperate situations where once normal people who had lost everything now scrounged and scratched around in the city for survival. Many of his tales were grim but, to Jenny, Oliver's world seemed somehow more real than her own. That was until the evening she first experienced Oliver high on drugs.

* * *

She had been dropped off by Joey and had done a little shopping, not for her but for Oliver. She walked down to his 'residence', new parka coat in a bag, together with a few jumpers and T-shirts. As she neared the spot she saw him talking with three others: two men and a girl. She would not have recognised him if it had not been for his distinctive eyes, and the place itself.

She saw a ghost of the man. His skin was pale and drawn, hair and beard longer and more unkempt, clothes even more filthy, and eyes glassy, shining with hungry intent. It was not a hunger for food. Drawing close she watched the four, shouting and circling round each other, then yelling and swinging punches.

'Oliver,' her voice seemed quiet, a whisper in a dream, 'Oliver, are you alright?'

They did not hear her but he did. Trance-like, he turned to face her, a look of shame spreading like butter upon his face. He spoke quickly to the others and walked towards her. She could smell him before she touched him.

'Oliver, look at you!' Jenny scolded him like a son. 'What's happened?'

He looked sheepish for a moment before the glint of hunger she had seen earlier reared again in his eyes. 'Look at me? Look at yourself! All dressed fancy and dandy coming to visit poor old Oliver in his living hell! Don't come here and judge me, Jenny. I don't need your pity! Give it to someone who deserves it, like your family!'

His outburst rocked her. She realised that something else was at work; maybe the heroin, maybe alcohol, it didn't matter. Whatever it was, this was the effect that it had on him. He had no idea what he looked like and he didn't care. The insults did not bother her… hell, yes, they did.

'Let me help you,' she pleaded. 'I only want to help you and for you to be my friend, nothing else.'

Something registered deep inside Oliver. Her words were a wand, seeking out his heart, his goodness and his hope. He knew what hope was. He lived with it every waking hour.

'I'm hungry,' he said as the tears not of a man but of a broken child surfaced.

Jenny threw her arms around him whispering, 'I'll get you some food. I'll look after you, Oliver. Please, come with me.'

He changed in a blink of an eye, the aggression replaced by a helpless young man, silent in his shame. Jenny took him by the hand and, ignoring the jeers of the others, guided him along the street. She headed for Rimini's without thinking.

The sound that greeted Jenny and Oliver from the high-class clientele of Rimini's was a blanket of whispers. As the well dressed lady entered with the tramp, voices, chatting previously about riches, dropped into a stunned silence. Before Jenny had got more than a few steps inside she was confronted.

'Madame Healy,' the maitre d' greeted her stiffly, 'you do not have a reservation.'

'I am aware of that,' she replied firmly, 'I can, however, see plenty of free tables, so perhaps you will guide us to one?'

As his face reddened, the manager of the restaurant appeared, looking a little embarrassed.

'Mrs Healy! Lovely to see you as always.' With a twitch of his neck and a shift of his eyebrows he motioned them to a quiet corner. 'May I have a quick word with you please?'

Jenny followed him, leaving Oliver staring around and the whole restaurant staring at him.

'Mrs Healy, we have a little problem with your guest.' He sounded apologetic.

'Not we, you,' she replied angrily. 'I don't have a problem at all, which is why I brought my brother in here.'

The manager let out the slightest gasp before composing himself. 'I see… your brother… I never knew…' The rabbit was in front of Jenny Healy's headlights.

'It is just…' he stuttered, '…our dress code, Mrs Healy; you must understand.'

Jenny glanced at Oliver. He was standing, arms by his side, head gazing upwards and around as he took in the sumptuous surroundings. She felt the fire in her heart burn.

'I understand your dress code and the appearance required to dine in such a place. I also understand that we, as a family, have used your restaurant for many years. If you turn my brother away, you are turning my family away.' She paused to let the ramifications sink in before she went on, 'I can assure you that my brother, Oliver, will not appear like this in here again. It is a private matter and one I would like to keep that way.'

Her speech was calm but direct, leaving him in no doubt of the consequences. To scorn the Healys could have costly consequences for the restaurant. He nodded, almost excusing himself, before saying a few quiet words with the maitre d'. Moments later, as the diners stared, they were led to a table which Jenny noticed was as far away as possible from anyone else. That would suit her just fine.

The voices gently rose as comments were passed around the corpulent clientele. Jenny found herself glowing. She had been strong and powerful, and for the right reasons.

At first Oliver looked awkward sitting across from her. It

must have been a long time ago, if at all, that he had dined in a restaurant. She gently took him through the process of ordering, explaining some of the dishes. He opted for steak, no doubt the only thing familiar to him on the menu. His 'what's this?' and 'what does that mean?' made her giggle as she realised that the menu that she found simple to understand was in reality a basic list of dishes that had been given continental names and fancy descriptions to underline the upmarket nature of the place itself.

Oliver ate the meal with surprisingly good manners, relishing every mouthful as Jenny found herself watching on. She couldn't imagine the last time he had eaten a good meal but the way his eyes rolled with delight, as if in some culinary dream, made it appear as if he had never eaten such sumptuous food, or it was simply too long ago for him to remember. His pleasure at every bite made her yearn to feel that good about a meal.

Afterwards, as they sipped some wine, Oliver expressed his appreciation for the meal. 'Thank you, Jenny.' He raised his glass. 'I will never forget this night, or your kindness to me.' His crystal eyes echoed a brief sadness. 'I'm sorry about earlier.'

'Please don't be.' She smiled. 'You know…sometimes I wish I saw the world through your eyes. The appreciation for things I class as normal, the wonder at kindness which I expect. It is I who should be sorry, for expecting you to feel and think the way that I do.'

Oliver's cheeks had regained their colour. On first appearances many would just see a down-and-out, a vagrant, but Jenny saw only that smile that lit her heart and those eyes that were so beautiful. 'We are different, Jenny, now, at this time, but I was like you once, not as rich maybe!' He laughed and so did she. He moved his hand across the table to hold hers. She did not withdraw it. It was not a romantic gesture but one of sincerity.

'One day I hope to become "normal",' he went on. 'My

"normal" is to not wake up craving a hit, to not fear sleeping for want of a bed. One day I will have that. That is my hope. For now...' his eyes filled with tears, '...for now, I have someone like you to give me hope, and the faith that when I do all these things then I will appreciate them all the more. I tell myself that this is just a trial and I have a meaning on this planet. Today, that may not seem the case. Not to those who pass me and see filth on the floor. At least they pick rubbish up. But I do know what your world is like. I do remember, and this world, the one I am in now, has taught me so much. Sitting here with you now, I know that. I see things you have forgotten to see.'

Jenny's glass trembled as she wept silently.

* * *

'Do you think England is changing, Oliver?' Jenny posed the question as they strolled along the quiet walkway. He stopped and she followed suit, waiting for a reaction.

They were now at the HMS Belfast which floats proudly on the Thames. Leaning on the railings Oliver surveyed the scene. 'The world is changing, Jenny.' He turned to look at her. 'I am changing, you are changing. It's all happening faster than we realise.'

She shifted closer to him. She felt secure in his presence. To the outsider, the lady and the tramp would be a humorous analogy. To Jenny, nothing at that moment in her life could have felt more natural.

'The ship is magnificent.' Oliver spoke, showing no awareness of her close proximity to him. 'It's where it should be now, afloat on this black carpet of water surrounded by glittering lights from the city; a showpiece, not a weapon. Wars are a thing of the past now, Jenny. Mankind has invented technology that it fears to use. Now the war is in money, as it has always been, but more, now it is in money wars. Economies can make countries and they can also bring them down.'

If it had been her husband or son talking about money she would have found the subject tiring. Now, however, she was intrigued. A small part of her resented that emotion. Oliver was homeless, but that didn't mean he was stupid.

'I know the anguish that money can cause,' she said in a soft voice.

He laughed loudly, the sound echoing out across the water. 'Really, you think you know what money can and cannot do?' He held back. 'Jenny, you will never have to worry about money. One thing we both have in common though is love…we don't feel it around us.'

She felt defensive briefly. 'I do have love. My children love me and Terry does…in his own way.' Oliver did not answer and she knew he was aware that she craved love. Only with Holly did she feel loved as a mother should. 'Besides,' she added gently, 'someone out there loves you; a family must love you.'

'Do, did, what does it matter?' Oliver snapped. 'They aren't here now, and for all I know they may even be dead.'

'Oh, Oliver, don't say…'

He spun around and began to walk away from her. 'I don't want to talk about it. Let's go home, Jenny, you to yours, me to mine.'

He paused, waiting for her to join him. She knew better than to push him anymore tonight. She had learned much, about him, and about herself. He stopped in the shadows, far enough away from the limousine so as not to be seen.

Jenny remembered the gifts. 'Oh, I got you a few bits earlier. I forgot to give them to you.' She offered him the bags. 'Don't be offended.'

He looked through them, smiling as he did. 'You are very kind. Thank you.'

With a look of tenderness, he kissed her on the cheek. As he did so, she did not smell his unwashed odour; instead she felt the kiss from someone she cared about.

'I'm glad you like them. Thank you for a lovely evening. I'll see you again as soon as I can.'

Oliver put the bags down and took both her hands in his. 'I'll look forward to that. You know where to find me.'

They hugged, filth against finery, before Jenny turned towards the waiting limo.

'Jenny…'

She turned her head.

'I… I just want to say, thank you.' His expression was one of sincerity. 'If I didn't know what an Angel looked liked, I would think you were one.'

The compliment lit her inside, a flame upon her soul. She cast that warmth back in his direction. 'You know what an Angel looks like?'

Oliver nodded. 'Oh yes, I've seen an Angel,' he replied truthfully.

Jenny smiled. She had no doubt that, whatever drugs he was on at the time, he was not lying now, at least not to himself.

'Goodnight, Oliver.'

CHAPTER TWENTY-ONE

'It is not what lies behind you, or ahead that is important. It is what lies within.'

(From the Scriptures of Galgliel)

After seeing off Pat, Harry and the boys at the station, Andréa and Steve returned to Boubin knowing it would be a long time before they left for England again.

Steve had not dreamt in such detail for a long time. In fact, the dreams had become a distant memory, as if their meanings had been explained fully. That night he was to dream once again.

The gentle slumber transported his mind into the familiar smooth passageway from previous dreams once more. He did not resist it, realising it was not just a passageway to the door ahead, but also from his mind into the vision he was about to have.

He let himself walk towards the room that he knew. Approaching the doorway he heard voices ahead, but felt no fear this time. His earlier visions had taught him that his mind was taking him to a place to which his body could not travel.

He pushed the door but it was stiff and would not open enough for him to pass through. Despite being unable to enter he could hear the voices within clearly.

'Should we let him see us, should we let him?' an unknown female voice spoke out. Then he heard a voice he recognised: it was the voice of Rose Gardener.

'He deserves to know. He followed his path. He is a part of everything that has happened, and will happen.'

There was a sneer at Rose's words before a male voice spoke loudly. *'He nearly made the wrong choice. He doubted too much. How will we know he will serve anyone well?'*

The first voice replied softly, *'He is human, and there is doubt in much of humanity. You know that there is distrust in anything else but what they see. It can only help for him to see us and to know more.'*

There was a silence filled with voices that did not speak, as those inside contemplated telepathically. The answer of their combined minds came after a moment. The door eased open emitting a ghostly guiding light. Steve walked slowly into the room that was now unfamiliar. There was no darkness, no chair in the middle of the room and there were to be no images portrayed. They had all been replaced now by bright light, not from a man-made source, but from those inside the room. Eyes focusing, he saw a circular court of Angels, sitting, floating and standing around a structure that was unfamiliar to his earthly eyes. If he had to describe it he could only say it was like a heavenly forum.

He did not speak as he came closer to the Angels. He seemed to have lost the power of speech. The masses of faces he saw had little meaning to him with the exception of Rose and behind her he now saw the figure of Helena. He noticed different tangents of glowing energy emanating from them all. Some appeared almost transparent, whilst others were solid and shimmering.

Steve felt conjoined with them, as if there was no further need to speak using words. The languages of many, from many places, all made sense in the telepathy he was aware of now. He absorbed and answered just by using his mind.

'The coin of Angels has moved on. Now we must wait for the one to come,' one voice spoke in his head.

'Will it find its way?' another voice asked.

'Yes, it will. It must. Love will guide it, as it guides us.'

'Why is the coin so important?' Steve spoke through his mind.

'It is the Angel coin,' a reply came from somewhere. *'It is our constant presence on Earth. It is powerful and just.'*

'What does it do?'

He felt gentle laughter. Not at him, but at the innocence of his infantile mind.

'The coin represents two things. I will try to explain but, suffice to say, that each person who comes into contact will only see one of the two sides of the coin, so to speak. One may see it to represent Angels, as you did. Others see it to represent a coin, money, value. It shows what it needs and the viewer sees what they see. It made sense to you and showed you the way.'

He understood yet his mind burned with questions.

'What of Dusana, the pendant, my mother? There is so much I do not fully understand.'

'You cannot, but all will come to you when the time is near.' It was Rose's voice. *'Soon we will not be able to cross the divide. Dusana is the chosen. She was born out of a near impossible love with the coin of Angels as the guide. She will grow pure and full of love. She will have the power to share her gifts with the world and, in turn, will defeat the shadows that are forming.'*

'Shadows, what shadows?'

She ignored him. *'The pendant was given to your mother as a child by a wise Angel whom she saw as a homeless man. She showed him love and he knew she would one day pass it to the chosen one. It is made from Rhodium, the most reflective metal on Earth. It will protect her from those who will suspect what she is. They will not see it in her eyes and she will be safe.'*

'How is Dusana the chosen one? What is she to do?'

Another voice, with a Czech accent, spoke. *'Dusana means spirit, soul. The world can have no more wars. Dark Angels created the technology to make weapons to destroy all but we knew they would be weapons that no one dared fire. We thought it would bring everlasting peace and, to a degree, it has. But now the Dark Angels wage a different war, a war of greed that will destroy many hearts and souls and in turn destroy all of us before you. It will try to destroy the one reason for human's existence: Love.'*

There was a calm. Steve tried to imagine what they could mean. He had felt the world changing but not as they said.

'How will we know the shadows and what are they?' he asked.

'The battle will not be between good and evil; it will be a struggle between love and hatred. Humanity has such gifts and such hope which only love creates. Those without it will seek it and find hatred in its place. The future is now in the hands of humans and the two half Angels.'

'That is enough.' He heard a voice form in his eardrums. *'You are here because you followed your path. Your search is over and you will have no further visions such as this.'*

He said nothing as he contemplated the thought: his daughter, a half Angel? He was overwhelmed as the room slowly began to dissolve in front of him.

One last voice answered the question he had not yet asked.

'She will not be alone.'

CHAPTER TWENTY-TWO

Terrance Healy had the look of a man who had won first prize only to find it was the wrong colour ticket. The six men left the lush office block of their Italian friends or, perhaps more appropriately named, prey. As they walked towards the waiting car, Terrance decided he needed some fresh air which meant they were all going for a walk.

He led them past the Spanish Steps, towards the Trevi Fountain. The entourage kept quiet, mumbling in whispers to themselves as their boss paced deep in thought ahead, occasionally twisting his neck to take in the throngs of people seated in the numerous bars, restaurants, pizzerias and trattorias.

Stopping briefly at the fountain, he flicked a few coins into the water as the group debated what he would be wishing for.

'It's certainly not going to be money,' said one.

'Probably some scheme of vengeance on that lot we just met,' another said sarcastically.

Terrance wandered back to the group and singled out the only Italian, a man named Alfredo, who had been hired in the latest recruitment drive for European business. His job had been to broker deals with large Italian companies for T Healy & Sons' European expansion programme. Now he stood there, meekly, waiting for an outburst from the boss he had only met yesterday, probably ending his short-lived career with the company.

Instead Terrance was amiable. 'Alfredo, take us to a good

bar with good food. We need to talk.'

Instantly the Italian felt a sense of relief as he joined Terrance at the front of the small crowd, leaving the others to raise eyebrows in unison at the calm outcome. 'Very unlike Terrance,' one quietly mentioned to another.

Terrance did not speak as Alfredo guided them to a particularly popular bar named Simione's. He organised a table outside for the six of them and a few moments later they were perusing menus whilst sipping on a range of beers and fine wines.

'So, gentlemen,' Terrance began, 'do we think we are going to do business with these Italians? You, Jimmy, what do you think?'

The man he addressed was one of the five buying experts he had picked out for the trip. The idea had been to broker a deal with the large producers of coffee and hams which would then give them a competitive edge to start opening a chain of American-style cafés across Italy. Terrance had long been an admirer of the USA way: big ideas, big expansion, and little time for small fry. He saw the American way of doing things as the future for England. To him, the Italian way was bizarre.

Jimmy shifted uncomfortably in his seat. The Italian owners had not been welcoming. In fact it had all turned rather hostile when one of them had accused Alfredo of being a 'traitor' to his own people. After a heated debate in which Terrance had thrown plenty of insults, the meeting had come to an abrupt end, leaving the six with no further business for the day and, as he saw it, no ideas on how to conquer this particular market. He weighed up the options before answering.

'Seems to me, sir, that those guys were a little backwards.' There were a few arrogant smirks around the table. 'We should maybe aim for another company, a competitor, and then bring that lot down.'

Heads nodded in agreement as Terrance ran his finger down the side of the glass of beer, creating a line of clarity on its frosted surface. 'I think not, Jimmy,' he replied calmly. 'In case any of you have not noticed, there are no chains of cafés around this place.' He focused on Alfredo as he went on, 'Tell us how it is, Alfredo.'

Alfredo found himself feeling isolated and a little bemused at the mannerisms of these Englishmen. This was not the way he and his countrymen did business. He coughed awkwardly and tried to explain.

'Well, sir, as we left one of the company men, he told me that he knew all about our operations and, well…' he struggled to find the words in English, 'they do not do business like that here. If you look around you will all see small cafés, family bars and restaurants and shops, all doing business and all supporting each other.'

Terrance leaned back in his chair and nodded, a smile forming on his face that said he agreed. He leaned forward and the others followed his lead, sheep to the shepherd.

'He's right, he's damned right. You see, gentlemen, this trip has shown us one thing. T Healy & Sons will not be doing business in this country.'

There was a silence as Terrance plucked a cigar out of his top pocket and lit it, letting the thick smoke rise upwards as he finally relaxed. Leaning back in his chair, the others followed his example again, looking bemused.

Jimmy plucked up the courage to speak. 'So what are we going to do, sir, go home and forget it? How are you going to explain that to your father?'

For the first time since leaving the Italians Terrance looked angry, livid in fact, his cheeks turning pepper red at the comment.

'I am not going to explain *anything* to my father, you imbecile,' he snapped. 'I am the buying supremo for this company and my father is tired. In case none of you have noticed…' his voice was now laced with disdain, 'I am taking this company onto new frontiers. We have over five hundred stores and shops, and if these greasy, illiterate, pathetic, yellow-bellied wops do not want to deal with us then we will piss on them. We will take our business elsewhere and we will succeed.' His eyes flashed with hatred and revenge as he went on. 'No Italian will work for T Healy & Sons, understand? That's your job when we get back home, Trevor,' he said pointing to another colleague. 'No Italians, none, nada, zilch, zippo, zero, geddit – and don't even mention human rights to me. Just get rid of any we have, and make sure we employ absolutely zero. *Capisce*?'

There was another, even more awkward silence as the men digested his demands. Trevor nodded, avoiding eye contact with Alfredo who sat, utterly shocked at the outburst. All of them sat there knowing that, although it was wrong, unjustified and illegal, it would be the policy and it would happen, or they would all lose their fat pay packets.

A waiter came over breaking the ice and Terrance gave his order to Alfredo as did the others. He translated and soon after a selection of tasty dishes came to the table. Throughout the meal Terrance chatted with a new sense of mirth, as if his decision had appeased him and all was good again in the world – his world. When everyone had finished he ordered some coffee and turned to Alfredo.

'Enjoy that, my friend?' He wore a Mona Lisa smile.

'Si, grazie,' Alfredo replied, wiping the olive oil from his moist lips.

'Good, I am so glad because you are special, Alfredo.' Terrance stared at him, seeing surprise registering in Alfredo's eyes at his words. 'You are special indeed, and you know why?'

Alfredo looked stumped. 'No, sir.'

'You are special because you are the last fucking Italian I will ever sit and eat with.' There was an icy silence before Terrance spoke once more.

'You're not deaf, are you, Alfredo?'

Alfredo shook his head, dumbstruck.

'Well…' Terrance spoke in a flat monotone, 'then you will know that we do not work with stinking, greasy Italians. You, my friend, are fired. Now fuck off.'

The rest of the group sat gobsmacked as Alfredo slowly got up, firing a look of disdain in the direction of his former boss. 'You are a rude, mean and selfish man. I am glad I will not work for you and I am glad my compatriots see you for what you are.'

Terrance simply raised his hand dismissively in his direction. 'Yeah, very interesting, wop. Now go and get a job pouring coffee and fuck off out of my face.'

* * *

Terrance froze. This young man who had it all was awestruck.

She was standing near the end of the bar, hands on hips, as she threw her head back in joyous laughter with the old man she was chatting to. They hugged and continued to laugh and Terrance wished, more than anything he had ever wished for, that he was the one she was laughing with.

He lapped up her figure. Around 5' 9", slender with perfect bumps in all the right places, but it was her exquisiteness that enraptured him. Her long black hair ran down her back, the fringe cut sexily straight across her forehead. Her eyes beamed large and chocolate, and her cheeks showed the sweetest dimples when she smiled. There was an aura about her that made his knees go weak.

Terrance watched her for a few more seconds as thoughts, both loving and lustful, cascaded into his mind. Without wishing to stare, he made his way rather awkwardly to the toilets. Inside, he tried to get a grip, splashing water onto his face and examining his features in the mirror as he did so.

He estimated that she must be a little younger then him, but not by much. As for looks... he stared at his reflection and saw a twenty-year-old man who, still with traces of acne, would pass more for a young William Defoe than a Leonardo Di Caprio. Usually he saw a powerful, driven young figure in the mirror, reflecting his own desires. Today he saw a shy, spotty child, more Adrian Mole awkward than Macaulay

Culkin cute.

Many things came easily to Terrance Healy. Amongst those were money, business and natural arrogance. But none of those fell into the bracket of charming a woman. Despite his desire, he dared not take the risk of belittling his good name and simply passed slowly by the girl, feeling as if she already knew his thoughts, notwithstanding the fact no one, apart from his cronies, probably gave him a second look. Here Terrance Healy was just another Englishman and his power was zilch. He wandered back to the table and tried to pretend he felt nothing. It was easier to immerse himself in idle chatter and his crowd were very good at that.

When the girl left, Terrance and his group were still sitting outside, deciding whether to stay and take in some nightlife, or head back to the hotel and relax before the flight home the next afternoon. Whether it was the gentle wolf whistle that emanated from Jimmy's lips as she walked past, or the sudden burst of courage mixed with desperation, Terrance never knew. All he did know was that one minute he was sitting down, the next he was standing in front of her.

Close up she was even more wondrous. He could now smell her as well as see her just a foot away. He stumbled over his words but heard something like '*Ciao*, er, hi, I wanted to speak with you a moment.'

Looking at him, she stopped before turning her pretty head to the table from which he had come from. There she saw a few men sniggering and cajoling each other. She grinned. 'Hi, I can speak English, just like you and your friends. How may I help you?'

In normal circumstances he would have been able to speak with an arrogant confidence, regardless of whom he was addressing. But this was not anything like normal circumstances and he froze.

'Well, er, I was wondering, do you have a boyfriend?'

She threw her head back and laughed, just like she had done in the restaurant. He wanted to kiss her, to hold her, like the man had done, but now he could not decipher the laugh. Was it at him, or with him?

'What's so funny?' he said, feeling exasperated.

'You are,' she replied, still laughing. 'That is a very forward question, don't you think? It's very English.' Her face showed her cute dimples and Terrance found himself smiling back.

'Yes, I guess it is. I'm sorry. I didn't mean to be rude or forward, it's just...'

'Just what...' she intervened.

He scuffed his feet like a child. 'Well, you are the most beautiful woman I've ever seen and I wondered...' Terrance glanced across to the table to see if any of the group were within earshot before continuing, 'I didn't mean to say it like that... if you had a boyfriend.'

He felt her stare, weighing him up, still smiling but calculating at the same time. Finally she spoke. 'Yes, I do have a boyfriend, kind of, but thank you, and now excuse me.'

No one finished conversations with Terrance Healy. He was the one that did the finishing – when he was ready. He was stunned, but somehow kept control of his temper simply saying, 'Where are you going? Where do you live?'

'I am going to San Piceno and I live in England.' Her answer was polite, but curt. He dared not say another word as he watched her move smoothly past him and out of his life.

* * *

'But what are we going to do?' Trevor's voice sounded confused, the earlier laughter now a thing of the past.

Terrance poked his head out of the back of the taxi. 'I don't care. Get laid, get drunk, go dance. Do whatever the hell you want and put it on the company tab. I'll meet you at the hotel sometime before we fly.'

With that, he instructed the driver to take him to a place called San Piceno, leaving the five men staring, open-mouthed.

'He never puts anything on the company tab.'

* * *

It did not take long to drive around the village, but it took more than two hours to locate the girl. Darkness fell suddenly on the village of San Piceno like a blanket protecting it from outsiders. After paying the taxi driver with a higher tip than he would usually give a five-star place back home, he watched from outside the window of the taverna.

It was getting late, too late to bound through the door, greeting her as if they were old friends. He was tactful enough to realise that. He needed a plan.

Inside he saw her sitting with a couple who, he assumed, must be her parents. The mother was pretty and the father seemed handsome in a typical Italian way, smartly dressed in a loose shirt and tailored trousers that complemented his Mediterranean looks. There was another man, a boy there, who sat next to the girl. He was not what Terrance would call handsome, for he did not allow himself to think of men in that way. But he was definitely not ugly. Terrance found himself suddenly muttering under his breath about the 'long poncy hair, wop greasy skin and overdressed smartness'. His dislike of Italians, men at least and this man in particular, had scaled new heights. They had caused him a strange emotion, jealousy maybe?

After a couple of people had walked past, staring at him as if he was an alien, he decided to hatch a game plan. He would stay here the night and then find out about the girl. Without realising it, Terrance Healy had become obsessed and it was not with work.

* * *

The following morning he woke up early, his mind alert. The small hotel was one of only two in the town and, although

Terrance was not used to such basic surroundings, he found the place overall acceptable, in a *backward* way.

Making his way to the piazza, a slab of pizza in hand, he looked around. The morning was gloriously warm. He wandered casually around the circumference of the piazza, exchanging good mornings whilst trying to find someone who spoke damned English.

Just as he thought he was out of luck, a female voice found him.

'You want someone to speak English for you?'

He glanced round and saw an old lady sitting alone on the bench he had just passed.

'Morning,' he replied, sitting down next to her with not so much as an introduction. 'I'm not exactly looking for someone to speak English actually. I am trying to find a young girl who speaks English.'

'Ah,' answered the woman slowly. *'I see… well, there is one girl I can think of. Can you describe her?'*

That was a piece of cake. Over the next few minutes he reeled off every feature of the girl in the finest detail.

When he had finished the woman gave a wise smile.

'Then I know who you are looking for. Her name is Francesca.'

CHAPTER TWENTY-THREE

'Fear love and you will never truly find it, for to love truly is to not fear at all. Love comes freely when it is felt and it will never run out, unless you fear it.'

(From the scriptures of Galgliel)

'I think it's a bit weird, Mum. I mean, what would you want to get involved with some down-and-out for? I never had you down as the saviour type,' she added in good humour.

'Holly, for starters, I am not *involved* with Oliver. Please do not use that word. And he is not a down-and-out.' Seeing Holly's doubtful expression she went on, trying to justify her secret to her daughter. 'Not down-and-out in that way. Yes, he has troubles, but he is not like that.' Seeing no change in her look, Jenny added, 'Perhaps you should come with me and meet him and make up your own mind.'

A mixture of sympathy and repulsion crossed Holly's face. 'Mum, if you want to see this man, then I know it is the right thing for you to do. Just not for me, please...'

Jenny grinned. 'Of course, you're always welcome though,' she smiled warmly, 'and thank you. That means a lot to me'

'What for, Mum?' she asked lovingly. 'You're always right in my eyes.'

She was glad she had confided in Holly, as she needed, wanted, to share her stories with someone. To be around Oliver had given her more pleasure than nearly anything else with the exception being Holly, of course. Time spent with

Terry had become harder. The seven years that separated them might as well have been seventy. Terry was still caring, considerate, at times, but the similarities ended there. He lived and breathed work. He had pulled back a little, saying he would be spending more time with the family. What he had not said was that family time would be with one person: Terrance. He got the prime-time slot, and that was simply because he was the next in line to the 'throne'. Terry's determination to make Terrance into the next him had not only meant that family time was in fact spent at work with just one member of the family but also that Terrance had become a harder, even more aggressive clone of his father. If Terry was a private man then Terrance was impossible to know. She could not even remember when or indeed if mother and son had ever had a chat about anything concerning the word 'feelings'.

Oliver was different. He wanted to talk about many things, from life on the streets to life across the world and so much more. As long as it was not his childhood, or anything to touch his past emotional status, he was a joy to speak with and when his eyes lit up, well, that was worth more than any diamond she had ever seen. It had crossed her mind that perhaps she saw Oliver as a replacement for her own son but, after analysing her reasons, she decided that the only thing she wished for from Terrance was even a modicum of interest in her. She got that from the 'down-and-out' as Holly called him. Sadly, not from the son she gave birth to. Perhaps one day that would change but, for now, she was going to see Oliver and tell him that she had shared her secret with her daughter. She felt he would realise how highly she thought of him and perhaps that would help with the one thing she had not been able to thus far: his drug habit.

* * *

A few of the 'locals' as Oliver called them had come to

recognise her and they would nod or grunt to her when she came to see him. Accepted was a word she would never have associated with the homeless but yes, she was accepted, at least by this tiny percentage of London's lost.

With Oliver nowhere to be seen at his Oxford Circus 'residence', Jenny searched for any familiar faces. A few words and gestures gave her an address and flat number off Fleet Street. Joey was waiting out of sight back near the Circus as he usually did when she went on her secret journeys. He never asked any questions and why should he? Jenny knew it would not be a good thing to be seen in this neighbourhood with a limousine, nor in any neighbourhood of Oliver's world come to that.

The block of flats that she had been guided to stood in front of her. A grey tower of pebble-dashed granite decorated in graffiti. The main door hung off its hinges, glass windows shattered as if the place had been abandoned. Jenny felt her skin crawl as she entered. She paused inside the grim lobby, waiting for her hands to stop shaking.

The stench of urine was the first smell that assailed her nostrils. A gentle hint of ammonia was the second. As she made her way cautiously up the first flight of stairs the malodorous atmosphere increased and she had to dip into her pocket for a tissue. No handbag with perfume here. No, Oliver had briefed her about such things as being seen with items that could 'feed' drug addicts. It was not the fact of her losing an item of value if she got caught in the wrong place, more the fact that the assailant wouldn't give a damn who they hurt or how much.

Her eyes blinked in sync with the flickering strip light of the hallway, and she whispered to herself, *'I thought these places only existed in the movies.'*

That might have made her smirk in another place. This was no time to be smiling now. What the hell was Oliver doing here?

At the bottom of the hall she came to number fifteen where

she stood motionless, her ears listening for any sound. What should she do now? Knock and introduce herself as Jenny, Oliver's pal, come round to say hello? The idea seemed ludicrous now that she was here. This place was not where she wanted to be, Oliver or no bloody Oliver.

She attempted to knock but could not make her hand obey. Her hands were shaking uncontrollably, fear coursing through her veins. She paused again, waiting for the breath that had somehow escaped suddenly to return, and for her hand to stop ignoring her command.

Eventually she found the courage. Her knuckles bounced off the door making a muffled vibration that barely made an echo. She did not need to knock again though. Her small clenched fist had made a discovery. The door was not latched shut.

The pathetic tap she had made moved the door a little, letting a slither of dim light escape into the hallway. She pushed the door forward slowly and heard her own voice reverberate around her. 'Hello?'

Silence answered, then a small sound, indistinguishable initially, until Jenny translated it: the shuffle of feet, not moving, just shuffling, scraping on the spot. Everything in her instincts told Jenny to turn now, to walk away and leave this place. That was, everything with the exception of the determination that Oliver had instilled in her. She moved forwards.

The first door on the right of the narrow hall was closed. The door to the left was open and within Jenny saw the source of the shuffling she had heard earlier: a figure, not Oliver's, sat, back against the wall, head moving to and fro, feet scraping in comatose melody with the head.

'Are you okay?' She waved a hand slowly in front of his face but there was no response. The man was oblivious to her. Whatever drugs he had taken had rendered him harmless. Somehow Jenny felt a surge of confidence that replaced the earlier fear. The pathetic figure in front of her was incapable of any aggression and, if that was the case with him, she felt she had nothing to fear of any other similar inhabitants of this wretched place. She just hoped Oliver would not be in the same state.

Two more rooms and four more people, all in a similar condition to the first man. Instinct now told her that Oliver was going to be just like the others, yet, when she found him lying on a filthy mattress which gave off a bouquet of smells made in hell, she was taken aback.

His face lay pointing towards the door. His eyes were what you could call half open, but he was not looking. There was not even a vagueness in his expression, just emptiness. She walked towards the lifeless-looking figure holding her breath inadvertently. As she drew near, she noticed there was little or no recognition of her presence. Kneeling down she touched his hand, running her warm fingers up his clammy, cold wrist onto his arm. There she found the puncture marks and, as she surmised the events that had led him to this place, he spoke.

'Mmm, hi,' his voice was elastic, stretching each syllable, 'it's the Angel. Hello, Angel.'

'Oliver,' she felt her breath rebound off his soaking forehead, 'it's Jenny.' She felt real desperation now. Her friend was in another world and she was the one that was suffering, not him. Tears streamed down her face. 'I'm Jenny Oliver, not an angel,' her voice cried in a whisper. 'There is no angel.'

Oliver twisted his body upwards, revealing the source of the stench. His matted hair was coated in pale-coloured vomit which, judging by the patch on his face had come from the mattress where he had been lying. She guessed he had collapsed in his own puke but he was as oblivious of his own appearance as he had been to her arrival. Now he attempted to stand, tottering as he tried to focus on her.

She let him look. The squinting eyes made him look like he was short-sighted, trying to concentrate on a piece of writing. Normally she would have laughed, pulled his arm in jest and received something similar in return; normally...

'What have you done to yourself, Oliver?' Her voice found

anger. 'Is this what happens? Is this what you want from your life?'

Perhaps Oliver had heard it all before, perhaps he hadn't. He made no gesture in acknowledgement of her tone and simply replied, 'Mad hit, babe, too mad really...'

He suddenly slumped onto the floor as if he had been shot in the back. As his face hit the bare concrete Jenny heard the crack of his nose breaking with the force. She let out the smallest scream along with 'Oliver!'

Blood trickled out from underneath his face as she tried to lift him up. She panicked. 'Oliver, Jesus! Oliver, please get up!'

She realised the seriousness of the situation and reached inside her boot, pulling out the mobile from the 'safe place'. Speed-dialling the number, she urged the person at the other end to pick up.

'Mrs Healy?'

She whispered into the mouthpiece, 'Joey, listen carefully...'

* * *

She crept back down the hall and made her way outside. There she waited until the bright lights of the limousine slid past. She watched the car turn round the first bend and out of sight. The shadows moved with various drunks and druggies before she saw the burly figure of Joey, a tatty jacket hiding his normally pristine suit. 'Where are we going?' he whispered, a glint of softness in his eye.

'I like the jacket. Had it long?'

'Ready for such occasions, Jenny.' She forced a smile as she heard her name. Good old Joey. She had taken for granted what a good man he was, a professional in every sense.

She led him upstairs to where Oliver still lay unconscious. Joey lifted him up in one move, leaning his head back and examining him as he did so.

'Is he going to be alright?' she questioned. 'Is this normal, Joey?'

She had not expected him to have any idea but his answer indicated he had know-how of some kind. 'We need to get him to a hospital or a clinic, Mrs Healy. The sooner, the better. I think he's overdosed.'

Jenny's earlier panic now returned as he delivered his verdict. Before her mind could race into gear Joey spoke calmly.

'I could suggest a clinic. A *private* clinic if you get my meaning. It would cost money but...'

'We'll take him there. I don't care about the money, and if no one will know it doesn't matter. Joey, can you carry him?'

Joey lifted Oliver effortlessly onto his shoulder and led the way out of the flat. As they left the building, a couple of people stared but a gentle growl from Joey turned their heads the other way. He lowered Oliver into the back seat with care as Jenny climbed in beside him. Soon they were driving to the clinic.

'Do we need to contact them, Joey?'

'No, Mrs Healy, they'll be fine. This sort of thing happens all the time. Just it's usually rich kids that go here, not, er...'

She saw his awkward grin and smiled back. 'I know what you mean. Thank you, Joey, for everything and, please, call me Jenny. I like it much better. I should have told you before about Oliver. I could have got myself into some serious trouble.'

'I am not sure if it occurred to you, Jenny.' Joey glanced back smiling broadly. 'It took me just moments to get through a pretty busy part of London to get to you.'

She let out a small gasp. 'You mean... you followed me?'

'Not entirely. I wouldn't put it like that at all. I was just doing my job. I knew if I was aware of where you are, I could always be on hand to assist. I've never interfered, until now, Jenny.'

She sat back as it dawned on her that Joey had known about her meetings with Oliver for a long time. He must have followed her before. Watching until satisfied for her safety. She felt closer than ever to him as she watched the street lights flash by. A bad dream with a happy ending – she hoped.

* * *

The limousine, like many before it and after it, pulled onto the gravel path and up to the security gate. Joey spoke briefly with the guard who looked inside the car and responded with a nod. The car glided up a long, tree-lined driveway before they arrived at the entrance of a large mansion. It looked anything but a clinic.

'I'll need your ID, Jenny,' Joey informed her as he lifted Oliver out of the limo. 'It will have to be validated before any treatment, you understand.'

'Yes I do,' she said firmly. 'No money, no help in this damned world. Here you are.' She shot him a sorrowful look.

Joey did all the official work while Jenny watched three men in pristine jackets pick up Oliver and lay him on a trolley which they wheeled up the ramp. She followed them into the brightly lit entrance almost having to jog to keep up, stretching out her hand to touch Oliver's. She glanced back to see Joey standing there. He had not moved and she understood why as one of the nurses said, 'Madam, I'm afraid we need to get the patient into intensive care.'

'Stop,' her voice commanded them and they did her bidding almost instantly, 'let me just say goodbye, please…'

They backed off a little. 'Quickly, please,' one replied.

Jenny leant over Oliver. 'Please, Oliver, take care. I'll see you tomorrow. I love you, you are a very special person to me, and I hope you know that.'

He clutched her hand, eyes closed and whispered back. Jenny could not quite hear the first words, but she deciphered the last. 'You are an angel in your own way, thank you.'

* * *

After a sleepless night Jenny made the call in the morning and was told that Oliver's condition was stable. He had taken many substances including heroin that had caused him to trip out. The nurse explained that he had been on the verge of an overdose and, judging by the amount of narcotics in his bloodstream, he was lucky that Jenny found him when she did.

Jenny felt utter relief. 'I want him treated and I don't care how long it takes. Money is not an issue.' Joey promised that as soon as they were allowed to visit he would take her and, before she could ask, he swore that it would go no further.

As the days passed the reports were more and more encouraging. Soon she would be able to go and see him and she had visions of a new man. He would be reinvigorated and ready to start a new life. Jenny had no real experience of drug addiction.

The day before she was due to visit, the phone call came.

'Mrs Healy, if you could make the payment now it would be appreciated.'

'I have no idea what you mean,' she answered in a puzzled voice. 'I thought I was able to visit tomorrow?'

The lady at the other end of the line joined in her confusion. 'You would if Oliver was here, Mrs Healy, but I thought you knew? He discharged himself.'

CHAPTER TWENTY-FOUR

His heart was beating harder than it had ever done before as he waited for her.

Terrance stood a little way from the house that the lady had described. He had no idea how long he would have to wait, but he knew he must wait. He could not go back now. He had watched the man from the previous night ride past him up the lane and into the house. In the two hours that went by, Terrance cursed him, wishing it was him. He hid as the man came out, gleeful that he was out of the way.

Standing at the front door, Terrance felt all his earlier confidence ooze out of him. When she saw him, she froze.

He acted fast to avoid even more shock. 'Francesca, hi, I had to come and see you. Please don't be angry.' The words were as unfamiliar to him as they must have sounded to her. He didn't do romance. He didn't do nice. But now he wanted to do it all.

Whether it was the innocence of her, or perhaps, unknown to Terrance, the fact that she and Domenici had just had a heated disagreement about where their future lay, she reacted in a way that Terrance was not expecting. She felt flattered.

'You are a persuasive man, Mr...'

'Terrance, Terrance Healy,' he prompted her.

'Well, Terrance,' she said in that silky voice he had craved to hear, 'it's nice to see you again and, I have to say, I'm flattered. What on earth are you doing in San Piceno?'

Although the whole romance thing was unfamiliar to Terrance he used his business acumen to interpret the true meaning of her answer. He prided himself on the ability to read people's responses and Francesca's told him two things. One was that this girl did not lie. So for her to say that she felt flattered was brilliant news. The second was that she knew what he was doing there. She was not that innocent.

'I'm here to see you,' he answered tactfully. 'Since I saw you in Rome, I can't get you out of my mind. Please, can I buy you some lunch?'

She toyed with the idea and decided it would do her no harm to perhaps be seen with this smart-looking Englishman. Perhaps it would shake Domenici into being more flexible. She felt a little guilty as she accepted. She had never done this kind of thing before.

She took him to a café on the fringe of the piazza and there they had paninis and coffee whilst Terrance ate every word she spoke as well as his food, listening about her life in England, and her love of Italy. He resented the parts where she spoke of Domenici as she showed signs of true feelings for him. He diplomatically agreed with the beauty of Italy over England, despite the fact he had cursed the people of the country less than twenty-four hours ago.

For her part, Francesca quite liked him. Not in a way like Domenici, he was her love, but she liked some of what he said. She was also enjoying the attention he was bestowing upon her. The further they went into their respective lives though, the more she found herself missing her man. She tried hard not to let it show, but Terrance sensed he was up against a mighty adversary.

* * *

'Thank you for the meal. That was very kind of you.' They walked together towards her home. 'It's been very nice to meet you, Terrance.'

Knowing he was running out of time, he tried not to sound too desperate. 'It was lovely to share your company. I'd like to do it again sometime, maybe in England?'

Francesca felt uncomfortable. She had no plans to see him again and did not want to give him the impression that she did.

'I don't know…' she broke the sentence to make it easier for him to digest, 'perhaps we will meet again someplace, randomly…'

Terrance may not have been a king of romance but he was smart enough to know the use of words and immediately knew she was not interested. He used all his guile to hide what his mind was thinking as he decided it was not that she was not interested; it was just that she was not interested – **yet**.

'Sure,' he answered easily, 'it's been magic to meet you, for real.'

He kissed her on one cheek in the English fashion. As his lips touched her skin, Terrance felt an overwhelming sense of desire that was difficult to control. The fragrant scent of her perfume lingered as he stepped back, faking a carefree smile.

'Take it easy, Francesca.'

'Ciao, Terrance.'

The two walked in opposite directions.

* * *

He made his way back the square, taking in the geography of San Piceno. He had an eye for towns and villages, born from his father's training of spotting the right location to build a new store. There seemed to be only two main streets into the village which had smaller veins of streets branching off them, with the river as the main artery. He saw a long, winding road feeding from behind the piazza. It seemed to trail up and round to the right before circling like a walnut whip up the edge of the largest mountain that formed the backdrop to the village. As he craned his neck, he saw the basilica overlooking the village. He grinned: the walnut on top of the whip.

Terrance snapped out of his store-building trance. A part of him had suddenly wanted to see the large sign of T Healy & Sons adorning the place, making Francesca squeal with delight that she knew the man behind the mask, so to speak. It was mid-afternoon by now and the previously busy plaza was now pretty much deserted. His dreams of the shop evaporated for a multitude of reasons: not enough people, he hated Italy, and Francesca would never be smitten by a man like him, using tactics like that. She was too pure and he knew it. He would have to either change as a man or change her as a woman. The latter sounded more difficult and the shop idea died there and then. He actually felt angry for thinking about the bloody business.

Terrance felt a total stranger and it unsettled him. He had to get back to Rome before the night flight home and he needed a taxi, fast. When he spotted the lady he had spoken to earlier that morning he found himself running down the street to catch her attention. He was gasping a little as he reached her.

'Hi, remember me? The guy you spoke to this morning?' He felt unusually out of breath.

She stopped, turning to face him whilst leaning on the walking stick that had been supporting her. *'It's the mountain air, takes it out of you if you are not used to it.'*

'Yeah right,' he replied, feeling the breath coming back into his lungs. 'Do you know where I can get a taxi, kind of soon?'

She pointed the stick ahead. *'Down and the last road on the right, there is a little place there with a couple of cabs.'* She smiled dryly before adding, *'If you are lucky, this is San Piceno, you know.'*

'Yeah, you could be right.' He nodded in agreement. 'Well, thank you.'

'How did you get on with Francesca?'

He had momentarily forgotten her. The woman's words brought her back into vision as he recollected the day.

'I'm not sure,' he said honestly. 'I think she's wonderful and we had lunch together but… you know… she has a boyfriend

201

and all that.'

He wondered if the woman already knew that. She seemed to know who the girl was, so why wouldn't she know she had a boyfriend in such a small village as this?

'Sometimes that doesn't matter in the long run.' Her answer told him she knew.

He felt a little irritated. 'What do you suggest I do then?'

She gave him a knowing look. *'I get the impression you don't like Italy too much, young man.'* Before Terrance could ask how the hell she knew that, she went on, *'The girl is Italian but also a part of her is from England, which you probably know. Therefore, I would suggest that you use your English romantic side to win her heart.'*

Aside from being slightly stunned that the woman had perceived he did not like Italy, he was equally confused about his English romantic side. He had never had one.

'I see,' he replied attempting to look like he understood her. 'So what would a man have to do to win a woman such as yourself with, as you put it, English romance?'

She chuckled and he felt like she had read his mind like a newspaper, an easy to read one at that. He felt flushed and a little silly.

A pause followed which made him feel even more awkward at having asked the question in the first place. 'Look, don't worry about it,' he mumbled. 'I'll work something out. I'd better get going.'

'Wait,' the woman responded thoughtfully. *'I would suggest if it were me, that is... I would suggest a man bought the woman he loved a gift. It would have to be a rare gift that represented their love, not just anything, but something special, something with meaning.'*

He paused, liking what she had just said. Money was not a problem, but his ability to choose the appropriate romantic gift was.

'That's brilliant! I'll go back and try to find something.' He felt warmth towards the woman.

'I was in London once, many years ago,' she continued, *'it was where I learnt English. Lovely days,'* she reminisced. *'There was a magnificent shop that sold rare items in the West End. Mmmm.'*

She looked up at the sky, her eyes watery, as if reliving a long-distance memory.

'Er, do you recall the name of the place, or where it was? I know the West End fairly well, you see. Perhaps I could find it.'

'Now then,' she closed her eyes, *'let me think.'* Terrance waited. A minute went by then another. He was about to intervene when she spoke.

'Do you have a pen?'

Terrance reached inside his jacket and plucked out a T Healy & Sons complimentary card with his name etched on it and a pen. 'Bingo!' he said, handing it to her.

She scribbled on the back and handed the card to him without taking any interest in his details. He glanced at the address. It was only a street name but he knew it.

'Thank you, ma'am, you've been a great help.'

'My pleasure,' she replied kindly, *'and good luck.'*

* * *

Luck appeared to be on his side as he found the taxi rank, or shed as it turned out. And one battered taxi to go with the driver who was sitting in a deckchair casually sipping coffee.

He arrived at the hotel with little time to spare. The others were waiting for him in the lobby, looking a little worried. Terrance tried to look unflustered as he grabbed his holdall from the neatly stacked bags next to Trevor. 'Well, come on then. Chop, chop! We have a flight to catch!'

A few hours later, as they settled on the plane, Jimmy dared to ask where he had been.

'I went out for dinner last night with that girl,' he lied. 'Then we stayed at this nice hotel on the outskirts of town before I spent the morning with her in bed, a bit of lunch and, you know, thought I'd better get back.'

He enjoyed their reaction and played on it. Laying out basic details of how good she was and how much they hit it off. As the questions kept coming, he kept answering, wishing more and more that it was actually true.

'One thing I don't get,' said Trevor, after they had had their fill of the lurid details of his lust-filled night, 'I thought you hated Italians? Does that mean we can still employ them?'

Terrance shot him a look of horror. 'Damn, no! Everything still stands on that!' He found himself grinning, the power trip of being Terrance Healy returning with the attention of his minnows. 'Well, I'll make an exception for her… if she asks for a job.'

They all burst into laughter.

* * *

Many miles away in the darkness a woman stood alone on the outskirts of a small village and whispered to the sky.

'Good luck, Terrance Healy.'

CHAPTER TWENTY-FIVE

'The hurt and pain of arguments can only cause misplaced pride. Do not let barriers be built. Be brave enough to always say how you feel despite the fear of rejection. Do not be the one to cry for unsaid words at the grave of someone you loved. For yesterday can never be changed and tomorrow may not come.'

(From the scriptures of Galgliel)

The festive season saw a rain-covered England. As people in all the major cities rushed to buy too many presents for their ever demanding children, the only winners were going to be the large stores. The big shots were going to make a fortune, none more so than T Healy & Sons together with its expanding non-food department.

The losers were the parents, their credit cards and their bank balances. Santa Claus was nowhere to be seen. That was unless you counted the endless amount of would-be Santas that got seasonal work while the rain lashed down outside. In London one benefactor was Oliver, for a very short time. Since Jenny's help in getting him cleaned up at least a little, in addition to 'having a word' with one of her favourite shopping haunts, it appeared Oliver would not only be earning some money but would also be in the warm. Sadly for them both, the meaning of Christmas had changed and Oliver quit after only two days. He couldn't stand the greed of the over-privileged while so many others suffered. It seemed, for Oliver at least, that some habits die hard and he chose to go back to 'his own people' as he told Jenny: 'At least they're like me.'

Christmas Day in the Healy household highlighted the ever growing cracks.

The run-up to Christmas had been hectic for both Terry and his son. For Holly and Jenny it had been a time of present buying and sharing each other's company. Holly wanted to be like her mum but, when Jenny suggested she go with her to meet Oliver, she found there was something in her make-up that could not face it. Part of Holly Healy was, after all, her father's. That part made her resent the homeless, even though she wished she didn't.

The big day arrived. Terrance glowed in the praise from his father as the family sat in one of Chelsea's most exclusive restaurants having Christmas dinner. Terrance, of course, took the plaudits for the growth of non-foods which had seen record profits. The fact that they sold almost anything that moved already and had started to move into other areas such as dry-cleaning facilities, home insurance, mobile phones, in addition to introducing in-house restaurants and cafés to many stores was by the by. Terrance chose not to mention that one of the main reasons for the ever accelerating growth was the strategy of shipping more and more in from the Far East at the expense of English production. He knew his father would not agree, nor any of his family, as a matter of fact. For Terrance it was an open-and-shut case of Merry Christmas, ho, ho, ho.

As the family of four ate the six-course meal, there was little conversation. After the meal there was even less. Jenny slipped into a daydream, wondering how Oliver was getting on in the shelter where they had promised him a dinner. She had spoken to him after the Santa Claus fiasco and cajoled him into going along. It was free after all and he needed a good meal. Humbly he agreed that he would, but only for her. When she asked why 'only for her', he simply answered, 'It's a lovely thought, but it is one day a year and the world runs for three hundred and sixty-five. I know as I eat there will be others like me not so fortunate and for the other three hundred and sixty-four days we'll be just as we are now. Society looks down on us on those days but the kind ones tend to feel guilty for that one day. I must sound so ungrateful but that's what it feels like.'

While Jenny pondered Oliver's outlook on life, Holly played with her phone, texting friends and telling them she was bored. Terry talked about business and Terrance listened, for a while. Soon even his obsessive business mind drifted off and, for the first time in ages, he thought of Francesca.

She would probably be in a warm house, full of love. He wished he was there with her. It wasn't the family thing he cared about. Even with his lack of perception Terrance realised his family were hardly *close*. No, he wanted her and, today of all days, it sank in more than ever. Father Christmas had not delivered the one gift he wanted the most and the one his stores didn't sell: Francesca.

They returned home late in the afternoon and opened their presents. Jenny had taken time to pick out gifts for the children and her husband whilst Holly had shopped for her mum. After opening a mass of prettily wrapped parcels, Holly jumped around madly, holding a beautiful diamond ring aloft. Even Terrance smiled as it triggered his memory of the old lady and her words. He would get something exclusive for Francesca and present it to her as a late Christmas present.

* * *

In January the snow came, a little late for most people but it came. For Terrance it meant a logistical headache. Whilst the children saw white streets and the chance to build snowmen and have snowball fights, he saw only slush and problems. He was not going to let that worry him though. He had given himself a day off which was unheard of. It was also unheard of for him to go shopping but, as he hadn't told anyone, he didn't feel embarrassed. When the limo pulled up just off Oxford Circus, he told Joey he was visiting an important new client and would call him when he was ready.

* * *

Terrance glanced at the card the lady had written on as he pushed the intercom button. 'Rare gifts, my arse. It's a bloody antique shop,' he mumbled irritably as the burly security guard came into view.

'Good morning, sir.'

'It would be if you would bloody hurry up and let me in!' Terrance barked in response.

A click of the lock and the door opened. Terrance found himself facing the hulking figure of the guard who would be guiding him into the shop.

'Please, follow me.' The guard waved a hand.

'How long has this place been here?' Terrance was not used to be guided anywhere. 'I'm not even sure if this is the right place.'

'Many a year, sir.' A cheerful voice came from within the shop. 'A very good morning to you. I am the owner, Harry Tobyn. May I assist?'

Terrance scanned the shop. It was upmarket, of that there was no doubt. Its interior was lavishly decorated, the walls covered with expensive paintings, the floor area filled with all manner of curiosities ranging from vases to statues, stuffed animals to war memorabilia. The shop seemed from another time. He could not imagine finding anything in here.

'Morning,' he replied as he finished his survey, 'I'm after something very classy for my girlfriend, something a little special. The name's Terrance Healy.'

He waited for the usual response and, when he heard Harry say, 'Terrance Healy of Healy & Sons?', he simply nodded and said casually, 'That's the one. What have you got?'

Harry knew the name of course. He was aware of them like many other big multinationals. He found himself wondering what a man like Terrance Healy would be doing in his shop. By his mannerisms, Harry deduced that the man before him had an arrogance about him which, in turn, made him wonder how he had a girlfriend at all. There was nothing about Terrance that struck Harry as handsome.

'That depends on what the lady likes.' Harry went for the sales pitch based on his assumption the female in question would have to be money orientated. 'We have some rare jewellery if that takes your interest?'

'Show me,' Terrance replied curtly.

Harry took him to the back of the shop where he unlocked a heavy-looking case which hung on the wall. Inside were a selection of old brooches, bracelets and necklaces that he had collected over the years. Some were pretty, most were expensive, and all exactly the kind of thing he would like Mr Healy to buy.

He watched as Terrance studied them. After a few moments Terrance looked up. 'Nah, don't like any of those. Have you got anything else?' He was already bored and his patience was running out.

'Do you have any idea what it is you're after?' Harry tried to sound concerned.

'I don't know,' began Terrance before checking himself. He needed to sound more assertive. He should know something about his girlfriend. 'Maybe a ring or a necklace…I guess.'

Harry guided him to a glass cabinet over on the other side of the shop. Inside were half a dozen rings, ranging from the early part of the century to post-war. His eyes scanned them and then below where he saw something.

'What's that?' He pointed to what Harry thought was an original African tribal piece. 'No, not that, that!' His finger pressed onto the glass.

Harry saw where he was indicating but he didn't like what

he saw. It was the coin. He instinctively tried to put him off.

'That's not a ring, or a necklace. It's an Angel coin, very rare but *very* expensive.'

Terrance's eyes sparkled. 'Well, may I have a look?'

Harry somewhat unwillingly undid the lock on the cabinet and let Terrance take the coin. He looked at it, holding it up to the light and flicking it in between his fingers.

'I like it,' he said, looking pleased. 'I think you could make it into a nice necklace. What do you reckon?'

Harry was not sure *what* to reckon. He was sure the coin was not supposed to be punctured with a hole. It was time for evasive action. He was supposed to know when to give the coin away. This definitely did not seem like the time.

'You *could* get it drilled and put on a nice chain,' he replied tentatively. 'But there are two problems with that: one is it would decrease the value of the coin dramatically, and the other is that I have a client who has shown an interest in the coin already…in its present state.'

The more Terrance looked at the coin, the more he felt it was the ideal gift. An Angel coin, rare and expensive, he cared not about puncturing it. He imagined explaining to Francesca its meaning. Only those special enough, of almost 'Angel status', deserved such a gift. He grinned to himself and hardly heard a word that Harry said.

He looked up. 'You say another client?'

Harry shifted uncomfortably before replying. 'Yes, I'm afraid so. I can see if we have something else similar.'

Terrance shook his head. 'No, I want this. How much is the other client offering?'

Harry created a figure on the spot: 'Twelve thousand pounds.'

Terrance baulked. 'Whew… that's a fair amount of money.' He looked at the coin once more. 'Tell me about it.'

Harry felt a gentle sigh escape. He remembered the last time he had described the coin. He wished it was Steve Bidante standing in front of him now as he spoke. 'They are now extremely rare. The coins are known to represent both good *and* bad luck. They were first introduced in France in the fourteenth century and are called "Angelot" or "Ange" coins. Later they were also made in England, but not until the late fifteenth century when they were reissued and first called "angel-noble" before they became known simply as "angel" coins.' Harry decided to add a bit at the end. 'As I said, they represent both good *and* bad luck.' He hoped that Terrance would opt for the bad luck scenario and leave the coin. As he waited for a response, Andréa's words repeated in his mind. *'You will know when the right person comes along.'* Up until now, no one had even looked at the coin and this guy seemed about the last person whom Harry would have put as *'the right person'*.

'I like the story.' Terrance smiled through thin lips. 'I'll give you twenty thousand for it, here and now.'

If Harry had been a greedy man then he would have been tempted. But money was not paramount, and his loyalty was solid. He reacted quickly.

'That's a very generous offer but I would have to confer with the other client and let them know we have a higher bid.' Seeing the disdain appearing on Terrance's face, he went on, 'You know how it is. I would of course do the same for you.'

Terrance looked at him for a moment, looking for a weakness. Harry remained silent. He saw none.

Terrance handed him a business card. 'Alright, let your client know and call me…today.' He turned and walked out of the shop. Harry breathed a sigh of relief.

* * *

It was several hours later when Harry dialled the number on the card.

'Terrance Healy speaking.'

'Hi, Terrance. Harry here from HTT Antiques. I've had a

word with my client and he's made a final offer.'

'Go on.'

'I'm sorry to say he has outbid you.' Harry prepared to lie convincingly as possible. 'Twenty-five thousand.'

He could not see him of course but Harry sensed Terrance's irritation. There was a pause and, for a microsecond, Harry felt the relief course through his veins. He was sure he was doing the right thing.

'Right,' Terrance sounded aggressive, 'thirty thousand if the answer is by today or thirty-five thousand if the answer is now.' It was his turn now to put the pressure on Harry. 'You don't seem a fool. Good business sense should tell you I'm offering a substantial amount of money. Your choice.'

There was no way out. Harry knew Terrance was not going to let go and the thought gradually crept into his mind: What if this was the person he should sell the coin to? He had always imagined 'giving' the coin to someone who would seem the ideal candidate, but what was ideal? It now occurred to him there was no such person. He had to make the choice. The simple facts were that, with no one else even looking at the coin, this was the **only** choice.

'What's your decision?' Terrance's voice cut into Harry's thoughts.

'I'll tell the other client. The coin is yours. When do you want to collect it?' Harry crumbled.

'Wise choice.' Terrance's tone had an arrogant edge to it. 'I'll have someone collect it from you in the morning. I take it that it comes with a gold chain?'

'Sure,' Harry replied. 'I'll pick a good one. It's the least I can do.'

* * *

After picking out a chain that was both feminine and classy, Harry paced the shop. He felt uneasy. He looked through a clutch of calling cards in the top drawer of his office desk and dialled the number. After a few rings the voice he needed to hear cut in.

'Speak now, or forever hold your peace.'

'Pat, it's Harry, I hope it's not inconvenient.'

'Not at all.' Pat's Irish lilt oozed warmth. 'Good to hear from you, Harry. Everything okay?'

Harry explained what had happened and described Terrance Healy. Pat had heard of the company, of course. After Harry had told him of the fake bid and his refusal to give up, Pat gave his opinion.

'Well, it seems to me you didn't have a lot of choice. Andréa asked you to decide and not to call either of them on the matter so the choice could only be yours.'

'I know,' replied Harry uncertainly, 'I just figured it would be someone more…'

Pat chuckled reassuringly, his soft voice soothing Harry. 'You've done the right thing. I see it like this: a man comes into your shop with the intention of buying something after being tipped off, right?' He didn't wait for Harry to agree. 'So you don't show him the coin BUT he eventually comes across it, sees it and wants it. Pretty spooky, eh?'

Harry smiled. 'Now you put it like that, Pat...' He could see why Steve thought so much of this man. Listening to his calm voice, Harry was reassured.

'Add to that, the fellow offers a silly amount of money for something you were looking to give away, right?'

It started to make sense somehow. 'I'll give the money to Steve and Andréa, for Dusana.'

'Great idea,' agreed Pat. 'You've made the choice and so it must be the right one.' He laughed and Harry felt convinced. 'Steve might have told you, I like to believe everything is for a reason. I heard you're a man of logic, so between us we seem to agree.'

'Thanks, Pat, I owe you one,' said Harry feeling much better.

'My pleasure, we'll have to catch up for a pint. Till then,

God bless.'

* * *

The following morning Joey arrived with two heavies to collect the coin.

After they had left Harry stared at the large packet of money. If it had been anything else sold from his shop, he would have maybe jigged around out back at the stupendous piece of business he had just done, but somehow he just felt sad.

The coin had gone, the choice of new owner his alone. Whether he looked at that decision based on his own logic or even attempted to view it with the faith that Pat Reilly seemed to show, there was little comfort. He had left the fate of Andréa's wishes in the hands of a man called Terrance Healy, the big shot in one of the most cut-throat companies in England.

He groaned as the haunting reality hit him. 'What have I done?'

CHAPTER TWENTY-SIX

2007

The February air was clear and crisp and the Hampstead mansion surroundings looked sugar-coated in the early morning frost. Jenny shivered as Joey swung the limo as close to the front porch as he could to allow her to step into the car avoiding any ice. She spoke briefly, instructing him to drive to the usual place – the usual place nowadays anyway.

It had been over a month since Oliver had disappeared. At first Jenny had been beside herself with worry. She had expected to meet with him after Christmas, to exchange stories of the big day, to laugh as she saw his eyes once more, felt his smile, heard his words. There had been none of that. He had simply vanished causing her to panic initially and then followed by days of looking, asking and worrying. After a month had passed, Jenny had even begun to accept that she may never see him again.

Holly had been harsh, she felt. Her view was simply: 'Well, Mum, what did you expect? You're not his fairy godmother, you know. A drug addict doesn't just change overnight.' The words had hurt her. Holly had never met Oliver so she could not know of his kindness and inner self. She was just judging him as a stereotype, wasn't she? Joey had been more careful with his words and wiser in his assessment. 'If you felt right, Mrs Healy, then you did right. You have to understand that some people can be helped and others can't. If Oliver wants you then he'll find you.'

It was true. Oliver had left of his own accord and not so much as a mention or a note left for her. Hardly the sign of someone who wanted to keep in touch. After many days of wandering around like a lost soul on the streets of the West End, Jenny accepted the advice as likely the truth. Oliver, as good a man as he was in many ways, was not there to be controlled. The drugs would be there for the foreseeable future and whilst they ran through his veins so would the craving and desperation to chase them. Sadly, Jenny knew that Oliver was unable to love anything else.

* * *

Francesca hesitated. 'I'm fine, Domenici, just tired.' It was a half lie. He had sensed something in her behaviour and it seemed more than just distance that separated them.

'I'm missing you more than ever, Francesca.' His silky voice and adoring tone sent a spasm of guilt to her stomach. 'I can't wait for next week. I really can't.'

'Me too, sweetheart.' She conjured up the thought and tried to push others to the back of her mind. 'Me too.'

After the call had ended, she breathed a sigh of relief. Her mind and heart were at war and hearing Domenici's voice had brought that to the fore. She had to speak to someone, but feared the reaction. Her life had been simple until Terrance had come along. Okay, not quite true, she reasoned as she paced round the bedroom. It had been complicated to love a young man who lived so far away. So many days apart and nights alone but she had coped. That was before her head was slowly turned by the Englishman and his charm. She could have never imagined it. The past weeks had been fun and she had been treated well. Terrance had taken her to some amazing places and treated her like a queen. At first it was easy. Something to pass the time and her youthful innocence had seen nothing wrong in casually dating a man whilst still holding deep feelings for another. 'It's just a phase,' she had told herself. Now that phase had instilled guilt and confusion into her. Others had noticed the subtle change in her character, the secretiveness of her actions, and now Domenici was suspicious. It was time to talk and time to make choices.

'Hi, Mama, can I ask you something?'

Nicole looked up from her book and, seeing the look of concern of her daughter's face, stopped reading. 'Of course you can, honey. Come, come and sit with me.'

Francesca joined her on the couch, wishing she could find the courage to ask outright, but instead deciding to go for a more roundabout approach, her trademark of late.

'Do you think Domenici and I will ever be properly together, Mama? I mean, do you think it can work with the distance?'

Nicole studied her face. 'Are you having problems with Domenici?'

'No! No, not really. It's just that sometimes I get lonely and then I wonder, I suppose.'

'Lonely!' Nicole laughed. 'Sweetheart, I would hardly say you get lonely! You're out most of the time with your friends. We hardly ever see you!'

The time was right, there was no escaping it. Francesca could not lie easily at the best of times and especially not to her mother. To not say her time had been spent with another man had not been a lie; she simply had not said anything. It was time to take the plunge. She could hide things no longer.

'I know what you mean, Mama. But there are different kinds of lonely, at least to me.' Her eyes seemed to sparkle with innocence. 'When you were younger, before Papa, did you not have more than one boyfriend sometimes?'

Nicole gave a knowing look. 'Ah, I see! You have an admirer, don't you?' Her smile put Francesca at ease. Why hadn't she said something before?

Francesca nodded, grinning shyly.

'You are a young, beautiful girl, Francesca. It's natural that men will find you attractive and some will chase you. As long as you feel right with it then it's up to you. My advice is to be careful though, you know?' Nicole's look said it all: sex.

'It's not like that,' Francesca replied hastily. 'Mama, please keep this our secret. I don't want to hurt Domenici or Terrance. I just don't know what to do. They're both lovely but in different ways.' She hugged her knees tightly to her chest. 'I am so confused!'

'Terrance, ah, a very English name!' Nicole laughed, taking Francesca's hand in hers. 'Listen, honey, you are young enough not to have to make any choices.' She smiled softly. 'One day you will decide what you want and who you want to love. It will seem easy then.'

Francesca thought for a moment but nothing seemed clearer on her feelings for either man. She liked them both but differently, straightforward as that. A part of her wished time would hurry so she would know exactly *what it was* she wanted.

* * *

'Good morning, Mrs Healy, a very cold one, I must say.'

Jenny smiled weakly and made some small talk for a while. The shop was busy as usual, full of female faces with credit cards and free time to spend. There had been a time when she had craved this environment. Now it seemed as alien as the weak, meaningless conversation of the shop assistant who homed in on her spending power rather than her personality. Jenny didn't enjoy these places anymore. In fact she resented them.

Forty minutes and four carrier bags later she left the shop. Outside, the cold air slapped her face after the artificial warmth of the shop that matched the artificial warmth of its staff in her mind. As her eyes focused on the flurry of activity in the street she saw him.

It was a unique, almost romantic event, which sent her heart racing and heightened her emotions in the blink of an eye. Regent Street was full of life. Throngs of people of all types and ages walking, rushing, running, this way and that. Yet they all vanished in that instant to be replaced by one person who shone out.

Oliver was dressed in simple black trousers and a parka coat, his hair tousled, neither tidier nor messier than before, but somehow more noticeable. His face wise and his eyes, his eyes, they bored inside her from the twenty metres' distance between them. She must have dropped the bags as time froze. Then he was there, offering them to her as one would as a gesture of kindness.

'Oliver,' the name sounded like sweet music as she said it, 'where have you been?'

He did not reply but simply offered his hand to her. She took it and began to walk with him. Guiding her between the throngs of people he paused outside a coffee bar. He did not speak but simply squeezed her hand softly to signal his intent. She replied by running her thumb inside his palm. They entered the café.

It was as they sat face to face across the small table that she acknowledged the change in him. He had shone out more than anything in the crowded street, lighting up her soul and sending her heart skipping. It had been a magic moment which she now saw in its true light. Something had changed in him. The Oliver she once knew had died that night in the cold, damp, stinking flat, to be replaced by the man across from her. He was full of one thing that the others in that street had forgotten how to emanate: life.

'I want to show you something, in a while.' He smiled and she remembered the artificial heat of the shop which had none of the warmth of his smile. 'I'm sorry, Jenny...for leaving like that...after all you tried to do for me.'

She went to reply, to tell him it didn't matter, but they both knew it did. She had never imagined how much she loved the man.

'I came to your house, to tell you, but then I wasn't ready. I couldn't do it.' Oliver grinned faintly. 'You know, Jen, me being me and all that.'

She translated his words with ease. He had not knocked on the door of her home because of her, because of the reaction it may have caused. He had nearly done it and that meant more than any gift she could remember. He had cared enough to find her, yet thought enough of her to be selfless and turn away.

'How did you find me?' was all she could say as tears came to her eyes.

'Joey drives like a gentleman, Jenny.' He chuckled softly. 'I put some of the money I've begged to good use and followed him.' Seeing her start to smile, he added, 'It was like something out of the movies, honestly!'

'I wish you had knocked, Oliver. I mean, I know why you didn't but, I don't know, I just wish you had.' The tears resurfaced and began to run freely down her face. 'I missed you, you know.'

She knew he could be a man of no emotion whatsoever. She knew that drugs were perhaps partly behind that, together with the harsh life he faced each day, yet Jenny now saw him crack. Just a fissure, not a full-blown explosion, but enough to know he cared. As if she needed to know at all.

'We should go. I have to show you something.' His expression became strained as he struggled to hold in his emotions. 'Can I get a lift with you?' The atmosphere changed in an instant as both laughed at his request.

Joey gave a simple yet knowing courteous greeting as Oliver got in the limousine. 'Can you stop here please?' Oliver asked gently as they neared the heart of The Strand, Theatreland.

'Are we going to see a show, Oliver?' Jenny looked bemused.

He ignored her comment. 'Thank you, Joey, and thank you for your help before. I owe you.'

Jenny noticed a silent respect between the two men as Joey replied, 'Any time, Oliver.'

'Come, come!' Oliver sounded excited as she felt her arm being tugged. A moment later they were in the street facing the Lyceum Theatre.

He took her hand and walked towards the theatre but, as they approached the doorway, he veered off slightly to the left where the narrowest of alleyways appeared between the two buildings. Their footsteps rattled off the cobbled artery until it opened into a courtyard of Tardis-style. There a large building, nothing like a theatre, stood in front of her.

'What is it?'

'It's home, Jenny,' he replied smiling, 'for now.'

The building was faceless. Square and bland on the outside but, as they entered, she found a new world within its walls. Rather like a hospital was the first thought that came to mind. Never a fan of hospitals and their sterility, she had been surprised and touched by the first children's hospital she had visited. This was that sort of place, only for homeless people. It was warm, cosy and clean. Every face she now saw had a story to tell. She instantly knew Oliver liked it here and that made her like it.

'Oliver, how did you get here?' She questioned as he motioned for her to sit at a small table that was set against the wall, a few feet away from a single bed. Jenny noticed a small dresser at the far end of the room covered in sheets of paper filled with handwriting. It looked liked he had been busy. She smiled as she added, 'How did you find this place?'

Again he showed emotion, this time stronger than in the café. 'I found it because of you, Jenny. You saved me that night.' His eyes closed with inner pain. 'I could have left this world that night. I had had enough, but you saved me. When I left the clinic I was in a typical state – well, I suppose, typical for a drug addict. Aggressive, craving, and claustrophobic of my surroundings and the attention, I checked out and left. Then came the hard part.'

'I don't understand.'

'Normally I would have run back to the streets…my home… you know, Jen. It's not the first time people have tried to help me.' Sympathy for her shone in his gaze. 'But, with you, it was different. After Christmas, everything was different. I owe it to you and…the Angel.'

'Oliver,' Jenny interjected, 'I have to ask you something about this angel. You mentioned it that night. I thought you meant angel-dust. Well, I did when I found out what it was.'

It was his turn to look amused. 'You researched angel-dust? PCP? Ha, ha!' He laughed until he started to cough and Jenny had to slap his back.

'Sorry!' His face red with laughter. 'That's funny, yet it's not at all. Oh, Jenny, if only I could tell you everything of my life. All I can say is take a look around you. You don't have to believe in my visions, and it doesn't matter. Just don't believe that everything is so straightforward. That's patronising.'

'I never meant it to be. I…'

'You watch shows on TV with people sharing the other side with others. You hear people talk of their Gods and pray in their churches.' He looked at her intensely. 'Can it be that hard to believe?' Leaning back, he added, 'Or is it because I'm a drug addict? Just another trip and angel-dust fits the bill. Who's the mad one here?'

Jenny flushed as she digested his reasoning. 'I'm sorry. I guess it's just my beliefs and…you're right. I doubted you, sorry.'

'No need, Jen,' he answered, his eyes looking deeply into her. 'Sorry doesn't get us anywhere at times. I've said sorry too many times in my life. I know that. I'm not going to make that word easy to use in future, especially where you're concerned.'

'What do you mean?'

He swung his arm around in the air as he spoke. 'This place; I'm here because I enrolled in a rehab program. I'm finished with it, Jenny. No more drugs, no more streets. I'm going to beat it.'

His eyes shone with the life she had felt earlier. She wanted to leap across, to hug and kiss him, but she refrained, trying to take it in.

'That…that's brilliant, Oliver! I'm so happy for you.'

'It means I'll have to leave for a while though.' His expression darkened a little. 'I've been accepted, two weeks' time, Scotland. I hope it won't be for long but I can't say.'

Jenny saw the first tear drop onto the table. 'I used to think it wouldn't matter. Time, people, no one would miss me, or I them, but now…'

An inner strength came from nowhere, laced with the despair of losing him so quickly after finding him again. 'It will be worth it, Oliver. I'll come and see you if you'd like.'

He shook his head, the emotions now overwhelming him as he reached for his top pocket. He slid a piece of paper across to her and turned away. She unfolded the letter and read:

Dear Oliver,

I received the biggest surprise of my life when I opened your letter. Six years had passed and not a day has gone by when you have not been in my thoughts. When you left I cried for days, as I did when I read your letter. I am still in shock to be honest.

You say that things have been hard but are getting better? Oliver, I would love you to come home but please do it when you are ready. You mentioned that you have some things to do first. I have waited long enough to see my son and I will wait that bit longer, knowing you are safe and well.

To say I miss my only son would be an understatement. Life has not been easy these past years. I know it cannot have been easy for you but I felt I had lost you and that made a part of me die.

I am your mother, Oliver, and I will always love you. Please know and believe that. I may not be perfect and some of my choices may have affected your life, but there is no one on this earth that loves you like I do.

Please write again soon. You said this address would not be yours for long so please tell me where to write to each time and I will.

You broke my heart, Oliver. To read your words and think of you has begun to mend it.

All my love,
Mum xxx

'Oh, Oliver,' Jenny smiled through her own free-falling tears, 'that's wonderful! You contacted her?'

'I owe it to you, Jenny.' He gave a watery smile. 'You gave me hope and found something that I thought was long dead – the will to go on.'

Jenny squeezed his hand. 'I didn't do anything really. Before that fateful day that I saw you, well... let me just say that you found me and changed so much for me. Up until then my life was grey and meaningless. When you vanished, I...' she breathed in to control herself, 'I know how your mum must have been feeling all this time, Oliver.'

He dropped his head a little, almost ashamed. 'I know. I should have got in contact earlier but...' He looked up, eyes ablaze. 'Do you think my mother would have wanted to see the person that you saw that night? Don't you think that would have destroyed her even more? For her to see me slowly dying in front of her? Jenny, I've only felt strong when you've been with me. I couldn't know it at first. Lots of people try to be nice, but you, you were different.' His eyes softened. 'Do you remember that first time, Jenny?'

'You wouldn't take the money from me,' she said tenderly.

'Exactly,' he replied, shuddering. 'I wanted to. The drug part of me wanted to. But I saw something and felt something different.' He leaned over the table to get close enough to whisper. 'It was just after I saw the Angel in the street, Jenny. You don't have to believe me but it made all the difference. She came and I could see her and then she sent you to me, to save me.'

His quavering voice sent spiralling sensations through her body, quashing any uncertainty that had been there before. She now knew that, if it made sense to him, who was she to judge. After all, she had found someone truly special. Someone who had awoken a part of her that had long lain dead inside.

As they parted a few hours later, she held him close to her, feeling his warmth and inhaling that familiar 'Oliver' smell that she had missed beyond belief.

'I'll let you know when I'm back, Jenny, but I may not write or anything. I have to do this part on my own.'

Saddened she replied in a hoarse voice, 'I'll miss you very much. You've become my soul mate, Oliver.'

He paused, the energy flowing freely. 'Soul mate, I like that.' He ran his fingers through her hair and she shivered at his touch. 'And you are mine. Until all this happened, I'd forgotten I had a soul.'

CHAPTER TWENTY-SEVEN

'Belief – a word of such power and diversity. All your life you will be told to believe in many things. Remember that belief has no boundaries. Those with dark hearts will try to taint and corrupt this, forcing you to fear much. The next time you stare to the dark night sky and see that shooting star you will know that it is true, for you will be watching an Angel in flight.

'But you already knew that Angels could fly, didn't you? Because you still have belief.'

(Taken from the Halls of Angels)

The limousine pulled up outside the house in South Kensington. Francesca giggled as she pulled her clinging black dress down a little, taking a brief look in the mirror running a brush one last time through her flowing hair.

'You look lovely, darling.' Nicole's voice came from behind, startling her. 'Is this our Terrance outside then? Are you going to invite him in?'

Francesca's phone throbbed from within the small silver handbag, telling her he was there. 'No, Mama, not yet. I'm not ready for that.' She kissed Nicole and, grinning like a child, added, 'I'll see you later, Mama, and please... not a word to Papa, okay?'

'Alright, but remember what we said, sweetheart.'

She glanced back, laughing. 'I know, be careful.'

* * *

He had selected his most expensive Armani suit and spent a fortune on the best aftershave in the shop, in addition to over an hour in the barber's. Terrance Healy was looking as good as he could. This was the big date. This was the time to tell her of his true feelings. The trip to the barber's had been the toughest thing to do. At twenty years of age he already had a complex about his thinning hair, which was gelled back on both sides, leaving a kind of point in the middle of his forehead. Holly, when she was being annoying, called it an arrow pointing in the direction of his brain: i.e. his mouth. She could not know how insecure he felt about it and that is why he had never had his hair cut outside the house. Now though, it was time to take a gamble. The barber, who he had paid handsomely, had done a good job. His hair actually looked thicker, at least to him.

He saw her walking elegantly towards the limo. She looked stunning. 'Bloody hell, Joey,' he muttered out loud, 'I am so in love with this girl.'

She greeted Joey with a shy smile which he returned with a touch of his cap as he held open the door. Sliding into the back, she gave Terrance an equally shy grin. Her family was not short of money by any means. The new business had seen to that. Yet she still felt a little awkward in the company of the Englishman who seemed to have more than enough, and was not afraid to spend it lavishly. At least it had appeared that way to her.

'You look stunning, Francesca.' Terrance leaned towards her, lips pouted. As he did so Francesca turned her face, offering her cheek. He sensed her body language and gently kissed her warm cheek as he wished for the day he could embrace her fully. *'Patience, Terrance,'* he told himself as he leant back in his seat smiling graciously. *'Tonight may just be that night.'*

As planned, they headed for the city's most exclusive private club-cum-restaurant. Roberto Burrs was *the* place to be seen in. Set in Mayfair, the Burrs was built in the style of an old English farmhouse which made it stand out even more from the buildings surrounding it.

Francesca gasped as they entered. The decor was sumptuous. Crystal chandeliers hung from the aged oak-beamed ceilings whilst medieval-style torches adorned the richly painted walls. A huge chimney breast sat in the middle of the club, each side of the vast pillar housing a glowing log fire adding ambient warmth and an overwhelming sense of romance. Exactly the reason Terrance had selected the luxury venue.

'Do you like it?' He looked to her for approval.

'It's very beautiful, Terrance, and...very romantic.' Her answer was just what he had hoped for.

The table that the smartly dressed waiter took them to was the best in the house. She had a direct view of one of the beautiful fires with enough privacy for Terrance to weave his magic. She just needed to submit to his charms. He had taken her to many places over the last month or so, but this was his master plan. A quiet word and a fat roll of notes had ensured they would receive the best treatment throughout the evening.

The meal went well. Terrance kept the conversation flowing in tandem with the wine as he tried to find a chink in Francesca's willpower. Gentle Italian music played softly in the background, captivating the mood. As Terrance saw Francesca smile, he knew what he wanted more than ever. He truly wanted to win her heart. Never in his short life had Terrance wanted anything more than the young lady across the table. It was time to lay the foundations and bare his soul; something he had never had to do before and something he feared greatly.

'That was delicious. Thank you, Terrance.' Her eyes shone in the light and with the wine. 'You always make me feel so special.'

'You're worth everything and anything, Francesca,' he replied, feeling now a confidence fuelled by the drink as much as her compliment. 'How are things with Domenici?'

As he said the name of his love rival Terrance knew it was a gamble. To speak of Domenici now could work against him but he needed to know what chance, if any, there really was.

Francesca was a little taken aback. Terrance had never really asked much about Domenici and he was not aware of the games her heart seemed to be playing with her. She felt thrown temporarily. Should she tell the truth about her recent doubt? Tell him things she had never shared with him before? She cared, she just was not sure how.

'Domenici is fine,' she said as casually as she could muster. 'I'm going to Italy next week and we will spend some time together.' She waited for the reaction in his eyes. It was instantaneous: they almost glowed green. An unknown desire to keep Terrance interested suddenly surfaced as she added, 'But that's then. For now I am here, with you.'

As she said the words she felt betrayal race through her mind. She was cheating on them both. The impulse to please Terrance had surprised her. She felt, at this moment, that a part of her heart was with him yet she loved Domenici. Francesca was giving a little to both men, but neither was getting all of her.

She was involved in a game she had never played before. Terrance, for all his bravado in the marketing game, had no idea how to deal with a woman who could melt him at a glance. He just smiled and sipped some wine as he tried to think of his next move. She gave him that opening with another flirtatious comment.

'So, you know that I am going to San Piceno. I have to ask why, if you know that and you know of Domenici, that you like to be with me so much, Terrance.' Her stare was long and deep. 'What is it *you* want from me, from this?'

There was no more time to waste. He pushed his hand towards hers. She took it as he spoke as sincerely as he could. 'Francesca, I know that you have strong feelings for Domenici…love even.' He paused to capture the word that referred to how he felt. 'I cannot ask you to be anything but yourself. I look at you and see the woman I want to spend the rest of my life with.'

'Terrance…that is…'

'Please,' he said in a gentle voice, alien even to him, 'let me finish. I may not be the man you want and I cannot make you care for me. All I can do is to tell you this. I'm in love with you, Francesca. I was from the first moment I set eyes on you.'

Although she was not prepared for it, she saw honesty and sincerity in him. She could not say the same to him yet something registered. She did not know what she felt anymore.

'You don't have to say anything.' He tried to make it easier for her and she felt the pain in his voice.

'It's not that I don't have feelings for you, Terrance,' she answered, trying to find the courage to say exactly what she meant. 'I do, I'm just not sure what they are, or what they mean. I need time to think about all of this.'

An arrow straight from the bow of Cupid hit his heart. Not destroying it, but sending it into a crazy spasm of inner joy. There was a chance! He had a chance to win her love! The coin cried out to be held, to be given. Events happened in slow motion. Terrance kissed her hand. Holding it firmly he slipped his other hand into his pocket. He felt the chain touch his fingers as he looped it around his index finger. As their eyes met, he felt a powerful, dazzling emotion overwhelm him.

'I want to give you something.' He held the coin inside his clenched fist so as not to show it before he had said what he needed to say. He saw her look a little shocked and realised she may be thinking something major was about to happen. It was his ace card. 'It's not what you think.' He let the smile drop from his lips. 'I'm not going to ask you to marry me or anything so drastic!'

She laughed, as he had expected her to, her guard suddenly

dissolving. Now was the time to deliver his well rehearsed speech.

'When I first met you, I felt something special. I followed you because I had to at least speak with you, to find out something about you.' As his hand squeezed the coin, he gained conviction. 'All my life I have never wanted for anything, Francesca, until you came along. Suddenly I wanted to be with you every waking moment. The more I know you, the more time I want to be near you. It's because of this that I've bought you this gift. I didn't just go out and buy anything. I waited for something special, something as special as you.'

'I'm truly touched.' Francesca could not think of anything else to say. At that moment that was how she felt.

'After looking, after a long search, I found a gift worthy of you, or should I say, it found me.' He let his fist unclench. The coin shone out, its chain flickering in the firelight. He watched her slim fingers move towards it, her eyes focused on it. He knew she liked it even before she said the words.

'Terrance, it's beautiful.'

'It's yours, Francesca, forever.'

The coin seemed to glow in the radiance of her palm, its glint turning and touching her with each movement. He was certain her eyes were suddenly brighter.

'I love it, I really do,' she said finally, a look of deep gratitude on her face. 'I can't thank you enough. It's gorgeous and these markings, what are they from? They're stunning.'

If Terrance had rehearsed a thousand times he could not have wished for a more perfect prompt. He drew a deep breath.

'The coin is very rare,' he began, 'it's the coin of Angels, Francesca, to be given only to those special enough to realise it, someone like you...the Angel coin, for the Angel of my heart.'

'That is the nicest thing anyone has ever said to me.' She gave a gentle sigh and he knew she felt something. The electricity had not been a trick of his mind. 'I will treasure it,

Terrance. Thank you.'

She leaned across the table and let her lips touch his. Her mouth opened, ever so slightly and his tongue pushed inside with no resistance. As they kissed, Francesca felt both love and confusion in one instant. Temptation and charm were about to go to war with innocence and young love.

* * *

Her waking thought was one of alien surroundings. The first images of the morning brought with them the hazy memories of the night before. The smooth ceiling she looked up at was a warm yellow and the sheets wrapped around her a cream silk.

Her sleepy eyes saw nothing familiar until she turned her head to the left. Terrance lay next to her, eyes wide open, face aglow.

'Good morning, Francesca,' the voice was warm but it made her feel uneasy, unnatural, she should not have been here, 'did you sleep well?'

She shifted slightly in the bed, easing her back up to the headboard and pulling a pillow behind her head as she did so. His arm moved across her midriff, his eyes still fixed on her.

'I did...I think.' She tried to smile but it was difficult. Her mind searched for a clear picture, her mind drawing a blank as to the events of the night before.

She attempted to deflect the attention. 'I have a headache, I know that!'

She watched as he slid from under the sheets and walked to the bathroom. His nakedness made her stomach feel contorted with the guilt of a drunken night. She could only remember the car and laughing on the way home and... kissing and...

'Here, take these.' He sat on the edge of the bed as he offered her some tablets and water. 'They'll soon fix you. So, did you have a good night?'

She sipped the water slowly, using the time as an

opportunity to think, but it was to no avail: her mind was too cloudy, too mixed up, to have any clarity. She tried to answer truthfully, at the same time expressing her current feelings.

'It was special and I enjoyed it,' she began unhurriedly. 'I go away in a few days though, Terrance, and I have much to think about. I hope you understand that.' Her dark eyes searched for understanding, receiving a little, but sensing a confidence that scared her. 'I can't give you any guarantees,' she added as gently as possible.

Terrance smiled as he got up and purposely picked up his boxer shorts which lay on the floor near her side of the bed. 'You don't have to, Francesca. I know a little of how you feel and that was wonderful.'

She got up and dressed like the shy seventeen-year-old she was. He watched her and she wished he wouldn't, but she didn't have the courage to say so. Within the hour she was in the back of the limousine with just Joey for company and a million thoughts racing through her mind.

'Please drop me here.'

Joey swung the car over to the kerb one street away from her road. 'Are you sure you want to stop here, Miss?'

'Yes, I am, thank you.' She felt a note of panic in her voice as her hand fumbled with the door handle.

She saw him come to the door, opening it with ease. 'As you wish, Miss. Perhaps we'll see you again soon.'

'Thank you.' She forced a nervous grin. 'Perhaps you will. Goodbye.'

The car drove off leaving her alone on the street corner. Her legs felt like they were going to buckle beneath her, her breathing suddenly erratic with the shock she felt at herself. What had she done last night?

Approaching the house, she was relieved to see nobody was at home. It would have been bad enough to see her mother's car on the driveway, but her father's? She dismissed the thought of that. She would have never been able to go back in.

She slid the key gently in the door and listened carefully for a moment, just to make sure. Only silence greeted her. Something she usually may have been disappointed in but now she felt grateful for the stillness. She ran straight upstairs and into the bathroom, only stopping to twist the lever on the shower as she tore her clothes off. By now her efforts to remember what had happened only succeeded in sending her into a panic. Tears began to stream down her face as she stumbled into the shower cubicle. She fumbled, closing her eyes to shut out the feelings, but it was no use. The alcohol had numbed some parts yet the images of Domenici, her mother and father all stood out in her mind as if they had all just found out that she had slept in the bed of another man. Disappointment was etched on her mother's face as she spoke to her. 'Didn't I tell you to be careful?' Her father's expression was one of both anger and almost heartbreaking acceptance that his precious daughter was lost while Domenici…She sobbed as the water rained down on her like his tears of confusion and hurt. The words whispered from his lips, 'Why, Francesca?'

She slumped down to the floor and let the torrent from above drench her hair and body until, after some time had passed, she calmed a little. The images were her making, weren't they? Reason fought doubt and started to come through. She could not remember anything. But that didn't mean anything had happened, did it? Gathering herself, she stood and finished her shower with meticulous detail. Each stroke of the sponge seemed to cleanse another part of her until, seeing some of her skin redden, she slowed and let the sponge drop to the floor.

Afterwards, she selected some of the plainest clothes she could find and plucked up the courage to look in the mirror. Her reflection was no different to the day before. It made her feel better inside. And then she noticed it.

The coin sat on top of her V-necked jumper, its chain glistening against her neck. Pausing, she looked a little longer before letting her hand move up to touch it. 'It's beautiful.'

She spoke aloud, analysing the images with her fingertips. 'It feels so right.' An idea came into her head and she let the coin drop back to her neck, feeling its touch upon her.

The computer whirred into life and she waited impatiently until the search page came up, typing in *'Angel coin'*. There were various descriptions with all sorts of meanings so she searched further until she found the image that matched her own. 'There it is!' she whispered as she waited for the page to load.

It told her that the Angel who was spearing the dragon of evil on one side of the coin was the Archangel Michael. On the other, the image represented a ship with arms and rays of sun at its masthead. Slipping the chain over her head gently she held the coin close and compared the writing that circled the rim of each side. Looking at the Angel, she read the words out loud: *'Edward di gra rex Angl Z Franc.'* It matched the page she was looking at and below was the translation. 'Edward, by the grace of God, king of England and France.'

'Mmm, very nice too,' she commented to herself. 'Means nothing to me.'

She turned the coin over and read out the other side, scanning the web page as she did so: *'Per crucem tuam salva nos Christe redemptor.'*

Francesca whispered the translation as the strangest of feelings washed over her. 'Thy cross, save us, O Christ, our Redeemer.' She trembled slightly, absorbing the words.

'Francesca!' The voice broke the spell and brought her back to the present. 'One moment, Papa!' She closed the webpage just as her father entered the room.

'Hi, darling.' He greeted her in his usual way before catching the look on her face, 'Are you alright, Francesca? You look as white as a sheet.'

'I think so,' she replied slowly.

Nothing could have been further from the truth.

CHAPTER TWENTY-EIGHT

'You go away next week, Francesca, and I won't get a chance to see you. It's been a long time and I thought it would be nice, that's all.'

Francesca could not help but smile at her father's request. It was true: they had not spent as much time together of late and a break at Point Clear was always lovely. Her confusion regarding Terrance and Domenici meant the timing could not have been more perfect. Not that her father could know that. She hugged him and beamed. 'I would love to, Papa.'

As he watched her leave the room Stefano afforded himself a knowing grin. There were more secrets within his family these days, of that he knew. And his daughter's behaviour had him worried. He could tell it had not gone unnoticed by Nicole either. Yet she had chosen, for reasons he could only surmise, to keep things quiet. Now he would have some time alone with Francesca. He was going to use that time to unveil a secret plan of his own.

* * *

Rusty watched Jan walk up the hill and sussed out his mood instantly. He saw hunched shoulders and a drooping head; something you might associate with a downpour of rain in the Dales. The thing was, there was no rain and Rusty, despite his outlandish dress style and behaviour, was no fool. Rusty waited for his friend to arrive whilst looking as if he had not a care in the world.

'Hey.' Jan made a move to acknowledge him. Not to do so would have been rude. 'What are you doing here?' Rusty had positioned himself in front of the gate so Jan would have to step around him to get through.

'How are things?' Rusty responded in an even more casual tone than usual. 'You seem deep in thought.'

Jan dropped his guard momentarily. 'I am, about many, many things. It is so hard to…'

'Live away from home?' Rusty paused, sensing he should not have interrupted. 'Sorry, look, you don't have to tell me. It's your business and… well, if you do need anything, anyone to talk to, I'd be happy to listen, Jan.'

Jan felt a degree of relief, someone to talk with, someone who cared. He went to speak, feeling his throat go dry as he said the words, 'My father is dying.'

Rusty outwardly presented a calm persona even when he was feeling some inner turmoil. This relaxed manner made it easy for others to share their burden with him and many others loosened their tongues in his company meaning he knew a lot more than people gave him credit for. His worry had been of something completely different than Jan's father. He had been worried that Jan's problems stemmed from his sister rather than his father. Rusty had heard enough recently to know she was the subject of undue and potentially harmful interest, yet now did not seem the right time to speak of such things.

'I'm sorry, Jan,' he replied sympathetically. 'How bad is it? I mean, how long have you known?'

Jan looked at Rusty and saw someone different for the first time. He saw beyond the dreadlocks, tattoos and body piercings that many, including himself, could make a stereotypical assumption about. Now, seeing him in this light, made everything drop into place. Rusty always seemed happy enough, an amiable, carefree soul, yet his most important character trait had remained well hidden until now: depth.

'I do want to talk about it, Rusty. There's no one else I can

237

talk to,' he went on, shrugging his shoulders. 'That's if you want to listen.'

'Of course I do,' Rusty replied, wrapping an arm around Jan's shoulder. 'Come on, let's take a walk and you can tell me anything you want. I am your friend.'

As they walked, Rusty remained silent, contemplating Jan's worries, whilst weighing up what he knew. Basia had become the focus of many of the workers' attentions recently. He surmised that, because of Jan's worries about his father, he had not noticed anything himself. Basia, naïve but beautiful, had noticed nothing and, as yet, nothing had happened. Rusty knew he was going to have to keep a careful eye on developments.

They stopped by a small patch of grass where there was an old swing and slide which Rusty assumed, from the red rust on both, must have been here for many years, probably from when William was just a boy. Jan slumped on the swing, rocking it gently back and forth as Rusty sat on the tip of the slide nearby and waited. He watched as Jan struggled with his emotions and the words to describe them. Eventually he lifted his tearstained face and began to talk.

'It was three years ago, 2004, a year after arriving here, that I heard the news. My mother was beside herself with worry. To her, my father was going to die.' He swallowed hard trying to hold it all together before continuing, the pain evident in his voice. 'I had planned for us to leave, Rusty! To return home to the place I never thought I would miss! When I heard the news, everything changed…my mother thinks I've told Basia but I never have. All my plans turned to dust on that day and my heart was torn apart. To perhaps never see my father again and work so he may have a chance to live or…to return home and almost certainly watch him die.' Looking through moist eyes he added, 'Not much of a choice, eh?'

The suffering of this young man was apparent and Rusty felt a deep sorrow for him. A boy, turned into a man in a country he did not know, someone who had followed a dream, only to live the reality of a nightmare. No words could do justice to his plight.

'So you still have not said anything to Basia?' Seeing Jan shake his head, Rusty went on, 'Perhaps that's for the best, but one day soon you will have to, Jan. If things are as you say then one day soon you should go home as well.'

There was warmth to his voice yet Rusty was thinking ahead as he spoke. Jan needed to tell his sister which, he hoped, would mean them going home. Despite the sadness that would await them, Rusty knew things would be much worse for Basia if they stayed.

Unaware of his thoughts, Jan contemplated the options.

'I think you're right, my friend,' he replied finally. 'A part of me says I should keep working and keep sending money but it has done no good, has it?'

'You have done it for the right reasons, Jan.'

'Worked here for three years for nothing?' Jan retorted angrily. 'That's the right reasons? I could have stayed in Karczew and everything would still have been the same. None of this has made any difference! All the pain and frustration and having to work like a dog for that bastard Ethan. It has all been for nothing, Rusty!'

As Jan leapt from the swing, eyes dark with years of pent-up frustration and rage, Rusty stood up blocking his escape. At first he thought Jan was going to lash out, to vent that fury on him, but he didn't; he couldn't. Instead he threw his arms around Rusty's bulky frame and sobbed freely.

Holding Jan's shaking body, Rusty felt tears of his own. 'You can't blame yourself, Jan. You've done all you can. I'm sorry it may not be enough but, to me, you are someone special. You've given your father years of life that he may never have had. Your mother will always know that and you must never forget that.'

He felt Jan nod, letting all his days of hurting escape, his head pressed firmly into Rusty's shoulder as the two remained entwined in sorrow. As dusk fell upon them, the two silhouettes could have been mistaken for a loving couple under the light of the moon. Sadly, nothing could have been further from the truth.

* * *

'Smell the air! You can never cease to wonder at the beautiful smells!'

Francesca laughed. 'Papa, you are still like a child!'

'I am indeed,' Stefano smirked, 'but the smell of the sea air is invigorating, don't you think? Deep and soulful, like that of the mountain air in San Piceno, yet there is a difference.' He poked her playfully. 'Tell me you cannot notice that, wise daughter?'

'I cannot argue with you,' she replied, trying to leap onto his back. 'Point Clear and San Piceno are both beautiful places. I know that, Papa; now let me get on!'

'You're too big now!' Stefano laughed as she attempted to jump onto his back once more. He looked at her lovingly as he added, 'My sweet daughter, all grown up now.'

The past days had been joyous for Stefano: a break from work, and time with Francesca which had been wonderful. Despite the chilly February day, they had decided to head into nearby Clacton and visit the old pier. The last time they had been there was when Francesca could easily leap upon his shoulders. Family breaks to the apartment in Point Clear would not have been complete without the seaside fun of the pier. He felt ten years younger and hearing Francesca's giggles made him feel she did too.

Their steps quickened naturally on the steep road leading down towards the pier. As they passed under the arched bridge that led to the gardens above Francesca tugged at her father's hand. 'Race you!' she laughed before sprinting off.

Francesca was like a whippet and arrived at the entrance to the pier a good ten feet in front. 'I win, Papa!' She smiled as he reached her. 'You're not as fast as you once were!'

Stefano grinned as he caught his breath. 'Maybe not, but I'm still strong enough to teach you a trick or two!'

'I know, Papa,' she replied affectionately, 'and I love you for that and a million other things. Come on! Let's go!'

In the years before when they had visited, the pier had had turnstile gates which you had to pay at to enter. The change in tourism, and indeed the pier, had meant they had gone. Now it was a wide entrance, adorned above with a huge sign spelling out the words 'Clacton Pier'. The busy days may have gone, especially at this time of the year, but it mattered not to Stefano or Francesca. The pier was still there and their memories would always be intact.

Long lengths of solid wooden planks stretched the whole way down to the end, over a thousand feet of ageing wood supported by steel girders underneath to protect it from the watery waves below. The sound of splashing sea was only drowned out this time of the year by the mixture of sounds venting from an array of rides and arcade machines, all vying for custom. Stefano watched as Francesca danced her way, Broadway style, to the dodgems, only glancing back to make sure he was following her. Two tickets later and that distant yet familiar smell of electricity from the dodgem cable fizzing against the wire ceiling filled their nostrils with delight.

'That was brilliant!' Francesca enthused stepping off the dodgems as Stefano checked for bruises. She had won her fair share of bumps during the ride and received the odd glare from the attendant for her ferocity of driving. Stefano found himself chasing after her again as she headed toward the sweet-smelling candyfloss and doughnut stall, her hair shining as much as her smile as she presented him with the pink fluffy stick of sugar.

'My treat, Papa,' she beamed taking his hand. 'Come on! Let's go to the end. I want to see what's changed.'

They made their way past small hoopla stalls and sideshows towards the larger attractions. Queues were forming at the Sea Aquarium and helter-skelter while screams of excitement rang out in the salty air from the Twister Ride and roller coaster. The wind picked up as the two walked onto the uncovered part of the pier.

Now they were on the last stretch that used to house the Jolly Roger restaurant many years ago. Stefano reflected on many a good meal there, whilst Francesca's attention was diverted by a small booth to the side of the now vacant building.

'I never saw that before.' She smiled curiously. 'What is it?'

He glanced in the direction she indicated, seeing the medium-sized structure. Silk-coated on either side with a hand-painted sign above a makeshift curtain acting as a doorway. The sign simply said 'Madame Rosie' together with an image of two hands clasping a clear crystal ball.

'It's a fortune teller, darling,' he replied, somewhat amused. 'They tell you the future, or at least that's what they say they tell you.'

Her eyes lit up. 'Papa, I want to go in!'

'Francesca…'

Her mind was elsewhere. 'Please, Papa…'

He melted, as she knew he would. Shrugging his shoulders, he took a handful of floss before grinning with acceptance. 'Alright, alright. Enjoy and I'll meet you at the end of the pier when you are done, okay?'

With a glint in her eyes she ventured off into the booth leaving Stefano smiling at the moment. *Fortune tellers indeed*, he muttered as he twisted more floss in his hand and left her to it.

* * *

A musty smell greeted Francesca as she pulled the curtain back and stepped inside. The booth, or room as it was really, was no larger than a decent-sized garden shed. The scent was a mixture of the pier's natural smells combined with faint lavender and a hint of dampness. She shivered a little as she made out a small table with an object covered in cloth and a chair either side. The light came from behind, a pale bulb hanging crudely from the corner. There was no sign of any fortune teller.

She coughed as loudly as she could and waited. A cough returned hers before she saw the woman shuffle in from the side of the makeshift palace of fortunes. Madame Rosie peered over half-moon glasses, almost in surprise at her new client. Francesca wondered if she got many customers this time of year, or any time of the year judging by the state of the place. She saw a hunched woman, perhaps sixty or more, with gnarled features and a witch-pointed chin. She looked like a woman with hardly any good fortune at all.

'Sit, sit,' Madame Rosie repeated as she snuffled and shuffled her way to the other chair. Francesca did as she was told and found herself facing a lady who suddenly reminded her of The Wizard of Oz and that Witch from the East.

'Five pounds please.' Her hand appeared from beneath the shawl draped around her shoulders. Francesca fumbled for a note and placed it in her weathered palm. 'Thank you.' She spat the words out with venom. 'Now, you want your fortune told, ah?'

Francesca was sure this was a rhetorical question but, now she actually thought about it, she was not sure if she did want her fortune told. Before she could give any answer however, Madame Rosie continued.

'Mmm, Italian, I would guess. No children either and no husband.'

'That's right.' Francesca gave a gentle sigh. If her initial fortunetelling was supposed to impress her, it didn't. Anyone could guess she was perhaps Italian and the fact she was still seventeen would indicate no children. Madame Rosie seemed not to notice and, after letting her glinting eyes run up and down Francesca's face, she pulled the cloth away to reveal a crystal ball on the table.

Her hands seem to grow as they wrapped themselves around

the ball, sliding and caressing it. She mumbled to herself as Francesca watched on. She was rather intrigued by the ball. It was what had probably made her go in there in the first place. Now, as she watched the old woman, she strained to see what magical images she was mumbling about. After minutes of silence, the only images she saw were the light of the dull bulb seeming to move with Madame Rosie's bony fingers.

'My future looks rather bland really, doesn't it, Madame Rosie?' She tried to make the comment sound like a casual joke. She was ignored for a few more minutes and the frustration of watching someone stare blankly at something started to irritate her. Just as she was about to give up Madame Rosie stopped abruptly.

'Rather dull, you say?' *She has a good memory at least,* Francesca thought. 'Not at all, my dear, not at all. Would you like to know your fortune now?'

Trying not to laugh, Francesca nodded. 'That would be nice.'

'You come from a strong family. Italian blood but English home, correct?'

'Yes, but…' She had pretty much said that before.

'Sshh!' she glared at Francesca. 'I haven't finished! You are young, yet you have choices that worry you. Confusion shines out from you, I see it clearly. You do not know what path to take and, because you are so young, you do not think you can make any choices yet, do you?'

Her words grabbed Francesca's attention. Perhaps she was worth listening to. No one could have known that, unless… the old lady was guessing. Francesca decided to keep her guard up.

'I am not sure what choices you mean.'

'Oh really, is that so?' Madame Rosie's weathered face cracked into a smile. 'Well, perhaps I can help you to remember. The ball says your heart is clouded. Two loves, but of different kinds and you are not yet grown enough to define which is which. One love is here and another far away.' She watched Francesca gasp a little before adding, 'I would say the other is in Italy, your *real* home. Would I be right, young lady?'

'Er, yes, that's right.' She was actually starting to believe this crazy old lady.

'Well, that's easy then.' Madame Rosie lifted the cover back over the ball indicating the session was finished. 'The answer will come to you because the choice you make is **very** important.' She gazed seriously at Francesca. 'I'm glad you came and I could help. The answer will come from the sea.'

'The sea?' Francesca replied, looking puzzled. 'What, you think because I live by the sea I will get the answer from there?' Her mind was working overtime and she felt suspicious suddenly. 'I don't live here. We have a place in Point Clear, but that's hardly by the sea! And in Italy there is just a river, no sea, Madame Rosie!'

'Don't be so foolish, child,' the fortune teller retorted. 'I know all that already! The answer will come from the sea, like I said. It doesn't matter where you are when you find it. You will know in your heart,' she gripped Francesca's arm firmly, 'I promise you.'

CHAPTER TWENTY-NINE

'The gift of a smile… The young lady passed the stranger on the corner. He looked, she looked. They said nothing. A month later she saw him once more. She smiled and he smiled back. A friendship was born, just from a smile.'

(Taken from the halls of Angels)

The first signs of spring were in the air and the farm was busier than ever which, in turn, allowed the workers little time to dwell on other things. That was perhaps with the exception of two: Rusty and Jan. Rusty had heard a couple of comments since his chat with Jan that made his skin crawl. Men can be many things sometimes, especially when in a group and the macho image comes to the fore but this was more than that. Ethan, who had confessed to wanting to give 'the little Polish whore a good seeing to' in front of a group of subordinates, had not only shown his true colours, but he had also drawn further unwarranted attention to the attractiveness of Basia. Since then Rusty had heard others talking in the same manner and it worried him. It really was time for Jan and Basia to go home.

Jan, on the other hand, had his own concerns which still made him totally oblivious to any attention Basia was receiving. Even Ethan's snide remarks in front of him went unnoticed. Whether that was pure vindictiveness on Ethan's part, or the fact that Jan had become numb to any remarks by his superior, no one could tell.

Jan had just one thing on his mind. He had to tell Basia about her father. He had hidden his illness from her for too long. Then they had to return home to see their mother and father. He was not sure which part was going to hurt the most, probably all of it.

Basia was sitting cross-legged in the caravan sewing as he entered. She briefly glanced up at him with a welcoming smile.

'Have you had a good day?' The routine was always the same.

'Not bad,' Jan answered as he looked at his little sister. Her hair was pushed behind her ears and clipped at the back exaggerating her facial bone structure. She was, even in his brotherly eyes, becoming quite a stunning young lady. 'Have you had a good day too?' he added, attempting to snap out of his daydream.

It was too late. She had noticed his look and realised something was on his mind. 'Is there anything wrong? You look a little strange.'

'It's nothing,' Jan began before cursing his words. 'Well, it is something actually…Basia, we need to talk.'

'Fine, then talk.' Her reply was cheerful as well as curious. She put the sewing to one side and gave him her full attention. It only made it harder for Jan to find a way to say what he had to.

Jan took her by the hands as he began. 'Basia, I have to tell you something and I don't want you to get upset.' He paused to gather his composure, seeing that Basia's expression had changed from one of carefree to concern. 'It's about father.'

Over the next few minutes he told her all that had happened: from the first phone call and the illness itself, to his decision not to tell her and why.

Basia's eyes darted back and forth as he spoke. She almost aged in front of him as the innocence of her previously protected world was torn, word by word, from her. When he had finished there was a stony silence as each looked in desperation at the other.

Eventually Basia spoke, a new found anger in her tone. 'Why are you telling me now, Jan? Why didn't you just wait until he was dead and then let me know?' Her voice was filled with pain.

'Please, Basia, don't be like this,' he pleaded. 'Can't you see why I kept it from you? To protect you, that was all I ever wanted for you. What good would it have done to tell you if father had got better?'

She felt the sadness envelop her as she whispered, 'You haven't answered me. So why tell me now?'

He paused as the guilt of it all washed over him. 'Because… I don't think he will live for much longer. I cannot say for sure, but I know the medication is only helping, not healing.' He stared through leaden eyes to see the broken girl in front of him as he went on, 'I had to tell you now, Basia. I could leave it no longer. I hid it from you because I hoped he *could* get well.' His head dropped in anguish as he added, 'I'm running out of faith now.'

Jan tried to move closer to her but, as he did so, she almost pushed him back, eyes ablaze. 'I followed you, Jan!' she screamed now. 'I left them both and followed you and our dreams, *our dreams*, not yours! I did everything you asked of me and I believed everything you said to me! I did all that but you couldn't tell me something so important because *you* decided it was right, *you*! I'm not sixteen anymore, Jan, and you are not my God! I deserved to know before! He's my father too!'

Again there was a silence only interrupted intermittently by Basia's gentle sobs. Jan stood motionless as his insides contorted with regret. He had known of the choices he had made. There was never going to be a right one and he had hoped for salvation for his father, rather than this, the burden of an empty soul.

He saw Basia thinking, shaking with floods of thoughts and emotions. When she stood up to face him he wished he could escape the nightmare, to wake and find it had all been a dream. Now her icy stare told him no such thing would happen. This was as real as it got and the Devil himself could not have made it more terrible for him as he saw her love for him evaporating with the seconds that passed.

'So tell me, brother,' her voice was laced with rage and sarcasm combined, 'you, the money keeper, the dream maker, how much longer had you planned we worked here while our father is dying? How much money do we have to make a new life for us all?'

He knew she had realised what he had done with the money. He knew he should have told her now. 'We have enough to go home now, Basia,' he answered weakly.

The skin on his cheek stung as her delicate hand lashed out, slapping him with all her force. Before he knew it she was upon him, her fury unleashed, her nails digging into his face, her screams into his heart, as he tried to hold her, to calm her.

'You bastard!' she yelled, clawing at him, kicking at him, 'I hate you!'

They fell upon the floor as he soaked up her anger not attempting to fight back. He cried as she rained down blows upon his crossed arms, screaming obscenity after obscenity at him. He remained silent, letting the storm come whilst whispering in his mind: *I deserve it.*

Her energy sapped, Basia slumped next to him, her face turned away. He could hear her panting for breath as he dragged himself up and stroked her hair gently.

'I'm sorry, I'm so sorry, Basia.'

'So am I, Jan.' She lifted her face and he saw hatred etched upon it. 'You'll do something for me now. You'll go home alone. I won't go with you. I want nothing to do with this anymore.'

'But, Basia…'

Her eyes flashed and he stopped. 'It's what you wanted then,' she snapped. 'Be man enough to show some honour now.'

He nodded. She was right. Dread filled him at the thought of returning home without her. Watching his sister he reflected on the choices he had made. Their father was dying. He felt at that moment he had killed a part of both of them too.

* * *

The plane landed relatively smoothly on the runway at Pescara Airport. Outside, Francesca saw a warm sunny morning yet, inside, nothing had landed smoothly at all. The sun was not shining in her heart. In fact there were clouds which showed no signs of shifting.

As the other passengers began to switch their mobiles back on, she checked for the umpteenth time that hers was off. Terrance had bombarded her with messages during the week leading up to the trip and even more so at the airport. He was bordering on the obsessed, and it made her feel a little edgy and, indeed, guilty. The problem was she did not know quite who to feel the most guilty about.

She realised that her usual bubbly smile was not present as Domenici met her.

'Are you alright, darling?' were his first words. With a quick adjustment to her expression, she grinned sheepishly and replied, 'Hi, sweetheart, it was a bad flight.'

The drive to San Piceno was filled with the noise of the little Fiat's engine and the sound of Domenici's excited voice as he explained all the events in the village. Francesca listened and nodded, trying to sound as interested as possible, while also trying to force her mind to concentrate on something other than her confusion.

'What do you think then, Francesca?' The question was innocent enough but, because of her inner thoughts, it caught her completely unawares. She turned her gaze from the window. His face was etched with curiosity, waiting for her answer.

'Er,' she smiled, 'sorry, I missed that. What do I think

about what?'

Domenici looked hurt. 'What do you think about what I've just been telling you for the last ten minutes? I passed my final exams and the fact that I've been accepted into Art College!'

'That's wonderful. It really is!' She could feel herself shifting awkwardly in the seat as she faked interest. She had truly heard nothing of what he had said.

He gave her an exasperated look before he smiled softly. 'Don't worry, darling. I know it was a bad flight. You probably need to rest.'

As his hand touched hers, Francesca wanted to both hold it yet push it away.

* * *

'So, sir, are you happy with the plans?'

'Sir?'

Terrance switched back on. His mind was far away from the conference and he had paid little or no attention. 'What? What did you say?' His voice was snappy.

'The plans, sir,' the voice repeated, 'for the new store in Stebdon. Are you happy for us to go ahead?'

Terrance looked at him blankly before glancing around the table. Seven other faces waited for his reply with intenseness, the same intenseness which he had been feeling. Only his was simply for a text message. He felt flustered.

'Yeah, sure,' he answered vacantly, 'let's go with them. Nothing out of the ordinary, is there?'

Brendan saw that he had not heard any of the conversation and tried to cover his boss's tracks. 'Only the fact that many of the town are opposed to the new store.' With a sly smile he added, 'Nothing out of the ordinary at all.'

Terrance slid back from the chair at the head of the conference table. 'Good. Then that's all. Get it done, get the shop open as planned, and call me if you need me.' With that he stormed out the room grabbing his mobile as he did and

251

double checking for a text. He saw none. 'Fuck.'

* * *

'Why won't you stay?' The question was an obvious one. She had flown out to see him and a few months earlier it would never have been asked. The cracks had been showing all day and now Francesca was running out of excuses. She had been expecting it, but that made it no easier.

'I just want to stay at my grandparents.' Her reply sounded feeble. 'I haven't seen them for a while, Domenici.'

Domenici may have been easy-going but he was not stupid. The reasons he had been making for her behaviour were wearing thin. 'You have plenty of time to see them. What's wrong? I've been talking since you got here about us, about the chance of being able to paint. To be able to plan a future, and yet you've hardly said a word.'

She knew he was right, but that made it no easier. Their eyes met and she feared that he would see the confusion, the sense of deceit in them. He only saw dark brown eyes that he adored as he waited for a response.

'I'm sorry for seeming distant.' Her hand slid onto his, the effect instantaneous. 'It has just been a long day.'

Domenici moved near. 'It doesn't matter.' His lips moved close to hers and she accepted them, she had to. 'I understand.' He spoke softly into her ear before kissing her more passionately.

She let him in. Her hands stayed where they were but his moved with the passion of his mouth, shifting, touching and searching. She felt powerless to stop him and, before she knew it, she was half naked on his bed. He was going to try and make love to her. She sensed his intentions as he groaned and moved and touched her all over. Still she did not respond, except to kiss him but he was unaware, rampant now, the testosterone taking over. She could feel him slip his trousers off and, as he moved back across her, she felt his leg push hers

252

apart. Then he was facing her, looking into her eyes with a fervour that broke her will. Any moment now he would enter her.

'No!' She grabbed his hands and turned her head from him briefly. The impact of her cry made him freeze.

'Francesca, what is it? What's wrong?' He looked like someone found guilty of a crime he had not committed.

'No, Domenici.' The panic set in now. She had no answer but she just could not let him go any further. 'I'm not ready, not tonight...please.'

For a moment, his expression was sympathetic as he stared at her. Then his gaze shifted away from her eyes and downwards. She froze.

'What's that?' His voice had changed and it was no longer soft.

'It's an Angel coin.' It was all she could say.

CHAPTER THIRTY

The journey had been long and tiresome but, most of all, lonely. Jan had left Sonnings with unlimited leave on the say-so of Edward Sonning himself. Apart from Rusty, and of course Basia, Edward was the only person he felt he could trust. It had been good judgement on Jan's part. Edward had been not only kind, giving him some money towards travel, but also ingenious by devising a 'task' which needed a young Polish man to meet some potential new workers for an 'induction course in London'. Even William had not smelt a rat.

Basia had not said goodbye, and that had hurt. She knew he had to leave on the last train from Stebdon but had purposely become scarce. He had wished for that last hug for many a mile and now, as he arrived cold and alone in Warsaw, he wished for her to be by his side more than ever.

Using some of the extra money, Jan checked into a basic bed and breakfast near the bus park. It was too late to travel any further and, besides, he wanted to experience some of his native land before the hours of pain ahead. After several shots of vodka and a few meaningless conversations with people he would never meet again, he staggered back to his room wondering where his future lay. He had no feeling of warmth to be back in Poland at all. As far as his heart and soul felt, he was in no-man's-land.

* * *

Punching the number into his mobile, Terrance stamped up and down the corridor whilst waiting impatiently.

'Mr Healy, good evening,' the voice answered. 'Are you calling to proceed?'

'Damn right I am,' he snapped back angrily. 'Is she with him?'

'They are currently in a small apartment block just south of the village centre, sir. She's in there, they're both in there. We can keep you posted on any changes.'

Terrance felt his face flush as jealousy took hold. 'Don't fucking bother to fill me in with details. Just get it done as soon as she leaves, understand?'

'Consider it done, Mr Healy.' The line went dead.

* * *

'Who bought it for you? Francesca, look at me! Are you seeing someone else? Francesca!'

Domenici's voice resonated through her mind as she wished she could vanish. She had switched off the phone in order to avoid the relentless text messages from Terrance. She had tried to hide things from Domenici. Yet she had left the one thing he would have surely noticed hanging right in front of him. Love had found her out and now she must explain.

'Domenici, it's not what you think. Yes, it was a gift and yes, it was from a man but it's me that has changed. Not because of someone else.'

Her explanation simply brought more confusion. 'Why, Francesca, why do you need another man? I love you. I want to be with you. What have I done wrong?'

She could almost feel his heartache as she saw the devastation she was causing. 'You haven't done anything. It's me, all me.' Her voice tailed off before gaining a sinister strength, a strength almost of self-detonation, knowing that each word she was about to say would cut deeply into Domenici's heart. 'I can't be sure of what I want anymore,

Domenici. I need time, I need to go home. If you can't give that to me then we're over.'

The coin felt hot on her throat as she spoke. That heat transformed itself to her eyes which lit up, ablaze with defiance. Francesca sensed her power as he reeled back at her outburst. The suffering of a man scorned was instantly apparent. She pulled her clothes on and stood up to leave.

'Is that it?' He asked the ultimate question.

She turned to see his distraught expression as he waited for the final blow. Never before in her short life had she felt such uncertainty.

'I can't say.' There was deep remorse in her tone. 'I'll call you when I know. I'm sorry.'

* * *

Stepping off the bus at Karczew, Jan's first impression of home was one of surprise. It was such a barren place. He had grown up here. Spent endless days looking, finding things to do. Now the mainly empty streets backed by empty fields and an empty grey sky brought home to him what he had always known: there was nothing for him here.

He met no one he knew as he walked to his former home. The years had changed him but not this place. It could have been another planet as far as he felt. Ahead he would see his parents once again. He knew that was going to bring him nothing but more pain and heartache.

The small area of scrubland in front of the house had not changed since he had last played there. Instead of walking straight up to the door and knocking, Jan hesitated. He was not brave enough yet. He would walk around the house. He would take in the smells and sights that would give him courage. Yes, that would help.

His own instincts could not prevent him looking though. He had planned to edge cagily past the window. To not spare a look that would surely change everything. But he could not

256

help himself.

The fire flickered and danced, its glow illuminating the scene. There was the figure in its rightful place, as he had left it: his father. Sidling up to the edge of the window he instinctively took in the scene. The grey pallor of his father's skin was evident, even against the orange glow of the fire. The canisters that jutted out from the side furthest from the fire looked exactly as they were: ugly objects that had no place in the room apart from to push their content into the tubes that ran up the side of the chair, filtering through the oxygen that was so easily attained outside, directly into the mask that added to his father's disfigurement.

Jan could not stop looking. He watched as his father slowly coughed and breathed. Gasped and coughed, sucked and coughed. He saw those eyes that had been strong for his family once. They now stared into nothingness filled only with prolonged agony. Was this what all the money had done for him? Given him a death sentence?

Helplessly, Jan watched the scene before him. Then he saw his mother. She padded into the room and stopped before the chair. Jan observed how much she seemed to have aged. She stopped and adjusted the mask, checking the tubes as she did so, before taking perhaps half a minute to look at her husband. To check everything was as it should be before it got too much for her. She wiped her hand across her face before she turned and then, for the briefest moment, he thought she stared straight at him, her expression haunted with grief. He saw the two ghosts of his parents in that instant, one dying and the other dead already.

Grief encompassed him and he did the only thing he could possibly do at that moment: he left.

* * *

Fate had no control. It would not have mattered if Domenici had remained there for the night. They would still have been waiting. There was only one thing fate did that night: it just speeded up the inevitable.

Perhaps it would have been more difficult in daylight, but there was always a way round that for the two hired professionals. The tough Scot Ian Neil nudged his compatriot, the equally tough Ken Douglas. It was the latter who was responsible for reporting back to base and it was Douglas who nodded that it was time.

Silent steps meant Domenici heard nothing before the arm wrapped itself around his throat. In a smooth motion, a fist crashed into his stomach, knocking the wind and any chance of calling for help out of him. A fraction of a second later and he felt a mask tighten around his face before another punch sent him into unconsciousness.

Domenici came round to a voice in his ear. 'Listen carefully, boy.' Trying to focus, he realised the mask had been removed. Now he saw the faint silhouette of one of the men, arms folded standing before him, before he felt his shoulder jolt. 'You see the girl again and we see you. If we see you, you won't be seeing much else after.' Domenici could sense the alcohol-fuelled aggression in his tone.

There was a slight pause and Domenici was sure he heard a chuckle before he felt a fist smash into his nose. Everything blurred into watery pain now as the men began the awful beating.

* * *

Terrance's hand moved with the speed of a cowboy at a shootout on the first ring on his mobile.

'So tell me.'

'I think he understands.' The gruff voice of Douglas hit the line. 'She left. We arrived. He knows what will happen if he sees the girl again. He's in a rough way, but nothing too serious.'

'Perfect.' Terrance's voice carried a tone of satisfaction.

'Well done.'

Ending the call, Terrance poured himself a glass of wine and crossed the lounge to the far bay window. There he gazed outwards raising a toast to himself and smiling broadly.

'To love and all that it can bring.'

CHAPTER THIRTY-ONE

'The human has no sorrow that an Angel cannot heal.'
(From the scriptures of Galgliel)

The April showers that are traditional in Britain did not come. Instead, the month was replaced by the beating sun, setting records on a daily basis whilst engaging the nation in idle chat about the weather that was not so idle. Talk of the environment was on the tip of everyone's tongues as TV screens showed images of normally empty beaches, now scattered with sun worshippers.

For Stefano and his family, the news should have been an early blessing. Orders arrived via fax and e-mail leaving the company short of stock and staff. That, combined with the sale of the café in March, meant Nicole was busy with the last details of the handover and Francesca... well, Francesca was lost.

She waited patiently while her father spoke with Darrell and some of the staff. They had agreed to work longer hours. Stefano explained to them all that it was paramount that they honoured each order from T Healy & Sons, the penalties of failure possibly being the cancellation of the contract and job losses as a result. It would be a good year, it seemed, but only if they could keep up with sales and the business was very much in sync with the seasons. The seasons however seemed to be changing.

'Papa, may I have a word?' She caught him as he burst out

the office, face concentrating on tasks ahead. Hearing her voice, he stopped abruptly.

'Francesca, what are you doing here?'

She grinned warmly and saw it melt her father's stare. He smiled back. 'Sorry, just busier than we can cope with at the moment. Have you come to help, darling?'

'I wish I could, Papa,' she replied honestly. 'I've actually come to ask for your help.'

'Really?' His face had a bemused look. 'My young daughter after her father's help? That doesn't sound good!'

'Papa!' She giggled slipping her arms around his waist. 'I've asked Mama and she agreed.' Her eyes widened. 'Now I just need your permission.'

Knowing that Nicole had agreed meant that he would agree too. Whatever it was, Nicole only made choices regarding Francesca that were solid and in her interests. However, he was not going to let her know that straightaway. Trying to keep a serious face, he replied, 'You need my permission? Permission for what, Francesca?'

She wanted to be honest. 'Papa, I need some time away. Some time to think. Things in my world have been moving very fast, too fast.' Her eyes opened wide as she spoke earnestly. 'I want to know if it's alright if I stay in Point Clear for a while. Alone.'

Stefano wanted to laugh at the joys of being young and the dreams of young love but he had sensed more than that of late. Francesca was as important to him as the air he breathed and that is why he himself had taken her away for a while. Despite the fact that she was still a teenager, he also knew she was old enough in her ways, and that there were genuine reasons for her wishes. 'Of course you can, sweetheart,' he replied with that look that only a father can give. 'I'll take you there when you're ready, and pick you up when you want to come home.'

'Thank you.' Her eyes sparkled with gratitude. 'You really are the best, Papa.'

He grinned. 'I know.'

* * *

Terry was doing less and Terrance was doing more. That's the way it seemed to Jenny Healy, yet she spent the same amount of time with both of them as before: little or none.

'I thought Dad's new role as ambassador was going to mean he spent more time with us?' Holly brought the subject up over another girls alone breakfast.

Jenny could only shrug. 'I did too, darling. He tells me the trips to the city and the grand openings of more stores are very important for customer relations.' Shrugging again and making Holly grin, she added, 'What can I do about it?'

'Well, Mummy,' Holly laughed as she spoke, 'at least you don't have to spend any time with Terrance. I love it that he's hardly here.'

'Darling, don't be like that,' Jenny gently scolded. 'He is still your brother, you know.' She pondered as she said the words. 'Come to think of it, he hasn't seemed himself for the last few weeks.'

Now it was Holly's turn to shrug. 'That is because he's in love, Mum.'

Jenny looked astounded. 'Are you kidding me? We are talking about Terrance here!'

'Mum!' Holly wanted to tell her off but found her reaction amusing. 'I can't see how you haven't noticed! It's not been all work, you know, and for more than a few weeks! Tough boy, city slicker, businessman Terrance.' Holly feigned an apologetic look as she added, 'Oh, and darling brother, of course! Well, he's fallen in love with an Italian girl!'

Looking perplexed, Jenny stared at her daughter for answers. 'How did I not notice?'

'Don't beat yourself up, Mum,' Holly responded cheerfully. 'He didn't make it obvious. Dad has no idea, and not many at work do either. I am his sister after all and sisters notice things that brothers do differently. Like the aftershave, the suits...the haircuts.'

Before Jenny could ask more, their conversation was interrupted by the sound of the doorbell. Holly jumped up to answer and returned a moment later holding a parcel and a handful of letters.

'Mmm,' she commented as she perused the mail, 'looks like one for you, Mum. Parcel for Dad, nothing for me and...the usual junk mail.'

As Holly threw the letters onto the kitchen table Jenny took the one addressed to her. It was handwritten which immediately attracted her interest. Tearing back the flap of the envelope, she slid out a few notepad-sized sheets and unfolded them.

'Is it anything interesting, Mum?' Holly asked casually.

Jenny's eyes shot across the first page as she answered, 'It's from Oliver.'

'Oh!' There was a degree of interest in Holly's response. 'Read it out loud, Mum!'

Clearing her throat, Jenny began to read the letter:

Dear Jenny,

Sorry it has been a while since any contact. The last two months have not been easy, and to write has been the last thing on my mind. The good news, as you will read, is that I am strong enough to write now.

The amounts of methadone I am taking are becoming less and less which is what we both know to be the overall aim. I am clear in my mind that I will beat the addiction, Jenny. I was sure of that when I last saw you. Of that, there was no fear.

I can tell you now that the thing that scared me most about coming off drugs was the future. For such a long time, in fact until you came along, I had almost become comfortable with my existence. I smile as I write this imagining you thinking *how*?

Well, my dear Jenny, I will try to explain.

When you have nothing, there is nothing to be taken away from you anymore. The fear of loss is furthest from your mind. The days hold no worry and no requirements. I was just me, the homeless Oliver, dependent on no one except the element of my keeper, the kindness of others. I lost that awareness along the way, Jen. The ease of being homeless was one thing. I could suffer the cold and the hardships because I wanted nothing from this world. When drugs came into my life I welcomed them with open arms. They made me feel even more freedom.

A fool's freedom, of course, I know that now. That false dawn only drew me into a world of darkness, a place where thieves would steal from their own to fuel their habit. I lost my identity. I faded into the very person I did not want to be and then... I was rescued.

I am not sure if this will all make sense to you so I will write it as plainly as I can. Jen, I have been saved. Never more in my life can I see so clearly as now. I have been gifted by an Angel herself. I have been shown the light and, through that, I met you and also made contact with my mother. I feel redeemed.

We spoke of Angels and I know I cannot ask you to believe in all I say. Just know this. I have a debt to repay, and I will repay it when it is due. They tell me here that if I continue to recover as I am then I should be released by Christmas time. What a perfect time to begin a new life.

I must go now as I have to write to my mum as well. I think we will meet one day soon. Once all this is over. I miss you and all that you are to me.

Sending you a green-eyed smile to let you know I love you.

Oliver xxx

'I would have said that someone like him couldn't write like that. Either that or he is completely bonkers,' Jenny heard Holly's voice in the back of her mind, 'I have to say, Mum. That was a very beautiful letter.'

Jenny wiped the tears away as she folded the letter and held it in her hands. 'I know, darling. He is a very beautiful man.'

* * *

Jan walked along the high street of Stebdon, rucksack thrown over his shoulder, eyes focusing ahead, ears pricked at the unfamiliar cacophony of noises. The sun beat down relentlessly, causing him to stop and peel off his now sweat-drenched woollen sweater. It was a far cry from the last frosty breath he had taken as he left Poland.

He was following the street out towards the turning that led back to the farm. The last days had taken their toll. The torture of watching his father had hurt him beyond belief and made him question many things in his life. The decision to walk away had been partly through sadness but also partly caused by his guilt, the guilt at not being able to face his parents without the one he cared for so much: Basia. Had she gone with him he could have coped, been strong for her. Now he had to return, even more shattered than before he left.

The distraction ahead did exactly that: distracted him. At first the noise grabbed his attention. Stebdon was not a place where noise occurred. Just the sound of a siren would cause much inquisitiveness from the locals. This din was as loud as any he had heard apart from the hum of tractors and lorries on the farm.

The path he had been walking on ended now, to be followed by hard sun-baked earth. The line of trees that hid the stretch of disused land had been replaced by an outwardly never-ending run of corrugated sheets that blotted out the landscape. He walked until he came to wide metal gates pushed back to allow all to enter and leave and he watched in disbelief.

Mechanical monsters were lifting earth in their greedy mouths, tossing it up and away like a child throwing sand aimlessly. Yellow-jacketed men shouted and pointed towards the eyesore that dwelt in the middle. Thousands of square metres of harmless space had vanished, to be replaced by a brick shell of preposterous proportions. The fact that Jan had never seen a superstore being built made the shock all the greater.

Forgetting the scorching heat, Jan suddenly needed to know what had happened here. When he had left, there was nothing here. How could this have happened so fast? His mind raced as he turned and ran towards the farm and Basia.

* * *

As the car turned into the small estate of sixteen houses and apartments, Stefano parked up and began going through the final list of instructions as they entered the apartment, Francesca nodding in agreement as she checked them off on her mental list.

Keys – yes; heating switch – I know how to do it: locking doors at all times – of course; call us as often as possible just to let us know you are okay – you know I will, Papa. Hurry up and come home.

'I will, Papa. I promise, just as soon as I feel ready.' She hugged her father, feeling his strong arms doing the same. A tinge of sadness at seeing him go, combined with the adventure and peace of being alone, washed over her as she waved goodbye until the car faded into the distance.

The apartment overlooked the distant lapping water of the creek which was home to a bird sanctuary a mile or so out. It looked like a long stretch of golden sand from the window, dotted with plants and unharmed, unvisited wildlife. Occasionally, when the tide was out, Francesca and her family would wade out in their boots onto the muddy bank of the sanctuary and take a picnic whilst enjoying this unblemished part of the world.

'I must go out there one day,' she promised herself smiling. 'Yes, Papa, I will check the water tide times!' With a chuckle she let herself in the apartment and began the first day of her escape from men.

* * *

The outside of the farm's main gates were crowded. The first person Jan laid eyes upon was Ethan, standing on a large crate, surrounded by some of the burlier workers; all of them yelling at the crowd who were bellowing back angrily. Everything seemed to have gone mad.

His first concern was for Basia. Seeing no way through the throng of people, Jan darted around the side of the wooden office, unnoticed in the hullabaloo. His heart was thumping in his chest. What could have happened? Slipping through the broken fence at the far end of the makeshift path that ran by the side of their caravan, he rushed to the door. Flinging it open, he called out, 'Basia! Basia!'

There was no reply and no one else in sight. Crazy thoughts ran through his mind as he hurtled out of the yard. Sprinting as fast as he could towards the house he shouted out her name. William Sonning's face appeared at the window as he approached. His expression had fright written all over it.

Jan banged on the door repeatedly until he heard William's voice on the other side. 'What do you want?'

'Open up!' Jan screamed. 'Where's my sister?'

A fragment of silence followed as William weighed up the options. Whatever had happened had made him extremely scared and his reply echoed that.

'No, I won't open up. Basia is in the barn with the other women. Why don't you go and help Ethan contain the protest?'

Protest, what protest? He had no time to ask and simply shouted, 'Why don't you?' before dashing in the direction of the barn.

The doors were bolted shut. It took many minutes to get the attention of someone who knew his voice, and even then it took Basia herself to convince them it was her brother and there was no danger. Jan's eyes lit up as he saw her run to him.

'Basia, my dear Basia!' His voice trembled with relief. 'What's been happening? Oh God! I was so worried!'

They embraced. All before forgotten in that loving embrace of brother and sister. He felt her shaking in his grip before she felt his warmth and protection and calmed as she murmured a reply. 'It's been horrible, Jan. The villagers, some of them, are blaming the farm for the new store. They say it will kill the village. That we are supporting Healy's!'

Jan absorbed her words. So that was what it was. A new supermarket owned by Healy's! But it made little sense for the people to be angry, didn't it?

'What do they want with attacking the farm? Have they attacked anybody?'

'No,' Basia replied reassuringly. 'Many of the villagers who worked here are leaving. They want no part of this and they don't want the supermarket either. There have been massive protests at the village hall as well and windows smashed but the council, they have been paid off, Jan! Now the word has spread that the farm will hire more and more foreign workers.' She looked at him and he saw the fear of the future in her eyes. 'For now they are after William but soon, Jan, soon…'

'I will protect you,' he answered calmly. 'I will always protect you, Basia, and I will never lie or hide things from you again.'

She gazed at him and he saw that familiar love in her young eyes. 'I forgive you, you are my brother and all I have after all.' She gave him a watery smile adding, 'How was it…back home?'

'I could not go in.' Jan's head dropped. 'Not without you and not to see that. It was too hard, Basia, too hard.'

He did not want her to see him so weak, to see the tears roll down his face as he thought of that moment. She did not try to. Basia knew her brother only too well. She slipped her hand into his and let her soft voice soothe him.

'We'll be alright. We have each other, always.'

* * *

The mobile was still off. Terrance took his and flung it across the room watching it hit the far wall before smashing into pieces and hitting the floor.

268

'Fuck!' he yelled, storming across to the landline and grabbing the receiver. Two buttons pressed later and Reception answered, 'Mr Healy, sir.'

'Get me a new mobile phone up to my office now,' he growled before slamming down the receiver.

Taking a handkerchief he wiped his forehead as he walked towards the window overlooking the busy city below. In times gone by he may have gazed, power struck at the view, and thought of his empire out there. Those days had gone. Now all he could see when he looked out was that girl. She was out there somewhere.

A knock at the door was followed by an assistant bringing in a brand new phone. The attempt to make conversation was rebuffed instantly, Terrance's volley of abuse almost pushing her out of the door. Things were not good in his world. Since Francesca had returned they had seen each other just the once and that had been a near disaster. He had expected her to have heard about Domenici and his fractured cheek and broken nose. His only slight concern had been that she may have connected the incident with him. Nothing had been mentioned at all though. It had been worse than that. She had been as distant as the sun. Her body language and behaviour had made him feel rejected, generating emotions that had made him feel weak and powerless. She held all the cards.

He had agreed with her that she needed time, purely because he was under her spell and feared losing her. In reality he had no interest in much of what she wanted. He knew what he wanted. The time that he had spent with her had taught him something though. He would have to sing to her song sheet or risk losing her. The pain of not being in control of the one thing he craved the most was making Terrance Healy a very angry young man.

He could not hold back any longer. Slipping in the SIM card from the destroyed phone he dialled up the number. Ken Douglas replied, his abrupt response indicating he had been waiting for the call to act.

'Do you know where the girl is?'

'Of course, Mr Healy,' Douglas answered with a hint of arrogance. 'We could give you a list of places she has been over the last…'

Terrance butted in angrily, 'Don't bother giving me a bloody diary update. If I want one I'll ask, alright? Just tell me if she sees the Italian, okay?'

'Of course, Mr Healy, you're the boss.' Douglas's reply had sarcasm contained in its tone.

Terrance wanted to end the call there and then but obsession took over, and he felt the weakness come again as he tried to speak calmly.

'Where is she now?' He cringed at his own pathetic self as he waited for Douglas's reply.

'She's in a place called Point Clear, Mr Healy…alone.'

The gamble had paid off. Terrance Healy suddenly felt a lot better.

CHAPTER THIRTY-TWO

Pat Reilly made his way towards Westminster Cathedral. A self-confessed man of faith, he had always been open about and proud of his Catholic roots. Anyone that had ever met him knew that. Not everything had made sense in his life, but that faith had helped him through the worst of the many, many situations he had encountered, both as a human being and in his vocation as a surgeon. With the exception of Ray Skee's death, Pat had been able to understand, or at least reason with other events, but not this one.

Hurrying towards the Cathedral, Pat mulled over the situation. There was no solution, no righteous answer to the events of the past night. Pat Reilly did not have dreams. Maybe one or two as a small child, but those days were long gone and, being a bad sleeper as he was, Pat generally knocked back a dram of Scotch and the odd tablet which, like the whisky, helped to knock him out. Things were usually very straightforward in the world of Pat Reilly's dream patterns, until last night. His bulbous thumb awkwardly punched in the last letters of the text. He gave a sigh of relief and pressed the send button just as he entered the Cathedral itself. Now he hoped his friend would answer his message and in the meantime, well, Pat needed to talk to God.

* * *

The thing with a place like Point Clear that made it tranquil was the peace itself. The local community kept themselves to themselves. Francesca did not know anyone by name in the village. With just two shops and two pubs, the small population saw few outsiders except in the summer months when a thin trail of city folk headed down to the small caravan park set at the point of Point Clear a mile away. It was hardly a place to meet new friends, which suited Francesca perfectly. It also meant that anyone out of the ordinary would stand out a mile. So, when she saw them, she knew they should not have been there.

The supermarket was a good fifteen minutes walk from the apartment whereas a smaller shop-cum-sub-post office was just around the corner. It had quite a limited stock but held the basics, including the milk and coffee that made Francesca decide to stroll up there on that bright, warm morning.

Usually the light jangle of the bell as she entered would be followed by a greeting from the old man behind the counter or perhaps a nod if he was already engaged in conversation with one of the few locals that popped in, as she did, for an essential item. The two men she saw sidling out of the small entrance to the shop looked as out of place as two cherries on a dung heap. In the split second of eye contact she saw a look of surprise on the face of one while the other was too busy looking at his mobile to see her. The seconds that passed allowed her to take in their features. One had wiry hair matching a wiry frame and his face had a hard exterior which was exaggerated by a fearsome scar on his right cheek. The other was bigger built. He had a shaved head which made him look like a hooligan straight off the football terraces. The tattoo on his neck simply added to the illusion. It was the skinnier of the two that saw her and his startled reaction told her more than words could say. Her natural instincts went into overdrive as she sensed danger sending her senses tingling.

The door closed behind them leaving just the shopkeeper and her. He grunted a greeting as Francesca turned to see the men outside huddled together and talking while staring in her direction. Taking the milk and coffee she pretended to look at some greetings cards which were set in a rack near to the window. It gave her time to ponder the meaning of the two strangers. She watched them glance at her suspiciously. She felt her sixth sense inside her jangling like the bell of the shop. They were somehow something to do with her.

To the outside world the young lady that left the small shop whistling gently looked totally innocent. She stared ahead as she turned and began walking casually to the end of the street.

There she turned right and stopped, opening her handbag and slipping out a small make-up bag which contained a mirror, some lipstick and blusher. Francesca casually let the tip of the lipstick touch her lips as she raised the mirror to her eye line. To anyone else, including the two men following her a little way behind, nothing seemed out of the ordinary. For the girl whose eyes looked in the mirror it was a perfect way to survey the men behind her. She watched carefully whilst pretending to finish her make-up. Her suspicions were confirmed. The men had slipped inside a bordered driveway, the larger of the two poking his head clumsily around the conifers every few seconds.

It could only be the work of Terrance. That was the assumption she made whilst performing her surveillance. Even that explanation seemed extreme. Why would he have her followed? She had explained that she needed time alone to work things out and she had asked him to respect that. The calls had ceased but the texts had not, and despite her not replying they still cascaded into her inbox. That was until a day ago. The jigsaw pieced together in her mind: a day ago, maybe when these two men were sent to watch her. The thought of Terrance taking such drastic action made her stomach turn.

As a final test Francesca made a neat diversion to test the water. The road followed round to the left whilst the apartment was on the street veering off to the right. She passed that turning and carried on to the bottom of the road which she knew to be a dead end. If her theory was correct and they were not from around here then they would not know this as there was no sign. She knew there was just a small piece of disused land which had been part of a through road project that was never completed.

Francesca held the small mirror at a careful angle. It showed them following her from about twenty metres away as she reached the end of the street. There she walked onto the patch of land and waited. The stakes were high. If these men were anything to do with Terrance she would be safe. If not, it was a massive gamble.

Both Neil and Douglas looked gobsmacked as they turned the corner to see Francesca staring at them, hands on hips like an actress in the theatre playing out her scene.

'Seems you two are a little lost.' Her voice carried a confidence that belied her fear. This for her was really 'showtime'. 'I guess Mr Healy is going to be pretty jacked off when I tell him you two spoofs have goofed!'

Their reactions made her want to laugh. Neil looked awkward and lost whilst Douglas looked plain angry at having 'goofed'.

Francesca suddenly felt calm. She was now the boss and the two men had not even said a word yet.

'It seems we've got ourselves a little lost, lady. Perhaps you could give us some directions?' Douglas tried to sound menacing whilst looking totally unconvincing. It was time to act out phase two, the cunning plan. She remained silent for at least a minute, eyeing both men up and down as if they were her guards or, worse, guard dogs. Neil looked lost, conversation evading him like a candlestick out of wax. Douglas just waited.

After the pause, Francesca let loose. 'For those of limited intelligence like you two, I'll make the choices easy for you to understand.' Seeing Douglas bare his teeth in an attempt at a snarl she grinned. 'No offence intended, but you really are in an awkward position.'

'Seems to me that it's you in the awkward position, you stuck-up Italian bitch!' Neil's voice carried the harsh Scottish accent with added aggression. It had worked many a time before. If the pen could be mightier than the sword then Neil believed that the accent could be stronger than the voice. This time however he had underestimated his opponent.

'It would be helpful if you could keep the monkey quiet, Signor Organ Grinder.' She shot a smile towards Douglas. 'Or should I ask you to keep his mouth Jock-strapped, no pun intended?' Although nervous, she was enjoying herself but she had to be sharper, had to keep the upper hand. It was obvious that Douglas was the man to talk with of rules. 'I'll put it like this to you. I know who you are and what you're doing here. I'm sure that my "boyfriend" who's having me followed would be slightly aggrieved if he should find out that I've not only met you both but am also so angry with him for the intrusion that I end our slightly tense relationship on the basis of that.' She paused to let the penny drop. Douglas looked thoughtful, Neil blank-faced.

'I have no idea what information you may have been given on your "mission" but here's how I want to play things out. Terrance thinks I'm seeing another man, an Italian like myself.' She briefly cast a look of derision in Neil's direction. 'Terrance is worried that it could affect things but... there's no Italian here, gentlemen. I can afford to give you that information and do you know why...?'

Neil looked beaten. 'No idea? Why?'

'Because he would never believe you if you told him that we had met like this and I had told you that!' She laughed confidently, feeling a sense of power before slipping in the ace card. In boxing terms, she could see that both men's guard was down; time for the knockout punch.

'So, you see, we are both in a tricky situation.' Her voice gathered sweetness like a stick collecting candyfloss. 'I suggest this...I can tell you the truth as it's in both our interests. I am going to be here for some time, but for just how

275

long? Well, I don't want you to know, as we don't want any potential agreements broken before they're made, do we? What I will say though is this: you're being paid to watch me, to not let me out of your sight, so to speak. To watch out for any visitors…'

The silence confirmed everything she had surmised.

'I have no idea where you're staying but I do know it's near. Perhaps within a street or two so as to see any would-be *visitors*. My deal is this. Move yourselves up the road, a good mile or so out of my sight so that I can feel the peace that I came here for. In return I'll give you a mobile number which I'll use to let you know when I'm leaving here. That way, gentlemen, I am in fact almost doing your job for you.'

Douglas gave a thin, mean grin as he took in the deal. Neil simply blurted out his thoughts. 'So you're going to lie to your own boyfriend?'

Douglas weighed up the options before replying, a crooked smile on his pock-marked face. 'It seems good enough for me, little lady. We don't seem to have much alternative, do we?'

With a laid-back grin, Francesca nodded. 'Good, it's a foolproof agreement, even for two fools. You repeat one word of this conversation to your boss and he'll have no option but to sack you on the spot before trying to call me and explain.' Feigning sincerity, she added, 'I don't want him to know my whereabouts so…if I say anything, it'll be the same.'

'Agreed.' Douglas turned to leave, motioning for Neil to follow before shooting an inquisitive glance at Francesca. 'Just one thing. Why?'

She knew she had won this battle and the adrenalin begun to subside as she replied softly, 'You have no idea what it is to be followed by someone who says they love you, do you? Is that love? I need time to think and, more importantly than that, I need peace.'

* * *

The text had sounded urgent enough, and the fact the mobile was switched off when he decided to call was enough for him to close up shop and head straight there. Now, as he entered, it took a moment to adjust his vision and spot Pat amongst the many shapes hunched in prayer.

Harry eased himself along until he was sitting close enough to Pat to grab his attention with a well-timed clearance of his throat.

Pat acknowledged him with a nod as he broke prayer. 'Thanks for the invite, mate.' Harry showed his wide toothy grin. 'Though you could have told me it would cost me ten quid to get in!'

Pat smiled dryly as he whispered a reply. 'It doesn't cost you if you're here to pray. It's a church, Harry.'

'Ah, I see,' Harry countered. 'Well, I haven't quite got that far, Pat. So, can I ask why you sent me that rather strange-sounding text? I never thought you would ever need me.'

Sitting upright, Pat's expression showed a more than usual glint of mischief. 'Well, needs must. You were the only one I thought I could talk to. You know, with Steve not here and all that.'

'Thanks for the compliment.'

'Let's get out of here. It's easier to talk.' Pat signalled to leave. Harry nodded. 'You know, Pat, I think that was the quickest ten pounds I've ever spent.'

Outside Pat led them to a small bar where he ordered two Guinnesses and began to explain.

'Last night I had the most vivid dream of my life, Harry. It's one thing that shocked me because I don't dream.' As he took a sip of the black stuff, Pat saw Harry raise his eyebrows but he said nothing, waiting for Pat to continue. 'But, being a man of reason, I could have addressed that issue. The fact that the dream showed me clearly watching Ray Skee save my parents in graphic detail in a scene I had no knowledge of witnessing, well, can you imagine that?' Another quick gulp indicated he expected no reply. 'That's then followed by seeing myself,

myself, Harry! Trying to save Ray that tragic night. Well, there's no explanation for that at all.'

Harry thought before replying, 'It could be a suppressed subconscious, Pat. You know, coming back. It happens.'

Pat knocked back the rest of his pint and glared. 'If there were two images I didn't want to conjure up in my mind, they were the two, Harry.'

'Well, mate,' Harry shrugged, 'I'm no expert on such things but I can't see any other reason.'

Pat was not yet finished. 'As if that wasn't bad enough, I then saw Steve talking with two women somewhere I've never seen!' Seeing his blank stare Pat went on, 'I know, Harry, it's crazy.'

Harry was not sure what he thought or what to say. 'What were they doing then?' It was the only response he could muster.

Pat signalled for another pint. 'He was asking them why I couldn't save Ray and one of them replied, *He will save many more lives.* I mean…' Pat paused seeing the waitress coming up with his pint. Harry took the first sip of his.

Once she had moved out of earshot Pat continued, his face full of concentration. 'Then the moment that woke me bolt upright, mate! One of the two women he was watching in the dream turned to me as if I was actually there in that place!'

Harry was now transfixed. 'You are bloody joking! What did she say?'

Sitting back in his chair Pat recited the words clearly. '*All life is sacred, Pat Reilly.* She knew my name, Harry. Can you believe that?' Knowing it was a rhetorical question, Harry simply looked amazed as Pat closed his eyes to think before continuing, '*But you will save a most precious life and the balance will be restored.*' As he opened them again, Harry saw a crazed passion in his stare as he added, 'Her eyes warmed me as much as her words froze me. I almost wanted to speak but she understood my mind and the last words she uttered were, *You tried your best with Ray but it was to not be undone.*

You must understand.'

Harry watched as Pat rotated his glass on the table, the black liquid spinning with his thoughts as he travelled alone in that world briefly. Gulping the remainder of the drink Pat stared sombrely. 'Bejaysus, Harry, I spoke to God a while back and he had no answers to such madness.'

* * *

Her thoughts ran like rain down a window, cascading freely, uncontrolled droplets of emotions. The experience of a few days ago had left Francesca feeling differently about many things. Things she had formerly not even been aware of. The discovery of being followed, watched, on account of someone else's wishes, someone who was supposed to care for her. She felt a natural anger at that and wondered why she had not just confronted Terrance there and then. Blown the two men's cover and be done with it. Finished any contact with Terrance on the basis of that.

As the time had passed, she had come to terms with the reasons why not. Sadness that he could feel that possessive of her; a realisation that she too had warm feelings towards him, or at least she did before they were punctured by something she could never have thought. She felt both a fool and an idiot for letting even a minute part of Terrance Healy inside her heart. She had perhaps forfeited Domenici to become entangled with the Englishman. Now she felt empty and foolish and even more confused.

What to do now? The warm May morning found Francesca wandering down to the foreshore, a small picnic packed in her bag together with a pen and pad. She planned to work things out before she could face the *old life*, to write down all her emotions and face them full on.

It was a beautiful day, sky azure blue, grass Irish green, air vibrantly fresh. She settled down and began to scribble in no particular order. Things that made her smile, moments of joy, feelings that needed categorising. The first sheet filled and overflowed onto the second as the sun rose above like a reading light.

She had no idea how long she had been writing but hunger pangs interrupted her thoughts. Unpeeling the foil from the food, she took some bread and cheese and poured a little red wine into a plastic glass. Slowly she let the flavours of the bread and cheese combine with a sip of wine, washing the food satisfactorily down her throat. The warm air gently swirled around her, playfully lifting her long skirt in small pocket pushes, combing her hair with its invisible fingers, touching her face with its beauty. Today the winds had dropped, the air calm and, as she relaxed, so was Francesca.

After eating the food and drinking two glasses of wine, she felt at peace with the world. She let the landscape take her focus. The water around the creek stretched its blue fingers out onto the horizon, its watery folds caressing her ears with its bubbling sounds. The sanctuary that broke its pattern looked like a beach just out of reach. It was then, as she let her vision drift along the sandy ground, that she saw the man. Her heart jumped, making her snap out of her dreamy warm state instantly.

She had not seen either of Terrance's henchmen since that day. Now, straining her eyes, she could make out the shape of just one man, his blank face looking in her direction. She saw the boat, rocking clumsily on the far side of the sanctuary as if it was struggling to stay in one place, knowing it should not be there. He must have seen her looking. He moved swiftly towards the boat and clambered in.

Francesca felt coldness wash over her. The sun was still beating down but now it was cloaked in some kind of shadow, the shadow of panic. Francesca wanted to get up but could not move. Panic and fear at being watched like that were restrained by anger and curiosity. The boat moved away from the sanctuary and the shape grew larger. Oars for arms, a two pronged octopus, its tentacles creating a splash either side of the boat as it swung and headed towards her.

As the boat drew near she heard herself gasp. A gust of wind lifted the sheets she had written, tossing them upwards like confetti into the sky. She did not attempt to get them; she could no longer move.

CHAPTER THIRTY-THREE

'Let love flow through you and you will find that you cannot help but smile and laugh. For the one you love will be able to create such magic within your soul that it will be uncontrollable. There will be no word to describe so much. But, to make sense of it, you will call it love, true love.'

(Taken from the scriptures of Galgliel)

He came into focus but not close enough to be recognised. As she saw through the autumn yellows and browns that were bruises on his face, Francesca gasped, letting the name slip from her lips as if it had never been spoken.

Domenici…

The boat's stern thudded against the dry mud of the bank and now she stared at the man she could never have imagined in this place. His face was distorted as if her eyes were seeing him through a bottle-glass window. As he stepped from the boat his stare was fixed upon her. A smile cracked, making it look like another larger cut to add to the ones that scored his face. He began to walk towards her, a dream from the past alive once more. She saw him as he had been way back when. Long curly hair, the white shirt, the black trousers, and the voice that now called out to her: 'Hey, give me your hand!'

Stumbling forwards, Francesca let the dream engulf her. She fell into the boat and his arms in one movement. Her breath escaped from her as she felt his arms wrap around her shoulders. They held each other, desperately, longingly, forever, in just that moment. Every emotion she had felt that morning now washed into the water around her, to become instantly diluted and meaningless. The next thing she knew the boat was moving and she faced her past, a smiling face, cracked like a car window after a collision, his previously soft brown complexion now scratched like a gnarled tree.

'What happened to you, Domenici?' She finally broke from the dream as if realising she had the power of speech.

He forced the largest smile he could in her direction momentarily lighting up his face and joining the long cut that had scabbed over giving the impression his whole face was smiling. 'Shh, not now, when we are there.'

Francesca asked no more. The short journey to the sanctuary was as beautiful as she had ever experienced. The memories of her first meeting with Domenici fired through her body as she watched his strong arms lift each oar up to the sky and down to the water. It was like a journey of Nordic kings on their final passage to Valhalla yet her heaven was here and now and it was not to be a final voyage. Of that she hoped more than anything.

* * *

Greed is good. The saying made famous in the movie Wall Street and epitomised by man. Greed is simply that, greed. It distorts the mind and soul. It replaces kindness with cynicism, honesty with treachery. Greed starts as an idea to get something more. It forms as a raindrop before becoming a pool of thought which then becomes a torrential waterfall. Greed came to Stebdon, intent in destroying all in its way.

When Terrance Healy cut the ribbon to celebrate the opening of Stebdon's first, and only, superstore, he was not completely there: physically yes, mentally, no. If Albert Guild had wandered up and reminded him of the trip to his toy shop all those years ago, Terrance would have stared vacantly at him. Albert Guild did not come that day and Terrance had little recollection of the day. He cut the ribbon, faked a smile or two for the local press, and shut out any sounds of protest that reached him. It was business as usual, another store, and another town. Terrance Healy's synonym of the word greed was progress.

He left after an hour, his mind full of a woman and a phone call to say when she had left and where she had gone. Waiting was not a word he liked to be associated with. Like the company itself, Healys did not wait. They conquered. When he was gone from the village he did not even remember it remained, its heartbeat now squeezed by the new word in town...progress.

Sonnings Farm now thrived, thanks to the T Healy & Sons contract and another new store could only add to trade. The store opening was just one of many that had already opened that year across the country. More stores meant more work, meant more money. Greed...its clammy reach stretched into the hearts of men and women alike, filling them with false dreams of futures they could never imagine, and would probably never see. For now, progress meant more money, at least for William Sonning and his parents. For the farm it meant more work for the workers and a greater influx of outsiders to satisfy the demand. The villagers initially boycotted the supermarket. The outsiders cared not. Items were cheap, imported, good value, made the wages stretch further and improved their lifestyles – for a while. There is a rare moment when dusk can seem like dawn, when the soft sun lies on the horizon in the same fashion as it rises.

It is known as – *a false dawn.*

* * *

Domenici did not want to speak of the event that had led to his injuries. He did not want to speak at all. He just wanted to look into the eyes of the woman he had loved from the first moment they had found themselves touched by fate. Francesca understood that now. As they lay close on the sandy sanctuary, she understood everything. She knew, without words, how he had been hurt. Terrance had given her the answers already. She needed no words.

The warmth of the day was overridden by the heat of their bodies as they made love. The chain holding the coin slipped down onto the sand as they caressed and touched, each movement bringing them closer, each breath saying so much of the love they felt for each other. After a time, when their half-naked bodies glistened under the light of passion and desire, Francesca lay on her side, looking up at Domenici, whilst the coin remained hidden in the grains of sand around her.

The hours till dusk moved as if under a spell. Hardly a word had been spoken, only talk of love. Only now, as she was standing at the foreshore, did she find the need to speak.

'How did you find me?' Her voice had a commanding tone.

'I had to find you, or lose myself,' Domenici replied, eyes distant as he turned his head to the coast behind them. 'I came from the boatyard across there. I asked for help, and it seems that there were many willing to give it, Francesca.'

She contemplated his words and let the curiosity disperse. It did not matter really. This day had answered everything. He came close, his hand stroking her cheek, his eyes sad.

A panic surfaced. 'Where are you going?'

Dark eyes, lit with fire, stared back at her. 'I am going, Francesca. I am going home.' His finger moved to her lips, about to break open but now hushed by his motion. 'No, please, say nothing. I love you. I love you with all my heart, but I need to go, and you know where I will be. You asked me to wait and I have. You said you needed time to think and I want you to do that.'

'But, I think I know.' Her voice was faint. 'Please, Domenici, I have had time and I think I am ready.'

She stopped. His expression made her mouth shut tight and

she fought to stem the flow of tears.

'Think, Francesca… You say you think, but I know you need more time.' She saw the hurt now. 'We both know how we drifted apart and why. When…if…I see you again,' his voice trembled like a teacup in an ageing hand, 'I want it to be with a full heart. I want it to mean forever.'

She wanted to answer now. A part of her wanted to plead, but nothing happened. She felt her voice betray her, just as her mind and heart had. She let him turn and climb into the boat. Her pirate, her hero, her man, her love. She heard the oars cut into the water like knife blades into her soul. Splashes that followed, the sound of a giant's tears. And she watched him row towards the moon before she found the courage to speak once more, the words tumbling out, too quietly and too late.

I love you.

* * *

The impact of *progress* came like a ghost to Stebdon, translucent yet whole and meaningful. It began as a whisper in the night that became a voice carrying a message – progress.

Slowly the force gained momentum. It was the small delicatessen that went first. Forty years plus it had been there, three owners, same shop, selling the same things. Local produce from ham to honey, jalapeños to jams, all good things, all locally made by the loyal inhabitants of Stebdon. People who had forsaken change because change meant leaving and leaving meant change. Loyal people let down, changed, by progress. Glass windows full of produce became whitewashed windows full of white. Other shops followed like sheep.

Albert Guild saw the storm coming. He had that instinct after years of experience. The toy shop was just that: a toy shop. Albert Guild was not a building. He had senses, senses that could smell change in the wind. His fingers were chilli pepper red. Once it had been through the labour of his craft but now they were from pushing through his rough grey beard whilst he was deep in thought. The future was decided. He knew his hours of craft and wisdom had been wasted. He knew that a long time ago yet, for some reason, perhaps belief in humankind, he had toiled, shaped and created those puppets, that doll's house, that fort with those hands, tired and worn, yet loyal to the cause. He sighed that day. A deep sigh, signifying the loss of that belief, a breath of air from ageing lungs, once full of hope, now just empty dreams in an empty shop. It was not that his skills were not cherished. It was simply the fact that they cost too much, and the prices were key to the customer. Why buy something that was three times the amount when you could buy a copy of that same thing, albeit much lower quality from a place like Healy's? *The customer is always right, they say.* 'Long live the customer.' Albert let the words drift like ageing dust, blown from the cobwebs that sat on the old beams above. 'If only there was a customer.'

A few months later, October to be precise, Albert Guild's last effort at craft lay in the fountain pen that his skilful hand held. He pushed the ink against the white sheet, old style, old ways, drawing a picture in words that etched, gravestone like, against its opposite: **'NOTICE: Last week of trading, thank you for all your support over the years. 50% off until 1st November 2007'**

It was to be Albert Guild's epitaph. When his shop died, a part of him died as well. He closed the door that one last time and heard the jingle of the bell. Its rhythm had represented so much, for so many. The sound faded and the magic left him that day. Albert Guild, toymaker supreme, kind as a man could be, the shopkeeper most remembered by children died two weeks later aged sixty-seven. He was not an ill man and many who attended the funeral remarked on his death as that of a 'broken heart'. The truth was that Albert Guild died because he had done all he could on Earth and now it was time for him to take his craft onwards. The Angels needed him more than those below.

* * *

Jan Kowalik had never seen such a store in all his young years. Before Healy's came to Stebdon he had believed that all the other shops and stores, cafés, bars and pubs were similar to those back in Poland, just larger. When the change came, he noticed it more than most. He saw the extra workers, all manner of cultures and nationalities, learning from each other, clashing with one another but all working together for the beast that was their lord and master. Smaller contracts for the smaller shops were pushed aside. Deliveries less accurate, deadlines dismissed. Sonnings Farm did not need tiny orders anymore. They were just tiresome and time-consuming. The accounts lessened, but the work increased. Jan saw it all. Yet he did not see the inevitable evil coming.

* * *

She was just shy of twenty on that night. Blonde-haired, bright blue-eyed, chiselled Baltic features, a slim figure with artistic curves, her saucer-shaped eyes saw the world for all its beauty, innocently unaware of hers. It had to happen.

Darkened eyes, bristly stubble on weather-beaten face, thoughts aplenty, all as dirty as the mud he stood on. His mind filled with instructions from his loins. Temptation rife, resistance at an all-time low, knowing it was wrong yet yearning for it for as long as he could remember.

She felt the hands first, one around her mouth, the other around her neck, tightening like clamps on steel. Sounds exploded inside her but there was no way of letting them free into the night air. Her body dragged like a deadweight along the soft muddy ground leading to the small shed, eyes wide open with the horror. She breathed desperately through her petite nose. Her ears were suddenly aware of even the slightest sound as she was dragged into the shed, door creaking open, door creaking shut, and then a fragment of silence before she became aware of the noise, so much noise. Hers loud and fearful, his a laboured panting, laced with anticipation.

One hand moved now, trailing from her neck downwards, clumsily pawing at her breasts. She could feel his breathing increase, almost panting as the rough hand touched soft bosom skin, nipples, before he paused, paused to think. One hand only was all he could use unless…unless he struck her down, knocked her out, knocked her dead. She could touch his thoughts now, feel what he felt. One hand only or… The hand left her breast moving down to her skirt, pushing it upwards. She felt her bare thighs being scratched by his sharp fingernails, upwards, upwards. Pain and fear as he touched her there and then…

He stopped. She could almost feel his thoughts, sense his fear now. He could not do it. He could not hit her, kill her even, in order to fulfil his perverted desire.

She wanted to cry, to scream, to beg for mercy, but one hand remained over her mouth whilst she felt the other loosen its grip on her thigh. Basia prayed silently that the momentary signal of guilt would fester, that he would save himself from this act and, in turn, save her. Seconds passed, and then, he removed his hand from her thigh.

She heard him wipe his lips, swallow and gulp. The hand moved again, to the door, a gentle creak ringing like nails on blackboard through her mind. Then he pushed her downwards, her face connecting with the mud of the floor, soft and cool, a face mask made by a demon.

She waited. Waited for some other sound but there was none. Still she waited, terror coursing through her veins. Slowly she turned her face from the mud, so slowly, to glance behind. He was gone. She sat up in the blackness. He had gone. Tears came, a gentle crying of torment at what had just occurred. Relief that it had not happened, innocence destroyed.

He slid out into the night, eyes darting from left to right, surveying the yard, safe now. Creeping away from the scene knowing he had lost his nerve, feeling as filthy as he had become. Hard lump in trousers softening now as the terror of his own actions came into his conscience. Neither of them would ever forget that moment.

Basia crept out from the shed, a ghostly silhouette under the light of the moon. He watched her. The one that no one noticed, but that heard so much. He watched the shape move and confirmed its identity. Rusty was much cleverer than many gave him credit for and he liked it that way. He had overheard the man talk and now, having followed him, it had confirmed that his intentions were not just words.

He knew it had not happened. Not enough time. He knew that he could not go in the shed and comfort the girl. Could not risk that, not risk being the one to find her, the one she may have thought was the assailant. So he waited. From his hiding place he watched her peek out of the door. He watched her creep fearfully away, white of skirt becoming grey of distance, then black of out of sight.

He gritted his teeth and clenched his fists. Rusty knew wrong from right and he knew this moment was coming a long time ago. He felt hatred towards the man for bringing it to him. Involving him in something he wanted no part of. Now, as he watched from the shadows he faced his nemesis. To be the one to tell Jan. To be the one to speak with her. Or to say nothing and feel as guilty as the bastard who had wanted to rape Basia.

He knew then, at that moment, on that night, that so much in his life, their lives, was about to change.

CHAPTER THIRTY-FOUR

Holly shrieked out as she ran into the house, her face aglow with happiness. Jenny heard her first and rushed out to see what was happening.

'Oh my God, Mum! You'll never guess what?'

Jenny saw the portfolio in her hand and guessed what. She did not let that show though. Her daughter's expression willed her not to.

'Tell me,' Jenny feigned surprise, 'I can't begin to guess!'

'Well, Mum,' Holly sounded breathless, 'you remember that portfolio I had done on last term break?' She did not wait for anything more than a nod from Jenny. 'Well, there I was. Me and the girls having lunch in the King's Arms in Knightsbridge and this guy, he approaches me and asks me if I have done any modelling. Well, I say kind of, right?' She giggled as Jenny smiled. 'So I tell him, and he makes a call to the agency where I had the portfolio. He gets it couriered down to the pub while we're having lunch. Can you believe that?'

Holly's whole appearance looked so astounded that Jenny could not help but feel amused rather than impressed. 'With you, darling, anything is possible! Go on, so what happened?'

Flapping the portfolio in one hand while waving the other, Holly tried to remain composed. 'He got the package, sat on his own and went through the pictures and then came back over.' She breathed in and began to speak in a deep voice which sent Jenny into raptures. ' *"Very impressive,"* he said, *"just what we're looking for."* So I asked what it was about and guess what? I have a modelling shoot this Friday! For a well-known brand of body and facial creams.' She put a finger to her smiling lips as she added, 'Can't say who at this point, Mum; company thing, you know.'

Jenny gave her a hug. 'I'm very proud of you. Do you know what type of modelling it will be?'

'Well, creams, Mum.' Holly pondered. 'He just said it's going to be me and a very dark-haired girl apparently.' She shrugged. 'No idea who, he just said it was a kind of black and white thing, darkness and light, me being the lightness, of course!'

Terrance entered the room as Holly ran her fingers through her long blonde hair and began dancing around the room à la Cinderella.

'What's got into you?' he growled.

'I am going to be a model, dear brother!' She laughed as she sang out the words. 'A model with a degree, that is to be me!'

Terrance looked disgruntled. 'You're going to be a model? Wow. Cosmic stuff, sister.' He looked at his mother. 'Seen anything of Dad?'

Holly ignored his rudeness as she leapt in front of him. 'No, but I want to speak to him and tell him about this!'

'Shut up!' Terrance barked out the words, his eyes glinting with anger which made Holly instantly silent. 'I need to speak to him, about business. You know the thing that pays for everything around here! You can tell him your little fairy tales later, alright?' With that, he muttered something under his breath and stormed out, leaving Holly looking bemused and upset.

Jenny put her arm around Holly to console her. 'Don't worry, darling. He doesn't mean it. He's just been a bit tense these last few days, must be work.'

'Don't defend him, Mum!' Holly retorted angrily. 'He's an absolute jerk! All he cares about is himself and please, don't think it has anything to do with work! I bet it's that girl! I bet she's seen what a complete idiot he is and wants nothing to do with him. Well, he deserves everything he gets!'

Before Jenny could say another word, Holly had slammed the portfolio on the floor and stormed upstairs tearfully. Her pictures scattered across the marble floor leaving an angry and confused mother to view a montage of her daughter.

* * *

The weeks that had passed had left Francesca to her own thoughts. She knew the answers, she always had really. Yet there was something that touched her deeply. Something that almost defended Terrance's actions: perhaps pity, perhaps his total interest in anything she did, perhaps his flattery, perhaps, she thought one day as she stared in the mirror, it was his gift of the coin. It mattered not anymore. She had made her decision to go to Italy, and her discovery earlier that morning had simply strengthened her belief.

Somehow she had never contemplated taking the Angel coin off. Now she considered it.

Unclipping the chain she let the coin slip into her hand. She loved it very much. Its beauty, its gleaming glory, the way it touched whatever light came its way and reflected it into golden. For a moment she felt lost without it and found herself wishing that it had been Domenici who had given it to her. It was the feeling that it gave her. It was as if she was *meant* to wear it. The indecision made her smile. She slipped it into her coat pocket where it nestled alongside the pregnancy-testing kit.

* * *

The conference was tiresome, the temperature blazing hot. Outside, in the Bordeaux streets, the flowers wilted and the tar became sticky. Sitting outside was not an option and inside, even with air conditioning, things were barely comfortable.

Terry was tired. Tired inside, and tired of events such as this. As an ambassador of the company, he had envisaged an easier lifestyle. Less hours, more time at home with the family, happier days. At fifty-three years of age, he had worked the life of someone double his age and it had caught up with him. Healy's had almost six hundred shops with plans for another one hundred and fifty a year in the UK and vast expansion in all the major cities in Britain before laying siege to Europe over the next decade. That was to be Terrance's mission. Young, determined, aggressive: all the qualities required to survive and prosper. Why was it then, with all the success, all the money, that Terry felt a little disappointed with things, disillusioned even? He saw his family rarely. The trips could be a week long, sometimes more, and when he did return home it was almost like meeting a new group of people. Terrance had become someone he was not sure he even liked. His own fault really: too cut-throat, too aggressive. When a conversation took place between father and son he knew what it would be about: work, one word, one subject, always.

Holly hardly spoke to him but at least she was warm when she did. He blamed himself for that as well. Neglecting her so much over the years, and Jenny…the wife who had loved him so much, agreed with his decisions to move, to buy, and to decide. He didn't even know her anymore.

He looked around at the faceless suits meandering nearby in the conference room. Aimless stares, repetitive conversations about money, power, stocks, products, all wanting to get where he was now. He hated the people suddenly. He hated the room and he hated Terry Healy. Making a brief excuse, not that he had to, Terry left the room and went to the toilets. A wave of nausea washed over him as he walked into the cool marble tiled washroom. Heading for the sink, he pushed his hand onto the tap and let the cool water spurt onto his palms. Unable to concentrate, his face stared into the mirror, the reflection unrecognisable. The water splashed onto his face, as his stomach twisted, sending a spasm of anxiety from his diaphragm. Questions came with dark answers now. His arm tingled and a pain surged through his chest. The water ran down from his forehead, mingling with perspiration, heading for his startled eyes. Hands went to chest in shock as fear overwhelmed him.

Crashing onto the floor, Terry felt his chest become tighter, his mind sending messages of poison, scrambling his thoughts, rendering him useless. Then, the pain stopped almost as suddenly as it had begun, leaving him sweating profusely and gasping for air. There he remained for a few minutes trying to gather some sense of composure as the reasons ran riot in his mind.

A short while and a good wash and smarten up later, Terry returned to the hall, whispered some instructions into his assistant's ear and walked out of the conference.

* * *

The journey had been uneventful enough. After speaking with Stefano and Nicole, the latter had taken her to the airport, a quiet smile on her lips at her daughter's impulse to go and see Domenici. Francesca said little on the journey, her mind overflowing with excitement tinged with doubt. Hours later, Francesca arrived back in the small Italian village. The day was warm and fragrant. Summer flowers blossomed all around her as she headed towards the river. Once there, she took the small path that ran alongside and made her way to where she knew he would be.

Domenici sat on a grassy verge under the bridge, his head bent, studying the canvas, brush in hand. Francesca walked around and approached him from behind, taking in the two images as she did so. One on canvas, one he was drawing from, the difference minimal. The swans that nuzzled necks in real life were briefly joined as one before they swam away from each other, the moment caught on canvas. The plants moved by the air that shifted them gently.

'It's very beautiful.' She said the words softly. Even so, he almost dropped the brush as he spun round, narrowly avoiding the easel with his knees. 'I'm sorry. I didn't mean to surprise you.'

'Well, surprise me you did.' His face was alight. 'Francesca! You've come back.' He paused, a slant of doubt visible on his scarred expression. 'Does that mean…you've decided?'

Kneeling down by his side, she kissed him on the cheek before they embraced fully. 'I knew that moment you came to Point Clear, Domenici. I knew then. But now it is you who must decide.'

He let his grip on her loosen so that he was holding her at arm's length. 'If you're sure, Francesca, then so am I. I always was, even when I knew someone wanted your heart.' His head dropped a little, the thoughts weighing him down as he whispered, 'Even then, darling. There is nothing for me to decide. I love you. I want to be with you…forever.'

Running her fingers delicately through his hair, Francesca's eyes shone with tears of happiness. 'Then I am the luckiest girl alive to have you, and I hope that you will be proud when I tell you that you are to be a father, Domenici.'

The words illuminated his expression. 'You're pregnant? Francesca, you're pregnant?' As she nodded, he leapt up, grabbing her hand and swinging her around as he yelled out with joy, 'I can't believe it! I can't believe it! This is the best news! Does anyone know? Have you told your parents? When did you find out? Oh my God, this is amazing!'

She laughed with him as the relief rushed through her body. 'I haven't told anyone, darling. I had to see you first. I had made up my mind that day in Point Clear but you told me to take more time and then…yesterday morning, I did the test. Domenici, we made a baby! We made it that day you came back for me!'

He hesitated for a moment and she saw the slightest flicker of doubt. 'What? What is it? Please, Domenici, what is it?' As she said the words, she felt his thoughts. 'No, Domenici, nothing happened with him. I do not want him. I just want you. I'm going to tell him as soon as I get back.'

The doubt extinguished as quickly as it had arisen. His eyes softened, almost thanking her. 'I am so happy, Francesca. We are to be a family.'

* * *

He sent the text message and then made the call.

'I'm sorry, sir. Your father has cancelled all calls to his mobile and office. He is taking some time off and does not want to be disturbed.'

'Yes, I understand that, you already said that, but I'm not any bloody one. I'm his son and I need a word with him!'

'I am aware of that, Mr Healy. I'm simply following instructions. He made it quite clear that he was not to be disturbed by *anyone.*'

'Right, well thank him when you speak to him next and tell him his son says hello!' Terrance's voice was laced with anger and sarcasm. 'Thanks for nothing.'

He cut the line dead before she could say another word and dialled up another number, pacing impatiently as he did so.

'Yeah, Trevor, hi, Terrance, look. I'm going to have to skip the meetings today. Something's come up.' He became more agitated as he heard Trevor's reply. 'Yes, you idiot. I know they're important but that's what I pay you for! Just tell them what they want to hear and push the plans through! Offer the councillors new roads and all the usual stuff, damn! Offer them a bloody new school if that's what it takes! Just do it. I'll call you when I can.'

Arrival of a text message vibrated on the phone as the call ended. Flicking through to his inbox Terrance opened the message eagerly.

It was to Italy as you suspected. She returns on the late plane tonight. Arrival at Gatwick at 23.30 Flight no 22349.

He closed the phone knowing that by the end of the night his world was either going to be complete, or shattered. For once in his life Terrance had lost control and it scared the hell out of him.

* * *

He saw his world collapse as soon as they made eye contact. He had watched her walk elegantly through Arrivals, her walk as light and happy as her expression, until she saw him. Then that look vanished immediately, as did any hope of her wanting him. He knew it before a word was uttered.

At first Francesca thought about walking straight past him. As soon as she caught sight of him, her heart had sunk into her stomach. Terrance moved from the railings towards her. It was going to have to be now, before her mother arrived.

'What is happening to us? What has happened to us?' His arm grabbed her wrist as she came within reach. His face contorted, a lover scorned. 'You never told me you were going to Italy, to see him.'

Francesca snapped back as frustration and anger overflowed. 'Let go of me!' Her voice was loud enough for bystanders to hear. He released his grip. His eyes pleading for her to talk, she was in no mood. She was going to have to be cruel to be kind.

'It's over, Terrance.' Her words cut him down without hesitation. 'It never really began. I love Domenici. I'm sorry. Now, let me go.'

'But, Francesca,' he had lost all senses, 'I love you. We belong together, please, I'll do anything.'

'Then let me go.' Her reply was firm.

His world came crashing down on him at that moment. As Nicole arrived and hugged Francesca, he watched in silence. Hearing nothing, seeing only the loss of the woman he needed more than anything.

There was a brittle silence as Nicole looked at Terrance, then back to Francesca, waiting tactfully for someone to say something. Pride kicked in suddenly as he wiped his tear-stained face. Francesca went to speak, but hesitated at the last moment. It was enough. Terrance turned and left the airport.

* * *

Stefano was called into the office at last. His palms were a little sweaty with anticipation. This was going to be a crucial moment for him, for his family, for their future. He had been unable to speak to Nicole about it. It had always been his choice. Now he would have to make the biggest decision of all, alone.

The bank manager shuffled through the wad of papers before him before giving a glance of acknowledgement in Stefano's direction.

'Well, Mr Riza, we have taken a careful look at everything and your request has been accepted.' He cleared his throat as he picked out three sheets of freshly printed paper. 'Based on your forecasts, we feel the loans can be met without too much problem. That is, of course, as long as business continues to keep up.'

Stefano felt both relief and tension at his words. It was a massive gamble but one that would secure everything. 'The figures and sales are there for you to see. It's simply a case of expansion. Our biggest client is growing at an astounding rate.'

'I agree,' the bank manager replied, a look of concern present. 'We feel that it is good business with the only risk being losing the contract.' Raising his eyebrows he added, 'That could happen, Mr Riza, we have to be aware of that.'

'Of course, but the loan is accepted, you say?' Stefano knew the risks.

Another cough, almost habitual it seemed, before the manager answered. 'Yes, in principle. We simply need a degree of security as I mentioned before. Now, looking at your assets, it seems that the two properties in England should provide enough security along with the business itself, of course.' Stefano saw a last chance to change his mind as the manager glanced up. 'Are you happy with that, Mr Riza?'

The pen divided the two men, along with the dark mahogany table. Stefano nodded as he took the pen, its content ready to deliver a binding agreement. One that would change all for better or worse, but change all. He signed the forms.

CHAPTER THIRTY-FIVE

'Nothing is as complicated as you see it. For an Angel, all is simplicity and simplicity is all. The night sky is black, the stars are bright. The darkness of evil is that sky and we are the stars. Your soul is your inner beauty. Listen to it and always cleanse it, for when you leave this Earth it will be all you are.'

(Taken from the halls of Angels)

News of Francesca's pregnancy was the main topic of conversation in the Riza household. Nicole had been delighted, as had Stefano. He tried to keep a positive outlook on things, but inside he was worried. The summer months had proved to be some of the strangest in many a year. After a heatwave in April the rains came, relentless and harsh. The summer was over before it even began. For some people, it made little difference. For Stefano it made him even more edgy. The funds were in the account but the orders were not forthcoming anymore. He kept it quiet. He had no one to speak with. All around him was happiness and plans for a bright future. He held the keys to that future. They were beginning to feel more like a heavy chain.

* * *

Jan was becoming a little concerned with his sister's new introverted behaviour. She seemed withdrawn, quiet, and almost reclusive.

He was not the only one who had noticed it. To bear the burden of knowledge was becoming even harder for Rusty. Something needed to be done, something needed to be said.

It was in late August that Rusty found his moment. He stood outside, watching carefully as the office emptied. Then he went in, leant against the counter and waited.

'Evening, Rusty.' Billy looked surprised. 'You come for an early sub on your wages?' His smile made Rusty want to retch.

'No, I'm fine for money,' Rusty replied easily. 'Plenty of work here at the moment. I'm here to help you as it happens.'

Billy laughed. It was meant to be a confident laugh, but as the two men faced each other Rusty detected nervousness, the slightest hint of that deeply submerged guilt.

'Help me? I don't think there's anything you could do to help me, my friend.'

Rusty smiled back. 'Is that so? Well, perhaps I can try. Let's see what I know. You're a married man, I believe. Been on the staff for many a year. Well respected, well liked, for the most part.' Rusty let the words sink in. He watched Billy's expression as the shame began to soak through his pores. 'I think I can help you. I think I can help you save yourself, Billy Jones. What do you think?'

'I don't know what you are talking about,' Billy replied nervously. 'I haven't done anything.' His look reeked of culpability.

'Really?' Rusty's gaze was assured, offering an almost compassionate smile. 'I suppose that's one of the things I have been wondering since that night actually. Why you didn't follow it through? It's your call, Billy. Just remember, the camera *never* lies.'

His bluff worked instantly. Billy lost the last remnants of his composure. The strain showed clearly as he spoke. 'I didn't do it, Rusty! I didn't do anything! God, I nearly did and I was so ashamed of myself that I couldn't go through with it.' He pleaded now. 'You must believe me!'

'I do. Only because I was there,' Rusty replied sternly. 'Why you, Billy? Of all the people, why you? She's a bloody kid, for Christ's sake! A young girl who's never hurt anyone! Jesus, if Jan were to find out…'

Billy brushed past, closing the door and slipping the lock before turning to Rusty, his voice trembling. 'I beg you, please, don't say anything! I know it was wrong but I did have my reasons. I shouldn't have done it. I was tempted, I admit. But I didn't hurt her, Rusty, I didn't…' he spat the last words out, 'rape her.'

Rusty flung out his hand, grabbing Billy around the throat with a power that belied his appearance. 'Now you fucking listen to me, Billy Jones. Those poor kids left their home to come here and find a new future. Their father is dying as we speak and if it just so happened that Basia was hurt, well…' His eyes showed a menace that made Billy cringe. 'I, Jan, anyone who cared, would be sworn for revenge. Now you tell me what reason you can possibly think of for taking that girl and scaring the innocence right out of her? You tell me that!'

The grip loosened, leaving Billy to cough and splutter for a moment. With a trembling voice he forced out a reply. 'I was going to tell her, Rusty. That was my plan. I'm not a bad man, I swear!'

'Tell her what? If you want this to disappear then this better be good!'

Billy dropped his head as trepidation seemed to take hold. 'I can't say, Rusty.' Looking up through fearful eyes, he added, 'If they found out…I would be…'

He felt his head pulled back as Rusty grabbed his hair in one hand, the other producing a gleaming sheaf knife. He pushed the tip of the blade against Billy's throat, letting the edge push into his flesh enough to draw blood. 'I should have told you from the start, Billy Jones,' Rusty whispered in a sinister tone. 'You don't have a fucking choice. Say what you have to say or I'll cut your throat and end your life where you stand.' He kept his eyes fixed on Billy as the blade pushed a little deeper.

'You say you're not a bad man. Tell me what you know.'

Billy nodded. Rusty loosened the grip of the knife. 'Talk fast, Billy Jones.'

Sweating profusely, Billy said, 'They're going to hurt her, Rusty. Ethan and a few others, I heard them talking about it. Filthy stuff, vile ideas, they're going to get her. I heard, and I smiled as if I agreed with them. Ethan thinks she's cheap, worthless and good for one thing only. When I heard, I said to myself I would grab her first one night. Pretend to scare her but whisper a warning to her. Tell her that this was not real but it would be next time.' Sobbing now, he went on, 'I…I…I got her, that night. I took her there into the shed but then even I was tempted, for a moment, just a moment. I felt the guilt and got scared. I never told her anything about the warning. I just left. I'm sorry, I'm so sorry!'

His voice trailed into gulping sobs as Rusty looked on, his mind working furiously. He let Billy contemplate his guilt before he spoke again.

'No one will know of this night, Billy Jones, but you must swear one thing to me. I'm going to try and get Jan and Basia to leave here before anything bad happens to her. You must promise that you will let me know about any plans, or **anything** you hear, alright?'

'Yes, yes, I will.' Billy looked up gratefully. 'Thank you.'

'Don't thank me,' Rusty answered with contempt. 'You may have saved that girl's life, you know. One thing's for sure though. You've just saved yours.'

* * *

'Terrance, we need to address a few issues so if you can just spare half an hour?'

'I really am not in the mood, Trevor.' He replied to his assistant's request with venom. 'Why don't you try and get hold of my father and have a word. You might get more response out of him than I have.'

Trevor sighed as he poured two stiff drinks from the decanter. 'This is important. The summer has been a disaster and the quarterly profits are going to be damaged massively. All I'm asking, sir, is for a little time to go through some of the figures and stocks and decide on a strategy.' Offering a glass to Terrance, he added gently, 'Please, sir. This is not for me. It's important for all of us.'

Terrance knocked back the Scotch in one, pushing the glass back towards Trevor. 'Alright, let's make it quick. What have you got to say and what do you suggest?'

While he leaned on the desk of the spacious office, Trevor thumbed through some pre-prepared notes. 'Right, the main products that have suffered are obviously seasonally related.'

'Obviously, Trevor, tell me something I wouldn't know.'

'Well, sir, let me see,' Trevor continued undeterred through the notes. 'There are a few large suppliers who we buy from: BBQs, garden furniture, that kind of thing. I suggest we contact all of them and advise that the figures have not reached their supposed potential.' He shot a sly smile in Terrance's direction. 'We'll *suggest* that we receive a price reduction for next year...or...be forced to look elsewhere for a new supplier.'

Terrance grinned. 'I like it, Trevor, I like it. You know that some of them will come back with *"Well, it was due to the weather"* of course?'

'Of course, sir,' his expression laced with humour, 'but we reply, *"Well, we're not responsible for the weather, are we?"* It's a choice they'll have to discuss at their next board meetings. Amuse us, or lose us; what do you think?'

Terrance walked over to him, pausing a moment before slapping his back, a grin appearing. 'I think it's tops. That's why I employ you, Trevor. How many companies do you have on the shortlist?'

'About fifteen so far but maybe more once I scan through the computers. One thing though, sir...' he glanced up, 'one of these companies is Italian. I thought you felt...'

'I fucking hate Italians!' Terrance's eyes bulged with fury as the word cut into his pride. 'Let me take a look.'

Trevor passed the notes over and waited as Terrance scanned the sheet. His expression suddenly became taut with bitterness.

'The owner is a Mr Stefano Riza.'

'Sorry, sir, that means nothing to me.' Trevor looked bemused.

'It doesn't matter.' He spat the words out. 'This company, I want gone.'

'I thought you would, sir, Italians and all that.' Trevor scanned the contract. 'They still have one year left though, sir. That could cause legal complications. We can't break that unless…'

'Unless bloody nothing!' Terrance screamed. 'Break the contract! Find a reason. Bad sales, bad service, bad anything! Just cancel this contract and do it today!'

Terrance approached him and tore the contract from his grip, his face riddled with scorn as he screwed it into a ball.

'I'll look into it, sir,' Trevor replied fearfully.

With a thin-lipped smile, Terrance unfolded the crumpled piece of paper, shoving it into Trevor's top pocket.

'Look into it?' Terrance snarled. 'That's good, Trevor. You do that, because your job depends on it.'

CHAPTER THIRTY-SIX

Stefano sat alone. His gaze was fixed on the glass of wine that he held almost tenderly in his hand. In the background the soft sound of Classic FM wafted around the penthouse apartment he was in for the weekend. One of three properties Stefano owned. The house in Knightsbridge was home for his wife Nicole this weekend, while his daughter Francesca would be relaxing now in the farmhouse in Italy with his parents. He wished he was there right now, in San Piceno, at home.

He sighed before gulping down the glass of Montepulciano in one hit. It did not taste anything like as nice as normal. No depth, no character, no feeling. Stefano Riza felt the sad similarity to his world. The glass of wine reflected him at that moment.

Instead of hurling the glass at the vast mirror that adorned the rear wall of the spacious lounge, he softly lowered his hand to hear the sound of crystal glass on crystal table creating a reverberating 'ting' that is normally associated with celebration. Not now. The phone call had changed everything.

Taking the envelope in his hand he stood and walked over to the French doors. Pushing them open, he stepped out onto the vast balcony to view the Point Clear summer evening. He had loved this place when he and his family had come to view it; Point Clear, what a beautiful name, which surely did justice to its location. A quaint seaside village set seven miles from the town of Clacton-on-Sea. It had exclusivity but also the beat of life close enough to touch.

With numbness he had never experienced before, Stefano gazed out at the golden sands which filled the eye like a never-ending carpet waiting for the red of the sunset to turn the landscape into something any film premiere would be proud of.

The beautiful creek stretched out beyond, separated only by the small sandy stretch of land, home to a bird sanctuary. The only images that broke this constant arc of peace were a simple wooden rowing boat moored up with ageing rope and a crooked jetty that connected the land with the water. Tranquillity reigned supreme. It was, and always should be, a place to reflect, relax and refresh. Yet, at that moment, he hated Point Clear. He hated England. He hated himself.

Leaning over the iron railings, Stefano peeled back the lip of the envelope which had remained sealed for twenty-seven years and slid out its contents. Breathing in deeply, he began to read.

LAST WILL AND TESTAMENT OF ME STEFANO RIZA

He scanned the address and then noticed the flat he was living in back then was as much a part of history as the content that followed.

I hereby revoke all former Wills and testamentary dispositions hereto before made by me and declare this to be my last Will and Testament.

*I appoint **Emilio Riza** of Fourteen Via Escalo, Ascoli, 3157 Italia to be Executrix and Trustee of this my Will (hereinafter called "my Trustee") but if he should fail to survive me or be unable or unwilling to act then I appoint **Cesare Bertolini** of Via Terenza, St Piceno 2890 Italia to act as Executor and my Trustee pursuant to the provisions of this, my Will.*

Stefano paused and, for the first time in what seemed like forever, he smiled. It was not a smile we would be familiar with, not a smile of joy, or of happiness, nor contentment. Those days, those smiles had gone. This was a wry smile. He spoke softly and his breath carried his words out into the August night. 'Emilio, Cesare....'

The pain of the car crash in 1980 that had cost the lives of his brother and his dearest friend resurfaced and simply added to his desolation. Seven long years had passed from that horrific night before he had met Nicole Simione and rediscovered a love for the world.

Back then, his life had been so different and now here, of all places, he had opened up a can of long suppressed worms without even knowing it. Stefano cast his mind back to the day he was given the will. Emilio, smiling, long tousled hair, film star looks, laughing as he handed him his sixteenth birthday present. Stefano had opened the envelope then and stared, unsure of what exactly his brother had just given him. 'It is always good to have things planned out,' Emilio had said, laughing. Stefano knew then and knew even more now. Nothing in this world can be planned. Time allows only guesswork.

It was so long ago now, so long ago that even the memory of his comrades had faded like the sun, only to be awakened by the flimsy sheet he held in his hand. He had envisaged the end so many times. The journey from Rome to England, two people, two lifelong friends who were probably listening to music, chatting without pause, embracing the moment as they always did, before the lorry changed their lives, ended their lives, ended their friendship, stolen a brother, taken a friend, broken so many hearts along the way. The years that had passed from then until he met Nicole had been as empty as the darkness of space itself, yet now in this deep abyss he had been close to falling into, Stefano felt an emotion at last: tears of pain and suffering.

The moments passed as the droplets of yesterday fell.

Eventually the tears ceased to fall from his vacant stare. So much had been decided in that fragment of time. That was then and this was now; the years had been kind to him for he had met Nicole the saviour mother of his beautiful daughter Francesca. The prominent facts on the sheet of paper now screamed out at him: his will was outdated and pathetic. He had not thought of death for so long.

The night was as inky black as his soul. Tonight could not be the night. His plan could not be executed. It would not be fair, not until he had changed his will.

Suicide would have to wait.

CHAPTER THIRTY-SEVEN

'Be humble and take a moment to ask yourself which material possessions are that important. They are enjoyable, luxurious, but beware the person it can make you become. Material things can make material people and you will find yourself surrounded by others of the same ilk. But you cannot take material objects with you when you die. I, Galgliel, can tell you that in your last breaths on Earth all of your life will flash before you. You will then know how many people really cared and you will know whether your once material cravings actually made you. Enjoy material things, but remember that real things are much more precious.'

(From the scriptures of Galgliel)

His nights had been mainly sleepless. The dreams when sleep came were dark and haunting. The fabric of his world seemed to have frayed, eroded. Now he had to face oblivion, of his own making. Stefano looked in the rear-view mirror. He looked how he felt: shattered. The lights shone from within the house like the beaming pupils of the two people that were within whilst his own felt dimmed. Another hour passed until he had plucked up the courage to leave the vehicle. The day had been hell. It had all been hell since the phone call. One call that surely crushed his empire into dust, the empire he had built with his family and one that he and he alone had been responsible for.

The initial warm greetings lasted just a moment or so. Nicole turned from the hob, pasta simmering gently behind her, to give him the loving kiss that always awaited his return. Francesca was standing by the breakfast bar, her face warm and radiant at the sight of her father and her own inner happiness. Instantly they both knew something was wrong. Stefano watched the alarm cross their faces. He heard their words of concern before he sat at the table and buried his head in his hands.

'What's wrong, darling?' Nicole's caring voice melted into his subconscious.

'Papa, say something. You're scaring me!' Francesca's arms enveloped his neck bringing warmth and pain combined.

'I am so sorry.' He found the courage to speak. 'I've lost it all. I've failed you both.'

'Please, Stefano, what are you saying?'

He breathed in deeply and blurted out the news in colourless tones. 'I've been with the bank today. They are looking to close the business down. We may lose everything. The house here, the house in Point Clear, the business itself.' He shot a sorrowful glance at Nicole. 'I should never have taken that contract. I should have listened, confided in you. I am so sorry.'

'What has that got to do with the bank?' Nicole sounded bemused. 'What's happened with the contract? Stefano, what's happened?'

Francesca simply looked confused. 'Papa, what are you talking about?'

Stefano felt Nicole's hand slide onto his. 'Please, Stefano. Tell us what you've done. I love you. We love you. We'll understand.' Glancing at Francesca she added, 'Won't we, sweetheart?'

Through glazed eyes he saw Francesca nod. Their love made him feel even more wretched as he tried to explain. 'The contract we, I signed, along with the other business we have presented a new problem.' Stefano sighed. 'One I thought I could deal with. It was making things more difficult for cash flow. You know how long they take to pay, Nicole. I had to do something.' Biting his lip in anguish he went on, 'I went to the bank and extended our overdraft together with a new loan. A loan secured on everything, except our home in San Piceno.'

Nicole's jaw dropped as the impact dawned on her.

Stefano continued, voice full of torment. 'They called me – Healy's, that is. They said they were cancelling the contract immediately based on breach of conditions. I argued at first. I told them we had not done anything wrong! We hadn't, Nicole, we had done nothing! The summer had made things hard, but with the money we would be okay. They said they weren't happy and were taking their trade elsewhere, just like that.' Stefano slid his head into his hands as he felt the impact of his own words.

Nicole was speechless. She felt neither anger nor sorrow. Just numbness that her husband looked so destroyed. It was Francesca who broke the silence.

'You said Healy's, Papa? You had a contract with Healy's? Why did no one say anything to me?'

It was Stefano's turn to look bemused. 'Darling, it was between your mother and me. Why would we want to concern you with such matters?' A faint smile of affection found its way onto his lips as he added, 'You have your own things to be concerned with. You're going to be a mother.'

'Don't either of you realise?' she replied in a shocked voice. 'This is not to do with you or your company! This is to do with me! The man I was seeing was called Terrance, Terrance Healy! I finished it with him and somehow he has found out about you and the connection, Papa.' Her voice reverberated with anger. 'This is his attempt to hurt me, don't you see?'

Stefano stared at his daughter whilst Nicole let out a gasp of disbelief. Before Stefano could respond, Francesca was shouting at the top of her voice. 'It doesn't matter! It cannot matter! If this is what he thinks will hurt us then he's a fool. Isn't he, Mama, Papa?'

Her tears ran into their hearts, her sincerity and honesty into their souls. Suddenly nothing mattered. Nothing could harm them. They had each other.

'Yes, darling.' It was Nicole that answered. 'He cannot hurt us, ever, can he, Stefano? We are stronger than that, than him.'

Stefano watched his wife and daughter hug, each comforting the other, before they turned and hugged him. The relief was infinite, indescribable.

'I love you both so much.' His voice cracked with emotion. 'So much.'

* * *

Jenny let the Range Rover slow down gently as she approached the building. It did not look anything like the image she had of a rehabilitation centre. She had imagined a daunting building, grey stone walls, barbed wire, electric fences even. The building she faced was more of a castle, picturesque and homely, set against the backdrop of a loch. Had she not checked the address once again, she would have believed she was staring at a place more akin to a Scottish hotel for lovers than a home for reformed drug addicts.

* * *

She almost did not recognise him as he walked towards her. It was only those green eyes that brought familiarity and that smile...The rest was so different. His hair had gone. Both facially, and from his head, leaving a shaven crop. His clothes were clean and he looked smart, handsome. She grinned like a child as he approached.

'Hi, Jenny, it's good to see you. What do you think?'

She laughed as he gave a twirl grinning from ear to ear. 'Oh, Oliver, you look fabulous!' Gazing sincerely she added, 'I am so happy for you. I've thought about you so very much.'

He motioned for them to walk. Jenny followed him into the gardens and, as they strolled through the greenery, he told her of his time in rehab.

'At first, it was very hard but the staff, they are so caring and human. My methadone supplements went down gradually and now…now, guess what?'

'What?' She smiled with the hope that seeing him had given her.

'The words I have been longing to say, Jenny. I'm clean. No more methadone. No more drugs. Been over a month now, and I have never felt so good.'

She threw her arms around him, beaming. 'That's the best news I've heard this year! I am so proud of you, Oliver. So, when will you be back?' She paused suddenly as the thought occurred. 'Will you be back, Oliver?'

'For a while, Jenny,' he replied with a gentle look. 'I have some things to do in London. Promises to keep, you know? Then, then I will go and meet my mother and after that…perhaps I will find my father.'

She found herself amazed at the change in his character. 'That would be so brilliant – your father! Have you spoken with your mother about it then?'

'A little.' His response was positive. 'She said he left when I was just a baby, but she didn't say why or how. I didn't push too much but she seemed to know that I would one day want to find him. I guess it's natural, Jen.' Shrugging his shoulders the brief frown vanished and his eyes sparkled with curiosity. 'So, tell me about your world! What has dear Jenny been up to?'

The months ran through her mind. 'I have to say, not a lot!' she surmised smiling. 'Not compared to you anyway. Holly got a modelling contract. She had the first shoot a while ago and she's doing well. Terry…well, Terry has been subdued recently. He doesn't seem himself and Terrance…well… he's in a black mood most of the time.' She shrugged her shoulders. 'He met a girl, fell in the love with the girl and then lost the girl. Since then he's been even harder to be around.' She felt some bitterness surface. 'It's sad, I know, but that's my world summary.' Trying to look more positive than she now felt she went on, 'It's not so bad. So tell me. When will you be back, and for how long?'

He grinned at her innocent expression. She was like a child waiting for the answers. 'I estimate...' he replied mischievously, 'I will be in London by the end of the month and as for how long...' letting his eyebrows rise in tandem with his thoughts, '...as long as it takes.'

Jenny giggled. 'And may I ask how long what takes?'

Putting one arm on her shoulder he stared deeply into her eyes. 'Don't ask questions with answers you would not want.' Seeing a tinge of hurt, he kissed her warmly on the cheek as he spoke softly in her ear. 'You don't want to know, Jenny. I promise you that.'

* * *

The fax came through into the converted office of William Sonning. Whipping it out of the machine, he shot a casual glance at its contents before halting in his tracks.

'Jesus Christ! This is impossible!' His voice carried real panic as he hit the speed dial on his mobile.

'Hi there, can I have extension 932 please?'

He waited for a moment until he heard the call connect. 'Hello there, this is William Sonning of Sonnings Farm account number 346873. We've just received an order for which I have a query.'

The voice at the other end of the line confirmed his details before asking, 'What seems to be the problem?'

'Well,' William tried to reply in a calm voice, 'this order is for at least three times the usual amount. We're going to have difficulty in honouring the amount.' Glancing at the sheet he added in an exasperated tone, 'Especially on a week's deadline!'

The reply was bland and direct. 'I suggest you do your best, Mr Sonning. You know our terms and conditions of company policy. Are you saying you cannot honour an order?'

It was not a threat, more a shrouded warning. 'Er, no, not exactly,' his answer feigned confidence, 'leave it with me. I just needed to be sure it wasn't an error.'

After the call William searched out his father and told him of the situation. 'Dad, they want ninety thousand lettuces by next week! We've no way of producing that!'

Edward looked solemn. 'I warned about these types of companies, William. They're an animal that's impossible to tame. We've struggled enough with the accounts on their delayed payments, let alone the cheap prices and...' he stared sternly, 'if you hadn't noticed, we're losing staff. Some of the locals have given in and gone to work for Healy's store. I did warn you, William.'

'Well, that's a great help,' William replied defensively. 'I figured you might have some ideas. Don't worry, Dad, I'll ask someone else.'

With that he left the room barging past Hayley on the way. She looked at Edward in confusion. 'What's got into him?'

Looking sombre, Edward answered slowly. 'The animal he could not tame is now becoming the beast that will end it all.'

* * *

The presentation awards were supposed to be a celebration of the company's profits and performance. In years gone by, Terry had overseen the awards followed by a hearty banquet and a few short speeches aimed at improving team morale. Now, under the command of Terrance, things were different this year, much different.

Negative media coverage was what Terrance blamed it on, but it was much more than that. Healy's had been putting up stores at lightning speed. Initially the larger towns had not seen too much of a change – *initially*. The smaller townships and villages had been rocked however. Many small shops had suffered or been forced to close and now, as time went by, even the high-street stores were feeling the pinch. Not only were Healy's selling a massive range of products as part of their expansion, but the majority of it was imported. From the sweatshops abroad straight to the man on the street, bypassing any production costs in the UK, you could see why T Healy & Sons had become public enemy number one.

The centre of theatreland had been chosen for the venue. Many of the hotels were taken for *achieving* staff as the company paid for accommodation for the awards. *'Good tax losses'* as Terrance smugly put it on the way to the Hilton. The crowd that waited outside jeering and taunting made the occasion a theatre event in its own right.

Terrance could handle the taunts and shouts of the baying public. That was one thing. He was protected by the cordon of police that lined the path into the hotel. The rotten eggs that thumped against his suit were something else. 'Don't they know who I bloody am?' he shouted to Trevor over the din.

'They certainly do,' Trevor whispered through clenched teeth, 'public enemy number one.'

Inside the building waiters awaited the guests' entrance, champagne ready, the occasion as planned. Shaken staff members were pampered on the way through to the *'hall of ceremonies'* as Terrance had wished it to be called. After a few drinks and talk of profits and futures, many forgot about the hullabaloo outside.

Following a meal for the four hundred or so chosen staff, awards were presented before the main man himself took to the podium. Terrance straightened his replacement suit and faced his minions.

'I would like to thank you all for being here today,' he began confidently. 'You all represent what we as a company represent: success. T Healy & Sons has grown with the economy and now stands proudly as the number one retailer in the country. That is thanks to people like you.'

He waited for the applause to die down before continuing, a wide grin appearing. 'You'll be aware that some people do not like success.' Motioning to the window he went on, 'Those people who chose to share their feelings are not part of our adventure. They do not like change and they do not like progress!'

His voice gathered pace as he spoke, ending in a political tirade. A brief silence ensued before gentle applause followed his speech. Undeterred he continued in a booming tone.

'We must remain focused. Over the next years we aim to become the biggest and most successful company in Europe and then what? Who knows? The world perhaps.' Spreading his arms he added in a celebratory voice, 'That is because of people like you! You are our future and we are yours!'

More applause rang out, drowning the hall. As the last hand clap sounded, a voice from the back of the hall rang out.

'What of you, Terrance Healy?'

His eyes immediately snapped to the source of the voice as heads turned in unison. The familiar voice rang deep in his heart as he turned to see her walking boldly now towards the podium. Terrance went to open his mouth but no sound came.

She was close now, her face flushed, her voice strong. 'I have a few questions for you to answer, Terrance. What will you do when you have bled this country dry of manufacturing? When you have closed down the shops that have been here for years? When the people that work hard and honestly no longer have jobs? What will they do then? Where will they find the money to go into your shops?'

He saw Francesca's glare as she came within feet of the podium, tears of anger streaming down her face. From the wings of the hall he saw security guards appear, heading towards her. As they approached with the intention of removing her, Terrance found his voice at last.

'No!' the word echoed above the mumbles that had grown into voices, 'let her speak.'

The guards stopped in their tracks and waited for something to happen. Terrance cleared his throat.

'I will happily tell you all,' he said in a loud confident voice, 'of our future plans for the company and the country. We care as much as anyone about that, young lady.' Smiling he whispered just loud enough for her to hear, 'It's good to see you, Francesca.'

Francesca bared her teeth. 'Well then,' she shouted, turning to face the astounded crowd, 'can you tell these fine people why you cancelled your contract with my family, just because **I rejected you**?'

A silence fell as quickly as Terrance's expression. Turning back to him, hatred written across her face, Francesca spoke quietly. 'I will embarrass you no further. I just want you to know that you will never hurt my family by trying to hurt me. I will be with Domenici and I will love him.' Her eyes ablaze, she went on as he stood stunned, 'I'm pregnant, Terrance, and I have everything you do not. I never loved you. I never could. You represent everything I detest in someone.'

She turned away and walked proudly down the hallway past the astonished congregation.

Terrance saw the faces staring now, waiting for him to say something, anything. He glanced towards Trevor to take over, before swallowing hard and mumbling into the microphone, 'That's it from me. Enjoy your day.'

CHAPTER THIRTY-EIGHT

'Sit down, son.' His voice commanded obedience. Terrance obeyed.

'Read that.' He slid the newspaper across the table.

Terrance saw the headlines:

T HEALY & SONS – BRITAIN' S MOST HATED?

'Dad, do I really have…'

'Yes!' Terry's voice barked out. 'Read the story.'

Normally he might have retorted something sarcastic, but not today. This was not normal and he had never seen his father like this. Yesterday had changed so much. He read the print.

Events at yesterday's fiasco involving T Healy & Sons were nothing short of ridiculous, as our reporter Mandy Neal explains:

There has been a public outburst over recent months concerning the expansion and monopolising of T Healy & Sons. Nothing however prepared me for the events at the Hilton, London.

Arriving at the venue, I witnessed almost riotous crowds outside the foyer baying for answers. When Mr Healy Junior arrived he was greeted with insults before being hit by some rather unpleasant-smelling eggs from one particularly irate protestor. The reasons, it seems, are many. Healy's growth has been nothing short of a revelation within the industry, yet their popularity is at an all-time low. The backlash was predicted last week when government figures showed a rise in unemployment in addition to credit borrowing. You would think a company such as Healy's was not to blame, but in the eyes of many they and the government are part of the reason. It is no secret that Healy's import over 70% of its products (figures 2006-07). This, along with rumours of local 'sweeteners' being paid in return for local council planning permission, has seen the giant move into the very heart of Britain's countryside. The results have been devastating.

Now that Healy's is officially the second largest landowner in the UK behind the Royal Family, the public want answers. Why has the company bought so much land, (much of it unused at this juncture), if they are not planning more and more expansion? Why have they decided to import many of their products from abroad, leaving the economy in shortfall with money leaving the country? Why have they forced UK companies to agree to an almost ridiculous set of terms and conditions which have resulted in many going bust, due to the inability to match their cashflow with these payment terms.

The answers are easy for many to see. Yesterday the pent-up anger of the masses spilled over onto the pavements of London. So why has it got this far and what does the future hold as the UK slides towards a recession?

We asked our business analyst, Carol McCarthy for her verdict:

The land ownership is obvious: to build more stores in the future and put pressure on local councils to pass plans. In one town I know of, they have been rejected three times already due to public outcry. Their policy is

'if we have the land, eventually we will have the store.'
The import issue is extremely dangerous. It has created a false dawn for our economy because the larger companies such as Healy's become, the bigger the problem will be. Imports from abroad simply mean that they are buying in much more cheaply and therefore are able to slash prices. The downside of this is twofold. Firstly, the standards of products are rarely as good as products made to British standards. Secondly, the consumer is led into a false sense of security as many of these products remain at the same retail price as they did with a previous British supplier. The final nail in the coffin is once more twofold. The terms offered to British suppliers are bordering on the ludicrous and it is an established fact that over 10% of companies dealing with T Healy & Sons went into liquidation or filed for bankruptcy last year alone due to these terms. Secondly, the imported goods have damaged UK manufacturing beyond repair over the last decade. You will not find a fence panel made in this country. Neither will you find a nail made here. That is just the tip of the iceberg. All we need now is for the nail for the coffin to be hammered shut and the damage will be complete.

Carol, how do you predict the future as things stand?

The future looks fairly bleak unless either government reforms are put in place or the attitude of these giants changes. The main reason has to be the stock they are selling. It is money which is leaving our shores and the profits going solely in the companies' pockets. The domino effect will mean that one day Mrs Brown, for example, will see Mr Brown return from the factory without a job due to the factory or shops etc closures. She will have less income and eventually it will not matter how much cheaper the products are. They simply will not be able to afford them. Put in simple terms: major recession.

The protestors seemed aware of that outside but inside events took a further twist when Terrance Healy's speech was interrupted by, we believe, an ex-lover. An unconfirmed source stated that the woman, who was described as Mediterranean-looking, entered the room shouting obscenities at Mr Healy. Our source stated that: 'He looked like he had seen a ghost. He wanted the earth to swallow him whole.'

It appears that the majority of people in Britain would like to see just that.

Folding the paper dismissively, Terrance shrugged. 'Storm in a teacup, Dad. They must have run out of decent news.'

Terry said nothing but began to clap gently, slowly at first, before gaining momentum.

'What are you doing that for?'

'Irritating you, am I, son? Isn't that the sound you adore: applause and adulation?'

Giving his father a frustrated look, Terrance replied curtly, 'Stop it, Dad. You're not funny.'

The fist slamming on the table stopped him in his tracks. 'I'm not funny?' he yelled in as loud a voice as Terrance had ever heard. 'I'm not funny? Well, let's look at you, shall we? The Boy Wonder who has managed to bring the company, a company I worked my fingers to the bone for, to its knees in terms of popularity! Do you have any idea of the damage you have done?'

'Like I said, Dad,' Terrance answered shakily, 'it will blow over. It's just a matter of time.'

'That I very much doubt,' Terry retorted furiously. 'You...we are going to make changes, son. I don't want the name of our family dragged through the dirt! The changes start here, **now**!'

Terrance suddenly felt defeated. His father had always been his role model, despite his own personal agenda. Trying to look reassured, he attempted reason.

'Okay, Dad, what do you have in mind?'

'Don't bullshit me, son!' Terry's voice was scathing. 'I'm not one of your brown-nosing skivvies who privately hate you behind your back by the way! You saw what the girl thought of you and I don't bloody blame her! You're an embarrassment!'

The words hurt deeply as his father delivered them with conviction. 'Alright, alright, I'm sorry!' He felt the confidence seeping away. 'What can we do, Dad?' With a lump in his throat, he added, 'I want to put this right.'

'Mmm,' Terry paused, 'it is a mess, son. We need to do this.'

'So what shall we do to start with?' Terrance saw his father had calmed. He also sensed within himself a long dormant emotion of interest in something other than himself. He wanted to listen.

'No more building in small villages and towns for starters. I also want to look at selling some of the land you have attained...' Terry glared as he added, 'without consulting me. Then I want to look at scaling down foreign purchases and supporting companies within Britain, perhaps with a labelling campaign or something proactive. We need to do something fast, Terrance. You have made our name mud.'

His father's words hit home and instead of snapping as he would have done normally, Terrance thought carefully before reacting. 'I agree. The land we can look at, Dad, and the new building of shops,' he gazed sincerely, 'it will cease. The foreign thing, I will look into.'

'What do you mean, look into?' The reply was edged with rage. 'You're the one that was the chief buyer! You brought this upon us!'

'Yeah, yeah, I know, Dad. I'll get something done. Just as soon as the current contracts are up.' Seeing his father glare in response, he continued looking ever more sheepish, 'It was a new idea. To get companies to sign longer-term contracts in return for lower prices. We can only cancel if they fail orders.'

Terry shifted forward. His eyes focused directly ahead.

'Sounds like the most stupid idea I have ever heard of,' he growled. 'Not familiar with the gentleman's agreement, I guess?' Seeing Terrance look away he moved even closer. 'Just one other thing then. I heard about the girl who confronted you. I heard you cancelled their contract. Would that be because they failed, Terrance?'

'Not exactly, Dad.' His reply was as dry as his mouth.

He watched his father get up and saw the strain on his face, the shame even. A cascade of guilt rose within him as Terry spoke in a solemn voice.

'I suggest you take a good look in the mirror, son, and decide what you want to become. I can tell you what I see in that mirror. Someone even I don't like very much.'

* * *

The day had been frantic for William Sonning; a day spent making endless phone calls, trying to pull in favours from fellow farmers, had resulted with just one option available. As Ethan had put it, 'Desperate circumstances call for desperate measures.' These were indeed desperate measures.

The order had been impossible to complete. William knew that as soon as he saw the fax. The farm could produce thirty thousand lettuces, perhaps forty if he pulled workers off the fields to help pack, but ninety thousand…impossible. After discussions with Ethan, they had decided to take the only course of action available: buy the lettuces elsewhere. This had opened up another can of worms. After making plenty of frantic calls to other farms, they had discovered the costs of buying were astronomical in comparison to their own. In addition, the amount of farms that could supply them had dwindled substantially since William had last taken the time to check up on his fellow suppliers.

'It's going to have to be Eastern Europe.' Ethan frowned as he contemplated the thought. 'I know of a couple of places that can supply us. It won't be cheap though.'

'I don't care about that,' William replied somewhat reticently. 'We can deal with losing money on this order. That's not my main concern, Ethan. It's what happens with the next order, and the one after that?' Worried, he gazed out of the window. 'We're going to have trouble. We've lost enough staff recently to the supermarket and, if you hadn't noticed, there's friction between some of the workers. It seems racism is alive and kicking.'

'Well, that's just one of those things.' Ethan looked indifferent. 'We pay them a lot bloody less anyway and I think if we get another order of that size then we should look to expand a little more.'

William looked unsure. 'I don't think my dad would be too pleased. Let's get this lot ordered in and take it from there.'

* * *

Trevor stared in disbelief. 'Sell the land? That's preposterous! Has your dad gone crazy, Terrance?'

Terrance returned his statement with a glare. 'Not really, Trevor, and I would watch your tongue. That's my father you're talking about. He created all this and I think we should listen. We're hardly flavour of the bloody month!'

Trevor looked confused. 'I think we should sit on some of the land, for now. As for your other idea on UK suppliers, there aren't so many around, sir.'

'Well? Why do you suppose that is?' Terrance shouted in frustration. 'Perhaps we had something to do with that?'

'You're the chief buyer, sir,' Trevor replied meekly. 'You make the major decisions, I have to say.'

If looks could kill then Trevor would have been a dead man. The thing was Terrance knew he was, in essence, right in what he said. He had made many choices without giving a thought to the repercussions. He waited for the red mist to clear before answering in as calm a tone as he could muster. 'I'm aware of that, Trevor. From now on, I will be concentrating on changing some major buying areas.' He rubbed his chin in time with his thoughts. 'I want to get British products marked with promotions and flags. Let's get some patriotism back to the company name.' Seeing Trevor's bemused reaction, he added hastily, 'So, what about this idea you had about slimming down contracts, etc? Have you started on that? Because I think we should review that strategy.'

Trevor found it hard to believe the change he was witnessing. 'I've put in place a mailshot for all accounts to the end of the month, sir.'

After pondering for a moment, Terrance rose from his seat, eyes filled with confidence. 'Right, well from the end of the month I want to review all accounts that are British-based and I also want to get rid of the contract system.' He saw the shocked look as he added, 'Things are going to change, Trevor. No more Mr Bad Guy.'

Whatever had happened was beyond Trevor's reasoning. He simply nodded in agreement as he replied, 'By the end of the month, sir.'

* * *

Three days before the end of the month the shipment arrived at Sonnings Farm. When William was called into the vast barn set aside for packing, he was astounded.

'Jesus bloody Christ, Ethan!' He stared at the rows of boxes. 'They look nothing like our lettuces, and what the hell is this label?'

The trays contained lettuces that looked shrunken by comparison to the ones grown via hydroponics. The label was in an Eastern European language and as William tugged at it he saw the cellophane peel with the label.

'This is awful!' he blasted 'Get me the kid, Jan, in here!'

A few minutes later and Jan arrived. William threw a lettuce towards him. 'Can you read this label?' Jan thrust out a hand to catch it. He gave a quick look and nodded looking puzzled.

'Of course, it's in Polish, but…'

'Don't worry about whys and whats, Jan,' William interrupted. 'Just read it out please.'

Running his finger over his native language, Jan read out the few lines.

'Fresh lettuce,' he found himself grinning, 'produce of Poland. Sell by date the seventh of December.' He looked up and shrugged. 'That's all it says.'

'Oh God almighty.' The colour drained from William's face as he turned to Ethan. 'We're in big trouble! The labels will take days to get off and the sell by date? Why the bloody hell have we bought with a sell by date that short?'

Ethan looked grim. 'We had no choice. We'll have to ship them as they are.'

'I don't know, Ethan. I mean, look.' William held a home-grown lettuce alongside a newly delivered one. 'Little and bloody large!'

'William,' Ethan's voice was hushed, 'we have no choice. You told me about the rules of the contract. Do you want to risk that?'

Looking downcast, William gave the only reply he could muster. 'You're right, we don't have any choice.'

* * *

As darkness covered the village in a moonlit blanket, the temperature dropped suddenly, a gentle frost forming on the kerbside. Jan was oblivious. His eyes stared ahead only at the deserted street. He passed through the main artery of Stebdon, once thriving, but now a parade of boarded up windows with signs repeating the same phrase: 'closing down sale'. Nothing deterred him until he arrived at the ageing red telephone box. There he stood shivering. Not with the rapid chill, but with the rawness that his heart felt. He held the door ajar, staring at the black receiver within; it almost felt like a direct line to God that would tell him of his father's entrance to his domain.

He did not make the call. Tears of pain streamed down his face and he let the door swing slowly closed before he slumped to the floor. In his hand he held the crumpled letter. Four years earlier he had held a similar piece of paper, yellow and full of dreams and promise. Now he held what could only be described as a death certificate.

Wiping his eyes with the sleeve of his flimsy jumper, he unfolded the letter to read for the umpteenth time the few lines that had torn him apart.

My dear Jan and Basia,

I weep as I write to tell you of the saddest news. Yesterday morning at 7.15am your father passed away. It has been the hardest year of my life and for him. I can only pray that the pain has ended. For me, it has just begun. Please call me as soon as you can. Please come home as soon as you can. I need you both.

Love Mum xx

He let more tears fall. The letter was dated nearly a week earlier. He had not called as he usually did. Now he would never see his father again and nothing would ever be the same. The dream was over. It had never really begun. It was time to go home.

* * *

Rusty woke suddenly late into the night. He was not sure why: a bad dream? No. He turned over in bed and, as he went to check the time on his watch, he saw him looking in through the window. The silhouette of Billy Jones stared at him, his expression full of tension, despite the black shadows of the night that shrouded him.

'It's going to be tonight. I heard them talking,' his voice whispered, the fear evident as Rusty opened the door. 'I think it will be Ethan alone though.' Billy added cautiously, 'I warned the other two. When I left he was drinking heavily and boasting of his intentions. Hurry!'

Rusty focused instantly. 'Where's Basia? What about Jan?'

Billy was shaking, his nerves in shreds. 'It's Ethan. He said that Jan had gone into the village. That's why it's to be tonight.' Eyes wide, he went on, 'I couldn't say anything, couldn't do anything or he would find out and then…'

Seeing the fear, Rusty put a reassuring arm on his shoulder. 'You've done your bit. Let's hope it's not too late.'

CHAPTER THIRTY-NINE

*'You may think you do not need to be loved. You may think you are
strong. The fool on the hill who spends his days counting money
worked all his life for it. The troubled child, now a man and a
murderer, craved his whole life for it. Let your defences down, for
it is not weakness at all. Love is the strength of humanity and it's
the only chance of survival.'*

(Taken from the hall of Angels)

The two men made their way towards the farm. Odd lights lit
the darkened mass of caravans and farm buildings, like a strip
torn from the stars above. Billy motioned to the small building
set behind the packing barn. 'I think it's in there,' he
whispered in a frightened voice.

Rusty considered the planning of this attack momentarily. It
would have had to have been discussed more than once: the
sinister plot to tear, to *rape*, Basia's innocence from her. He
fought the inevitable anger, trying to replace it with a clear
head. Now was not the time to be irrational. Unbeknown to
them, Jan and Basia were relying on him. Coming to a halt
fifty yards from the building, he turned to face Billy.

'I need you to go home, Billy. I need you to go home and
never to repeat anything of this night.'

'But, what if…'

'What if nothing,' Rusty replied firmly. 'There could be
many scenarios in there, Billy. None of them are likely to be
good.' Gazing sincerely at the strained moonlit face, he

continued, 'I need you to forget this night, *whatever* happens. It's for the best, Billy. Can you do that for me, for you?'

As if digesting the possibilities, Billy remained silent for an instant, before nodding and gulping a reply. 'If it's for the best, I want no part of this.'

As Billy slipped away into the night, Rusty crept as quietly as possible towards the building. Nearing the doorway he could just make out the faint glow of what appeared to be an oil lamp, its dull illumination peeking through the crack of the frame. As he got closer, he checked for the sheaf knife inside his pocket, his body tensing with each step. There was no sound emanating from within. Not initially, but now, now he could hear something... the faintest sound... of crying.

Was he too late? That was the last question Rusty asked himself as he peered through the door. After that everything became a haze.

* * *

The caravan door was ajar. Jan's senses tingled. Something was wrong. Basia was not there. Instinctively he went to the small drawer of the kitchen cabinet and pulled out the gleaming blade as the possibilities ran through his mind. The first question was not why the door was open, but why Basia was not inside.

Heart racing, he ran from the yard towards the house. There were few lights on. Most people were either tucked up in bed or relaxing indoors, so when he saw the figure dash across the field, Jan knew it was part of the answer. Mind racing, he contemplated chasing, but decided on locating the place he was running from. If Basia was not with him, she could be where the man had just left from. It was a gamble, but there was no time for further thought. Every instinct he had spelt out danger.

Jan saw Ethan Dobbs push Basia against the wall. He saw him slap her hard across the face, cursing in a drunken tone, before forcing her to the floor, pushing his strong frame onto hers, muffling her sounds with his hand. Frenzied, Jan pounced. He saw Basia's eyes widen as she watched his arm move with venomous grace. He saw the horror in them as she watched her brother slide the blade across Ethan's throat. The following seconds were clouded in red as the knife did its deed. Ethan spat raw choking sounds as the crimson spurted in different directions

The blood fell, as did the perpetrator of evil, his blood leaving his body in time with his life. A moment later he was dead.

Jan stood still, encompassed by the rage that had driven his mind to perform the deed. Basia looked up; no words were exchanged. They both read the other's mind.

It was over; so many things were over.

* * *

Pushing the door gently open, he witnessed the horror. He was too late. He saw Basia and Jan holding each other in trembling arms, Basia's face marked by the struggle with Ethan. Neither seemed to notice he was there.

He approached the motionless figure of Ethan Dobbs. Face down, just a foot or so away from them. He saw the blood that had trickled from the wound before he turned him over. Ethan's eyes stared into nothingness. Wide and surprised as the knife slit his throat, the gaping wound still leaking the last drops of blood.

'Jan,' Rusty pieced together the story, 'Jan, are you alright?'

At first the mad gaze was simply that. Traumatised eyes turned to stare at Rusty. They were filled with the insanity that the discovery of Basia must have brought. Slowly Jan focused, realising that Rusty was not a danger. He spoke in a soft voice as he stroked his sister's hair. *'Father has gone to heaven and now we must go home. Father is in heaven, now we must go home.'*

'Jan.' Rusty attempted to break Jan's trance-like state as Basia rocked in his arms.

'This place, these people, evil people,' Jan snapped in a threatening tone. 'It's William's fault! He brought us here! He did all this! He'll be next, and he'll know what pain feels like!'

Kneeling beside them, Rusty stared compassionately into his eyes. 'No, there can be no more killing, Jan. You have to go home now. Do you understand? You have to go home.'

Rocking to and fro, Basia sobbing softly, Jan showed little acknowledgment as he answered. 'He never got her, you know? He tried, but I got here in time. I made him pay for his wickedness. I sent him to hell, Rusty. *I sent him to hell.'*

Rusty saw there was no remorse for his actions. How could there be? He also knew there was little time. Others would not understand, or even see things for what they were.

'You've done what you had do, Jan. He left you no option, I know that.' Seeing Jan respond with a gentle nod, he went on, making sure to keep a calm voice. 'I'll do what I can to protect you, but you must leave…tonight.'

'He's right.' Basia's voice interrupted them. 'I want to go home, Jan.'

Her tearful eyes would have brought down an empire. Jan forced a smile as he kissed her. 'Yes, yes, we will, Basia, tonight.'

* * *

They sat in silence as Rusty drove the pickup truck deep into the night. With the first signs of dawn, the battered vehicle reached the station that would take them on the first leg of the journey home. Rusty took the bloodstained clothes from which they had changed, and slipped them into a bag. A last glance at Basia was rewarded by a knowing look of thanks.

Jan offered his hand.

'Will they come for us, Rusty?'

Shrugging as they shook hands, Rusty replied, 'I'll do everything to make it difficult. Besides,' a confident grin emerged, 'there are enough people that knew you were not here last night. As far as they know, Basia was with you.'

'Thank you for all you've done. I will remember you always, Rusty.'

They watched as he drove the chugging vehicle away, their last goodbyes carrying in the wind.

* * *

Sirens filled the morning air as the body of Ethan Dobbs was discovered at dawn. It seemed that the entire police force of Stebdon arrived that day. Questions fired like bullets amongst the villagers. A sense of deep shock enveloped the small community.

The names of many, including Jan and Basia Kowalik, were mentioned as suspicions ran rife.

Rusty waited for the opportunity to mention quietly to Edward about Jan's father's death the week before and his decision to return home two days earlier. He used the timing of the situation along with Billy Jones's agreement to verify the facts. Billy cemented the alibi by producing payslip documents which stated the termination of employment the previous week. From would-be prime suspect, Jan slipped away from consideration, set free by a good friend, and a trusted employee in Billy who simply had no other option but to agree to the instructions given him by Rusty.

Amid the commotion, William stood stunned by the news. His most loyal employee was dead. With no inkling of Ethan's seedy intentions, he could only surmise a fight or something ridiculous that could have led to such action. Nothing like this had ever happened in Stebdon before, and William was unprepared for it. The next days were a living hell, only made worse by the news that followed.

* * *

Edward watched from the window as he pushed the empty breakfast plate to one side. The steady row of lorries trundled up to the loading area. He watched William, Billy at his side rush over, faces etched with distress. Edward waited. He glanced at the faxed sheet on the table. He could make out the scribble of T Healy alongside the wording – 'chief buyer'. Hearing the sound of steps approaching the door, he paused, looking up to see his son burst, panic-stricken, into the room. 'You won't believe it, Dad! They've sent nearly the whole lot back! We have had it.'

As William collapsed onto the chair, Edward drew breath and began to read from the sheet.

It is with regret that we, T Healy & Sons, inform you of serious breach of contract on supply number 09/254. We have found a large section of the goods to be substandard, in addition to being purchased from another source outside our contractual terms. Under the ruling within the terms and conditions of our contract, we will return the faulty stock to you with non-payment. In addition to the above and in accordance with terms and conditions note paragraph seven, line sixteen: 'Our contract is null and void due to serious breach.'

'It's over, William,' Edward said quietly.

* * *

The effect was as dramatic as the death of Ethan Dobbs. Unbeknown to anyone on Sonnings Farm, just three more days may have saved them. The new ruling for no further contractual business was implemented on the first day of

December. Pale-faced and stricken with guilt, William told the hundreds of staff the news. Many locals left within days, returning to the village where they resided in search of work. The majority ironically ended up at the supermarket they used to supply. For the foreign workers, and there were many, it was a case of finding somewhere else to go. The next months would see a rise in crime within the village and consequently the eventual closure of T Healy & Sons supermarket, the first of its kind. By the time the last dregs of outsiders had moved on in mid-March of the following year, the village was more or less a ghost town, shrouded in shadows of days gone by.

When Terrance Healy signed the document he took little notice. It was to be one of the last he signed for the closure of a UK business. His decision cost a village its prosperity and, eventually, cost so much more.

The lost business followed Jan Kowalik into Eastern Europe.

CHAPTER FORTY

December 2007

'Well, you'd best just get your glad rags on and come, you silly bitch. Dad wants us to represent the family and this could be big business!'

He stood there, face contorted with rage, as Holly returned his look with a hatred of her own. 'I don't want to go to a sad fucking party, full of obese filthy men and women. People whose noses are as far up in the air as those idiots you call friends are up your bloody arse!'

Terrance looked as if he was about to blow a gasket. No one spoke to him like that, no one. He stormed across the bedroom and pushed his face into Holly's. 'Listen, little sister…,' his voice carried menace, 'it's Lord Chavry's bash. I *have* to go to this goddam party and so do you, whether you like it or not. Dad has too much on, and you know it's not his thing. Good diplomacy is crucial for the family name, especially now after the bad publicity of late. If we want to expand into Europe then these are the sort of places we have to go and the sort of people we have to meet. So, rather then piss Dad off, be a good girl and get ready.'

'Piss Dad off?' Holly retorted angrily. 'He doesn't care if I go or not! God, Terrance, you get worse by the day! It's *you* that wants me to go, not him. You're to bloody blame for the bad publicity anyway! You want me to go just so we all look nice and cosy, and probably so half the people that no doubt *hate* you there won't be rude enough to say it in front of me!'

One person, well, one of two people that Terrance had no control over was Holly. His mum he could deal with and his father he could cope with, at least until the recent outburst. Only Francesca and Holly caused him trouble with their refusal to be manipulated. He paced for a moment, calculating his next move. That was it! He turned to face her, eyes gleaming with mischief.

'I tell you what, darling sister. How about we compromise? You come with me and have a good time like a good girl, and I'll keep a lid on your little drug habit?' He leant back against the bookcase looking triumphant.

Holly's reaction was one of shock. 'What? How? Shit!' He had thrown her completely off guard. 'You don't know what the hell you're talking about, you piece of shit!' Her mind raced as the impact of his words hit home. 'How did you know?' Her voice was distinctly weaker.

'Dear, dear me,' Terrance said casually, 'you wouldn't think that a caring brother like me wouldn't protect his sister, would you? I have friends in Loughborough, Holly. Friends who talk and all I can say is that my interests are in your education, and the family's reputation. What was it now? Sweet Holly's words, ah yes: pills for thrills and coke and a smoke?'

Holly felt repulsed as she remembered the night she had said that. Flashbacks of her standing on the table, feeling on another planet as she yelled out to the crowded room, top off, watching the boys baying. It had been fun but now she was in trouble. She knew her brother well enough to know that his words carried a sinister meaning. He had the power and the know-how to make her life hell. She was defeated.

'Alright,' she said bitterly, 'I'll go. Just don't expect me to hang off your tuxedo all evening.'

He smiled confidently. 'There's a good girl.' Opening the door he glanced back. 'Don't worry. Your secret is safe with me. I'm sure you'll have a good time,' he chuckled. 'Bound to be plenty of drugs there.'

She wanted to spit at him.

* * *

Joey was waiting with the limousine at seven thirty. 'Good evening, Miss Holly. You're looking lovely tonight.' He glanced at Terrance. 'Evening, sir.'

Holly pulled her light cream jacket over her shoulders. She wore only a thin black cocktail dress, with silver sequins that glittered under the lights outside making her look quite captivating. She smiled at Joey but, before she could thank him for the compliment, Terrance chipped in.

'Why, thank you, Joey. You're looking swell yourself.' Grinning in a cocksure manner he added, 'To Lord Chavry's place at Westminster, Joey.'

Joey nodded and held the door open for them. Holly remained silent throughout the journey. She wondered to herself how Joey remained so calm and polite with such an idiot as her brother around.

'Make yourself busy, but be around for when I call,' Terrance barked as they arrived outside the house-cum-palace of Lord Chavry.

'Yes, sir,' Joey replied with a hint of sarcasm. 'Have a good evening, Miss Holly.' He shot her a warm smile before driving off.

They walked close together, despite being a million miles apart. Holly felt she was climbing a mountain as they walked up the large marble steps leading to the great oak doors of Lord Chavry's home. There they were greeted by his welcoming committee of butlers and security guards.

'Good evening, Mr Healy, Miss Healy.' The butler smiled faintly. 'So pleased you could come. Please, let me take your coats.'

'Ta,' said Terrance, throwing his in the direction of the butler. 'Thank you,' added Holly with a rather embarrassed smile.

She followed as Terrance strolled into the vast main hall. Off the hall there were countless doorways, each leading to elegantly decorated rooms depicting the richness of the mansion. Instantly they were served drinks by one of the many waitresses that were floating around. Even as she took her first sip of champagne, Holly found that plenty of eyes were already on her. Terrance was oblivious, of course. He was too busy shaking hands and greeting the gentle parade of rich and richer that wandered over ready to talk figures and profits.

While she faked the smiles and accepted the kisses on her hand, Holly sensed she was attracting looks from some of the 'friends of the family'. She could feel the eyes, inspecting her body from top to toe. Filthy, powerful thoughts flowing through the minds of men who could afford to buy sex, which made it even more fascinating for them to ogle at a pretty rich girl like her. She felt completely alienated.

When Lord Chavry made an appearance, Holly actually felt a sense of relief. The dull, mindless conversation about money and business was becoming unbearably repetitive. She watched as he strolled over towards them. He was a rather portly figure, probably through too much rich food and parties such as this. His crisp white shirt bulged a little from within his tuxedo and his thin grey hair was matched by a ferret-like moustache which made him stand out from the crowd. The marble and gold cane he held was more of an 'I am rich' statement than an aid for walking. She both admired and detested him at the same time.

'A good evening, Lord Chavry.' Terrance cut off his conversation with a bloated colleague as he drew near, his sickly smile practised for such occasions.

'A good evening to you, young Mr Healy.' Lord Chavry smiled with the arrogance of someone who knew he was the only person there who was more powerful than the young upstart. 'And this must be your beautiful sister,' he oozed. 'A pleasure to meet you, Miss…'

'Holly,' she intervened as was intended. 'It's very nice to meet you, Lord Chavry.'

He gently kissed her hand before shaking Terrance's who was acting more politely than Holly had ever seen him.

'A superb home, sir, and a great turnout, I may add.'

'Thank you, yes, there are some good people here, and... some idiots.' He winked at Holly who could not help but grin.

'So, young Healy,' Lord Chavry held a cigar which was lit by a waitress who appeared from nowhere, 'it seems T Healy & Sons are now the largest in the UK. Congratulations are in order!'

Terrance looked smug. 'Thank you, sir, it's been a long road. We've had to work hard and I...' Terrance shifted his tie proudly, 'I personally have had to oversee many changes. But now we are where we want to be, sir. Our buyers are performing well, and our suppliers are being as competitive as any.'

Lord Chavry puffed on his cigar sending a plume of smoke in between the two. 'Yes, I've heard. Seems most of your buying is abroad now. From the Far East?'

'Business is business. It's all about price, all about value,' Terrance replied curtly.

'Perhaps it is, Healy, but I don't necessarily agree.' He gave Terrance a knowing look. 'It seems the company reputation is a little tainted. I heard that the last of the cutlery producers in your father's home town went bust recently. I don't suppose you dealt with them though?' Lord Chavry smiled wryly. 'Shame, they probably would still be going now. But business is business as you say.'

Holly found herself enjoying her brother's sudden awkwardness. She knew that Lord Chavry was one of the richest men in Europe and had been successful in the steel industry as well as many other projects. It was a cloaked dig to which Terrance reacted squeamishly.

'I was sorry to hear about that, sir.' He tried to sound sincere. 'I think it's a simple case of competition, sir. If we can

343

get the same product from abroad for less it makes good business sense. Don't you agree?'

'I don't,' Holly found herself intervening. 'If we all buy from abroad then more places will shut down, won't they, Lord Chavry? Then the people who worked at them will have lost their jobs. Eventually, there will be less money for people to buy anything.'

'Exactly, my dear.' Lord Chavry smiled. 'And that's what could well happen.'

'Of course, I understand your point, sir.' He was looking flushed now. 'We have, my father and I that is, we have addressed these issues of late and will be concentrating on UK promotion more than ever. I'm sure if our two companies do business within Europe, sir, well, I'm sure you will see the change in our strategy.'

'Perhaps, Healy,' Lord Chavry replied as he stubbed his cigar out on a nearby silver ashtray, signalling the end of the conversation as he did so. 'We shall see, and time will tell. Enjoy your night.' He gave Holly a polite nod and walked off leaving Terrance fuming.

'Why did you say that, you silly bitch?' he whispered. 'You could have screwed everything up!'

Holly looked at him with distaste. 'I said what's true. Your policy has only been good for your bank account. It has had no benefit for people in your own bloody country. You've just been greedy and now people are seeing you for what you are.'

He looked as if he wanted to hit her, but instead pushed his mouth close to her ear. 'I wish I had never brought you here! If this deal goes down the tubes, you'll be the first to regret it, I promise you.'

Holly felt the fierceness in his tone. She tried to counter. 'If the deal goes wrong, it'll be only you to blame. You should have thought a little less about yourself and margins, Terrance. It's not all about profits. You know that we're never going to be poor.'

A part of him knew that his sister was speaking the truth. His stubborn pride, however, took control. Instead of agreeing, even giving a little leeway, he felt that uncontrollable anger in his reply.

'I don't need a kid like you to tell me how things should be done! I suggest that you go and find some drug-taking friends and do what you do best! I swear, Holly, if things go wrong tonight because of you, I will make sure you never model again!'

Before Holly could answer, a group of men wandered over and began talking to Terrance. She watched them smile falsely as they went through the same rigmarole of profits, money and power. He was right about one thing. She needed to take herself or, at least, her mind away from here.

* * *

An hour and an Ecstasy pill later and Holly felt much better. She had found some rich kids whilst wandering around and integrated easily. A few more drinks and the pill had a warming effect on her. The offer of some cocaine and some fun upstairs was just too tempting.

As she talked the idea over with the young group of youths, she saw Terrance heading towards her not looking too happy. He ignored the others and tugged Holly away.

'What are you up to?' he snapped. 'You're supposed to have been here to promote the family, not hang around with these misfits!'

'I was promoting the family until you told me you wished I wasn't here!' she retorted in a raised voice which made him grimace. 'These people are more fun than the idiots you've been talking to, and by the way…' she gave him an ironic smile as the drugs inside made her feel more powerful and daring, 'you can stick your threats up your pompous arse because I couldn't give a toss! You might own plenty of people but you will *never* own me!'

'Shh, keep your voice down!' Terrance was looking both

345

shifty and livid at her outburst. He grabbed her by the wrist, hurting her as he pulled her close.

'Listen, you little druggy, you can get yourself a lift home because I'm leaving! You're an embarrassment to me and, believe me, you will pay for it! I may not own you, but I can disown you.'

He snarled and stormed off leaving Holly gulping for a moment before returning to the group with a weak smile. 'Sorry about that, just family stuff.'

* * *

'No Miss Holly, sir?' Joey enquired as Terrance flung the door open.

'No, she's staying on with some friends, Joey.' He glared into space before adding, 'And don't wait up for her. She said she's going on to another party.'

'Of course, sir.' Joey pondered his words and wondered just what had happened.

Holly's rage made her dangerous. She had always been independent enough, but her brother's attitude had made her even more determined. She was going to have a good time and, she thought, screw him. After over a dozen lines of cocaine and another two pills she simply grinned and followed the man as he guided her upstairs.

She was led into a room at the west end of the long hallway. There she saw a huddle of people who looked vacantly at her as she entered. She had never tried crack cocaine but, when the man asked her, she shrugged nonchalantly as if it was nothing new to her.

After drawing on the heavily laden pipe she joined those around her in a stunned, glazed haze as the euphoric hit of the crack cocaine ran through her veins.

She had never felt so elated and any images of the earlier tension with Terrance evaporated completely as she floated in the joy of the drug.

346

Time was irrelevant now but it did not seem long before she felt strange. No one was taking any notice of anyone else; spaced out on various substances, they were oblivious to her growing concerns. A desire to ask for help, to show fear came over her, but the faces that stared blankly showed no interest. A wish for Terrance to appear washed over her as she left the room and somehow staggered into the bathroom. The drug now took hold sending a spasm of anxiety which, in turn, made her fall headlong onto the floor. A terrible awareness came over her as she lay there. It felt as if her skin was crawling with minute insects *from the inside*. She itched and scratched as panic set in and the drug began to crash, sending her mind and body into overdrive.

Her thoughts were in turmoil, littered with panic and a need to vomit. *'Too much, too strong, reaction...'* The words never left her mouth.

* * *

'Jesus Christ!' Lord Chavry stood in the doorway of the bathroom. 'Is she...?'

'She's dead, sir,' was the reply from his most trusted butler.

'What about the boy? When did he go?' He wiped his glistening forehead with a handkerchief.

'We saw him leave a few hours ago, sir,' the butler answered calmly. 'Chances are he would have no idea.'

'Right,' Lord Chavry was calculating, 'bloody shame, she was a nice-looking girl.' He paused, before finally coming to a decision. 'Right, well we can't have her being dead here, can we?'

The butler knew what his master was thinking. It had happened before, but in one of the nightclubs he owned, not in his own home. 'No, sir, not a good idea at all.'

'Make sure that the girl left just after her brother. Get hold of our security boys. You know the ones that *deal* with this kind of thing.'

'Yes, sir.'

'Good man.' Lord Chavry took one last glance at the corpse as he left. 'Like I said, bloody shame. Well, let me know when things have been cleaned up.'

'Of course, sir.' The butler locked the bathroom door. 'Leave it with me, sir.'

Lord Chavry was worried about one thing but kept it to himself. What if their driver came back to pick up the girl? What if he had been told she was still there? It was the only chance of a problem. Little did he know that Terrance had unknowingly already created the alibi when he told Joey not to return. Unbeknown to him, Lord Chavry had little reason to worry at all.

* * *

The two burly men did not see Lord Chavry. They were shown the girl and went about their business.

An hour later and the two silhouettes quietly supported the third along the dark street on the way to Westminster tube station. No cars, no contact, usual instructions. They knew what to do. A short trip on the tube and no suspicions raised before the body of Holly Healy was dumped. No need to rape her for effect. It would be a typical drug overdose.

When the call came to the house, Lord Chavry politely informed her worried mother that Holly, that pretty girl, had been seen leaving a little after Terrance. Perhaps he knew where she had gone? He forced a wry smile after convincing her he did not.

Putting down the phone, he pondered the night's events as he dissolved the microcosm of guilt that had been bestowed upon him. *'It's just like you said, young Healy. Business is business.'*

CHAPTER FORTY-ONE

'Possessions do not bring happiness for they are just that:
possessions. Possessiveness will not make someone love you.
Think of the word possess as having the happiness and joy not to
possess anything and you may find you have it all.'

(From the scriptures of Galgliel)

'Thank you for a wonderful evening.' Francesca hugged
Simone goodbye at the doorway before wrapping her soft
pink scarf around the woolly black coat she was wearing.
Pulling her hair back, she glanced in readiness towards
Simone's husband Ivor who kissed his wife gently on the
cheek whilst whispering the words, 'I won't be long.' She
walked carefully down the set of old steps leading down from
the apartment, her hand holding the rails for support. She felt
both merriness and delicacy at that moment. Just a couple of
glasses of wine during the evening had sent her head spinning
a little earlier. It had been a long time since she had touched
any alcohol but tonight she had enjoyed it. Her own discipline
had steered her away from drink but it seemed no sin to share
a glass or two with good friends, especially at this time of the
year.

As Ivor joined her on the street, she smiled and linked arms
with him, out of their strong friendship and also the feeling of
dizziness that craved his support. They walked down Kestrel
Street and past Canary Wharf towards the nearby tube station.
Ivor chatted cheerfully along the way about life in London as

she asked questions about this building and that building. She asked out of that inborn curiosity that now heightened her senses. The icy evening made their steps slower as Ivor realised a slight tenseness in her usually confident walk. He smiled and answered as informatively as he could.

The streets were fairly deserted now, leaving a ghostly feel to this part of London. Above and ahead, the Christmas lights flickered in tandem with shop displays, guiding the path towards the tube station. The two saw only a few party revellers no doubt celebrating a Christmas bash and now also on their way home as the clock turned past midnight and towards the early hours.

Francesca looked and took everything in. Even the cold slabs that her feet echoed upon were a subject of thought. England was her home in name but, in her heart, it had never truly felt like that. Before the pregnancy, she had to be in this country, but it was not here, not now, not ever, that her heart lay. She admired much of this old country, with its Englishness, tonight especially. She digested the soothing voice of Ivor, together with the euphoric feeling of the alcohol, still very much in her bloodstream. So she listened, not for one but for two, and while she did she shared the thoughts with her unborn child. It would not be long before they were with Domenici back in San Piceno – home.

Ivor, having realised the tenseness in her step, held her arm more firmly as he chatted. It was with a genuine affection for his wife's beautiful friend that he did so. He had known Francesca for just a few years but, his wife apart, he had never met such a woman with a wholesome, wonderful attitude to this world. He truly cared for her, and now his eyes scanned around the empty streets with wary concern.

Francesca had asked to walk to the tube station in order to clear her head. After much debate over a cab, which she refused stiffly, it had been him that suggested he walk with her. Even now he regretted it. She had only agreed on the condition that he would walk her just to the tube station and no further. When he suggested accompanying her to South Kensington she would have none of it. The last tube ran at just after quarter past midnight and that would mean Ivor would have to get a taxi all the way back.

Francesca's sheer obstinacy meant that she would not change her mind. They had agreed to disagree which meant he would leave her at the station.

For now he was her strength, her guardian, for both of them and his friend Domenici. Soon that task would be over, leaving a short span of time before she would contact him with a text message: a message informing of her safe arrival home but, until then, that loop of time would stretch like elastic inside him. He tried not to show his uneasiness as they approached the station but Francesca sensed it.

There were a few people milling around outside. The majority were smoking before they took the steps down to the various platforms. Ivor suddenly fell silent. Sensing his emotions, Francesca stopped abruptly, her arm indicating Ivor to do the same. She slid her mobile out of her handbag and flicked the front open before pressing a button or two and holding the phone to her ear. 'For you, my dear Ivor.' She smiled, bringing the phone up.

He watched her as her smile lit up the street. Her dark innocent eyes sparkled as her soft voice spoke in response to the call connecting.

'Papa.' He watched her as she paused, her eyeballs rolling upwards softly as she listened. 'I'm sorry for waking you, Papa. I know it's late but I need a favour.'

A moment later she tucked the phone back into her bag. 'I hope that's enough for you, Ivor. Papa will meet me at the other end, okay?' She could not help but let a cheeky smile slip from her pretty face.

He soaked up her smile, finding he could do nothing but return it in kind. Her call had its desired effect. He felt better, knowing at least she would be in good hands sooner rather than later. They embraced gently before she planted a kiss on each cheek and bid him goodnight.

* * *

Canary Wharf tube station was at its quietest. As Francesca dropped the coins into the ticket-dispensing machine, the only sounds came from the whirring of the ticket being processed, along with a sudden gust of icy breeze from the main entrance. She shivered a little as she took the ticket, before walking carefully towards the barrier. The sound of her heeled boots now punched the floor, resounding much louder than before. At least it seemed so to her. She felt a little unsteady in her step without the supportive arm of Ivor to cling to.

A deep breath and a positive thought of home and she felt a surge of confidence. An escalator trip and three more turnings later and Francesca stood on the platform. At least ten feet away stood a couple, which made her feel more secure somehow. She did not have to wait long. The tube arrived two minutes later and she boarded, taking one of the many empty seats.

As the carriage and tube in general swayed from side to side, Francesca calculated her stop to switch lines. She would need to change from the Jubilee Line at Westminster. Six stops. Flicking through a discarded paper, she took in little of the headlines that stared at her in bold black ink. Her mind tried to shut out the tube's stench from a day gone by as she reflected on the evening.

It had been lovely to see Simone again and worth the journey, despite her condition. Simone was the same Simone she had grown up with in England, and Ivor was the perfect husband. Their life in the city was one of richness yet they still held time only for each other. Despite Ivor's high-profile job, he was not one of the London folk. Too many of the people at the gathering had been only interested in commenting on her looks, in between pouring expensive champagne and harping on about income and material objects. Francesca cared for neither.

Her thought pattern was broken as the tube slowly ground to a drumming halt at Westminster station. She glanced at the couple remaining on the carriage who were now in a drunken embrace. Her last vision of the tube as it slid back along its journey was of their lips against each other's. It made her smile and think of Domenici.

Taking the steps over to the next platform took just a minute or two. She could hear the sound of Big Ben chiming as she walked: one o'clock in the morning. She would just catch the last tube. No one passed her and, as she arrived at the Circle line platform, she found herself alone. Glancing up at the digital display, she saw that it would be four minutes before her tube arrived and then...home.

Small scuttling movements made her eyes snap towards the track. She saw little rats moving speedily along. A feeling of anxiety suddenly crept across her, almost as if one of the vermin below had crawled up onto her bare skin. Biting her lip, she breathed in again and concentrated on positive thoughts.

The eeriness of being alone on the platform was one that could easily overwhelm a person in the wrong frame of mind. Francesca was not such a person. Even when the sound of crisp steps from above vibrated downwards she remained as calm as possible.

She tried to picture the person before she saw him. The emptiness made the sound of their footwear echo tenfold, as each step came closer, closer...

She did not turn, but simply waited and concentrated on the clicking of shoe on concrete step. Her ears told her that the person was at the bottom now. A sly fleeting look told her it was a man. He must have glanced himself before taking three or four steps to the left, away from her, a sign of non-intrusion – perhaps.

Another quick look told her more. Her talent for taking in information rapidly served her well now. The man was just less than six feet tall, well built, with fine hair which was balding slightly on top. He wore a long coat that went down to his knees, covering what looked to be an expensive suit judging by the trousers and shining black shoes he wore. *Probably made in Italy,* she surmised with an inward smile that only a female with her inner strength could think at this place, this time of night. She was vulnerable but, having taken the snapshot of the man, she felt better than she had before the slow steps of his walk had rung in her ears.

From within the tunnel the sound of the tube resonated, bringing its underground thunder closer and sending the night beings below, scuttling away into their darkness once again. Many of the carriages had a few people within. Francesca took the one closest to her, sensing relief that it was empty. It felt safer somehow. The doors had already slid shut, before she even noticed the stranger in the same carriage. Before she had a chance to contemplate he walked towards her and took a seat just one away from her. Fear suddenly rose and caused her to cast a look straight into his face. He returned her look with an almost shy one as he nodded and gave her what could only be taken as an awkward smile.

Now as the tube bumped and jumped along the track Francesca found her mind playing games. She fought emotions as her brain raced, craving the end of the journey. Her eyes once more looked at the tube map above her. She did not need to this time. She knew how many stops, just four, but she wanted to look busy. She needed to feel busy.

One stop, then two stops went by. The man seemed to have absolutely no interest in her. He was reading from a document he had taken from his briefcase, head stooped, each time she had shot a look. Calming with each second that passed, she found her hand running up inside her coat and over her belly. The tube stopped once more and she noticed the man look up. She followed his eyes and saw why. Three people boarded the tube. Francesca let her eyes take in the new passengers.

There were two men and a girl. Francesca guessed the girl

was a similar age to herself. She was wearing a small cocktail dress, with just a skimpy jacket hanging over her shoulders. '*Much too little for this time of year,*' she thought. She must be cold but Francesca doubted that mattered as the girl looked drunk to the point of unconsciousness. The men had hold of her in either arm, each supporting her weight as they cajoled her through the doors. They moved along the carriage a little but did not sit down despite the room. The two men glared towards Francesca and the stranger before whispering to each other. Neither of them wore coats which was a little strange but then, judging by the girl's scanty evening wear, it was not so surprising. Francesca imagined a long night out, one where the girl had one too many drinks leaving her two friends to carry her home. She compared being in that situation and felt sick inside. She would never allow that to happen. Her hand responded on her belly. '*Especially now,*' she thought.

She was sure that she heard one of the men speak but the vibration of the track distorted any voice so she could not be sure. Then she heard a voice about which she could not be mistaken.

'Get off at the next stop.' It was a whisper, but strong enough to carry to her. 'Your life could depend on it.'

Her eyes saw his and they met for an instant. Francesca's gift of seeing people in a snapshot kicked in as his crisp blue eyes spoke to her. '*He means it and he's not a threat. He's scared.*'

In the time that remained to think, she could only weigh up two men and a girl versus one stranger. That stranger had just told her to get off the train. Before she had anymore time to consider why, the tube slowed at Sloane Square. As the doors slid open, she shot a glance at the stranger. His eyes pleaded with her as he rose and in one motion walked off the tube. Instantly she chose. She hurried off with him and, as she did so, her eye caught a glint of shining metal at one of the men's waistlines. It was not the gleam of a belt. It was the butt of a gun. She did not look back.

The doors slid shut and she was alone. Just her and her baby, alone with a stranger based on a second's instinct. She felt sick. The sensation of alcohol had long since worn off to be replaced by a sense of uncertainty and vulnerability.

His voice spoke again. This time he moved close and his presence did not scare her. In fact she felt a strange sense of relief.

'I'm sorry to have scared you.' The tone was soft and rich. 'Please follow me and let's get upstairs.' He signalled to the staircase leading upwards out of the station. Without a pause he turned and began to climb the steps. She followed automatically. The closer she got to the entrance, the safer she felt. More people would be there.

After a moment the two of them stood near the entrance of the station and then the man spoke again. 'Are you alright?' he asked, his voice full of concern. Francesca nodded somewhat confused. She was far from it.

'I heard them speak. They were not going to let us off.'

Francesca thought of the glint of the gun and as she did so his next words amplified in her mind.

'One of them had a gun.'

Their eyes met once more as she tried to speak through dry lips. 'I don't understand.'

He saw her fear and spoke slowly so as not to inflame it further. 'Neither do I, young lady, but I do know one thing. That girl they were holding...' he paused, '...you can be sure she was dead.'

Francesca swallowed hard as the reality of what had just happened sank in. How did he know? It mattered not. Whoever he was, he had possibly just saved her life, their lives.

'Shall I get you a taxi? Do you live nearby?' His soft voice brought her back to the present.

'I...I...my father is meeting me at South Kensington station. I'll call him,' she whispered.

'Then I'll wait with you until he comes,' he replied. 'If that's alright,' he added carefully.

'Of course, thank you.' Francesca forced a weak smile of gratitude as she pressed the redial on the phone. A moment later and she explained to her father that she was not at the planned tube stop but one two stops earlier.

'He'll be twenty minutes or so,' she told the stranger as she put the phone away. 'I said I would meet him by that coffee bar over there.' Francesca giggled suddenly. 'You just heard me say that on the phone anyway.'

He smiled back at her. 'Then I say let's get a coffee. We both need it.'

'A cappuccino and...' he glanced at her, 'espresso please.'

He indicated they should sit down at which Francesca frowned. She was starting to feel her old self once more. He looked bemused.

'You don't know much about Italy or Italians, I take it,' she said laughing. 'Two things: to drink espresso we stand. It's rude to sit. Also we only drink cappuccino in the mornings.'

He looked at her with amusement and suddenly they both started to laugh at their situation.

A voice broke into their laughter and Francesca turned, a look of relief suddenly spreading across her face. 'Papa!' she shouted out loud running towards her father before hugging him tightly. Stefano looked confused but happy to see his daughter so affectionate. As the hug broke, he looked towards the stranger and then back at Francesca.

She realised his confusion. 'I will tell you all later, Papa. Please, we must both thank this man for looking after me.'

Stefano did not question her. He knew her too well and trusted her absolutely. Taking a few steps forward he held out his hand with a warm expression. 'Thank you for taking care of her.'

The stranger shook his hand and nodded. 'It's nothing. I was glad to help.' He added nothing more, sensing Francesca's look.

She gently put her arms around him and kissed him on both

cheeks. 'Thank you so much. I...' A tear came from nowhere as she looked into his kind blue eyes. 'I feel I owe you my life somehow.'

He said nothing for a moment as if searching for an answer that was right. In the end he muttered, 'It was all I could do and I did it.'

She wiped the tear away and kissed him once more. 'I will never forget you.'

'And I will always remember you, pretty lady.' He grinned back.

'Francesca!' The voice behind them told her that her father had waited long enough.

'I must go,' she whispered.

'Goodbye,' he replied.

She took a few steps towards the door before spinning around. 'I'm so sorry! I didn't even ask your name!'

The man smiled enigmatically. 'The name's Pat, Pat Reilly.'

CHAPTER FORTY-TWO

December 2007 – beginning of 2008

'No, God! Please no! Please no! Oh Jesus! No, no, no…'

Jenny crumpled to the floor in a broken heap. Terry knelt beside her, his heart decaying. Terrance stood, stunned and shamefaced.

'Please, Jenny, Jenny, my love.' Terry tried to comfort her, his voice shaking with the shock.

'No, Terry, it can't be true. Not Holly, not my darling Holly.' She shook uncontrollably in his arms, her tears soaking his neck as he too broke down and sobbed with her. Two parents who had loved their child in different ways but loved her unconditionally nonetheless; the worst kind of tragedy engulfed them.

Terrance was glued to the spot. When the news came that Holly's body had been found, the guilt imploded within him. Three days had passed since the party and two since she had been placed on the missing list. Those two days had been hell. His father's look of disdain that he had left his sister in the first place. His mother's anger that he could be such an uncaring, unloving brother. Her face told him that she would rather it have been him.

What had followed was the guilt. The guilt of knowing that he left her there, of knowing that she was taking drugs, and of knowing that it was strange that she had left the party alone. Nothing added up and a thousand thoughts pounded his mind as to her last moments. No one at Lord Chavry's had any answers and that sickened him. It sickened him because they did not care. It repulsed him that he was one of those types of people. The thought would not leave him now. He felt totally responsible for her death. If he had stayed, she may still be alive. He knew it, and he knew that his parents knew it.

* * *

The funeral was to be held in Worksop. Terry had, for the final time, made the family decision. 'For the family,' he had said. 'What family?' she had screeched, sobbing in reply, 'We haven't been a family for years.'

Darkness had set in the Healy household. The death of Holly had blackened their souls and left a void, never to be replaced. When the argument started on where her daughter should be buried, Jenny simply didn't have the energy to fight. There was no winner. They had all lost, her the most.

Terry arranged everything. Jenny said nothing. Terrance was an empty shell. Before Holly's death, the rejection of Francesca had wounded him beyond words. He had realised that, for all the power he had craved and all the power he had gained, none could conquer love. Money could not buy the love of one girl, or the life of another.

The day of the funeral came. The Healy family, along with many friends of Holly's from school and university, made their way to Worksop. Black shapes crowded below a barren grey sky as they filed into the church. Amongst the tears and anguish were words of her life, set against the only colour from the elaborate coffin which shone gold and silver against shining wood. The music muffled sobs as the song 'Return to Innocence' by Enigma played to the pallbearer's slow march to her graveside. As Holly Healy's young body was lowered into the hole in the ground, it left a hole as dark and black within Jenny's broken heart. All watched, grief-stricken, as Holly was laid to rest. Terrance forgot everything else at that moment and cried uncontrollably.

* * *

There was no Christmas or New Year in the Healy household that year. There was no talk of work or business as Terry instructed his staff to 'take care of things', and Terrance booked himself off on leave of absence. To Jenny, the only good thing that came out of all the agony was to see her husband and son actually caring about something else *but* business.

When the New Year was done with, Jenny informed them that she was going away for a few days to spend time in Stebdon with her family. There was no suggestion of an invite for either of them and neither questioned her.

* * *

The frost was crisp on the ground the morning of her leaving. Terry had asked if she wanted Joey to drive her down which she bluntly refused. She wanted to be alone. As she pulled out of the driveway she noticed a familiar shape a short distance away on the heath. She gasped before stopping the car.

He sat huddled under a tree, his face lowered but his eyes looking beyond her in the direction of the house. She could see he was shivering like a drunk, his parka covering his shaven head but there was no doubt: it was him.

Jenny got out of the car and walked slowly toward him.

'Oliver?'

He did not respond but muttered a little as she drew close enough to touch him.

'Oliver? Can you hear me?'

She heard his mumbles now. 'Must stay close, must watch, must wait, must protect.'

'Oliver, you're scaring me. Are you alright?' Jenny half knelt, pushing her face close to his. He snapped out of the trance-like state and flicked his eyes in her direction with such ferocity it made her heart skip a beat.

'Jenny,' his voice was focused, 'I am so sorry. I heard the news…how are you coping? Where are you going?'

'I'm going to Stebdon, Oliver. I need to spend some time with my parents, to spend some time at *home*.' The words comforted her as she heard them in the chilled air.

'That's good, Jenny,' he replied slowly, 'that's good. I'll stay here and watch and it will all be alright.'

'Watch, watch for what, Oliver?' she replied worryingly. 'Why don't you let me drive you to the shelter, take you in the warm?'

He swayed his head in confusion. Nodding back and forth and muttering again before switching his gaze back on her clearly.

'Can you take me to either London Bridge or my place in Oxford Circus? It must be one of those two places.'

'Of course I can. Come on, let me help you up.'

Jenny pulled him slowly to his feet. She could feel ice on the parka crack as she lifted him. He must have been there for hours. The desire to leave for Stebdon wavered for a moment as she helped Oliver into the car and headed for home, his home at least.

'Why did you come here, Oliver? Where have you been?' Jenny fired questions as they made the journey.

Oliver did not look at her as, gazing out of the window, he replied, 'I had to come, not to see you, mind; just to make sure.'

'Make sure of what? You're not making sense.' Jenny felt a tinge of frustration. Could she really just leave him now, like this? Oliver made her mind up for her.

'Jen,' he gently slid his hand onto her shoulder, 'I know you have things to do and so do I. It's for a reason and, for now, I can't tell you about that reason. Just know one thing, I never stop thinking of you and I feel so sad about Holly…' He looked away once more and Jenny saw tears as she quickly glanced away from the wheel.

Of course, she thought, Oliver would have known, would have found out. That was Oliver and he was right: now was not a time for talking. He had his reasons, she had hers.

She left Oliver standing on the kerb in Oxford Circus and made her way to Stebdon.

She could not concern herself with thinking too much about him now. Her mind was full of the places she would visit, for her, for Holly, for the happy times. She would look up Albert Guild in his shop and she would visit the dance hall where she had spent so many carefree nights. She would walk the pretty streets and breathe in that special air that would remind her of youth and heal her heart.

But she would in fact do none of those things.

* * *

Stebdon was no more. She sensed it as soon as she passed the sign, welcoming any passer-by to Stebdon. The 'Please drive carefully' was difficult to make out under the black graffiti that was sprayed across it. The road into the village had unkempt grass and she saw broken glass littered around. Jenny drove slowly, the shock of each terrible new discovery seeming more awful than the last. She came to the village hall and saw the sign which said 'Temporary shelter – 2 weeks'. More graffiti stood out, and away in the distance she could see row upon row of what appeared to be caravans. Had the village been invaded by gypsies?

She searched for answers in the village centre and there she found some. The streets which she had grown up on now lay empty. The shops she remembered were gone. Boards covered them or blank whitewashed windows. As she approached Guild's Toys her heart sank. It looked as though it had shut down.

She stopped the car and got out. Walking to the shopfront she saw that familiar paned door and imagined the ring of the bell in her mind. A handwritten sign still adorned the window. It's writing now faint. **'NOTICE: Last week of trading, thank you for all your support over the years. 50% off until 1st November 2007'**

Jenny swallowed back the tears as the sorrow enveloped her. What had happened? Where had the Stebdon she grew up in gone? She thought of Holly and it simply compounded the loss. Running back to the car she screeched away to find her parents and get some answers.

* * *

'What's happened to the village, Mum, Dad?' Jenny let loose as soon as she entered the house. Her shout made her mother jolt in her chair as her father tried to soothe her.

'Dear Jenny.' Her mum tried to comfort her. 'I know you're upset about Holly, of course you are, love. Come and sit down. Don't you be worrying about silly things now.'

Jenny didn't want to talk about Holly. The loss of her daughter was why she had come here; to escape the sadness, to return to a place where she had such beautiful memories, to return 'home'.

'I can't believe it.' Jenny sat down. 'What has happened to the village? Dad…?'

'Things changed, Jenny. Things changed fast.' His reply sounded uncertain in itself.

'I don't get it!' She felt anger surface. 'Why didn't you tell me?'

Her mother looked away and her father looked downwards as he answered. 'It's hard to say this, Jenny…' He didn't have to; Jenny's mum intervened, 'Because of your husband!'

'What the hell does that mean, Mum?' Jenny was shell-shocked.

'To put it in a nutshell,' she looked sternly at her daughter, 'we thought *you* would know.'

'But, Mum, I had no idea. Do you think I would have

wanted *this*? Why didn't you say something at the funeral?'

Her father shook his head. 'No, it's not our business and we're keeping ourselves out of this. If some of the people of the village knew,' he gave her a worried look, 'it was our family then…'

'What are you saying, Dad?'

'He's saying that the farm on the hill got a big contract from *your* husband. All very fine to begin with.' Her mother's voice had a sarcastic edge to it. 'All the local villagers had plenty of work and Mr Sonning and his wife… well, fine people. The son is nice enough but he got greedy, see? Got in with *your* lot, fancy big contracts and too much to cope with so what does the farm do? I'll tell you! They bring in more workers. Firstly from outside the village and *then*, outside the country; bloody foreigners, as if we didn't fight them off all those years ago!' She became enraged.

'Marge, calm down.' Jenny's father, Bill, tried to soothe her.

'I will not calm down! She deserves to know!' Jenny's mum paused for a brief respite before continuing more calmly but still with a burning fury. 'So, the farm lets them stay on their land in exchange for payment, therefore earning more money. To begin with, it wasn't so bad, was it, Bill?' He nodded grimly. 'That was before your shop opened here and shut down any competition *and*,' the rage returned to her voice, 'it was before your son decided that the farm had failed on a delivery so he kindly gave the business to another company.'

'I can't believe it,' Jenny said quietly.

'Well, you should, Jenny,' she answered stiffly. 'As soon as the farm lost the work, the workers had no jobs and as soon as *your* shop shut the others down then more people lost their jobs.' Marge slowed. A tinge of remorse surfaced. 'That son of yours, he's not so clever, you know, giving the contract away. Now there's no work. There's no money, and people have nothing to spend at your shop so now that's closed down!'

'I had no idea, Mum, honestly, I had no idea,' Jenny said in a shattered voice.

Bill put his arm around her. 'We're not blaming you, dear. You probably had no idea. We know that. It's just such a shame. It's not just happening here, mind. It's happening across the country, you know.'

Jenny multiplied the thought in her mind, feeling sickened as she did so.

'Fools,' she whispered to herself, 'if there are no jobs then who will buy anything?'

'Like I said earlier, dear,' her father said in a composed voice, 'times are changing.'

Jenny looked at both her parents and joined in their sorrow. 'Yes, Dad, Mum, times are changing, and I am going to make sure of that.'

* * *

'Do you remember where we met, Terry?'

The iciness in her voice startled him. He poured a cognac as he chewed on the steak, giving his mind a chance to reflect on the question.

'Of course I do, love. The dance hall.' He gave a smile as he sipped the drink. 'You always were a good dancer, Jenny, lithe and pretty.'

Her silence led him to believe it was part of the event. She had asked, no, forced the issue of a meal alone together. She was right, of course she was. They spent too little time together and even now, after the tragedy of Holly's death together with his much emptier schedule, they still spent a fraction of time together. A foreign emotion emerged: something reminiscent of guilt perhaps, of time lost that could never be recovered. Gulping the cognac, the brief sentimental feeling passed as he refilled the glass and gazed across the candlelit table at his wife. She looked beautiful. Sometimes he felt he had forgotten just how much.

'Do you remember *where* we met, Terry?' Her eyes met his. 'The dance hall, yes, but *where*?'

'Ah, I see!' He smiled as the penny dropped. 'Of course, love, in Stebdon.' He pushed a combination of steak and mushrooms into his mouth as he added, 'Mmm, never forget that place, or that night.'

In romantic terms, it could have been classed as a compliment from her husband. He rarely said anything along those lines. Jenny remained unfazed.

'Do you remember the last time we went there together?'

Still chewing he shook his head. 'I can't say as I can, love. You've been back plenty though, haven't you?'

'I certainly have.' Her answer was icy cold. 'I was there just the other day, Terry. I saw one of your supermarkets there as well. You never mentioned that to me, did you?'

'I had no idea.' His face showed genuine surprise. 'I'm not involved with that side so much anymore, love…expansion. Honestly, I had no idea.'

'Well, darling,' Jenny leant forward, adding to the impact, 'I suggest you go there and see what the effects of a T Healy & Sons have had on a small village. It certainly had an effect on me.' Glaring she went on, the fury prominent upon her face. 'I would imagine it has had quite an effect on the people of the village as well judging by what I saw.'

He had never seen her look so enraged. He reflected on the chat with Terrance about the protests and the newspapers. Things had got out of control but could be undone, of that he was sure. This, however, this was more tricky.

'Jenny, I had no idea. Tell me, what's happened?'

'Gone! It has all bloody gone!' Her eyes filled with tears. 'You! You!'

'Please, love, calm down.' His voice fell on deaf ears.

She looked through him as the anger rose. 'There's going to be change, Terry, and I'm going to make it. I want change.'

A panic gripped him as he tried to digest what she was saying. 'Anything, love, we can work anything out.'

As she stood, Jenny felt overwhelmed by the sadness of it all. Holly came to the forefront of her mind followed by a cascade of images over her lifetime that flashed by: happier days, hopeful days, not days like today. Her voice faltered as the pain of it all came forth. 'I'm going away for a while. I need to think. I'm not sure what I want anymore.'

The impetus of her words hit home. For the first time in all their years together he cracked like a brittle bone. 'Please…please don't leave me. I love you, Jenny, I always have. I only ever wanted the best for you. Please…'

She could not hate him even though she had so wanted to before now. It was not him that had destroyed her town. It was the company. It was not him that had left their marriage empty and emotionless. It was the company. Not him that had totally created the son she resented. That too, was the company. And Holly…? She swallowed hard as she turned away. Was that the company? What if she had not gone that night? It was too much to bear.

'I don't know anymore, Terry. I'm sorry.'

CHAPTER FORTY-THREE

'The pendulum swings. Much has been lost and much will be gained, just as the light of Holly Healy has become dark, so will the dark become light. The balance will be restored. Let the Angels walk upon Earth for the last time; the clock is ticking.'
    (Galgliel's scripture entered into the chronicle of Omniangels)

'Mum, I can't ask anymore except that you think about it, *please.* Dad's lost without you and I am worried, *seriously* worried. He looks ill. He's not eating. Mum, please.'

Jenny paced the London hotel room as Terrance pleaded with her. The past week had been heart-rending as she had faced up to the choices she had. Since the death of Holly, nothing had seemed the same. The grief was total.

'I'll think about what you've said,' she replied after a while. 'I appreciate you coming here, Terrance. It must have taken some guts.' She gave him a loveless glance before continuing: 'You have to understand that for the last God knows how many years I've felt alone. Only Holly gave me something to hold onto and…' She fell into silence at the thought of Oliver. No, she was not about to get into a conversation about the vagrant that had given her more real feeling than her husband and son combined. She wondered about him suddenly as Terrance spoke.

'I know how you felt about Holly and deservedly so, Mum. She is…' his voice faltered, 'was…a beautiful girl and I miss her deeply.' Jenny saw his earnestness as he went on, 'Dad

369

and especially me have missed the point for too long but for us, for Holly, please, Mum. Don't let our family come to this. I beg you.'

'No guarantees, Terrance. I need more time to put things together.' Jenny motioned towards the door of the plush room. 'Now, if you don't mind.'

The kiss that he left on her cheek remained in her mind for some time after he had gone. Lying on the bed, Jenny closed her eyes and tried to shut the world out.

* * *

The evening drew the darkness in early, the crisp chill sending people indoors as quickly as possible. Dog walkers and passers-by were at a premium on Hampstead Heath as the ghostly mist spread across the park.

A shadow moved through the blue-black night, its breath unnoticeable now against the blanket of thin fog, steps as silent as space itself, purpose absolute. Steering away from the street lights he watched in silence. The empty street across from the park held his goal. He checked his inside pocket. The gun was there. A quick pinch of whisky from the bottle that had become his crutch and he was ready. Soon he would be able to face his demon.

* * *

The bar on London Bridge provided a welcome refuge on a freezing night. Terrance had paced the streets for a few hours after speaking with his mother. Recent times had set his mind awash with dilemmas and concerns. As the foreign girl struggled to understand his order for a drink, he found himself wondering about the business. He had not thought of work for some time but now, seeing her blank expression, he almost let a wry grin slip from his lips at the changes around him. England was selling its soul for the price of a profit. He, of all people, should have seen it coming.

He sat alone. One drink became two which became three. No one made any attempt to make contact with him. No one gave him a second look. Here, in one of the great cities of the world, he was just another human being. He was nothing special at all; in fact the city lights just magnified his irrelevance. He listened in on passing conversations as he watched the clientele predominantly of suited young men, fresh-faced and vibrant, discussing margins and life in the City. He saw the odd cluster of ageing men and woman wearing ageing suits, holding on to the last strands of youth as they attempted to fit in with a world that was ever changing. He saw the drawn lines on their faces from one too many nights at the office and he saw the emptiness that he himself felt inside. A hollow interior, borne of work-induced fervour, which had left their families far behind and alien to them. Their worship of money had seen to that and now, trapped in the loop, they had spent plenty of that money on a range of anti-ageing products in a world that was purely cosmetic. Their exteriors painted with products and treatments afforded by the wages that were their Gods. Now though, as he watched these people, he could almost see the cracks forming as age, strain and a slow realisation crept over them. He remembered a saying from his father: it's the person that makes the habits but in the end it's those habits that make the person. They may be surrounded now by their little groups of business friends, but once that time came to go home, he knew they would be as lonely and as unwanted as he was now.

The drinks did little to help. Instead the emotions heightened and the clarity seemed to absorb him. In all his years, he had cared for little but the business and the status it had given him. Only Francesca had meant anything, and he had lost her to his own greed and gain. He wondered about her, and reflected on her beauty and strength. Something he had never seen in a woman before. As time was called in the bar he made his decision, whispering to himself as the bouncer ushered him unsteadily to his feet, 'It's never too late.'

Starting out by the HMS Belfast to head for the tube station, Terrance was suddenly distracted by the pretty display in a nearby flower shop. The first thought that ran through his mind was *'Open late? Yeah, I bet those people nip in to buy forgiveness from their loved ones.'* He passed the shop glancing at the array of flowers within, pure and fragrant. At the corner he checked. Another thought entered his mind. It was borne out of the thing that had troubled him all that night: love.

A few moments later and he left the shop carrying a beautiful bouquet. He noticed now the odd glance from people. People, like him, who probably figured he was just another statistic of the City, eager to please the lonely partner that he had deserted for the evening. Terrance found himself humoured by the irony. He knew where these flowers were going. He would have loved nothing more than to be taking them home to the girl he loved. Nearing the tube station, he stopped to pick up a bottle of water from a vending machine. As he fumbled one-handed for change, he recollected the girl's words in the shop as he had paid for the flowers. At the time they had not registered, but now, they had a new meaning.

'They're lovely. She must be a lucky woman.'

The girl behind the counter was, he guessed, in her early twenties, plain yet attractive. Mary Jane meets Peter Parker kind of plain. He laughed as he handed over the money. 'I guess she is.'

He now recalled her gentle sigh, like a bird that had lost its song.

Impulsively he retraced his steps back towards the flower shop and moments later stood in front of the girl smiling awkwardly.

'These are for you.'

She did not sigh this time. Instead, a smile lit up her face as she began to laugh.

'That is so…you shouldn't have. I didn't mean to… why?'

'I got them because you made me believe in something: how lucky I actually am.' With a smile he added, 'I'll need another bouquet though; something different, they're for my mother.'

'Of course and, like I said, she's a lucky lady.' The girl's face reddened as she picked out another bouquet and gave it to Terrance smiling shyly. 'And thank you.'

Terrance paid and walked towards the door before pausing. He turned back to see the girl looking at him. 'I just want you to know,' he smiled warmly, 'I got them because I wanted you to know that you're special.'

A warm sensation crept through him as he left the shop to deliver the other bouquet leaving a total stranger touched by his kindness.

* * *

The brass knocker thudded into the night, its echo carrying into the street. He waited, first feeling the glare of the outside light as it flicked on before watching as the door opened to reveal the face he had not seen in years: the face of Terry Healy.

Terry did not recognise his visitor as he stared blankly. 'Can I help you?'

'You most certainly can, Mr Healy, you most certainly can. Would you mind if I borrowed a moment of your time?'

'At this time of night, I think not!' Terry replied irritably. 'Who the hell are you?'

The mood changed in that instant as the man leapt forwards, shoving the door and him backwards. Seconds later and he was inside.

'You always were pretty blunt, weren't you, Mr Healy.' His voice reeked of sarcasm. 'Your way or the highway, as I remember.'

Terry looked mystified. Trying to gather composure and

control, he raised his voice in reply. 'I have no idea who you are! Take what the bloody hell you want and go, before I call the police!'

Producing the gun the man spoke quietly in reply, a sickly smile appearing. 'The police, you say? Oh, Mr Healy. How apt, how very you.'

Levelling the gun in front of Terry's face, the man's expression remained fixed on Terry who took a step backwards, alarm bells ringing in his ears as he stuttered, 'Do...do I know you?'

Waving the gun in his direction, John answered apologetically. 'Sorry, Mr Healy, bad manners on my part! Does the name John Parsons ring any bells?' He watched for a reaction and, seeing none, continued in a more sinister voice. 'Let me help you along, Terry. The last time we had any dealings was, let me see,' he feigned thoughtfulness rubbing his chin, 'oh yes, twenty-eight years ago. I worked for you, Mr Healy, drove a lorry for your company. Rather smaller than it is now, I must admit. I'm surprised you don't remember?'

Terry stepped back again, his mind in turmoil, as he tried to make a connection between the shabby-looking man in front of him and his statement. Just as the pieces began to fall into place, John spoke again with a new found antagonism. 'You see, Mr Healy, I crashed a lorry driving for you.' Looking down briefly he added, 'Not your fault, of course. I killed four people, Mr Healy. Four innocent people.' He returned his stare which was now full of remorse as he relived the moment. 'I've lived with that pain for the last twenty-eight years, you know. A heavy burden, wouldn't you agree?'

'Yes, yes, I would. But I don't see how...'

Sadness was replaced by fury as John interceded. 'I didn't think you would, Mr Healy. Can't see how that has anything to do with you, and to a degree you're right. You weren't driving the lorry, were you? You weren't over the limit, were you? No... I understand your view. So, let me tell you why I'm here, shall I?'

Before Terry could reply he felt the cold steel of the gun barrel against his forehead.

'I would suggest you stop edging towards the phone, Mr Healy. There, that's a good man. Now, where had I got to? Oh yes, why I'm here. I'm here to tell you what happened to me after that night. Of the twenty-eight years since that awful event, I have spent eleven of them inside a prison cell repaying a small proportion of my debt. I can never repay that debt fully though, Mr Healy. I have to live with that every waking moment of my miserable life.' Looking at Terry through tear-filled eyes he went on, 'And that's where you come in. I lost my freedom for my crime and accepted the sentence given to me. **You took the rest from me!** I could have carried on the business if you hadn't immediately distanced yourself from me.

'Not for me, Mr Healy, for my family, my wife and child! I could have got someone to carry the business on so they would have an income and I would have been forgiven.' John moved the gun menacingly along Terry's temple, the release of passionate hate prominent on his face. 'I lost them both, Mr Healy, and I lost eleven years of my worthless life. Do you know what it's like to face that kind of loss, Mr Healy? Would you like me to show you?'

Terry felt the cold touch of the barrel against his forehead a split second before the pain hit his chest. A searing spear of death coursed through his veins as the heart attack came. Unable to find breath, the panic set in as his heart began to fail. John watched Terry's complexion change from a red-pink to a gaunt grey.

'What the hell? What's wrong?'

He watched, stunned, as Terry fell backwards, crashing into the sideboard sending ornaments falling as he hit the floor.

'Oh my God, I didn't mean for this to happen!' John yelled 'Oh shit! Stop! Get up!'

There was no response from Terry as his body fought against the attack. The seconds ticked by as John stood motionless. Then suddenly the debate was over as his consciousness kicked in. *'Get the hell out of here! He ain't gonna make it! If you get found here then you've had it!'*

Slipping the gun inside his pocket, John took a last glance at the spluttering figure on the floor. A quick look around showed no sign of his presence. As long as the old fool died, he had nothing to worry about. John Parsons had faced his demons and said his piece. Time to go.

As he pulled the door shut Terry struggled to clamber up. His throat felt trapped by the shirt, his chest clamped by veins that had become steel-fibred rope enclosing his frail heart. Somehow he made it to the phone and, grabbing the receiver, punched in the numbers 999. Seconds flashed by before he heard his own voice: 'I want to report a burglary! Yes, a burglary. My name is…' The receiver slipped from his sweating hand before he could speak further. A flash of colour hit his temple and then – everything went black.

* * *

'I would like these to be given to Mrs Jenny Healy.' Terrance placed the bouquet on the hotel desk counter as he added, '…please. Just say they're from someone who loves her, nothing more.'

The receptionist scanned through the computer records before she nodded. 'Yes, sir, I'll make sure that's done.' She flashed a look at the flowers then at him.

'I'm sure she'll like them very much. Do you want me to…?'

'No.' He smiled. 'She'll be asleep now. If you wouldn't mind keeping them in water, I'd like them delivered with her breakfast. She'll like that.'

'Of course, sir, leave it to me.'

It was a fair walk back to the tube station but Terrance did not mind. Something had happened to him tonight. He had discovered emotions that had made him feel light on the inside. Everything seemed clearer after watching so many people. A message had been delivered, and he understood that message. Tomorrow or today, as it was by now, would be a new day, a new beginning.

Stopping by the ship he gazed out across the Thames. The vast vessel floated calmly on the black carpet. The glittering lights of the city flickered, as if the starlit sky above had dropped down to his eye level. Inhaling deeply, Terrance felt a surge of crisp air hit his lungs. He actually felt good to be alive. Awareness encompassed him now, despite all that had happened with his family. Now was his chance to make a difference. A chance to prove he was capable of love, a chance to honour his beautiful sister. As he thought about Holly, he let the sadness engulf him in the stunning setting. He whispered into the night, *'I wish it had been me, instead of you.'* Crying silently he paid tribute to a precious life lost and vowed never to forget her. Never to forget who he really could and should be.

The icy cold was the only thing that made him aware once again. A glimpse at his watch told him it was only a short time before the last tube would leave. Pulling his collar up around his neck, he headed towards the station at a brisk pace, oblivious to the watching shadows. The world was changing. Not subtly, as in decades past, but as foretold by the Archangel. Darkness took the form of man, unaware of good intentions or kindness; only intent on its desire, its greed. Terrance walked towards the black hearts without a clue.

The two youths did not see a man who had made any difference that night. They saw prey in the form of a typical suit, easy pickings at this hour. All his life, Terrance Healy had been in a position of power. Tonight he was just another man in a suit, walking alone in a place where he should not be. Fate was about to strike.

Terrance was wondering about his father. He wondered if he would still be up, waiting to see what progress, if any, had been made by the visit to Jenny. He debated what to say. How to put things in a way that would offer hope, yet not become a false dawn. As he juggled the possibilities of each scenario, the shadows struck. Two shapes appeared behind him. The first he knew of the attack was a blow to the back of his head. The ferocity sent him forwards, slamming to the floor, as all around him became a blur. A voice, maybe more than one, sounded behind him as his hands instinctively reached out, clutching for something to hold onto, to save the fall. They only met with solid concrete which tore into his skin. Attempting to avoid further blows, he put his arms to his face. He felt his ribs crack, as the boot made contact. The air from his lungs burst out into the night, leaving a winded desperation for oxygen. He waited for the next blow, unable to shout out, unable to defend, unable to believe this was happening.

He heard more noise now, a crack of bone perhaps. His mind tried to make sense of the sound. It was not him being hit, but someone else. A yell of pain leapt into his earlobes, followed by a scream of rage, like the sound of a banshee which penetrated the darkness. Breath slowly came back to him. He turned on one side to see the three shapes in violent conflict. One was scampering away now, limping badly whilst the other two were embroiled in battle. Then it was over. A crushing sound ended the brawl as one hit the other, sending him against a railing which welcomed his skull with its steel bars. The last remaining man turned slowly around to face him.

The moonlight created a silhouette around him. Terrance saw the tall, lean frame of the man from his feet upwards. As his eyes climbed, they met a clearly defined shaven skull from which ice-emerald eyes stared in his direction before he heard the words.

'You have just met your guardian Angel, Terrance Healy.'

An onslaught of fear overwhelmed Terrance before he lost consciousness.

CHAPTER FORTY-FOUR

John reached the outside railings and tore down the street twenty metres or so, before he came to a halt. Gasping for breath, he began to think about what had just happened. During his life, John had seen his fair share of heartache and pain yet was he now totally ruthless? The thought of leaving a man to die alone was too much to bear. Even if it was Terry bloody Healy. If he went now, the chances were that he would not be found out. He could therefore carry on, living in the knowledge that the old bastard had got what he deserved. But would he? The battle of two inner spirits raged as John surveyed the options.

If he left now he would have to live with that for the remainder of his days, on top of the longstanding guilt from years ago. It would become another burden. If he went back, he would have to break in and that could add to his troubles. The only other scenario would be to call an ambulance himself and do the right thing. He knew the risk of doing that. With a sigh, he made the call from his mobile. After a few moments of explaining what had happened and having given them all his details, John trudged back up the road and waited for the ambulance to arrive. Within moments the flashing lights and sirens of two police cars lit up the area.

'Mr John Parsons?' The police officers approached him as he waited outside the house.

'Yeah, that's me,' John replied.

'Can you come with us please, sir? It's concerning Mr

Terry Healy.'

With a sigh of acceptance, he let the officers guide him to the car where he was handcuffed and bundled into the back. As they drove off, he saw the ambulance screech to a halt and two paramedics run towards the door. John Parsons gave a half-hearted smile. Terry Healy could have had that heart attack anytime. Maybe they could save him; he hoped so. After all the years, all the heartache, perhaps it would be him, of all people, who helped to save Terry Healy. A part of John wanted to laugh at the irony, another part to sob in despair. One thing he knew for sure: It seemed that every time he had the misfortune to be involved with Terry Healy, his world changed for the worst.

* * *

The white light paled a little to be replaced by a familiar face from long past.

'Mr Baker?' Terry mumbled as he saw the figure come into view. 'Am I…am I dead?'

The old man smiled kindly. *'Not yet, not in the way you think, young Terry. It's been a long time, you know.'*

'But if I'm not dead, how is it that I'm talking with you? You died years ago, Mr Baker.' He checked for a moment suddenly feeling rude. 'I apologise, sir. I'm confused, that's all. It's so lovely to see you again, but how?'

Mr Baker's face came closer, and it was then that Terry realised he could not move. He looked lovingly at his former boss as the old man moved close enough for him to breathe in the smell of his cologne.

'I am only here, because you allowed me to be, Terry. I have been around for some time, you know.' Mr Baker winked, just like he used to when Terry had done something good or right when he was younger. *'You shut many things out on your rise to the top, Terry. I suppose you would not believe in Angels if I told you about them, would you?'*

'Are you saying that you're an Angel, Mr Baker?' Terry's voice sounded unsure.

'Of sorts, yes, indeed I am. You could say a guardian Angel.' He gave Terry a knowing smile. *'We all have them, Terry. You just have to look hard enough.'*

'Why are you here now, Mr Baker?' He felt a tinge of fear as he asked the question. 'Have I messed it all up? I only ever wanted to do the right thing, Mr Baker, like you taught me. I only wanted to be a good man.'

Mr Baker scratched his chin thoughtfully as he looked at his young protégé. *'Listen carefully, Terry,'* he said after a moment. *'I watched over you as a young man. You have a good heart. I watched over you for many years, and I know that it is not too late for you. Many things on this Earth are changing. The call of the Angels will not be answered soon. In fact Angels of many types will face an exile of sorts.'* He saw Terry looking back, confusion written upon his expression. *'I will try and make it as simple as possible. I have wanted to appear before you for many years but your beliefs have made that impossible. There are Angels everywhere on Earth. Some able to cross the divide and appear in human form, others only in visions. It all depends on many things. Soon that will stop. There is a new darkness on the horizon, a new challenge that the half Angels will face. They are the hope for all things good and pure.'*

'I see,' Terry replied, looking unsure. 'I don't understand what that has to do with me though, Mr Baker.'

'Of course not.' Mr Baker chuckled. *'I am sorry. Let me explain. You are not going to die, Terry Healy. You have been spared, and the lessons of this moment will stay with you for the remainder of your healthy life. You are involved in all of this. You have been chosen, a small part to play, but a part nevertheless. Your life has had much impact on others. Your actions and the actions of others close to you have changed lives for the better and for the worse. Your own family has suffered but now is the chance for you to make a difference, to*

change things for the good. Now, when you have chosen for me to appear, is the time that you have opened your soul. It is not too late.'

An inner affection coursed through Terry's veins as he listened to the gentle tone of Mr Baker, a man he had respected and loved. He had forgotten how much he missed him.

'I have made many mistakes, Mr Baker. I should have slowed things down, concentrated on my family. I should have spent more time loving them.'

'Hush now, Terry.' The old man interrupted him with a warm grin. *'There will be a brighter day, and you will survive. You will make good choices and help to redress the balance. It will only be a thin slither of a fingernail on the hand of a giant, but, it will help to add to the message and lead the way.'* Terry watched as his expression became serious. *'You must do something very important when you wake up, Terry, very important.'*

'Of course,' Terry answered confidently, 'anything.'

Mr Baker moved closer and, although he could not see them, he could feel the hands of the old man softly wiping his forehead, sending a calming sensation into his mind.

'You must forgive the man who saved your life today. Without him you would now be dead.' Mr Baker nodded before Terry could say the words 'John Parsons'. *'You must repay him the debt you now owe. To do that, you must explain he saved your life and then tell Terrance that you need him to meet John Parsons. Do you understand, Terry? Tell Terrance, he must meet John.'*

'Yes, I will do as you say.' Terry felt his voice becoming quieter.

'Good. If you do not do this then much will fail. It is the balance. Do not fear. Terrance will know what to do.'

Terry felt the old man's fingertips upon his eyelids as sleep overwhelmed him. 'God bless you, Terry Healy.' Mr Baker's voice caressed his mind as slumber came. *'I am so glad you finally called upon me.'*

* * *

'He'll be alright, Jenny, broken ribs at worst. I got here just in time. Yes, by the HMS Belfast. He'll be fine, just shaken with a few cuts and bruises.'

Terrance regained consciousness to hear his mother's name being spoken. Glancing up from the floor he saw the man kneeling alongside him. He was holding Terrance's mobile to his ear and appeared to be talking with his own mother. Terrance tried to speak but all he could muster was a faint grunt as pain shot through his side.

'I told you I would be here, Jenny. You just didn't understand what I meant. I promised I would come back and be ready for this moment.' The man must have sensed Terrance moving as he looked round. 'Wait, Jenny, I think he's coming to. Alright, I'll see you soon.'

'What the hell is happening?' Terrance tried to sit up as a stabbing pain ripped from his ribcage.

Clicking the mobile shut, the man offered it back as he spoke. 'Hey, take it easy, Terrance. You've broken ribs and a pretty nasty cut on the back of your head. Let me help you up. We need to get you checked out at a hospital.'

Holding his arms up as a kind of shield, Terrance snapped, 'I'm not going anywhere with you until you tell me what the hell is going on! Was that my mother you were speaking to? Who the hell are you?'

He felt the dizziness surround him as he fell back to the floor. The man recognised this and caught his head as it slumped backwards. In a soft voice he tried to explain. 'Calm down, Terrance. It was your mother. She called to speak with you. I took the phone from your pocket and saw it was her so I answered. I know your mother. She's my friend.' The man moved closer now and Terrance saw concern in his eyes as he went on, 'She's on her way now. My name is Oliver. Do you remember anything about what happened?'

Terrance tried to recall the events. 'I was walking…thinking about my mother and then…it all happened so fast.' He looked at Oliver in confusion. 'I don't know… Please, tell me what's happening, Oliver.'

Kneeling down alongside him, Oliver spoke with assurance. 'I've known about you for some time, Terrance. What I am about to tell you will probably seem bizarre, if not crazy to you, but it doesn't matter. You'll know I'm speaking the truth and perhaps you will believe me.'

'Try me,' Terrance answered rubbing his head. 'Tonight has opened my eyes up more than you know.'

'It's strange you should say that,' Oliver replied. 'The man you see in front of you was someone you would have probably sneered at a few months ago. I was a homeless drug addict when I met them, you see.'

'Met who?'

'When I met your mother, and when I saw the Angel. They both changed my life and, unbeknown to me at the time, changed yours it seems, or at least saved it.'

Looking a little startled, Terrance tried to find the words to react. 'My mother never mentioned you!'

'I understand why,' Oliver retorted. 'She realised how you would have been, I suppose. She's a wonderful woman who has been left alone for too long. When the Angel spoke with me, I knew that I was destined to know Jenny, destined to save you.'

Feeling less confused, Terrance tried to make sense of what Oliver was saying. 'How is it that you were here tonight?' he asked in a bemused tone. 'I had no idea I would be!'

Oliver gave a small grin as he replied. 'I didn't know it would be tonight. I only knew that one day soon this would happen. That darkness would come for you. She told me that those with black hearts would find you, those who classed your life as worthless as that of mine. They would not only take your possessions but also your life. The Angel told me that I had to save you, for you have served them well.'

'Served them well?' Terrance's voice rang with scepticism. 'You're making less sense by the moment, Oliver. Served who?'

'The Angels, Terrance,' Oliver responded sympathetically. 'You found the Angel coin, didn't you? You took it to its rightful place and gave it to the one who will be mother of the half Angel. You are owed a debt which I have repaid on their behalf.'

'Francesca?' Terrance felt the agony as it all fell into place. 'But I loved…'

'No!' Oliver snapped. 'You were not capable of loving one such as her!' His eyes lit with a deep fury before settling in the light of Terrance's sadness. 'I'm sorry, it's the truth. Until you know love yourself, you will never be able to give it. Perhaps this lesson will change all that. But know that you did something very important, for yourself, for us all. You were never going to be with her, Terrance.'

Terrance felt the reality as he heard Oliver speak. He had always known that somewhere inside of himself. Perhaps that is why Francesca had become more than something he cared about. She had become something he craved to possess. Seeing the man standing in front of him knowing so much made him aware that so much was out of his control.

'So is that it?' Terrance stammered. 'Everything is fixed now? My task is done and so is yours? What now, Oliver? Where do we go from here?'

Before Oliver could answer, there was the sound of approaching footsteps. The two looked round to see Jenny accompanied by Joey. Jenny rushed into Oliver's arms as Terrance watched on.

'Thank you so much,' she whispered hugging him tightly. 'So this was what you meant about coming back?'

'Yes,' Oliver replied with a smile. 'I knew it would be hard for you to accept what I said before, especially when I was on another planet for the most. I doubted it myself at times,

Jenny, but as I got better, as the rehab began to work, I realised that the flashbacks were occurring more and more often. I knew I was chosen to do this.' Glancing at Terrance he added softly, 'I've done my bit, Jenny. It's him you need to look after now.'

As Oliver melted into the background, Jenny and Joey helped Terrance to his feet and began to guide him towards the waiting limousine. Seeing Oliver walk away, Terrance called out.

'Wait! I want to do something for you. How can I repay you, Oliver?'

Oliver looked back. 'There is nothing you can do for me, Terrance Healy, but thank you.' He shot a warm look in Jenny's direction. 'Your mother has given me enough. Now I have a life to make. See you again soon, Jenny.'

With that Oliver shrank into the shadows leaving Jenny to whisper, 'I hope so, Oliver. I hope so.'

* * *

When Terry came around, he saw both Jenny and Terrance by his bedside. The mass of tubes and wires did not stop the three embracing through tears and laughter, whilst the bandaged Terrance spoke of his attack and the kindness of Oliver.

As Terry listened something inside him registered.

'Son,' he intervened, 'I need you to do something very important. I need you to contact the police and ask about a John Parsons. He's the man who will have been accused of attempted burglary, and possibly something to do with my condition. Tell the police I want to make a statement regarding his innocence.'

Terrance glanced at Jenny who stared back blankly.

'But why, Dad, if that is what happened?

Waving a hand to intervene, Terry looked deeply at them both.

'You must do this. I know what I'm talking about. This man

saved my life. You must find him and take him to meet your friend Oliver.' Seeing the look on Terrance's face he shook his head. 'I'm not mad, son. Trust me. I just know this is what has to be done.'

Terrance looked again at Jenny for reassurance. She smiled, taking his hand.

'If that is what your father thinks is right, then you should do it, darling.'

'Alright,' he said standing up, 'I'll get it done now.'

Jenny leant over and kissed Terry softly as she smiled. It was a smile that she felt naturally, for the first time in many a year. Without knowing it, Terry had quietly won back the heart of his wife by his actions. The reason – she knew who John Parsons was.

CHAPTER FORTY-FIVE

'Life will change, as will you. There will be pain and hurt and anguish along your journey. Do not despair and do not let events make you afraid of facing them again. Love will test you, it will break you, yet it will be the one thing you will desire in your heart. If one day, you feel you cannot pick yourself up and love once more, just remember. If you are afraid to fall, you will never learn to fly.'

(Taken from the halls of Angels)

When Oliver returned to London, Jenny was there to meet him at the station. Emotions overwhelmed him as he spoke of his first meeting with his mother. As they made their way back to the house in Hampstead, Jenny listened intently as Oliver spoke in detail of the meeting. He was going to move back to Sheffield and look for work to begin with. As he finished the story she saw the faintest edge of sadness in his eyes.

'What's wrong, Oliver? You should be the happiest man alive. Your mum is proud of you. I'm proud. We all are.'

'It's nothing really, Jen.' He shrugged. 'I suppose the only thing now is to find my father.' Nodding to himself he added, 'Mum wants it too.'

Jenny smiled in acknowledgement whilst running the next few hours through her mind. She simply hoped it would all go to plan.

* * *

'I told you, I don't need any explanation from your father!'

Terrance sighed. It had not been easy to convince John Parsons that he should escort him to their family home. The fact he had been acquitted of all charges and a full explanation of the mistakes made still did not sit well with him. Terrance decided to try another approach.

'Listen, John, my father doesn't want to patronise you or anything of the sort. He only wants to say a few words, okay?'

John tossed his head upwards in contempt as he grumbled, 'He's said enough to me for a lifetime, thanks. I did what I thought was right and look where that nearly bloody got me.' He shot Terrance a sarcastic glance. 'No offence, Mr Healy, but I've seen enough of your family to last me a lifetime.'

As the limousine headed towards the house, Terrance threw his cards on the table. 'Mr Parsons,' he said sincerely, 'I know what has happened in the past and mistakes have been made, by all of us.' He watched John's reaction carefully, waiting for him to cast his mind back in time. Seeing the smallest chink of regret he continued, 'We can't get back those days. But, perhaps there are things we can do to change our futures. Please, just give my dad a chance to say and do what he wants to do and then, I promise, you'll never hear from us again.'

Terrance's words had the desired effect.

'Alright, alright, Jesus, the way you go on you make your dad sound like a bloody saint!' Seeing a slight grin appear on Terrance's face, John could not help but smile a little himself. 'Just make sure he doesn't fall over when he sees me this time.'

* * *

'Honestly, Jen, we don't have to do this. I'm quite happy to have some food, wander around the West End, and head back off, honestly.'

Jenny took his hand and held it reassuringly. 'I know you don't want to come to my house, Oliver. I'm asking you to do this for me.'

Oliver stopped as they came to the entrance of Hampstead Heath. 'I don't understand why though, Jenny. Before I did what I did, you had no desire for me to meet your family. I did it not just for you but,' he paused, an uncertain expression surfacing, 'well, for the Angel I saw too, you know.'

'That's exactly why you must come though, Oliver!' Jenny replied as she looked into his eyes. 'What you said, what you did. It meant a lot more to me after I saw things for myself. I *believe* in what you say, which is why you must now believe in me.'

Oliver grinned. 'Okay, Jenny, but I'm starting to wonder if you're acting a little crazy.'

'I'm not,' she answered softly, 'I promise.'

* * *

Terrance let John and his father talk in the front room while he sent the text to Jenny to say that they were there and ready. Afterwards he stared at his phone for a moment wondering whether or not to put into action what was in his mind.

'Sod it.' With fingers working furiously, he punched in the text message and pressed the send button.

A few moments later the sound of the key turned in the front door as Jenny and Oliver arrived.

'Hi, Mum, Oliver.' Terrance greeted them holding out his hand for Oliver as he smiled in his mother's direction. 'Good timing and, Oliver, thanks again for what you did.'

As Oliver shook his hand, he gazed up at the vast marble reception as Terrance nodded to his mother.

'Oliver,' Jenny interrupted his thoughts, 'please, come through to the drawing room. There's someone I would like you to meet.'

'Sure,' he replied glancing at Terrance. 'You don't have to thank me anymore. I did the same as you would have in the circumstances.'

Jenny led them into the drawing room where Terry and John were sitting at a large dining table.

'Gentlemen, sorry to intrude,' Jenny said in a relaxed tone as she walked towards them. She kissed Terry softly on the cheek before turning to John. 'You must be John Parsons,' she said as she held out her hand.

Looking a little taken aback, John shook her hand as he answered, 'Yes, I am and you must be…'

'I'm Jenny Healy, Terry's wife,' she replied. 'Please, I would like you to meet someone.'

John stood up as Jenny motioned to Oliver to come forward.

'Oliver,' she said, her voice shaking with emotion, 'I'd like you to meet John Parsons.' Seeing his look of bewilderment, she added emotionally, 'Your father.'

Aside from Terrance, whom Jenny had told, the other three men looked totally stunned.

Oliver and John stood looking at each other for the first time in thirty years before John spoke, his face taut with emotion as the words cracked from his lips.

'Are…are you my son?'

Oliver looked at Jenny, his green eyes washed with memories as a glaze coated them. 'How, Jenny, how did you know?' he murmured.

'Fate, Oliver,' she replied with tears in her eyes. She walked up to him and whispered in his ear, 'Remember the night you were so ill? The night we had to take you to the clinic? You told me your full name, Oliver. I now know all this is meant to be.'

The two men clinched in an embrace of words and feelings that the years had stolen. Terrance watched on for a moment before he turned and left the room quietly. He had hopefully repaid a fraction of his debt.

* * *

The hum of a text message distracted Terrance from his

thoughts as he sat alone in the garden. Flicking to the message, his heart leapt a little before calmness returned and he tried to focus on the courage needed. The message simply read:

'Yes, you can call me.'

His heart caressed her voice as he heard the simple 'Hello'. It seemed so long, yet a moment ago in his mind. A somersault occurred in his stomach as he spoke her name.

'Francesca.'

A short pause followed as they both listened to silence. To him, it was golden. She was at the other end of the line. They were speaking. He could say what he wanted to say.

'Terrance,' her sensual tone oozed down the line, 'I am so sorry. You know, what you said in the text, what happened?'

'Francesca,' he repeated her name softly, 'it has been so hard. I need to tell you how sorry I am for the way I behaved.' As sentiment came to the fore he wiped his eyes and went on, 'Holly, she was murdered. I wanted to tell you before but…you know. The way things were…' he paused, feeling a rush of confusion as he murmured, '…you know.'

It was her turn to sound mystified as she replied, 'I can't believe that. When did it happen, Terrance? I mean, I never met her but…that is so terrible.'

'December.' He could only just utter the word as a new sensation overwhelmed him. A feeling of remorse that had somehow been hidden now overwhelmed him as he spoke with the one true love of his life. Tears fell freely as he tried to keep control. 'It was in December. Oh God, I miss her, I miss you.'

She heard his sadness and felt it deeply. He had never spoken like this before.

'Are you alright?'

'Yes,' Terrance answered sombrely. 'I am, kind of, Francesca. Much has happened since me, since us…'

'Don't, please don't, Terrance.' Francesca readied herself.

Finding the strength he interjected, 'I need you to know

something. I need you to know that I want you to be happy with Domenici and I'm proud for you both. I was a fool with you, with many things. I know that now. I've lost a woman I loved, in you. I lost a sister I never loved enough, in Holly. I just want you to know that I will never be that man again. I will never make those mistakes again. I'm not even sure what I'm trying to say.' Teardrops blurred his vision now. 'I just needed to tell you. Of all the people on this planet, I just needed to tell you, Francesca.'

'Thank you,' she whispered, her fingers running down to the bulge of her stomach. 'I'm happy you chose to tell me, and happy that you feel this way.' Her voice broke slightly as she added, 'Terrance, I'll never forget you. If our paths cross again, I will always save a smile for you.'

A watery grin surfaced as he heard her speak. 'That's all I need to know. I will never forget you.' He readied himself to deliver the hardest of all words. 'Goodbye, Francesca.'

The last silence they would ever share followed. A silence full of flashbacks and images of the time together, before she sealed their worlds and shut the door forever.

'Goodbye, Terrance.'

The line clicked and the gateway to her world closed. Terrance remained outside for some time, weeping quietly whilst inside two people were bridging the gap of empty years.

* * *

Francesca lay on her bed for a while stroking her bump and reflecting on the conversation. She felt pleased they had spoken, but sad for his grief and humble at his honesty. Drifting into a warm afternoon sleep, her mind slipped into a dreamy state.

It was there that she saw the girl on the train, gaunt and colourless. Images tumbled into her subconscious as she saw the face of Pat Reilly and heard his words: *'She's dead.'*

It was not her father who came to meet them at the café bar in her dream. It was Terrance, his face contorted with anxiety as he searched for his sister. She went to speak but no words came out.

With the first gulp of waking breath, her heart beat fast. The dream had been *too* real. She felt sure, more than ever, that Pat Reilly had somehow been there that night to save her, but not just her. Shivering, despite the warmth, Francesca caressed her bump, contemplating the alternatives of that night. She knew one thing for sure. She had been one of the last people to see Holly Healy. She also knew a secret she could not dare to share.

CHAPTER FORTY-SIX

The Archangel Galgliel knew this day would come, as did all those who had left the Earth and become Angels in one form or another. It had been written many eons ago that this would come to pass. Even now, with the hour approaching and all in place, the sadness was evident in her eyes. From now until the challenge of darkness had been faced, there would be no place for Angels to walk amongst men, women and children.

She reflected back to the time. It had seemed the perfect end to the war between dark and light. To create a law for the good of mankind, to believe in humanity, to give it the optimum chance to flourish. Two types of Angel had sat across from each other, each believing that they had just created a law to end all conflicts. The Laws of the Angel would bind dark and light until only one could survive. Soon, all Angels would be powerless to touch upon the hearts and souls of humans.

With Rose and Helena by her side, Galgliel pondered what might have been if humanity had achieved what she and all others had forfeited. The gifts of peace were there to take. The advancement of technology was freely shared. The Earth, a place of unique beauty and balance, was their playground. It had seemed, after the last Great War, that mankind had learned from its mistakes. That was when the laws had been agreed between Galgliel and her fellow Archangels and those with hearts of black who threatened to infiltrate the souls of man. The bargain was struck in simple terms.

'If you believe by the end of the century that mankind will prevail into a loving society then Angels will walk unhindered and all things dark will fade forever. If not then darkness itself, in the form of many things, will banish you from Earth eternally.'

As the century drew to a close, all saw that humankind, with all its gifts, knowledge and power, was still destroying itself. Wars still raged as life became less important than oil and riches. Hunger and famine went unchecked, the media coverage limited to propaganda. Class still controlled class as the less fortunate suffered. Greed and selfishness won over kindness and equality. Religions clashed, and the environment became an ever growing concern. The Angels knew that their time was short. All seemed lost as the laws were implemented. Then the miracle happened they had been waiting for; perhaps the only chance of salvation for all pure Angelic life forms.

As if reading her mind, Helena broke into Galgliel's thoughts.

'Now we are so near, Galgliel. I have to ask you something. Something I have not been able to fathom completely. It is concerning Rose and the night that the Angelis Mortis touched her spirit and redeemed her soul.'

Galgliel smiled serenely, *'Pray ask, Helena.'*

'The Angelis Mortis told us of another and we knew our task. When she touched Rose she spoke of such things. I do not fully understand this though. If she would tell us, surely she would tell them?'

Galgliel turned to Rose. *'Do you wonder the same things, Rose Gardener?'*

'It is not for us to ask, but to do,' replied Rose peaceably. *'I believe they would not ask such things.'*

'That is correct. Those with elements such as greed and vengeance have no place for such questions. Their existence does not focus on asking, simply doing, gaining.' Galgliel paused, the slightest hint of strain showing on her porcelain

complexion. *'You both know much of the laws of Angels. It is our rules that state a half-century must pass before we can return to Earth in whole form. That period is to learn the meaning of divinity, and so guide those who are needed. It is so that you, Rose, were cast into involvement with Steve Bidante. The prize: your soul would be saved. During that time he saw pure love which resulted in your quest being completed.'* Galgliel looked warmly towards Helena. *'Your task was to show Andréa to the world and let her shine through with her gift of kindness and purity. For the one that saw it could be the one that would create the child. Dusana was born out of not general creation, but pure love. By two people who would never have been able to have a child without the other. Steve knew that, and Andréa doubted, but now that is gone from their memories. Now the second child will be born, and destiny will guide them towards each other from this day onwards.'*

Helena looked at Rose knowingly. *'The child, the boy, he is born of the coin also, Galgliel?'*

'The coin of Angels has passed on to guide the girl,' Galgliel answered softly. *'Its meaning to humans with no knowledge of its power is what made it so important. The coin represents just that to many. A coin of extreme value perhaps, but to any eye it has a beauty that they simply cannot avoid seeing. He was guided to it by both love for her and what it can bring in the form of greed. He would have paid anything for it. He could not know that it could never win her heart. Even with the intentions of love fuelled by power and greed, the result was all we could have hoped for. It guided the coin to her, and now it will link all together. It will be the bridge between the dark and the light, the power of love and the power of possession. The Angel coin will remain on Earth and continue to connect the chain of events.'* Galgliel paused as they reached the east side of the river bank before looking to Rose. *'Tomorrow will be more than a new day. You must travel this eve and speak for the last time with Steve.'* Galgliel let her

eyes convey the intent she felt. *'You must penetrate his mind and tell him what we know. He will understand now.'*

Rose nodded in silent agreement whilst Galgliel turned to Helena.

'If all goes well then you will feel the time, Helena. Act upon that. I will do what I can to make all things come true as foreseen.'

The three women touched fingertips with pure affection before Rose ghosted up into the night sky. To a wandering human they would have seen little more than a drifting white feather coming down to float upon the silky black river. The time was near.

* * *

Steve finished reading the last line of the book as Dusana's eyes tilted downwards into slumber. After kissing her gently, he made his way out of the bedroom and smiled briefly as he saw Andréa lying fast asleep on the sofa. He watched her for some moments, examining her features and inhaling her sweet odour.

'My wife,' he whispered in his mind, *'so beautiful and Dusana...'*

Walking to the window, Steve looked up into the night sky as the thoughts flooded through his mind. Something within had seemed strange today and now, alone to think, he tried to make sense of the alien emotions.

Pouring some wine, he quietly opened the front door and stepped onto the porch terrace. The sound of crickets flooded the night with a gentle harmony, whilst the moon, in full silver shimmer, set alight the stars above. Gulping down the first glass in one hit, Steve topped it up from the bottle and found that he was grinning in amusement.

'Well, Miss Wine, it's you and me again,' he said, looking at the quarter empty bottle. 'It's been a while.'

The bottle remained inanimate, but Steve cared not. He

wanted someone, something to speak with. As memories of years past returned, he began to look at the bottle for counsel.

After another glass he spoke softly into the night. 'Remember our chats, Miss Wine?' He felt his speech slur very slightly as the alcohol hit the spot. 'You've always been a good friend but much has changed.'

Gazing at the bottle for a reaction briefly, he continued, 'Something has happened to me today, Miss Wine. I don't quite know how to explain it. It kind of feels like I'm sad inside.' Letting his fingers caress the neck of the bottle he contemplated the statement. 'Perhaps not sad. Maybe down, maybe scared…'

Silence answered him. Miss Wine did nothing, except provide the remaining red liquid to the glass. After finishing the bottle and feeling a sense of relaxation, Steve went into the house, before returning with another bottle and planting himself on the rocking chair. The second bottle opened with a hungry ease as the contents coursed through his bloodstream, creating inner warmth that the day had stolen from him.

'You never say much,' he slurred staring at the second bottle. 'Never mind, you never did. It was always the dreams that spoke.'

Lighting up a cigarette, Steve blew puffs of smoke towards the moon whilst drinking more than half the second bottle. He felt a wave of euphoria wash over him before inevitable sleep pushed his eyelids down.

* * *

Galgliel sat alone by the river's edge. The inky night sky covered the village of San Piceno in a shroud of black, severed only by the glow from moon and stars alike, giving a silvery glint to the bubbling river. Galgliel let out a thought-provoked sigh which sent ripples downstream. These were to be the last days for her and her kind. The impact of the thought made her feel what a human would describe as a shiver.

How had it come to this? She, Galgliel. Free, to roam this universe after many millennia of distinguished service as an Archangel. She, the Archangel of Divine Will, Divine Harmony, Divine Authority, Divine Love, Divine Light, and Divine Power. Soon she would be mistress of nothing on this Earth as the darkness challenged all things sacred. Darkness in all its forms would attempt to fester and destroy all of humanity.

Galgliel let a pure white teardrop from her soul into the river as she remembered this holy place. The River Mesti where she saw the last of her human generation; her bloodline through eons fall in the War to end all wars. It had been then that she took the challenge. She, who could not seek revenge or redemption or any such black thoughts, had looked to the future with a vigour that the pain of loss had instilled in her soul. Now would be her first and indeed last act of influence for over three centuries. Then it would be in the hands of those who would not know, could not know, their power. The world was finely balanced on the scales of time. Only time would show if she had chosen the right path.

The tear settled on the film of water in front of her, a white speck on a dark watery blanket. Closing her eyes, Galgliel let the Divine combination of all that she was flow to her fingertips which she then slowly submerged into the river.

The wet liquid cooled her Angel heart as the river reacted. The tear became tears, and then tenfold, twentyfold, before expanding in a flood of white purity that filled the night with a burst of virgin colour.

Breathing in deeply, she let her eyes open to see the work was done. Withdrawing her fingers from the river she muttered the words: '*River of dreams, take me in your wake.*'

It took a few moments for Galgliel to raise her tired frame from the river bank, her energy depleted by her actions. Drifting into the shadows of the night, she left that place for the final time whilst leaving her Divinity to flow through the water that would soon become – The River of Dreams.

* * *

Steve looked around, realising instantly that this place was alien to him. He could not see himself. The realisation of a vision quickly calmed the initial fear that engulfed him. All around was empty and quiet as he gathered in the surroundings. Behind him there was a blank canvas of nothingness, whilst ahead lay a colourless path alongside a verge of lifeless grass. There was a feeling of desperation in the silent air. A feeling he related to the day. He was in that place now.

Experience made him walk along the featureless path in search of what might lie ahead. After a few hundred steps, he paused to focus on the doorway that appeared in front of him. It was not a doorway of typical size: something much larger. Approaching closer he saw the doorway was in fact arched. Two large aged wooden doors barred his way forwards. The sensations of the day now surged within. The sadness that had filtered through his mind was epitomised by the doors that he now recognised. They were the doors that he had walked through so many years ago, the very doors that had once led him to the funeral of his parents.

Swallowing hard, Steve fought the panic as he juggled the options. He could try and waken, but he had never felt that power before. He could stop here and hope that reality would come to his rescue. Or he could push the doors open and face whatever it was that had infiltrated his heart. The decision wrangled in his mind as positive emotions met negative. He did what only he could think of. He closed his eyes and focused on something beautiful. She came at that moment in the vision of the girl with the white hair and crystal blue penetrating eyes. Now she was real. Dusana said the word, and all fear passed as it echoed in his ears: *'Daddy.'*

With renewed strength, Steve pushed the doors open

forcefully and stepped through. The path was no longer there. Instead, he saw a stretch of road containing flashing lights and the noise of activity. Beneath his feet he saw a patch of concrete – a lay-by. To his left, a short distance away, he saw the vehicle that tore his heart out.

Police cars and fire engines flashed lines of blue across the landscape as the cluster of uniforms raced to the scene. In between the movement of hosepipes and cutting tools, Steve saw the wreckage of the car as his stomach lurched into an abyss of torture.

No one appeared to see him as he neared the vehicle. Able to walk no closer, he stopped ten feet away, frozen by hurt and pain. A sound of another siren briefly took his attention as the ambulance veered onto the lay-by. Paramedics jumped from the vehicle, instantly assessing the scene as they rushed to try and save the doomed.

A hollow numbness enveloped him now. The sounds melted into a silence that his subconscious released before a click of a door opening ricocheted like a bullet to the side of the car. Looking straight at the lorry, Steve saw a figure emerge from the driver's seat. The man let the door sway open as he glanced back at the front of the lorry, now embedded in the side of his parents' car.

The man walked over slowly and Steve felt the perspiration trickle down his forehead. He was staring at the man responsible for his parents' death. A man of no consequence, no particular distinguishing features; just an average-sized, average-built lorry driver who had stolen the lives of those he loved. As the rage grew he heard the man speak.

'So, you must be their son?'

'What?' Steve replied in a tone laced with confusion and repulsion.

'Their son,' the man repeated, coming close enough for Steve to touch. 'In there, the dead people. You must be their son, or you wouldn't be here now, would you?'

CHAPTER FORTY-SEVEN

'I could think of you and all of your qualities, but it would take me your lifetime and a river of tears to describe. I could speak of you until my life is over and the river is full of tears. You have your wings now, borne out of love and I will never forget your song. Though sadly missed on Earth, I know where Angels really belong. You are now a real life Angel and I am blessed for I can love you forever.'

(Taken from the scriptures of Galgliel)

The impulse to flail his arms at the face of the man was almost overwhelming, yet his words stopped the inevitable action. Glancing towards the lorry, Steve saw two firefighters attending to the vehicle. He returned his stare back to the man in front of him. As their eyes met he saw a glint, the tiniest chink of a sparkle that glowed with a deep red. Heart racing as the permutations ran through his mind, he replied in a careful tone, 'Perhaps I am but then, like you, perhaps I'm not what I seem.'

The man laughed a deep booming laugh that reverberated around him. But the laughter carried much more than that: its sound was laced with a sarcasm and despair that sank into the pores of Steve's skin.

'Don't try and fight what you know to be true, boy!' He spat the words out with venom. *'I just killed your parents! They didn't have to die but you did! Somehow things didn't quite work out, did they.'*

A flashback to his childhood overcame Steve as he remembered the day: of Granny and sandwiches, chess and fun, the decision to stay, and many years later on, her words.

'It wasn't me who asked you to stay that day.'

So the words of his grandmother were true. The thought that Cyril had spoken with her and made him stay that night had once seemed bizarre. But that was a long time ago. So many things had made sense since then and the fact that he was feeling, or seeing this now, made things all the more believable.

'Can you feel it?' the bitter voice interceded once more. *'Can you feel the anger – the sorrow?'*

The battle raged as Steve fought the powerful emotions raining within. With all his might, Steve raised a smile through clenched teeth.

'You are not the driver. You are what I felt today. I know what you are.' Biting into his lip enough to draw blood, he added in a cutting voice, 'I can see your soul: black and filthy and laced with deceit. I know what you are!'

The man buckled momentarily, the red glint evaporating to be replaced by a look of utter grief. *'I am so sorry,'* the man whispered before the glint of red returned to his iris.

'I know where your child is,' he hissed pointing at the wreckage. *'You know what fate can do. The choice is yours.'*

The thought hit Steve like a hammer blow. Trepidation sprang into every part of his being as he heard the threat. The resolve he had felt a moment ago was now replaced with a terrible fear for his daughter.

'What is it you want?' Steve mumbled in reply. 'Don't hurt her, I beg you, not her.'

Steve was sure he heard the man snarl the word *she* under his breath, before he moved closer to him, his breath and odour overpowering. As he spoke the stench of rancid decay flowed with his words.

'All I want to know is your name.'

Three things happened in that instant. A sound from above

of beating wings distracted his attention, while the surprise at such a request made him almost totter where he stood. Just as he readied himself to answer, a gentle tug from somewhere within stopped him doing so. He heard the words: *'Hold my hand.'*

'What?' The man was briefly caught off guard. *'What the hell?'*

He held out his hand as the man screamed *'No!'* realising that Steve had found an escape. The hand became dust as Steve left the dream.

* * *

'Hold my hand.' The words flowed sweetly before he awoke.

With a jump Steve sprang out of the chair, the nightmare still real, before he felt the warmth of her flesh and focused to see her there, hand in his.

'Roz?'

Rose Gardener smiled warmly as she let the flow of energy from her hand infiltrate his skin.

'You have learnt much since our last meeting, Steve. I could not bring you from your vision unless you realised it could be done.' With an expression of concern she added, *'Did you speak of much with him?'*

Still shocked and disorientated, Steve puffed out his cheeks in reply. 'You knew? I mean, who was that? Why did he want to know my name? It made no sense, Roz, but I knew...'

'You knew it was deceit, didn't you?'

'Yes, somehow,' Steve nodded, 'I felt something today. Something that I cannot put into words but now, now I think it was the apprehension of what just took place.'

Sitting alongside him, Rose looked kindly into his eyes. Instantly Steve felt better. That warmth that he remembered from her persona brought him back to childhood as he waited for her to explain.

'I have messages for you, Steve. You must listen carefully for

you will not see me again. Not on this Earth.'

'What?'

'Shh,' Rose silenced him with a finger, *'you have followed your path and learned much of what your destiny held for you. I can fill in some gaps but you will have to bear the burden of secrecy for you have your own tasks to fulfil. Are you prepared to do that?'*

Without wanting to interrupt her golden tones Steve simply nodded once again.

'The death of your parents was not so much of an accident, Steve. It was in the sense of the man who drove the lorry, but not in the events that led him to be there. To put it into clearer terms, you were supposed to be there as well as the other in the other crash.'

'Other?' Steve interrupted in surprise. 'I did not know there were others.'

Grimacing a little, Rose continued, *'A bargain was struck regarding humanity, between the Angels of both sides. Angels represent many things humans understand, but in essence, they too are both good and bad. The difference with sentient beings is the inability to fight, or declare wars upon each other. Instead, there is what you would class as emotions: love, hate, generosity, greed and so on. We know that love is the prime reason and instinct of human life. Both sets of Angels know that, as do humans to a degree. We are not there to directly interfere on matters of the flesh. It is our only power to guide or to influence.'* With a tinge of sadness Rose went on, *'That is our place in things but, of course, things are influenced by us, and fate itself. Now however, Angels of all kinds will leave Earth, only for one kind to be able to return when the clock is done. This has been decreed as "The laws of the Angel".'*

Steve stared blankly as she paused. 'I'm not sure I understand all of what you are saying. A clock? And,' he twisted his head to one side, 'what has this got to do with me?'

Undeterred Rose spoke softly in reply. *'A bargain was made between the two bands of Angels after the last great war. The stakes were simple: let humans find peace and love before the new century reached its first decade or all Angels would be banished until the clock reached its end. Only then could we return to whatever is left. Technology and intelligence would reach humanity giving them the chance to create their own paradise on Earth.'* Rose's voice cracked a little. *'By 2010, the end of the first decade, all Angels will be unable to have contact with this place. Despite the technology of so many things from cars to computers, from antidotes to aeroplanes and so much more, humans are in a delicate position. The planet is suffering as the environment is destroyed. People are starving, yet there is so much food. Diseases which could have been eradicated are not, to keep the population controlled and so much more. In essence, many hearts and souls of men and women alike have been tainted by the elements of darkness: greed, corruption, selfishness and hate.'*

Steve digested her words with a look of unease as he spoke. 'What will happen? What of the future for us, for our children, for Dusana?'

The name brought a faint smile to Rose's lips. *'Dusana – that is why you and Andréa were so important, Steve. Your path took you through fate and the coin of Angels to Andréa. Between you, both of you created a child born out of pure love.'* Rose tilted her head to one side. *'You were not able to produce children and neither was she. The prophecy told of two half Angels. One to be born out of pure love, the other from greed, both guided to each other by the Angel coins.'* Rose radiated pure energy as she added, *'Dusana is a half Angel.'*

'And the other?' Steve asked gulping, 'Who is the other, borne out of greed, can that be a good thing?'

'It was not the greed that the dark Angels had anticipated,' Rose answered gently. *'The coin found greed and that greed guided the coin to a woman. A woman so beautiful that even greed loved her. Her choice was to choose unknowingly*

between him and the man who could give her total love. She chose correctly, at least as far as we could have wished for. Like us, the dark Angels know of the prophecy. The man you met in your vision was there to find out your name. From there, he would find the name of your daughter and then, before we leave Earth, they would try and cause tragedy for both half Angels. They fear your daughter and they will fear the son also. If they find each other through the coins, then the elements of darkness will indeed have an enemy to dread.'

Rose stopped talking and sat back as if the energy was leaking from her. Steve noticed she looked less bright, less youthful this time, and he wondered if this could as a result of what she spoke. If what she said was true, then time was running out.

'Rose,' he said quietly as she closed her eyes in meditation, 'where is the other child? Can't you tell them of this also? What am I supposed to tell Andréa? She will be beside herself with worry and… what are we to do with Dusana?'

Her eyes snapped open as a last burst of energy emerged. *'The boy is to be born tomorrow. No one can speak of where and no one can tell another. Only the deceit of your vision could have made you tell a stranger such information and you did not. Dusana must be kept safe until her eighth birthday when the year is 2010 and we have left. Only then can she see the world and learn of her gifts.'*

Seeing the apprehension in Steve's eyes she added softly, *'Do not worry for you or Andréa. Dusana will learn so much and spread love. You already know she can reach the minds of humans. You saw her yourself, Steve. I can tell you only what I know, and that is if fate holds true then the coins will guide them to each other just as they did with you and Andréa.'* With weariness in her voice she added, *'This is all I can say, but I feel peace, knowing of your strength tonight. When we are gone your dreams and visions of such things will cease. Just know that in your heart.'*

Rose stood and walked to the front of the porch slowly.

Steve noticed that the aura that glowed gently around her now flickered intermittently.

'I must go now,' she said resignedly. *'I am sorry to burden you with such knowledge. It is important that you use it wisely, Steve.'*

'But, Roz,' Steve replied calmly, 'if I understand all you say then when the visions stop, that's it? I will not see my mother or father or Granny and Granddad.' His voice petered out with the sadness he felt as he added, 'I will see no one?'

Rose gazed compassionately as she answered. *'I am sorry but it is true. An Angel can only cross the divide after half a century, at least in a form you would associate with being physical. You will not see them, Steve; if the worst comes to pass then nobody will see them again. We will cease to exist in the minds and souls of future generations. So you see,'* her eyes sank into an abyss of sorrow, *'the darkness will have won and the soul will become extinct. Humans will become machine-like, or simply fade into the category of a dying species.'*

'I will do my best.' Steve said the words with conviction. He held out his hand which Rose took gently in hers smiling faintly.

'I know you will. Remember what I once told you about hope and spread that hope in your life. We can ask no more.'

'I have just one last thing to ask you. I need to know, in order to understand for the future.'

'Pray ask,' she replied glancing back.

'The clock, you mention the clock. What do you mean about the ticking of the clock?'

As her light failed around her, Rose took a deep breath acknowledging his request.

'You live by time, Steve. You all do, and so have become enslaved by it now, so much so, that your fate will be dictated by it. All events are marked on the clock of your universe. It will either be the mark of humanity or the obituary. So you understand let me tell you that in your terms. We will leave

Earth at ten minutes past eight – 2010. You understand now? The change will never happen in your lifetime but your lifetime and the birth of the half Angels will affect all time.'

Steve digested her words. 'So…the year 2400 would be 24.00. That is the end?'

'The judgement,' she replied softly, *'not necessarily the end. It seems a long time away, doesn't it? Yet humans know that in just half a century the environment will ail and suffer but they do nothing. Imagine a world aware of such a simple fact. It is right in front of them, if they only could see it. Three hundred and ninety years will determine much, but the next half a century will determine all.'*

Steve could feel the magic and sadness of the moment. 'What of you, Rose Gardener – Roz? What of you now? Is that it? You leave us now, me now? After all…'

She let her arms open and the two hugged softly. His lips kissed her cheek and he could feel the soft wrinkles now, the marks of age upon her face. He could feel her frame as he held her there, old and ready for no more work on Earth. He knew as he held her there in that timeless moment that Roz was ready to join her husband Doug, to go where she belonged.

'I will miss you forever,' he whispered as they took one last look into each other's eyes. 'You were and are a real-life Angel.'

'I am ready now. My work is done and I am tired. Never forget…always have hope.'

With a last warm smile, Rose pushed her arms upwards as if she was pulling the sky towards her. In an instant she was away and up into the night, leaving the single tearful silhouette below on the ground.

CHAPTER FORTY-EIGHT

Francesca eased her fragile frame onto the rug that Domenici had laid down for her. Despite the walk, which was only fifteen minutes or so, she felt the energy sap out from her under the weight of heavy pregnancy. It would not be long now, and the idea to return to Italy for the birth had suited them both perfectly. Domenici had taken a month off from his art studies and, with financial help from both families, the last week had been bliss in the little cottage they had rented for this special time in their lives.

As she settled by the River Mesti, Domenici began to unpack the simple fare they had brought for the day: bread, cheese, water and wine along with a sketch pad for Domenici and a book for Francesca. The late morning sun hung above them as they ate, cascading its warm rays upon the greenery, split only by the blue line of the river which now hosted an array of delicate sounds from nature. Contentment reigned supreme in this small paradise-like place.

After eating enough for two, Francesca lay back on one of the soft pillows Domenici had gently placed beneath her head. He kissed her softly before taking his pad and letting his fingers weave across the blank sheet. Francesca fingered through her book and breathed in the warm sweet-smelling air. As she felt the day's beauty wash over her pretty frame, her book slowly slipped from her hand as her eyes succumbed to the caress of the sun's warmth.

The sun had dipped somewhat giving a gentle nudge-like

chill that must have woken her. Glancing across, she saw Domenici, head buried in concentration as his hand glided across the pad. By his side many sheets containing images were neatly stacked under a smooth stone.

Francesca sipped some water as her mind came out of its sleepy haze. As she got up and stretched, Domenici paused to look up and smile at her affectionately.

'Did you have a good sleep, darling?'

'Wonderful,' she replied happily, 'this place becomes more beautiful every time I see it, sweetheart.'

Sauntering along the river's edge coloured with a kaleidoscope of summer bloom, Francesca let her eyes stretch as far as they could as she took in the scene. The river bubbled over rocks and pebbles until it reached the quaint bridge. There it slowed a little, its clear liquid climbing over the pretty rockery, before continuing its never-ending journey.

Peering into the crystal clear water, Francesca watched small fish darting around under the current. She let her hand ease into the cool water, casting a fleeting look back towards Domenici. He was oblivious to anything but the pad, creating the scene she was in on paper. Francesca smiled contentedly as the water gurgled refreshingly around her hand.

She cupped a handful of water and brought it to her face. A sense of exhilaration rushed over her as the cool liquid met warm flesh. As she gasped in enjoyment it happened. Francesca felt a gentle tug inside her stomach before it became a wrench and a shot of pain enveloped her body. In a flash, she had lost her balance and fallen forwards into the water. The shock was instant as her body became engulfed in the water which now seemed freezing. Gasping for air, the last thing she saw was Domenici still staring at his pad, unaware of her fall. Then everything went dark.

* * *

Helena made her way up the dusty main street of San Piceno.

412

Wearing a long brown cardigan with a pale cream scarf, you could easily have mistaken her for a gypsy. Her hair was unkempt but, despite that, the beauty of her mix of youth and maturity made her both unnoticeable yet, to the astute eye, compelling.

She entered the foyer of the whitewashed hospital where she soon found the reception area of this small but communal place. The receptionist looked up from her magazine with a slight look of surprise, as if she had been disturbed.

'Buon giorno,' Helena said with a warm smile. *'Dove Signor Baroni per favore?'*

'Momento.' With an inquisitive glance as the woman asked where Signor Baroni was, the girl picked up the phone and punched in an extension.

After a few brief words, she placed the receiver back on its hook. 'Signor Baroni, cinque minuti.'

'Five minutes? Thank you,' Helena replied as she moved away from the desk and waited.

She spotted Signor Baroni from a distance. As the lift doors opened, he walked slowly towards her, clipboard in hand, expression of concentration upon his face. He was a bald-headed man with a kind face. His broad shoulders seemed hunched, almost weighed down, as if the burdens of both his work and his humanity had taken their toll. The receptionist pointed in Helena's direction as he approached. A moment later they were facing each other.

'Good morning, Doctor Baroni, a wonderful day. wouldn't you agree?'

He smiled and steely blue eyes lit up as he replied, 'Good morning, you speak English well, I must say.'

'I speak many languages, Doctor Baroni.' Helena chuckled. *'You speak good English yourself, but I am not here to compliment you on that. It is with other news that I bring you your compliment.'*

'Really?' he responded smiling. 'May I ask what I can do for you?'

'It is said that you are the best doctor in the village. I have a somewhat strange request for you. I need you act upon it immediately. I need you to take a midwife and head to the river.'

'A midwife?' His answer was riddled with intrigue as well as humour. 'I do not even know your name yet you are asking such a strange thing of me? In my position, I think you would be asking the same question: why?'

Helena chuckled once more. She let her eyes bore into his. He saw many things all at once and in that instant the doubt disintegrated.

'My name is Helena Sekhova, Doctor Baroni. The reason I tell you this is because, within the hour, there will be a young lady who will need your help and that of a midwife. She is to give birth and she will need you both. It is vital that you act now.'

'Anna,' he called, looking over to the receptionist, 'call up to Freya and ask her to come down for a moment. I need a word.'

As Anna dialled the extension he turned back to Helena.

'Now, Helena, I need you to…'

There was no one there.

* * *

Francesca knew the pain was the beginning of the birth. Her body began to experience inner eruptions, her mind froze in panic, as she flailed her arms underneath the icy water. Then the blackness came and all around her fell into silence. When she came to, the water had calmed and become clear, as if she had reached the bottom of an abyss. Looking around, she realised that her eyes could see everything in the finest detail. Above, the surface appeared to be miles away. Yet it could not be. The river was deep, but not as deep as it now seemed. Then she saw the white drop in the distance. The tear of Galgliel that she had let fall from her eye into the river to

414

enable its enchantment. To Francesca, it initially appeared as a small white speck. A single star, studded against a sea of blue. All else left her mind as she watched its floating presence moving nearer, ever nearer until…

The whiteness was so bright now. It illuminated her being, transforming everything else into black, before it formed into a shape, the shape of a girl. White became hair, and blue became eyes. The silvery glow became the pendant which hung from her neck deflecting the blue forwards, directly at Francesca. She felt no fear, marvelling at her snow-white beauty as an overwhelming sense of love encapsulated her. Seconds passed as she stared powerlessly at the girl who now closed her eyes and held her hands, as if to pray just for them both in this place. Francesca felt a jolt inside as her heart leapt.

'I have seen you before!' She thought the words. *'When I was young, in London! I saw you! Who are you?'*

In return she received electric blue as the girl opened her eyes and uttered the word which sought its way straight inside her body, lifting her soul into rapturous beauty.

'Francesca…'

The word carried a power Francesca had never experienced. A feeling of uplifting clarity and closeness beyond anything she had witnessed before. The girl gazed with a wonder in her eyes as the two of them exchanged a silence full of emotion, yet laced with curiosity. The girl reached out a virgin-white hand. Francesca touched it, feeling soft warmth, combined with a slight touch of coolness. After a moment, the girl drew her hand away and all that remained in her palm was the reason for the coolness. It was her necklace with her coin, the Angel coin. Destiny ran through her veins. She knew the girl shared the same coin, the same knowledge. There were so many questions to ask, but no words could be spoken. She felt her body drift into a state of weightlessness as the image before her began to fade.

'Wait, please wait.'

'Francesca, Francesca.' She heard her name, but the voice

was not that of the girl. She felt her hand being pulled as the voice echoed in her mind and then…

'Francesca.' The voice was that of Domenici. 'My God, please let her be okay. Doctor, will she be okay?' The words had little impact as she lost perception of her surroundings.

The doctor laid her flat as he performed mouth-to-mouth resuscitation. By his side stood the midwife and Domenici who was in a state of utter panic. Francesca could hear his voice becoming ever louder as she left the place and returned to life. The soft, kind eyes of Doctor Baroni greeted her as he gave a relieved smile. He had followed the woman's instructions without a shred of a doubt and arrived just in time to see Domenici struggling to pull the girl from the water. As he breathed and pumped Francesca, he felt a wonder that such visions could still exist. How could she have known? As the first splutter of water was released from her lungs, Doctor Baroni knew he had just saved a life, two lives. Yet without the woman Helena, he would not be here now to save them. He heard the shouts of jubilation from Domenici as Francesca opened her eyes, the water now free from her body as she coughed and spluttered with the intake of oxygen.

Francesca felt the air upon her face like a blanket made of the wind, massaging and welcoming her back. She felt Domenici kissing her as he pulled her towards him and embraced her tearfully. Doctor Baroni wiped his brow as he heard Freya speak.

'Doctor, we need to hurry. Look. She is going to give birth.'

He saw Francesca's dress, the lower half stained in blood. With clinical action he went to his briefcase and produced a syringe as he nodded for Freya to take control. There was no other choice. The baby would be born here.

* * *

Some hours later Galgliel and Helena watched from a distance, knowing that their work was done. The river had shown, beyond all doubt, that Francesca was to be the mother of the half Angel. When its enchantment pulled her towards it, she could do no more than answer her own fate and slip below its waters to face her vision. The impression would stay upon her heart forever.

'It is time,' Galgliel murmured tenderly as the first cry of a new life sounded upon the river bank. *'We have done all that is asked of us. Now the fate of us all is for others to decide.'*

Freya handed the baby to Francesca wrapped in a towel. 'It's a boy,' she said joyously, the elation of birth glowing from her eyes. 'Now you just have to think of a name.'

Francesca took the infant and held him close. She gazed up to see both Doctor Baroni and Domenici smiling tearfully at her. Domenici glowed with pride as he spoke. 'A name, darling, we never thought of a name.'

Cradling the child into her bosom with one hand, Francesca looked into the palm of the other. There was her necklace. It had not been a dream. She let the mystery wash over her as she smiled calmly.

'I think the name Angelo would be perfect, sweetheart.'

CHAPTER FORTY-NINE

'It can defy science, religion and logic. It is stronger and more powerful than all other emotions as one. Yet its force can only be for good. It exists in all of us and we only exist to seek it. It is LOVE.'

(Taken from the scriptures of Galgliel)

Angelo Emilio Virone was born on 28th May 2008 to the proud parents Francesca and Domenici who became married in late August at a small but special ceremony on the banks of the River Mesti in San Piceno. The few that attended were close family and friends, in addition to more than a few unseen spirits that watched with pride and hope.

Francesca never spoke to Domenici about the coin and he never once again mentioned the gift from Terrance. He knew of course but, for whatever reason, he acknowledged that the coin was of importance to her and, after all, he had won the heart of the girl he loved.

For Terrance the next months were life-changing. The news of the child and the marriage of the girl he loved were difficult to face, yet he did so with dignity, deciding to put all his energy into firstly his family and then his work. T Healy & Sons announced a drive to support UK-based businesses that would reap dividends over the coming years, thrusting billions back into the country. Ironically, back in Poland, Jan Kowalik became a manager of the farm producing crops for the same company that had almost destroyed Sonnings Farm. The

Sonnings went back to serving small businesses and never again got involved with a multiple supermarket chain.

Oliver Parson's life changed for the better as he was reunited with both his mother and father and found a new purpose in life. In early 2009 Jenny Healy née Cross set up, with her husband's support, the UK Homeless Shelter. The fund would bring hope to many people, like Oliver, who had been caught up in the harshness of life, and offered both shelter and drug rehabilitation programmes for those who enlisted. Oliver became an envoy for the cause.

It would be another year (2010) before Steve and Andréa Bidante would return to England with Dusana who was now in her eighth year.

CHAPTER FIFTY

'Try to live your life like an artist adding colour to the canvas of your soul. Always take care in the pictures that you paint. For in old age, you will be left to view an exhibition of a lifetime's work.'
(Taken from the Hall of Angels)

December 2009

Whiteness of snow covered the country by day whilst unusual storms filled the night sky. To the experts, it was simply down to global warming, that much of the world was seeing such strange weather cycles for the time of year. Those, such as Steve Bidante, pondered the implications rather more deeply.

The last influence of Angels breathed its form upon mankind as the snows of the pure laid the blanket upon the planet and the souls of darkness raged in the night venting their anger at the forthcoming exodus of their kind. For those left behind, it would be remembered as nothing more than a freak winter.

Galgliel watched as the final links between her kind and those they were formed from were severed. The future of humanity now truly lay in its own hands. Fate, destiny, so often a gift or curse from another place, would now be written with the blood of man. She left Earth at the month's end, along with all sentinel beings, in the knowledge that only one person would know who the two half Angels were. He would indeed play his part, as it was written, in the joining of the two.

* * *

'You have yourself a merry Christmas, my friend, and not too much drink, eh?'

Harry laughed as the two walked towards the front of the shop. 'Chance would be a fine thing! I have to finish off here before I take the boys to the airport. It's going to be some frantic rush but I know they'll love it.'

'No need to have booked a trip to Lapland if you ask me. Not with this weather anyway,' Pat replied gazing out of the window at the snow-covered street. 'Could have saved a packet. Not that you need to on your income. I never realised antiques could be so profitable.'

'It could be worse.' Harry flashed his loveable grin. 'You're the one who probably needs to watch the drink anyway, Pat! You should know that in your profession! What do you have planned?'

'The profession is why I drink!' Pat chuckled in reply. 'Me? The usual, I guess. A few drinks with the parents. A few drinks with some friends, and a few drinks with people I have never met before. Oh, and maybe I forgot, a little dance or two with a fine lass, if I'm lucky!'

'I'm sure you'll have a good time. Please give my love to your parents,' Harry replied slapping Pat on the back. 'Have a Merry Christmas and a Happy New Year, Pat.'

Pat returned the slap, together with a grin as he let himself out of the shop. 'Will do my best, Harry. See you in 2010.'

Stepping outside, the icy wind picked up sending debris swirling around his feet. Pat pulled up the collar of his jacket as he took in the scene. With just three days to go before the big day, the streets were humming with people. He walked amongst the human roundabout of colour and creed, all coming and going to the sound of Oxford Circus's festive offerings. A small quartet played a stone's throw away from the shop, their booming instruments fading as he headed at a brisk pace up towards Oxford Street. There the sound was replaced by sweet voices of carol singers clustered together against the bitter cold.

Approaching the sanctuary of a nearby coffee bar, the cold already eating into his pores, he debated the beauty of the season. The snow fell steadily enough to prevent London's slush, making the scenes around him feel more meaningful than in years past. A man of belief, he had seen the changes. To him, this year appeared to have something more significant than Christmases gone by. That feeling was about to be multiplied by the sound of a voice.

'Pat! Pat!' He heard her shout, a voice from the past, now echoing through the crowd.

Turning around, it took a few seconds to identify her. By then, she was upon him.

Her face was alight as she pulled him into a warm clinch. 'Pat! My God, fancy seeing you here!'

'Well, I'll be blessed!' Pat blurted out the words with a sense of awkwardness at her tenderness, together with affection for it at the same time. ''Tis a blessing to be seeing you again, young lady.'

Francesca breathed out deeply as she stepped back so that she could look at Pat directly. The air created a momentary ghostly divide between the two as she spoke.

'I've thought about you so many times, Pat,' she said with a deep sincerity before stumbling a little on her words. 'It would take a long time to explain why really but…' She moved close as she whispered, 'Let's just say, you saved me, shall we?'

'It was nothing,' Pat answered humbly. 'I was just there that night. You know fate, Francesca. I just did what anyone would have done in the circumstances, but…' With a cheeky grin he added, 'It's always a pleasure to meet a pretty lady.'

As her laugh filled the air with both clouds and melody, Pat saw the contingent approach. Francesca grinned, a look of sweet shame on her face. 'Sorry! I should have said before,

Pat. This is, well, my family!' Her shyness evaporated instantly as she pointed to Stefano. 'You've met my father before, of course.' He shook Pat's hands readily with an eagerness that said more than words could.

'Pat, this is my husband Domenici.' She spoke with a love that made him instantly like the handsome man in front of him.

'A pleasure to meet you. You're a very lucky man.' Pat offered his hand to Domenici, smiling warmly.

Domenici grinned as they shook hands. 'A pleasure to meet you also, Pat.'

'And this,' Francesca pointed behind her, 'is my mother Nicole.'

As Pat turned to see the attractive woman smiling at him, his eyes moved down to the pram she was pushing before she held out an arm to him.

'I would also love to introduce you to our new addition!' Francesca oozed happiness.

'Well, I'll be star-struck! So this is the reason you looked a little chubbier last time we met.' Pat chuckled with good humour, kneeling down to stare behind the soft clear canvas that protected the infant inside. The boy's mop of black curly hair accentuated the big brown eyes staring back at him. 'Well,' he laughed, 'it seems you two can make a beautiful child.'

'Thank you,' Domenici's voice replied warmly, 'Signor Reilly. I heard of your kindness. I feel that I, we, owe you much. Before now, you were just an image in my mind from Francesca's description.' His eyes glistened. 'Now you are real and I thank you from the bottom of my heart.'

Pat absorbed the praise with the serenity of one who cared not for compliments. Inside, however, he felt truly touched. He saw Francesca for the briefest fragment of time in a different light before he spoke again. She was smiling, almost in awe, but his stare was now elsewhere. It took him down, past the flowing jet-black hair, the deep brown eyes, down towards the nape of her neck. There, resting upon her soft skin, lay the coin of Angels. He let out a gentle gasp as he heard the words within his subconscious – *Everything is for a reason*. His thoughts travelled back to that time when he had once doubted faith. The time when he watched Ray Skee die before him, powerless to prevent it despite all his will. Now, as he became aware of that voice once again, he realised: he had just seen the most precious present that Christmas could bring.

'We all thank you, Pat. You are a special man and we will never forget you.' Francesca's voice echoed warmly.

He tried to summon the words to do justice. 'No, let me thank you, all of you. I'm honoured to meet your son, Francesca, Domenici. He is a beautiful child.'

He knew the next three words before they uttered from her lips.

'He's an Angel.'

Author's postscript
I was honoured to be invited by Roz's family to speak at her funeral in June 2008:

I could speak of Roz and all of her qualities, but it would take me her lifetime and a river of tears to describe.

Our chats across the fence brought joy and warmth to us both and I learned many things about myself, the world, and all of you here today.

One such chat we had on a warm spring evening inspired me to write the book in her honour. The name 'In search of an Angel'.

Within those pages Roz shone like the stars, becoming the character that said so much of who she was to so many: Rose Gardener.

The proudest of moments was giving the finished book to Roz who simply smiled and said, 'You took your time! I've been waiting ages for this.' We laughed and kissed and that was Roz.

She loved everything with a pure joy. She cared about everything with a depth beyond any words.

She would speak of her daughter Jenny with kindness and love and, Susannah, she was so proud of you.

She would glow when speaking of Paul or Karen with whom she shared a special friendship.

Friends, so, so many. From her cute names such as the Captain and Chip shop boy and her friends Hazel, June, Cliff, Linda and countless others.

I could not begin to name you all, them all. But I saw her smile, that special Roz smile as she spoke of the many people who showed her the same love she gave so freely. Roz shared her energy and happiness with all of you because she saw the special part in all of you.

In later years she cared for her husband Doug with utter dedication beyond anything I have ever seen.

I could speak of Roz until my life was over and the river was full of tears. I will just say a few more words in a short poem which I hope will do some justice to an amazing person.

With her patience, kindness and warmth she taught us all,
A loving woman whose daily actions defined the very word
beautiful.
Always ready with that smile, everything would grow upon her
touch.
From her plants to our hearts, her wisdom would show us so much
To us all she was different to any other,
She was a neighbour, a friend, a mother, a grandmother.
She would say so many special things, just another reason to love
her.
So today we take time to reminisce
On a beautiful person who will be sadly missed.
And I will always remember her words:
We are each of us angels with only one wing,
To fly, we need only embrace each other.
Roz, you have your wings now, born out of love and we will never
forget your song.
Though sadly missed we all know where Angels really belong.
You were a real-life Angel. We will all love you forever.

Also by Martin Penalver

'In Search of an Angel'

Steve Bidante is eleven years old when events in his life leave him needing hope, when all he breathes is the oxygen of desperation. Forced against his will to make the transformation from boy to man, he clutches at a wafer-thin strand of belief that carries him through the darkness and into the body of a man.

Somewhere in his soul lies the belief that one day he will find what he is looking for. His quest from past to present is filled with passion, laughter and happiness intermingled with tragedy and despair when his beliefs are tested to the limit.

Share in the touching journey of an unassuming man who knows not *why* or *how* he will walk his lonely quest, only that he *must* follow the path that opens up before him.

It is a lonely quest, the search for an angel…

ISBN: 978-1-905988-15-0